Praise for *Before Lunch*:

"Angela Thirkell has a definite place among American readers. In her own subtle and delicate way, she is completely successful in portraying the ridiculous side of the English gentry of the period before the Second World War." —*Books*

"A first-class satire." —*Commonweal*

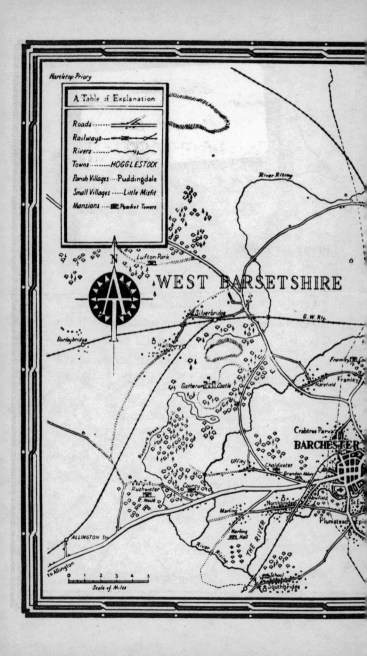

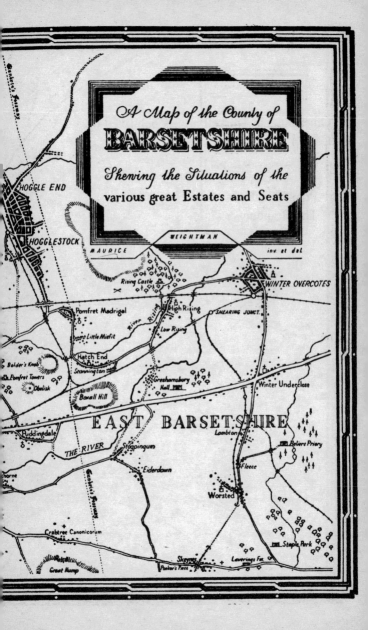

A Map of the County of

BARSETSHIRE

Shewing the Situations of the various great Estates and Seats

WEIGHTMAN

MAURICE   inv. et del

HOGGLE END

HOGGLESTOCK

Rising Castle

WINTER OVERCOTES

Pomfret Madrigal

High Rising

SHEARING JUNCT.

Little Misfit

Low Rising

Balder's Knob

Hatch End

Scannington

Pomfret Towers

Greshamsbury
Hall

Obelisk

Boxall Hill

Winter Underclose

EAST BARSETSHIRE

Ruddingdale

Lambton

Beliers Priory

THE RIVER

Stogpingum

Fleece

Eiderdown

Worsted

horne

Crabtree Canonicorum

Staple Park

Skeynes

Leverings Fm.

Great Hump

Parker's Pace

Other Angela Thirkell novels published by
Carroll & Graf:

Pomfret Towers
The Brandons

BEFORE LUNCH

LUNCH

ANGELA THIRKELL

Carroll & Graf Publishers, Inc.
New York

First Carroll & Graf edition 1988
Second printing 1992

Carroll & Graf Publishers, Inc.
260 Fifth Avenue
New York, NY 10001

ISBN: 0-88184-397-0

Manufactured in the United States of America

. . . Le temps adoucira les choses,

Et tous deux vous aurez des roses

Plus que vous n'en saurez cueillir. . . .

CONTENTS

❧ 1 ❧

MR. MIDDLETON IS ALARMED

❧

THE OWNER OF LAVERINGS LOOKED OUT OF HIS BEDROOM window on a dewy June morning. Not the large window that commanded a gently sloping view to the south of his garden, his meadows, and a wooded plain with hills beyond, but the side window to the east that overlooked the little lane. In his hand he held a letter, with whose contents he angrily refreshed his mind from time to time. Neither the mild June air, nor the beneficent warmth of the sun, could counteract the evil impression that the morning post had made. Everything conspired against him, down to the fact that the White House, whose garden marched with his own, was undoubtedly empty, so that there was no valid excuse for not letting it to people that he didn't particularly want as tenants. Not that he disliked his widowed sister, Mrs. Stonor, but her two grown-up stepchildren were an almost unknown quantity and might come bursting into his privacy with the ease of neighbours who are remote connections by marriage and annoy him very much. All he knew about the young Stonors was that the son was delicate and the daughter, as he shudderingly remembered her, not delicate at all, and at the moment both states of health seemed to him equally repulsive.

Giving his camel's hair dressing gown a petulant twitch he walked back to the table where his breakfast tray and his letters had been put. The cup of coffee that he had poured out ten minutes ago was now tepid with a crinkling skin on its surface. It was more than flesh and blood could stand. He strode to the door, opened it and bellowed his wife's name into the passage. No one answered. He banged the door to, spooned the horrid skin clumsily into the saucer, drank the tepid coffee to which nauseating fragments of milky blanket still clung, and looked at the rest of his post. Business, letters from the office, contractor's estimates. He slammed them angrily down again and returned to the east window, chewing the cud of his resentment against his sister, who by her inconsiderate wish to spend the summer near him had entirely and eternally wrecked his peace of mind.

Presently a creaking sound became audible, then the clop of a horse's hoofs at a slow walk, then a gentle clatter of harness and trappings, the encouraging voice of a carter. Round the corner of the lane came a bright blue farm cart with red wheels, drawn by a benevolent monster with long hairy trousers and a shining coat. The cart was laden with early hay, and one axle was in sore need of greasing. Perched sideways behind the monster's hind quarters was a middle-aged man, giving monosyllabic instructions to the horse, who took no notice at all, knowing by long practice exactly what his driver was going to say. On the side of the cart was painted in slanting white lettering,

J. MIDDLETON ESQ.
LAVERINGS FARM

At the sight of this equipage the watcher from the window felt an exquisite sense of peace and well-being steal over him. There are various degrees of fame. Some would give their name to a rose, some to a mountain, some to a sauce or a pudding, but John Middleton's secret ambition, ever since boyhood, had been to have a farm cart of his own with his name painted on it. He became vaguely conscious that earth held nothing more satisfying than to look out of one's window on a summer morning, warmed by coffee, glowing with anticipation of a visit from one's only sister and her stepchildren, and see a blue farm cart with red wheels, drawn by an imperturbable cart-horse, driven by Tom Pucken, containing fragrant hay, emblazoned with one's own name.

"Morning, Pucken," Mr. Middleton shouted from the window.

Tom Pucken looked up, showing a handsome, crafty, weather-lined face, touched his disgraceful almost brimless hat, shouted some pre-Conquest instructions to his horse, and was carried away towards the gate that led to the farm. Mr. Middleton, refreshed by this encounter, took off his camel's hair dressing gown, finished dressing, and went in search of his wife. But he did not, as one might have expected, go out of his bedroom and down the staircase.

In his earnest desire to make life really comfortable for

himself he had arranged his house in an unusual way. For at least four hundred years there had been a farm at Laverings and for most of that time it had been in the possession of the same family, passing sometimes to a son, sometimes to a daughter and the husband, so that however often the name may have changed, the blood was the same. Even so the farmhouse itself had been altered, pulled down in parts and rebuilt, added to, occasionally burnt, but had kept its own spirit and the name of its original builder. When the last owner, having ruined himself by building the White House and trying to be gentry instead of sticking to the farm, decided to sell the place and go to join a cousin with a motor works in Canada, most of the land had been bought by neighbouring farmers, but the house, with a few acres round it, remained derelict.

John Middleton, a rising architect, happened to pass Laverings on a walking tour, recognised it at once as his house, but could not afford to buy it. He had a simple confidence that he would always in the end get what he wanted, a confidence which so far had never been disappointed, though a generous habit of mind and an aged mother to support made it very difficult for him to save money. For ten years Laverings remained empty and desolate. At the end of this time a very unpleasant gentleman called Sir Ogilvy Hibberd suddenly made an offer for it. The county, who disliked and resented Sir Ogilvy because he was a Liberal and not quite the sort we want (though admitting that there had been some perfectly presentable Liberals only one didn't really know them), suddenly resolved itself into a kind of informal Committee of Hatred, with Lord Bond of Staple

Park near Skeynes, well known for having voted against Clause Three of the Root Vegetables Bill, in the chair. Lord Bond, who had more money than he knew what to do with, was pushed by his masterful wife into buying Laverings, together with the White House and four large fields, while Sir Ogilvy Hibberd bought "The Cedars," Muswell Hill, which had come into the market on the death of Mrs. C. Augustus Fortescue (Fifi), only child and heiress of Bunyan, First Baron Alberfylde.

Lord Bond had felt for some time that there ought to be a sound man at Laverings. What Lord Bond meant by a sound man no one quite knew, nor, apart from a strong feeling against anyone from Cambridge, did he, but a chance meeting with Mr. Middleton settled his mind for him. Mr. Middleton talked to Lord Bond for an hour and a quarter without stopping and Lord Bond invited Mr. Middleton to stay with him at Staple Park. On Sunday afternoon he walked his guest over to Laverings to see the repairs he was doing on the house. By Sunday night Lord Bond, a little dazed, had offered Mr. Middleton a long lease of the house at an absurdly low figure and promised to make all the alterations that his new tenant wanted. Mr. Middleton at once decided to have the east end of the house entirely to himself, using the original kitchen as a library with the old back stairs communicating directly with a bedroom, bath-room and dressing-room, which he also used as a work-room, on the floor above. His mother, who was unwillingly installed in the country, preferred a hipbath in her bedroom and soon languished and died. Her son mourned her sin-cerely with the largest wreath of expensive flowers that

Skeynes had ever seen, which was described in the local paper as a floral tribute, and then forgot about her, except when sentiment got the better of him.

For ten more years Mr. Middleton lived alone at Laverings in great happiness, going to town from Tuesday to Friday every week, working with concentrated violence on Monday and Saturday morning and talking to weekend guests from Saturday afternoon till late on Sunday night or well into the small hours of Monday morning. During this time he set up as a very mild amateur gentleman farmer and had lately added to the little herd of cows he already possessed the blue farm cart with red wheels whose acquaintance we have just made.

When Mr. Middleton met his future wife she was an orphan and over thirty and Mr. Middleton was nearly fifty, so it seemed a suitable marriage enough and they had a large wedding in London with a reception at the Bonds' town mansion in Grosvenor Place and the bride said Thank Goodness now she need never see any of her family again. So she never did, for they lived in quite another county and hunted. Mr. and Mrs. Middleton had no children, but as Catherine Middleton truly said, once one had got over the mortification it was really a very pleasant life.

So Mr. Middleton went out by the door that led to his little back stair and descended to the library, a large, low, sunny room, with a French window onto the garden, lined with books, furnished with one very comfortable chair, a few less comfortable ones, three large tables heaped with books and papers, and a piano which no one ever played. He looked at

the table where material for an article for the Journal of the
Royal Institute of British Architects was accumulating, put
his morning's post on another table and again bellowed
aloud for his wife. This time his appeal met with more
success, for Mrs. Middleton, who had been doing a little
gardening, heard his call and came across the lawn. Her
husband went out onto the flagged terrace to meet her and
affectionately kissed the top of her head. Not that Catherine
Middleton was a small woman, but Mr. Middleton's impressive bulk, topped by a slightly bald leonine head, was apt to
make everyone else look frail and insignificant.

"How are you this morning, darling?" said Mrs. Middleton. "You look very nice and peculiar."

"I fail to see anything peculiar about myself," said Mr.
Middleton.

"That is because you can't see yourself, Jack," said his
wife. "You really look very nice and I like you just as you
are."

Mrs. Middleton did not exaggerate in calling her husband's appearance peculiar, for ever since he had bought the
farm cart, he had thrown himself vehemently into the part
of gentleman farmer and, after a severe struggle with his
tailor, ordered his clothes accordingly. This morning he
was dressed in a blue shirt, a kind of shooting jacket in large
checks with pockets capacious enough for a poacher, orange
tawny plus fours, canvas gaiters and heavy nailed shoes. It
is true that no gentleman farmer off or even on the stage
ever wore so preposterous an outfit or wore it so unconsciously, but to go about looking like an eccentric gave Mr.
Middleton such unalloyed pleasure that his wife had not the

heart to point out to him the marks his nailed shoes made on the parquet floor of the library.

"I am glad you can tolerate me as I am," said Mr. Middleton, still suspicious, "for at my age it is very improbable that I shall change. Had I been a younger man when you married me, Catherine, a man more suited to you in age, you might have re-moulded my life, shaped me again to your liking. But you took pity on an ageing wreck, your young life twined itself round the rugged roots of a storm-shattered tree, and I cannot alter my way of living, I cannot change my spots."

"I do love the way you say everything twice over," said Mrs. Middleton, "and I would hate you to change your spots. What were you calling me for?"

Mr. Middleton's impressive face dissolved in a flash and became as formless as water.

"I called you because I needed you," he said, suddenly becoming a heartbroken child. "I called you once and you did not come."

"And then you called me again and I did," said his wife, whose adoration of her husband was unshadowed by any illusions about him. "Can I do anything?"

"It is my sister Lilian," said Mr. Middleton, recovering himself under his wife's bracing want of sympathy. "I had a letter from her this morning. It is here, in my pocket. No, it is not. You see, Catherine, my memory is not what it was. It is on the library table."

He turned and went indoors followed by Mrs. Middleton.

"Sit down, Catherine," said Mr. Middleton, seating himself in the one comfortable chair, "and I will read Lilian's letter aloud."

When he had done so his wife asked him to give her the letter as it was much easier to understand things if one read them oneself. Rather offended he handed over the letter with a pained and studied courtesy which Catherine ignored.

"That sounds very nice," she said as she gave it back to him. "The White House is quite ready and aired. It only needs the beds making up and it will be great fun to have Lilian and the children, and as she says she will bring her own maid there will be no difficulty at all."

"Children!" said Mr. Middleton.

"Well, Denis is twenty-five and Daphne is four years younger, and I could be their mother at a pinch. And at another pinch you could just be their grandfather, I suppose. I mean if you had had a son when you were sixteen and he had had a son when he was sixteen, that's thirty-two and you are sixty-two, so Denis could be thirty, which leaves him several years to the good."

"Why Lilian had to marry a retired Colonel who did nothing but die and leave her with two grown-up step-children, I don't know," said Mr. Middleton, determined to have a grievance.

"I daresay she didn't either," said Mrs. Middleton placidly. "One usually doesn't. Falling in love makes one do very peculiar things. Look at us. There couldn't be two people less suited, but we simply had to get married. I do love you, Jack."

Mr. Middleton looked at his wife and his face which had

been wearing an uneasy irritated expression melted to pure tenderness, a look that always pierced his wife's heart, though she did not think it good for him to know this, so she asked when Mrs. Stonor wanted to come. Her husband said next week and this was one of his working days and she must know that if he could not break the back of the day's work before lunch he might as well retire and leave his practice to a younger man. So she laid her hand on his shoulder and went across the garden to the White House.

LORD BOND when he bought the property had so altered and improved the White House that it made a very pleasant residence, forming part of the Laverings estate. Up till the beginning of the year it had been let to the widow of a retired General, and when she died Mr. Middleton decided to keep it as an overflow lodging for his weekend parties or to lend or let it to friends. Sarah Pucken, the carter's wife, was willing to oblige when the house was full and could usually produce a daughter for emergencies. Mrs. Pucken had been a kitchenmaid at Staple Park before she married and knew her place to quite an alarming extent. It still pained her to feel that her husband was one of the lower class, but she fed him very well and allowed him half a crown a week out of his wages for himself. Her three elder daughters were all in service in good houses. Two were still at home and showed rebellious symptoms of wishing to go into Woolworth's, but their masterful mother had already found a place as kitchenmaid with Mrs. Palmer at Worsted for Ireen, whom no one but Mrs. Middleton called Irene, and had her eye on a sixth housemaid's place for Lou. This youngest

scion of the Puckens had been christened Lucasta after Lady
Bond, who had with overpowering condescension per-
sonally stood godmother to her ex-kitchenmaid's child, but
it was well understood by the village that the name Lucasta
was no more to be used than the best parlour.

Mrs. Middleton went down the flagged path, through the
gate, across the lane and in at the White House gate. With
the key that she had brought with her she unlocked the front
door. To her surprise she heard voices at the back of the
house and going to the kitchen found Mrs. Pucken and Lou
having what Mrs. Pucken called a good clean. Everything
in the kitchen was wet. The kitchen table was lying on its
side while Lou scrubbed the bottoms of its legs and her
mother scrubbed out the drawer. Mrs. Middleton stopped
short on the step that led down to the kitchen and was one
of the architect's mistakes, and surveying the damp scene
with interest, said Good morning to Mrs. Pucken.

"I dessay you was quite surprised to see me and Lou,
madam," said Mrs. Pucken in the voice of a conjuror who
has produced a rabbit from a top hat. "I was just passing
the remark to Lou that Mrs. Middleton would be quite surprised to see me and her, didn't I, Lou?"

"Mum said you would be quite surprised seeing her and
me," said Lou, whom no efforts of her mother's could bring
to say Madam, although she had no wish to be impolite.

"Well, I am surprised," said Mrs. Middleton, feeling that
by making this confession she might escape a repetition of
the statement. "And," she continued hurriedly, "I was just
coming to ask you to give the house a good dusting as soon
as you had time, because Mr. Middleton's sister, Mrs. Stonor,

is coming down next week with her stepson and stepdaughter."

"There now, Lou, what did I tell you?" said Mrs. Pucken.
"When Miss Phipps at the Post Office told me there was a
letter from Mrs. Stonor gone up to Laverings I said to
Pucken, Depend on it, Pucken, I said, we shall be having
Mrs. Stonor down on us before we can turn round. So I
hurried up with Pucken's breakfast and brought Lou along
with me to give the kitchen a good clean out. When did you
expect Mrs. Stonor and the young lady and gentleman,
madam?"

Mrs. Middleton had long ago accepted Miss Phipps's
inquisitions into the mail bag and was indeed inclined to
admire her unerring memory for every correspondent's
handwriting. Miss Phipps took the broadest view of His
Majesty's Post Office regulations and would always keep
letters back at the shop instead of sending them up to
Laverings if Mr. Middleton telephoned that he was going up
to town by the early train and would call in for his. More
than once had she allowed him to hunt through the bag for
his own letters, open them and alter a word or a figure, and
if Laverings wanted to ring up any neighbour she always
knew if the person wanted was at home, calling on a neighbour, or shopping at Winter Overcotes where the chemist
would take a message. As she had never put her power and
knowledge to any but kindly uses no complaint had ever
been made and the Inspector, though he vaguely suspected
something, could not put his finger on it.

Mrs. Middleton said she expected the Stonors on Saturday
week.

"There," said Mrs. Pucken, sitting back on her heels, "it's a good thing I've got the kitchen clean. Monday me and Lou can do out the drawing-room and Tuesday the dining-room and Wednesday the best bedroom and Thursday—"

"But you did them out only last week, after Mr. Cameron had been here," said Mrs. Middleton, who had housed her husband's partner and another member of the firm at the White House for a weekend.

"I like that Mr. Cameron," said Mrs. Pucken reflectively, "and Lou wished she had his photo, didn't you, Lou?"

Lou giggled and set the table on its legs again.

"But I couldn't let Mrs. Stonor come in here not without I give the rooms a proper cleaning, madam," said Mrs. Pucken, suddenly becoming businesslike. "Come along, Lou. There's some nice suds in the pail and you can wash the scullery floor. I remember Miss Stonor as well as if it was yesterday, the time she came down to Laverings and the Jersey was ill. Miss Stonor was up with her all night and Pucken said she had a heap of sense, madam, not like some young ladies. Mr. Middleton quite took on about that Jersey, didn't he madam, Lily Langtry, that was her name."

Casting her mind back to the last visit the young Stonors had paid them three or four years earlier, Mrs. Middleton thought that "put out" but imperfectly represented her husband's state of mind at the time. His anxiety for his best cow, to whom he believed himself to be fondly attached, though he never knew her from her fellows, was combined with intense distaste for the medical details that his sister's stepdaughter poured out at every meal during her attendance on the invalid.

"And young Mr. Stonor, he was took dreadful," Mrs. Pucken continued, enjoying her own reminiscences. "The doctor come twice a day for a week and he looked like a corpse. I do hope he's better now, madam."

Yes, reflected Mrs. Middleton, that part of the young Stonors' visit had not been a success either. It was not poor Denis's fault that he had been delicate and still got bronchitis when other people were having sunstroke, nor was it his stepmother's fault that she had been in America at the time and could not come and nurse him herself. But Mr. Middleton, while generously supplying money for nurses and doctors, had deeply resented the presence of an invalid in his comfortable house. He had a kind of primitive animal hatred of any kind of illness, except his own occasional colds which were in a way sacred and drove every other subject out of the conversation. Even his wife's rare ailments drove him almost to frenzy with fear and dislike and it was tacitly understood that no servant must be seen if she was coughing or looked pale. The result of Denis's unlucky illness had been that Mr. Middleton nearly quarrelled with his sister on her return from America and had refused to ask the Stonors to the house again. Mrs. Stonor, who really loved her brother, had concocted with her sister-in-law this plan for taking the White House, hoping that at a safe distance he and her step-children would get on. If only Denis would keep well and Daphne would be a little less healthy Mrs. Middleton thought it might do, and she looked forward to the Stonors as next door neighbours.

"Yes, he is better, Mrs. Pucken," she said, "and working very hard. You know he writes music."

"Yes indeed, madam," said Mrs. Pucken pityingly, for as she afterwards said to Lou no one didn't *write* music. Play the piano, or the ocarina, or turn the radio on, yes: but write, no. Then she disappeared into the scullery with the nice suds and Mrs. Middleton went upstairs. The bedrooms looked spotless in spite of Mrs. Pucken's threats of cleaning. Mrs. Middleton automatically straightened one or two pictures which Mrs. Pucken would certainly put askew again as she dusted them and looked out of the window. Through a little silver birch, across the cheerful flower borders and the grass, she saw Laverings comfortably mellow red in the sunlight and could almost see, through the open library window, her husband wrestling with his article for the Journal of the R.I.B.A. Her heart suddenly swelled with affection for her large, overpowering autocrat, who bullied his clients so unmercifully and needed her own strength for his own weakness. How weak he was very few people besides his wife knew. Mrs. Middleton thought of them. Lilian Stonor had never admitted it, but Mrs. Middleton had once or twice caught a fleeting glance that told her how exactly Jack was estimated by his sister. Mrs. Pucken, of all people, knew it and stood in no fear of the roaring domestic tyrant at all. As for Alister Cameron, the junior partner of the firm, she never quite knew what he knew. For ten years he had worked assiduously and untiringly with Mr. Middleton, shouldering all the drudgery of the office and never putting himself forward. Beyond the fact that he was absolutely trustworthy, read the classics for his own pleasure, reviewed books on them with cold fury, and had rooms in the Temple, no one knew much about him.

That he loved and admired Mr. Middleton, she knew. How much his love was the protective pity that she herself often felt she did not quite want to guess. That her husband was a brilliant architect, a most unusual organiser and had an astounding gift for seizing the moment and making money for his firm she was well aware, but she feared that one serious check in his hitherto unchecked career might find him out. She had once hinted at something of the kind to Mr. Cameron. He had listened attentively and then said that success could make people very vulnerable. "But," he added, "he will always recover himself because whatever events may do, you won't let him down; nor, though that is a minor consideration, shall I." Mrs. Middleton had been much comforted by this remark and she and Mr. Cameron had become in a gentlemanly and unemotional way very fast friends. It was one of her treats when she went to town to have lunch in Mr. Cameron's rooms and exchange some ordinary remarks and share some unembarrassed silences before going on to a theatre, or a shop, or a hairdresser. And for her Mr. Cameron would occasionally drop his pose of detached tolerance and say exactly what he thought about women undergraduates or the Master of Lazarus's views on Plotinus, using his guest as an audience as freely as if he were Mr. Middleton himself.

She had sometimes in the earlier days of their acquaintance indulged in sentimental and romantic speculation about his past, imagining him like George Warrington, a blighting marriage or a dead romance in his background. But this pleasing illusion was dispelled one day when they were talking about husbands and wives (with special refer-

ence to Lord and Lady Bond) and Mr. Cameron had said he
had never yet seen anyone he wanted to marry and hoped
he never would, having had his blood curdled by two aunts
and a governess in early life.

After that Mrs. Middleton had with feminine perversity
felt obliged to gather the nicest girls in the neighbourhood
to Laverings for his benefit, but though he was only about
her own age they had all treated him as an uncle at sight and
flung their arms round his neck with a freedom that certainly did not betoken any serious feelings.

In the distance Mrs. Middleton could hear the stable clock
chiming eleven from Staple Park and roused herself. There
was shopping to be done in the village, the report of the District Nursing Association of which she was secretary to be
finished, and a dozen small household odds and ends await-
ing her. Alister Cameron was coming down on Saturday
week, the Stonors would be arriving on the same day and
perhaps he and Daphne—and then she laughed at herself
for trying once more to melt Alister's flinty heart and went
off to the garage to get her car.

❧ 2 ❧

GUESTS AT THE WHITE HOUSE

❧

ON THE SATURDAY MORNING OF THE FOLLOWING WEEK Mr. Cameron left the office with his weekend suitcase and made his way by underground to Waterloo. The one through train to Skeynes (for by all others you have to change at Winter Overcotes) was on the point of starting. The guard, who knew Mr. Cameron, held a door open and called to him to jump in, which he did just as the train began to pull out. The exertion of jumping in and the slight jolt as the train began to move caused him to stumble against some legs and he apologised.

"It's all right," said the owner of the legs, a girl who was doing a crossword.

Mr. Cameron put his suitcase on the rack, looked to see whether it was a smoking-carriage, and saw with slight regret that it wasn't. The 11.47 was always rather full on Saturdays and the only vacant place was next to the girl over whose legs he had stumbled. So he sat down in it and being rather tired after some late nights and heavy days went to sleep, or at any rate passed into a state of suspended animation which lasted till the train got to Winter Overcotes. Here some rather primitive shunting which was being done by a white horse harnessed to some good trucks made such a noise that he woke up and found most of the passengers had got out. A young man and a woman were in the two far corners reading and the girl next to him was still doing her crossword. As he had very good long sight he could not help seeing that she had made very little progress since Waterloo and the words she had tentatively filled in were in several cases incorrect. At the moment she was struggling with 7 down, the clue to which was "Tomorrow to . . . woods and pastures new (Milton), 5." With fascination he watched his neighbour think, frown, lick her pencil and finally write the word *Green* in block letters. He could hardly control himself.

"I say, Denis," said the girl. "This seems all wrong. If I put Green for 7 down it makes sense all right but the letters don't seem to fit. I mean I'd got Socrates for 5 across, because it says 'This call for help contains a large parcel,' which was pretty good work, but now it will have to be Socratee. Do you think they spelt it Socratee sometimes? I mean in the accusative or something?"

The young man, evidently Denis, said he simply couldn't think.

"Oh, but then it wouldn't be S.O.S. for the call for help but S.O.E." said the girl. "I expect the man that wrote it did it all wrong. Someone told me that they stick next day's crossword up in the office, I mean the squares of it, and anyone who comes along can put in a word, so someone who didn't know much about Greek plays put it in wrong."

"Sophocles you mean," said Denis.

"That wouldn't do," said the girl after a moment's hard thinking, "unless you spelt it like sofa; because it's only eight letters."

Mr. Cameron could bear it no longer.

"Excuse me," he said, "but I couldn't help seeing over your shoulder. It ought to be fresh."

"What ought?" said the girl, evidently willing to receive any new idea but quite at sea as to his meaning.

"Green of course," said the woman, who had come closer to the girl and was looking at the clues.

"Oh, you mean it ought to be *fresh*," said the girl, licking her pencil again and blocking in the word Fresh. "Well, they ought to explain properly and anyway they've got two letters the same. If I were the editor I'd see they did the crossword properly. Green woods is just as good as fresh woods."

"It's really Milton's fault," said Mr. Cameron apologetically.

"Oh, I did see it said Milton," said the girl, "but I didn't quite get the idea. Thanks awfully. Could you do any more of it?"

Crosswords were like drink to Mr. Cameron, who willingly took the job and finished it before the train had reached Skeynes, in spite of the Worsted tunnel where the railway company, in accordance with a tradition dating from the days of oil lamps, refused to put on any lights and the carriage windows were obscured with a sulphurous deposit that did not melt away till the train was halfway down the valley on the other side.

"Well, thanks awfully," said the girl as the train slowed down for Skeynes. "We're getting out here. Lilian, here we are."

The woman shut her book and put it into a small suitcase. As she stood up, Mr. Cameron saw her face properly for the first time and recognised it. He got out of the carriage with his suitcase and called a porter, whom he delivered over to his fellow travellers.

"Oh, thank you so much," said the woman, and then she looked questioningly at him.

"Yes, we have met," said Mr. Cameron. "It was stupid of me not to recognise you at once. My name is Cameron. I'm your brother's partner."

"Of course," said Mrs. Stonor. "I met you once at Laverings. These are my stepchildren, Denis and Daphne. Denis has just had influenza. Are you going to stay with Jack? I have taken the White House for the summer. I asked Catherine to send a taxi to meet us, so perhaps we could give you a lift."

As she was speaking they walked up the platform towards the exit, through which from the booking office surged the form of Mr. Middleton, intent upon meeting his sister and her party. He was in his country squire's dress, carrying the very large stick with which it was his habit to incommode himself on his walks. As he caught sight of his sister he raised the stick in greeting.

"Lilian!" he exclaimed, trying to throw into the name a wealth of meaning intended to disguise the fact that he didn't know what to say.

"That is very nice of you to come and meet us, Jack," said Mrs. Stonor, "and if you would put your stick out of Daphne's eye I could kiss you. Mr. Cameron, would you mind helping me with the luggage? I can't remember if I had twelve things in the van or thirteen, and the children are always ashamed of me in public."

She drifted away followed by Mr. Cameron.

"That's all right," said Daphne, as she got in under her step-uncle's guard and banged her face against his cheek.

"Wait a moment," said Mr. Middleton, slightly annoyed. "I will give the stick to Flora. She loves to carry it for me. Flora! Flora! Where are you?"

A stout brown spaniel who had been sending a crate of hens into hysterics by sniffing at the wooden bars, looked with kindly contempt at Mr. Middleton, wagged her tail and sat down. Daphne laughed a hearty laugh and said Flora was too fat to move.

"She is not fat," said Mr. Middleton indignantly. "She is twelve years old and needs her food. Flora! Come and take stick. Take stick for master."

Flora slapped the platform with her tail and smiled tolerantly.

"Dog won't bite pig, pig won't get over the stile," murmured Denis. "How do you do, sir."

Mr. Middleton looked coldly at his step-nephew, but could not ignore Denis's outstretched hand and had to shake it. Mrs. Stonor with Mr. Cameron in attendance was still fussing over her trunks outside the luggage van and Mr. Middleton had leisure to inspect the young Stonors, whom he had not seen for two or three years. They were much as he remembered them and his memories were unsympathetic. Daphne was certainly a very handsome girl but had what appeared to him a terrifying air of good-humour and determination. Besides, she had called Flora fat. As for Denis, he was even taller and thinner than in Mr. Middleton's recollection. Huddled in a long coat on a balmy June day, his large dark eyes ringed with the marks of suffering, he reminded his step-uncle too much of an organ grinder's monkey. When Flora waddled up and inspected the newcomer's legs and Denis, stooping, took off his glove and patted her, his long bony hand seemed to Mr. Middleton to increase the resemblance, and he felt the vague unreasonable distaste that always overcame him at the sight of illness. To make up for this uncharitable feeling he informed Denis that Flora liked him.

"I wish I could think so," said Denis, slowly straightening himself and putting his glove on again. "I am afraid she knows I don't like her. Dogs always come to me because they know I see through them and they enjoy it. They are such masochists. I am always polite to them, but I wouldn't care if I never saw another one again. What a charming station you have, sir."

Mr. Middleton became a prey to mingled emotions. To his mind, quick to grasp essentials, it was clear that Lilian's stepson was going to be a perpetual annoyance to him. He didn't like young men who wore gloves in the country and camel hair coats; people who didn't like Flora he could not away with. That a good many of his friends had no particular affection for her he was not aware, but so long as they veiled their true sentiments under a decent veil of hypocrisy he was willing to take a surface value. Young Stonor's analysis of his and Flora's reactions he found almost indecent. Nor did he at all like the easy way in which the boy had dismissed Flora and condescended about the station. He looked angrily round. Charming appeared to him the last word one would choose for Skeynes station. It represented what might be called Mid-Victorian functional railway architecture, as far removed from the Gothic romanticism of Shrewsbury on the one hand as it was from the modern station with circular booking office, elliptical signal boxes and stepped-back waiting-rooms on the other. There was a decent squat row of grey brick offices with wooden floors which were watered from time to time during the hot weather to lay the dust that they engendered; the booking office and entrance hall still contained one of those advertisements, now much valued by connoisseurs, of a storage and removal firm whose vans had the peculiar property of exhibiting one side and one end simultaneously; the station-master had a little office chokingly heated by a stove with a red-hot iron chimney and furnished with yellowing crackling documents impaled on spikes; there was a waiting-room containing a bench, a table, an empty carafe of incredible thickness and weight, two chairs and a rusty grate full of smouldering slack; the porters had a room called Lamps which was always locked; and at the end of the down platform was a tank on four legs from which local engines still obtained their water supply through a leathern hose pipe. There were a few little flower beds, edged with white-washed stones and containing varieties of flowers from penny packets of mixed seeds. On the wooden fence that separated the platform from the station yard was another prize for the amateur of railway art, enamelled on tin, a fine original example of the distich about the Pickwick, Owl and Waverley pens. The platform was sheltered by a corrugated iron roof with a wooden frill along its front and all the paint was an uncompromising chocolate colour.

From the foregoing description it will be easy to see how to Mr. Middleton and most of the inhabitants Skeynes was simply a station, while to Denis and some of his generation it was a period piece to be treated with protective reverence. When Denis, having done his duty by Flora and his step-uncle, strolled up to a chocolate machine and actually obtained a small slab of very nasty pink chocolate cream, he felt that a summer at Skeynes would not be unbearable.

By this time the luggage had all been put on a trolley and was on its way by the side gate into the station yard, where the Laverings car was in waiting.

"Oh dear," said Mrs. Stonor, giving way to despair. "Your car can never take all our luggage, Jack. Is there a station taxi, or could the station-master ring up something? We seem to have a frightful amount, but really for three months one does want everything one has in the English climate. I did think of not bringing my tweeds, but one never knows and it is such a nuisance if you haven't got your things when you want them. I always say if you *are* taking any luggage you might as well take what you need."

"It's only thirteen things," said Daphne, "besides the things we had in the carriage with us. The car could easily come back for the rest. I say, Uncle Jack, you've still got that nice chauffeur you had last time I was here. Hullo, Pol-

lett, how are you? You could easily get our things up to the
White House, couldn't you?"

Pollett touched his cap to Daphne and without making
any verbal reply, for he was a man of few words, favoured
her with an expressive glance in the direction of his employer.

"Oh, I suppose Uncle Jack's one of those people that don't
like luggage on their seats," said Daphne, accepting this
curious attitude towards the leatherwork of an expensive car
as one of the inexplicable facts of life.

"Perhaps some of it could go up on the porter's trolley,"
said Mrs. Stonor, talking aloud to herself and anyone who
was unable to avoid hearing her. "It's only a mile to the
White House and not very much uphill and if I said which
things we don't need so much as the others, it would do
quite well if we didn't get them till after tea, or even by
dinner-time."

"I'd love to go up on this," said Denis, who was sitting on
a suitcase on the trolley with his long legs dangling over the
side. "Yes, Lilian, I know I should get axle grease on my
trousers, but it is too late; I got it as soon as I came near the
thing. It exudes death-rays of grease, yards away. I'll have
to take them into Winter Overcotes and get them cleaned.
I can't think why we haven't a car of our own. No, darling,
I beg your pardon," he exclaimed, getting off the trolley and
putting his arm round his stepmother. "I know it's because
I'm such a damned expense with my foul diseases."

Mrs. Stonor gave him a glance in which some anxiety
mingled with a good deal of affection, pressed his arm, released herself and went over to her brother, who was now

talking to Mr. Cameron. But hardly had she begun to ex-
pound her plans for the luggage when a trampling, creaking
noise came round the bend of the road, resolving itself as it
approached into the blue farm waggon with red wheels,
drawn by the shining monster with hairy trousers. Mr.
Pucken, who was as usual seated sideways just behind the
horse, addressed a few words to his charge, who pulled up
and stood quietly waiting for the next job.

"There, my dear Lilian, is the answer to your questions,"
said Mr. Middleton. "Tom Pucken will take your luggage
up in the cart and I will take you all in the car, for it is
already past lunch-time."

"Never mind lunch," cried Mrs. Stonor. "We lunch at
any time. I must look at your cart."

Mr. Middleton, who lunched at half-past one and was
already annoyed at being late, herded his sister towards the
car. Pollett opened the door and Flora, bursting through
among everyone's feet, hurled herself into the car and sat
panting on the seat.

"Here, come out of that," said Daphne, hauling Flora's
unwilling dead weight out by a handful of her back. "She
needs training, Uncle Jack."

"She doesn't," said her owner indignantly, answering
Daphne back as if they were children of the same age.
"Come to master, Flora, and sit on master's knees."

But Flora, recognising in Daphne a natural dog-ruler,
was crouching slavishly at her feet with worship in her eyes
and turned a deliberately deaf and disobedient ear to her
master's invitation.

"Get in, Lilian," said Daphne. "I say, Uncle Jack, that's

the best cart I've ever seen. I always wanted to know someone who had their name on a cart. "J. Middleton Esquire,
Laverings Farm." It looks simply marvellous. Could I go
up in it, with the luggage? Come along, Denis."

Denis made a step towards his sister, but was stopped by
Mrs. Stonor, who begged him to be sensible and come in the
car. Denis, who was already feeling the effects of the heat
and the wait in the station yard, was secretly glad of an
excuse not to accompany his sister and obediently got into
the car, looking extremely green in the face.

"I shall go in front with Pollett," said Mr. Middleton hastily, not so much from unselfishness as from a wish not to be
in the back of the car if young Stonor was going to faint or
die in it. "Come up, Flora. Come up with master."

Flora bundled herself into the back of the car, and busied
herself in guarding Denis's feet from possible enemies. Mrs.
Stonor lingered for a moment to collect Daphne, but her
stepdaughter was standing in the farm cart like Boadicea
while Mr. Pucken put the luggage on board.

"I say, Mr. Cameron, it is Mr. Cameron, isn't it, your
name I mean," Daphne shouted, "come up in the cart."

Mr. Cameron looked from Miss Stonor to Mrs. Stonor in
some perplexity.

"Yes, do," said Mrs. Stonor in answer to his look. "My
brother will go mad if we wait any longer and I must get
Denis back as quickly as possible. Please don't let Daphne
drive the cart or ride the horse or go the long way round,
and could you make sure that there are *three* blue suitcases,
because if one is missing it is sure to be the one that is wanted,
and could you see that the brown hat box is the right way up

because I think some of Denis's medicine is in it and one of the corks isn't a very good fit and if the cork comes out—"

But Mr. Middleton, angrily saying a quarter to two already, snapped his watch to in a terrifying manner and told Pollett to start, so Mr. Cameron never knew what would happen if the cork came out of the medicine bottle and found himself deserted in the station yard with the masterful Miss Stonor. How he was to stop her driving the cart or riding the horse or going the long way round he couldn't conceive, and could only hope that his interference would not be needed. So he went over to the cart and told Daphne that her stepmother wanted to know if there were three blue suitcases.

"I expect so," said Daphne indifferently. "Come up and we'll get going. You'll get a lot of hay on your clothes because Pucken was carting hay this morning, but he gave it a good sweep out he says."

Mr. Cameron in a cowardly way gave up the question of the blue suitcases, and climbed into the cart where he sat on a holdall, feeling that Miss Stonor could deal with the situation far better than he could. Mr. Pucken was settling himself in his usual place on the shaft, when Daphne called down to him that she wanted to drive and would he chuck the reins up.

"All right, miss," said Mr. Pucken, "but mind you don't pull on them or he'll pull up. Just let them lay on his back, miss. He knows the way home."

Daphne caught the reins and flapped them on the monster's back. Mr. Pucken rammed the remains of his tobacco further into his pipe, lit it and prepared to tolerate the gentry

enjoying themselves. Daphne, taking his advice, perched
herself on the front of the cart and let the reins lie slack,
while Mr. Cameron wondered what subjects, if any, would
interest her. Suddenly he remembered Mrs. Stonor's second
request. Looking round he saw two brown hat boxes. They
were shaped like drums and to the lay mind there appeared
to be no reason why one way up should be more the right
way up than another.

"Oh, Miss Stonor," he said, "Mrs. Stonor said there was
some of your brother's medicine in one of the hat boxes and
she wanted to be sure if the bottle was properly corked. Do
you know which it would be?"

Daphne, who had been holding the reins with the air of
one guiding the whirlwind and directing the storm, pulled
them violently. The monster stopped. Daphne quickly
opened one of the hat boxes, rummaged among a confused
heap of scarves, woollies, gloves, silk underclothes, powder
puffs, anything in fact but the hats for which the box was
intended, and at last produced a small pink bundle with a
brown stain on it. This she unwrapped and held up a bottle.

"What a mercy Lilian told you," she said. "Denis hadn't
room for his medicine, so he gave it to Lilian and she hadn't
room, so I said I'd put it in my hat box and I wrapped it up
in my vest, but the cork must have worked a bit loose. Anyway there's hardly any of it spilt, but it's made a mess of
my vest."

She drove the cork firmly home, wrapped the bottle up
again, thrust it into the pocket of the loose coat she was
wearing and flapped the reins. The cart was once more put
into action and the monster breasted the hill up to Skeynes

village. Mr. Cameron then became aware that Miss Stonor was looking at him with what he felt, though he could not account for it, to be disfavour.

"I suppose," she said suddenly and rather defiantly, "you don't think there's anything wrong with Denis."

"Wrong?" said Mr. Cameron, playing for time. "Oh no, nothing wrong I'm sure."

"Well, you must have noticed," said Daphne severely, "about his medicine. You've just seen it."

"Yes, I did see it," Mr. Cameron admitted, "but lots of people have medicine. I have some awful stuff that I take myself sometimes."

"Well, Denis is *really* not well, or he wouldn't be having medicine at all," said Daphne. "He's always been like that and it's a frightful shame. There's nothing really wrong with him, he just can't help it. Sometimes people think he looks like that out of swank, but he loathes it and he can't bear people to talk about it. So don't tell him he looks rotten or anything like that because he can't bear it."

She ended her explanation with a flushed face and a break in her voice which Mr. Cameron found touching though a little unnecessary. She must be very fond of her brother to take him so seriously. He certainly looked pale and weedy, but by no means in mortal danger. However to be polite he said he was very sorry and he had noticed that Mr. Stonor seemed to feel the heat.

"Mr. Stonor?" said Daphne. "Oh, Denis, you mean. Of course he did. That's why Lilian wanted to get him to the White House as soon as she could. She's an angel. Not a bit like a step. I really think she married father so that she could look after Denis and take me about a bit, at least I can't see any other reason. Father found us rather a bore, because he was a Colonel and he wanted army children and I was a girl and Denis was never well, so that was a wash-out. Mother died ages ago in India. Lilian was really our friend first. We warned her what it would be like marrying father, but she seemed to like it all right."

In face of these interesting family details Mr. Cameron felt rather at a loss but luckily the monster turned into the little lane that led to Laverings and the White House, and all the suitcases lurched across the cart. Mr. Pucken, knowing that the horse would with Casabianca-like devotion go straight to his stable whatever Miss Daphne tried to do, slipped down from the shaft and went to its head, where he explained to it that a short halt would be necessary to unload the luggage, after which it would get its dinner. On hearing this the monster stood still, with one hoof delicately poised on the tip of its shoe like a ballerina.

Mrs. Stonor's maid, who had come the day before by motor coach, hurried down the garden path followed by Mrs. Pucken. By the greatest piece of good fortune Palfrey, which was the name of the maid, had taken a violent fancy for Mrs. Pucken and Mrs. Pucken for her. Owing to Mrs. Pucken's favourable introductions Palfrey was already on the best of terms with the village tradesmen and Miss Phipps at the shop, and Mrs. Pucken had spent the morning at Laverings drinking tea and doing a quantity of quite un-necessary cleaning, for the house was already spotless from her ministrations. Lou, to her eternal disgust, had been ban-ished to the scullery to peel potatoes and shell a few peas for lunch, while her mother and Palfrey, whom Lou was instructed to call Miss Palfrey on pain of death, discussed the major mysteries of life, saying what a shame it was Mr. and Mrs. Middleton hadn't any children, though Mrs. Pucken gave it as her opinion that Mr. Middleton was nothing but a big child himself and Mrs. Middleton had her hands full.

"Your lady hasn't any children not of her own, has she?" said Mrs. Pucken.

"Oh no," said Palfrey pityingly, "being as Colonel Stonor was a widower when she married him."

She looked Mrs. Pucken firmly in the face, as if challenging her to dispute this curious physiological phenomenon and such was her personality that Mrs. Pucken very slavishly nodded her head in a knowing way.

"The Colonel was very particular," said Palfrey, putting all the cushions askew on the sofa and chairs as she spoke. "Very particular indeed. I was cook there for two years before he died and I never cooked for a gentleman that was more particular. Now madam and Mr. Denis and Miss Daphne they don't hardly seem to notice what they eat, though I will say for Miss Daphne she's a hearty eater. But what Mr. Denis eats wouldn't feed a cat, Mrs. Pucken. A bit here and a bit there and as like as not leave it on his plate after all. That's why we've come down here, Mrs. Pucken, to see if the country does him good. Always playing the piano and going to the concert, in London. I wonder madam can stand it, I really do sometimes."

At this point Mrs. Pucken said she heard the car so she and Palfrey went to see if there was any luggage, after which Palfrey ran upstairs to clean herself and Mrs. Pucken received Mrs. Stonor and Denis, who said how do you do to her very charmingly and sat down abruptly on a chair in the hall.

"Would you like some sherry, Denis?" said Mrs. Stonor anxiously. "Jack said he had sent us some, and if Mrs. Pucken knows where it is and there is a corkscrew in the kitchen anywhere we could have some at once. I did put a corkscrew in my big trunk, the one that has your music in it, but it hasn't come yet, so that's not much use."

Mrs. Pucken said the sherry was in the larder and there was a corkscrew on the dresser and the sherry glasses were in the pantry and she could get a bottle and have the cork out in a minute and did Mr. Denis like the dry or the sweet as Mr. Middleton had sent over both. Lord Bond, she said, liked the dry best and she had noticed that gentlemen usually did, but it wasn't a mite more trouble to open the sweet if Mr. Denis liked it. And as a preparation for the festival she called to Lou at the top of her powerful maternal voice. Denis controlled himself with an effort, hoping that neither the effort nor his attempt to conceal it would be visible to his stepmother and said he really didn't want any sherry and would rather wait for lunch. Mrs. Stonor, who was acutely sensitive both to his fatigue and to his self-control, saw nothing for it in the face of Mrs. Pucken's determined kindness but to accompany her to the larder and there hold her in talk about sherry and corkscrews till lunch was ready, leaving Denis to recover himself as best he could. If only the cart and the luggage with the hat box and the medicine would come soon.

Very luckily Lou had so far exceeded her instructions as

to put the potatoes on, a phrase which should need no explanation, while Palfrey was cleaning herself. Her mind, if she can be said to have had any, was running on a bottle of bright red liquid nail polish which she had brought against her mother's orders and hidden in her other pair of shoes, so she naturally forgot to put enough water in the saucepan and just as Mrs. Pucken and Mrs. Stonor came into the kitchen Palfrey, summoned by a smell of burning, came clattering down the little staircase that led from the top landing to the kitchen and opened the door at its foot with a dramatic flourish. The storm burst over Lou's head, thunder and lightning from Mrs. Pucken and Palfrey, and Mrs. Pucken, sending her home to put her father's dinner in the oven, quickly washed a few of the smaller new potatoes and put them on so that they might be ready for the travellers as soon as possible.

By this time the sherry was forgotten and then the cart was heard and the staff rushed out to help with the luggage.

"Good-bye," said Daphne to Mr. Cameron. "I hope you enjoyed yourself. And don't forget what I said about Denis."

"I enjoyed myself very much," said Mr. Cameron truthfully, "and I'll remember. I hope I shall see you again while I'm here."

Then he went off to the right to Laverings, while Daphne went through the gate on the left to the White House. Here her stepmother met her, carrying an empty glass.

"Did you find the medicine?" Mrs. Stonor asked anxiously. "I told Mr. Cameron to ask you about it, because I wasn't sure if the cork was in properly."

Daphne pulled the vest out of her pocket and produced

the bottle. "Here you are," she said. "It's made my vest in a bit of a mess, but there's heaps left."

"Thank goodness," said Mrs. Stonor. "Will you take it to Denis, or shall I?"

"You take it," said Daphne. "I want to say good-bye to Pucken, but I wanted to give you the medicine first. Poor old Lilian."

Mrs. Stonor poured out Denis's medicine and took it into the drawing-room where he was standing at the piano, tapping a note here and there with one finger.

"To your great pleasure, Lilian darling, I will at once tell you," he said in the rather high voice which she knew so well as a danger signal of nerves, "that this little upright is quite impossible, so you will not be tormented with my playing at all. And a good thing too, I daresay," he added, shutting the lid with great care. "I always said I ought to compose without a piano and here is my chance. Oh, darling, you haven't got some medicine for me?"

"Daphne has just brought it," said Mrs. Stonor, handing him the glass. "It was in her hat box and if I had had any sense I would have told Pollett to put the hat box in the car, but I didn't think of it. I only thought of telling Mr. Cameron to tell Daphne to see if the cork had come out, and she wrapped the bottle up in her vest and it was rather stained."

"I don't know what I'd do without you and Daphne," said Denis, making a face. "This is quite the most disgusting medicine I've had yet. What a useless encumbrance I am."

His stepmother looked at him with mild reproach and took the empty glass.

"Quite right, darling," said Denis, laughing in spite of

himself. "Too much self-pity. But don't you ever wish you had let that odious, unhealthy schoolboy die a natural death? You wouldn't have noticed if I'd died then, but now it is quite a habit with you to take care of me and I think you would miss it. Do you know, Lilian, you've been standing between me and Kensal Green for nearly ten years?"

"Well, someone had to look after you," said his stepmother apologetically. "You looked such a wretched atomy, all eyes and bones."

"And someone had to look after Daphne, who was a quite dreadful giggling schoolgirl then," said Denis.

"And there was your father, who wasn't bony or giggling," said Mrs. Stonor almost sharply.

"Forgive me," said Denis. And then Palfrey disdainfully banged a little gong which stood in the hall and they went in to lunch where the new potatoes were much admired and Denis actually ate two.

After lunch Denis was ordered to lie on a long chair on the little stone terrace in the corner of the L-shaped house and get as much sun as possible, and he was tired enough to obey with very little fuss. The sun was very hot. A lawnmower at Laverings made a pleasant distant drone and scent from the sweetbriar hedge drifted in the air. Denis felt that he might be quiet at the White House, he might find a little of the inward peace which he so desperately wanted. Whenever, in his experience, his mind settled to some kind of equilibrium, his body would give it a twist or a jerk. How often Lilian had saved him only he knew. She had never pretended to understand his mind, perhaps never thought it worth while to try, but her kindness, her patience, her affection had been as constant as day and night. What she didn't understand she accepted, and so naturally that one had gradually come to think of oneself as an ordinary person that happened not to be very well, instead of imagining, as that bony schoolboy had done, that one was marked out as different from other people and being savagely proud of it. His gratitude to her was so much part of him now that he sometimes forgot it. He suddenly thought of the words he and his stepmother had exchanged before lunch. As usual he had said something stupid, almost cruel, rousing even her tolerance to a protest. He and Daphne had never cared much for their father. Or perhaps, if one delved deeply enough for truth, always an unpleasant work, he had not got on with his father, and Daphne, who could get on very well with everybody, had with her younger sister's loyalty come over to his side and lost touch with her father. Between them they had decided that Lilian Middleton had married Colonel Stonor so that she could be a good stepmother to two motherless children. But as he got older Denis had realised, with some shame, that Lilian had probably married his father because she was deeply fond of him and had taken on the care of two children not so much younger than herself, not because she thought they were misunderstood or unkindly treated, but because anything that belonged to her husband was dear to her. Denis was thankful to remember how Lilian had so tamed him that he began to have good manners to his father, which were accepted with surprise and silent gratitude, and from his real effort to please had come at last an understanding not deep, but good enough to make life easier for them both. Daphne, pleased to do whatever her brother did, allowed herself to be affectionate to her father and improved vastly under Lilian's hand. If Lilian had burst out before lunch about her husband, even as little as she did, it meant that her feelings were deeply touched. Denis flushed hotly as he remembered with what fatuousness he had said, or almost said, that she had married his father for his sake, and as an afterthought, for Daphne's sake. How could he have been such an oaf? He prided himself on a certain sensibility, but there was nothing to be proud of in taking for granted that a woman had not loved very deeply the man she married: gross insensitiveness, was the best name he could give to it. That Lilian never suspected an unkindness and never bore rancour made it all the worse. Denis began to feel his heart beating too fast and an answering pulse in his head which would probably mean what were known as "one of poor Denis's heads," as all this rushed over him. Five years ago he would have made a scene with his stepmother, accused himself, implored forgiveness, left her with a headache as bad as his own, but this at least he had learned, to keep his remorse to himself. So he lighted a cigarette and tried to think of his music, and gradually, though his head was no better, he was drowsy enough to hover not unpleasantly between waking and what was less sleep than a kind of blissful half-consciousness.

But meanwhile who can describe the rage of Mr. Middleton? Not only was he late for lunch himself, but when he got back, at two o'clock, he had to wait yet another fifteen minutes for Mr. Cameron. In vain did his wife offer him sherry or a cocktail. He was exhausted, a thing of no account, a mere purveyor of motors and general transport for sisters and nephews and nieces, and the whole world would have been taken into his confidence had it been there. As it was, he had to content himself with his wife and the parlourmaid for audience.

"No, no, Catherine, you well know that sherry is poison to me at this hour," he exclaimed. "And as for cocktails, this is no weather for them. There is only one thing that I could drink—"

"Well, if we have got it you shall have it," said Mrs. Middleton.

"—and that," said Mr. Middleton, "is beer."

"Shall I bring some beer then, madam?" said Ethel, the parlourmaid, who had brought in the sherry.

"When I say beer, none of you know what I mean," said Mr. Middleton.

"Yes please, Ethel, off the ice," said Mrs. Middleton.

"None of you are old enough," said Mr. Middleton, addressing his wife and the departing figure of Ethel and suddenly becoming a pathetic nonagenarian, "to know what beer was. Ah! the beer we used to drink before the war, long long before the war. It had savour, it had body, it was meat and drink to the thirsty body and the thirsty soul. Had Dr. Johnson drunk the beer we used to drink he would have amended his dictum to Beer for Heroes. You do not know what it was to come in after a long day's tramp, hot, sweating, tired as only the walker can be with a divine fatigue, stupefied with the strong air of the hills, the scent of gorse and heather, the salt tang of the sea, the sweet resinous smell of pinewoods above the fiords, the chill wind from the great glaciers, the glare from the sand dunes of the desert," said Mr. Middleton, who seemed to have done his walking in a very composite kind of country, "and grasping a tankard to feel the cool nectar slip down one's throat, grateful to the palate, to the throat, to the whole body. To relax the body in utter contentment and then to talk. Ah! how we talked in those days. Have I ever told you, Catherine, of my great, my epic walk with Potter and Bagshaw, both now with the great majority, men of infinite learning and humour, ascetics like myself, caring for little but the things of the mind and the use of a well-tempered body."

"Yes, darling," said Mrs. Middleton.

"I may have, I may have," said Mr. Middleton, "I know I repeat myself, for I get old, I have no longer the brain of the youth who could never be tired or worsted in argument, but bear with me, Catherine, while I repeat for myself, for my own enduring pleasure, the story of our walk up Kirkstone, over Fairfield, across to the long backbone of Helvellyn," said Mr. Middleton, drinking at one long draught the glass of iced beer that Ethel handed him, "—again, Ethel; that was good, you have iced it to a nicety—down across the end of Thirlmere, up and over by Armboth, among the mosses to Watendlath, then unspoilt by the hand or pen of man, down into Barrowdale, up the Stye Head Pass, across Green Gable where he saw the rainbow of Valhalla spanning the valley at our feet, down again to Buttermere—thank you, Ethel, thank you. This beer is the best I have ever tasted. Where do we get it? I must have a cask to hold my high revels."

"It's not in casks, sir, it's bottled, from the Fleece down in the village," said Ethel. "Light Lager."

"Catherine, we must always have this beer," said Mr. Middleton. "I know beer. Few men know it as I do and this is *beer*."

"It's what we always have, sir," said Ethel.

"It may be, it may be," said Mr. Middleton rather crossly. "No thanks, no more. It is not so good now as it was before."

With which Shakespearian echo he reassumed his fit of gloom.

But almost at once Ethel announced Mr. Cameron and they were able to go straight in to lunch. The meal was so good that conversation fell to a pleasantly low level and when they had finished their coffee Mr. Middleton carried Mr. Cameron off to the library to talk business.

"I shall go over before tea and see if I can do anything for Lilian," said Mrs. Middleton. "She looked so worried about Denis. That poor boy."

"I hope he isn't going to be ill again," said Mr. Middleton. "Ask them all over after dinner to-night, Catherine. After all Lilian is my sister. I may be busy, I may have to work, but she will be welcome, and so," he added battling with his lower self, "will her stepchildren. Do not forget, my dear Catherine, to order more of that excellent beer."

"I did, yesterday," said Mrs. Middleton. "The Fleece like sending on Saturdays, so I usually order on Fridays. What time do you want to dine, Jack?"

After a great deal of talk it was decided that after so late a lunch it would be agreeable to have dinner at a quarter past eight, and the two men went off to the study while Mrs. Middleton prepared to visit her sister-in-law, for it was already almost four o'clock.

❧ 3 ❧

GUESTS AT LAVERINGS

❧

IT WAS ONE OF MRS. MIDDLETON'S SPECIAL GIFTS THAT HER
servants stayed with her. In most households a sudden demand for lunch at a quarter past two and dinner at a quarter
past eight would have been met with sulks and followed by
notice. But though Mr. Middleton was entirely inconsiderate
of his staff, or perhaps because he was so whole-heartedly
inconsiderate, they all felt a protective adoration for him and
never left except to marry. The more people came for the
weekend, the more unexpected guests turned up for lunch,
tea and dinner, the more the Laverings kitchen rose to the
occasion. It was not the good wages, nor the large Christmas
tips, not the lure of seeing and hearing famous people, for
the Middletons' circle though very well known had not the
names that adorn the cheaper Sunday papers. There was in
it some of that rather sentimental British feeling for children, drunken men, very small things and dogs; not that
Mr. Middleton exactly surprised in himself, in Count Smorl-
tork's words, all or any of these elements, unless it was his
occasionally childish attitude. A great deal of the kitchen

contentment must have been due to Mrs. Middleton, who
had the excellent housekeeping tradition of her family, infinite patience in listening to stories of misfortune, and never
lost her head or her temper, unless deliberately. A story was
current in the kitchen that she had once thrown some Benger's Food, feeding cup and all, out of Mr. Middleton's bedroom window because it was not properly made. The
Benger's Food was by now in a fair way to becoming a leg of
mutton, or a turkey with trimmings, and added greatly to
her reputation in the village. Even Lady Bond, who kept
her servants by the reign of terror which the better class of
that race still admires as being a proof of good blood, had to
admit that Mrs. Middleton was a past mistress in the art of
keeping a staff.

Therefore, when Mrs. Middleton wanted dinner at a quarter past eight, she merely gave the order to Ethel and was
able to go over to the White House without any foreboding
or sinking of the spirit.

She crossed the lane and went into the Stonors' garden.
Everything was very quiet. Mrs. Pucken had gone home,
Palfrey was reading about the Home Life of the Royal
Family in the kitchen, on the other side of the house. The
only person to be seen was Denis, lying on a chair in the sun,
his hat tilted over his eyes, so whether he was dead or asleep
she could not tell. As a matter of fact he was neither, but
still in that state of blissful half-consciousness that only the
right time and place can bring. The slight noise of Mrs.
Middleton's approach broke this calm. He looked up and
saw what for the moment he took to be a stranger, for he
had not seen Mrs. Middleton since he had been ill at Laver-

ings some years ago. He looked at a woman no longer young, with a face that proclaimed good breeding, rather tired eyes and a mouth that told him nothing till it broke to a smile and he suddenly knew who she was and incidentally where he was, for his waking had left him for a moment confused. He sat up.

"Don't get up, Denis," said Mrs. Middleton. "I'm so glad to see you again."

Denis, fearing that he was being treated as an invalid, uncoiled himself as quickly as possible and shook hands. Mrs. Middleton was a tall woman, but she had to look up to see Denis's face. In it she saw more than she liked of the invalid whom she had helped to nurse, so she at once said that he was looking much better.

"Oh, I'm quite all right, thank you," said Denis. "I expect you want to see Lilian, don't you. She was going to unpack, but it's nearly tea-time. Will you come in?"

"I can't tell you," said Denis as they went into the house, "how sorry I was that we made Mr. Middleton late for lunch. It all seemed to be rather a muddle with our luggage and Flora and Mr. Cameron, and darling Lilian did so much explaining. I'll go and find her and Daphne."

"Wait a moment," said Mrs. Middleton sitting down. "I want to know about you. Are you really better? And how much do you feel like doing? Jack wants you all to come over to-night after dinner, but if it would tire you, please tell me. We have so many people at Laverings and I want you to feel free to come in when you like and stay away when you like. We have rather a good piano if that would amuse you."

"That's a hideous temptation," said Denis. "I was congratulating myself on the badness of this little piano, because I ought to work at composing without a piano, which this odious little affair would give me every encouragement to do. And now you mention a good piano and all my good resolves go flying away."

Mrs. Middleton suggested that he should give way to his evil impulses in the middle of the week when her husband was in town and so avoid disturbing him. In a few minutes Denis was telling her his plans for some ballet music that he had almost been commissioned to write. Palfrey, bringing in the tea things, was asked to let Mrs. Stonor know that Mrs. Middleton had come and in a very short time Lilian came downstairs and kissed her sister-in-law with great affection.

"You look very well, Lilian," said Mrs. Middleton. "And ridiculously young to have such grown-up children."

"It isn't as if they were really mine of course," said Lilian seriously. "I could nearly be their mother, but not quite."

"All this talk about mothers is sheer vanity and one of Lilian's favourite ways of showing off," said her undutiful stepson. "She likes people to think I am really her son so that they will say how surprising and they never would have thought it possible."

Mrs. Middleton laughed, but secretly she thought, with compassion, that though Lilian might look younger than her years, poor Denis looked far older than his. Then she asked about Daphne.

"Daphne was in a very good job with a doctor," said Mrs. Stonor. "She did secretary work for him and then he most selfishly died, so she wants another job, but I rather hope she won't find one just yet. It would be so nice to have her down here for the summer. She gave the greatest satisfaction to Dr. Browning and has a gift for adding up figures that I simply can't understand, besides knowing people when she sees them again. Oh, Daphne, here is Aunt Catherine."

Daphne embraced Mrs. Middleton, enquired warmly after Lily Langtry and was delighted to hear that her ex-patient, now a thriving grandmother, was well and had beaten Lord Bond's Staple Selina in the milk competition, though coming second to Mr. Palmer's Phaedra.

"What a funny name for a cow," said Mrs. Stonor.

"Mr. Palmer called her after some amateur theatricals they had," said Mrs. Middleton, which explanation satisfied everyone. "Jack wants to know if you will all come over after dinner. We shall be alone except for Alister Cameron, whom you know."

"Oh how lovely," said Daphne, "and we'll play Corinthian bagatelle. Or did Uncle Jack break it to pieces? He said he would when Denis was ill, the night you and I, Aunt Catherine, do you remember, and that nurse that was always taking offence made such a noise."

"Yes, Uncle Jack broke it to pieces himself. And then he repented, because the British Legion would have liked it, so he bought them a new one, much better than ours."

"But it was yours, wasn't it, Aunt Catherine?" said Denis.

"Yes, I suppose so," said Mrs. Middleton. "Lilian, all this 'aunt'-ing. Need your family be so polite? They call you Lilian, so I really think they might call me Catherine."

"I'd love to," said Daphne. "I always do except when I'm talking to you. It's an awfully nice name somehow."

Denis said nothing. Catherine was a comfortable kind of name, but he didn't feel he particularly wanted to use it. One could always manage by saying "you" to people. The Aunt Catherine who had been so kind to him, whom he had expected to see when his stepmother brought him to Skeynes, had mysteriously vanished. Her place had been taken by a stranger, charming enough, but someone he must get to know all over again. When he woke and found her looking at him his first feeling had been a faint resentment that he had been taken unawares. He so wished never to be treated as an invalid and she had stolen upon him, found him having what Nannie used to call a nice lay down, taken him altogether at a disadvantage. Then looking at her as his consciousness emerged from the confusion of a light sleep, he saw her eyes, and it had become, though he only realised it now, extremely important that they should look less tired.

Mrs. Stonor went back to Laverings with her sister-in-law to look at the improvements in the garden and the young Stonors were left alone. They went out onto the terrace and strolled into the little wilderness where a stream had been coaxed into miniature pools and waterfalls and planted with delicate clumps of flowers and shrubs.

"I call it very clever of Catherine to make all this," said Daphne. "She did a lot of it when you were ill at Laverings. I wish I were about six inches high."

Denis thought six inches would be too small. One wouldn't be able to cross such a roaring torrent, he said, if one were that size. He thought about a foot high, tall enough to enjoy the scenery without being frightened of it. Daphne pointed out a very good place for fording the river if there were a few stepping-stones and for the next hour they worked industriously at making travel easier for people one foot high and laughed so much that they didn't hear Mrs. Stonor coming towards them. So she stopped to look at them, full of gratitude that Denis looked so happy, hoping that it was a good omen for a successful summer. The one grief of her happy married life had been that she could not remove her husband's anxiety about the boy whom he loved and couldn't understand. If Colonel Stonor had lived she believed the understanding would have grown as Denis's health improved, and already there had been a hopeful basis of more toleration from the father, more patience from the son. Since she had been a widow she had devoted herself more than ever to her step-children, with a vague feeling that if Daphne had a happy time and the right clothes, and Denis was nursed and persuaded into better health, her husband would be pleased. It had meant a good deal of economy for they were not well off, but her own wants were few and she was not easily tired. She was one of the rare people in whom perfect health goes with real compassion for the weak and to Denis she had given from her strength with both hands.

Denis, perhaps unconsciously conscious of her presence, looked up and saw her. His tired lined face melted into the smile that always touched his stepmother to the quick, in which she saw all the affection and gratitude that the greediest woman could want; and she was not greedy. She came nearer, admired the stepping-stones and suggested one or two small improvements suitable for people a foot high.

"Oh, a dreadful thing," she said suddenly, putting the last stone to a flight of steps by which travellers would get to the top of the beetling river bank, "Lord and Lady Bond are coming in after dinner at Laverings. I did hope we would be alone, but they are agitated about something somebody wants to build somewhere and they said they must come and talk to Uncle Jack about it. If you feel too tired, Denis, Daphne and I will go and I will say you are going to bed, which will be nearly true because you will be going to bed sometime in any case."

"I remember Lady Bond," said Daphne. "She came to lunch the day the Jersey calved and she knows a lot about cows, but I had been reading the Stock Breeders' Gazette when I was sitting up with Pucken the night before waiting for the calf and I caught her out once. She is one of those people that ought to have been a Colonel's wife in India if you see what I mean."

"I'm glad she isn't," said Denis. "I'd love to see you arguing with her about cows and I certainly shan't go to bed. I shall read up Cow in the Encyclopaedia and confound her with my knowledge. Also I shall play the Ranz des Vaches to her on the Laverings piano."

Daphne said she betted he didn't know what the Ranz des Vaches was.

"Of course I do," said Denis. "It is the tune that Swiss waiters all over the world get homesick when they hear."

"When they hear it, you mean," said Daphne. "You can't

say It's the tune when they hear."

"Well, It's the tune when they hear it wouldn't make much sense either," said Denis. "You don't know English Usage, my girl."

THE party at Laverings were having coffee in the library when the Stonors came across from the White House. Mrs. Middleton told Ethel to bring three more cups and some fresh coffee, Mrs. Stonor protested that they had had coffee at home and didn't want any more, and after the senseless hubbub demanded by the conventions, got her own way. Mr. Middleton, who had made up his mind that Denis would arrive fainting, in a shabby velvet coat (for such was his rapidly conceived idea of an invalid who was a musician), was agreeably surprised to see his guest in a very ordinary smoking jacket, clean and tidy, his hair (which Mr. Middleton for no particular reason expected to have grown several inches since their brief meeting that morning) neatly cut. The boy was certainly no beauty, if not downright ugly, but he looked healthy enough in the waning summer light. And now that there was no danger to his own sensibilities, Mr. Middleton was ready enough to be sympathetic. So he asked Denis to sit by him, offered him a cigar which Denis refused and enquired how he liked the White House, and what he proposed to do during the summer. Denis said he liked the White House very much and hoped to write some music for a ballet.

"Lilian," said Mr. Middleton to his sister, who was talking to her hostess and did not in the least wish to be disturbed, "this boy of yours tells me he is going to write music for a ballet. That is excellent, excellent. The ballet is one of the best exercises for the young musician, for it gives him the rigid framework which is so necessary; the trellis on which the vine can put forth its luxuriant growth. The same applies to all forms of art. The picture must have a limit, hence the arbitrary shape, square, oblong, the lunette, the tondo. Sculpture too has its boundaries; the triangular pediment, the square lines of the tomb, even the actual shape of the mass of marble from which the skilled artist will release the imprisoned group or figure. Similarly with music it has been found necessary to impose upon it the form of the symphony, the sonata, to prune what is excessive that the plant may grow with more vigour. Alister!" he called to Mr. Cameron, who was happily talking to Daphne about a river in Scotland where he had once fished, "one moment. Would you or would you not agree with me when I say that of all the arts literature, at any rate in England, is that which stands least in need of bounds? That the strength of that glory of our country is such that it can climb and wander at its own will, careless of forms, or creating its own form as it goes."

Having thus forcibly attracted the attention of his whole audience Mr. Middleton, without waiting for the reply which Mr. Cameron knew him far too well to waste his time in making, was enjoying himself immensely, when Ethel, seizing a moment between two sentences, announced Lord and Lady Bond.

As her ladyship bore down upon the company Denis at

once recognised what his sister had meant when she said that Lady Bond ought to be a Colonel's wife in India. It was quite obvious that she would arrange the life of any of her friends or acquaintances without the faintest regard for their feelings, bully all the tenants for their good, be on every committee, and in short be a despotic benefactress to the whole country. Her husband, a little roundfaced man with a white moustache, followed her closely.

"How are you, Bond," said Mr. Middleton. "This is my sister's stepson, Denis Stonor. He is composing a ballet."

"Are you a Russian then?" said Lord Bond. "No, no, stupid of me, Middleton couldn't have a Russian sister."

"I'm quite English all over," said Denis, "and it's an English ballet I'm trying to do the music for."

"English ballet, eh?" said Lord Bond. "Now that's most interesting. I thought it was Russian ballet. I know my wife took me to something Russian last summer. Not much in my line, but there was a nice bit of music by that fellow that wrote the symphony—what is its name, the one my wife's musical friends are always talking about, the Seventh. You know I always think it's a funny thing writing a symphony and calling it the seventh. I knew a man, before your time he was, Abel Fosgrave, he had a very good taste in wine and called his first daughter Septima."

Denis said gravely that there must be something in the number seven. Lord Bond said he was probably right and the name of the fellow that wrote the symphony was Beethoven, but it didn't sound Russian, which seemed to depress him so much that Denis kindly offered to play him some of his own ballet on the piano. But before Lord Bond could answer, Lady Bond, having said what she considered fit to Mrs. Stonor and Daphne, demanded the attention of the whole room.

"Something has happened of so serious a nature that I felt I must see you at once, otherwise Bond and I would not have interrupted your family party," said her ladyship, whose habit of speaking of her husband by his name without a prefix was the admiration of all who heard her.

"You know," said Lady Bond, graciously including all her audience whether interested or not, "Pooker's Piece."

Most of them didn't, but they were too cowardly to say so except Mr. Cameron, who simply said No.

"No, you wouldn't know it," said Lord Bond kindly. "It is on the edge of my property, just above High Ramstead."

"Just where we march with Mr. Palmer," said her ladyship in a feudal way, "on the other side of the Woolram, above the hatches."

"Oh, you mean Overfolds," said Mr. Middleton.

"No, no, Mr. Middleton," said Lady Bond. "Overfolds is the name of that triangle where Mr. Palmer's larches come down the hill. Pooker's Piece is the part at the bottom, by the little lane that runs up past old Margett's cottage to Upper Worsted. Any of the old people would tell you its name."

"I thought—" Mrs. Middleton began.

"Yes, Mrs. Middleton?" said Lord Bond kindly.

"Oh, nothing," said Mrs. Middleton weakly, remembering that envious shepherds to whom she had talked gave that particular field a grosser name, though Lady Bond did Pooker's Piece call it.

"Well, that is the bit of land I mean," said Lady Bond firmly. "And what do you think we have heard?"

"Pooker's Piece," said Mr. Middleton. "The survival of these pre-Norman names, even so near London, is excessively interesting. Pooker, Pook, or Puck—"

"Pooker wasn't pre-Norman," said Lord Bond, "I found out all about him a few years ago. You know the living of Skeynes Agnes is in my gift. I had to go through the records of the church there and it appears that the Reverend Horatio Pooker was vicar from 1820 to 1843. He bought that field from sheer spite, because my great-grandfather and Palmer's great-great-uncle both wanted it, and left it to the Charity Commissioners."

"And that," said Lady Bond, determined not to be forestalled in her news, "is where the trouble comes. You remember Sir Ogilvy Hibberd?"

Everyone said Yes: some because they did, the others because they felt it would save trouble.

"Well, he has bought Pooker's Piece," said Lady Bond, "and wants to put a teashop and garage there. As soon as I heard of it I said to Alured that we must see you as soon as possible."

It was a tribute to the importance of the occasion that Lady Bond should have used her husband's Christian name, which was only wrenched from her by severe emotion. There was a brief silence of consternation, broken by Daphne, who asked who Sir Whateverhisnamewas was.

"A Lloyd George Knight," said Lord Bond, "something

in shipping, I believe, from Goole. I have had to meet him once or twice on committees but my wife does not know him."

"How did you hear about it?" asked Mrs. Middleton.

Lady Bond opened her mouth to speak, but Mr. Middleton, who had hitherto been silent, suddenly uttered the words, "This touches me very nearly."

Daphne said Why, but catching an appealing look from her stepmother, said no more.

"Pooker's Piece," said Mr. Middleton in an enormous voice, contemplating an unseen audience in a building about twice the size of the Albert Hall. "If I had been asked to name one place in which the spirit of England breathes, in which oak, ash and thorn still shelter who knows what woodland divinities under a rustic guise, untouched since the days of the Heptarchy, I should have named Pooker's Piece. Many is the tramp I have taken over wood and common in this countryside, with Flora enjoying every moment of it as much as I do, with that wonderful dog's instinct for what is best—not only because Master likes it, but best in itself. Many, I say, is the tramp we two friends have taken together, but none have been so wholly blessed to us as our walks over Pooker's Piece."

Having thus delivered himself he snapped his fingers affectionately towards Flora, who opened one eye from the rug where she was sleeping, looked at her master with complete lack of recognition or interest and went to sleep again.

"And now, Bond," said Mr. Middleton, "I would like to pick your brains. My man Pucken says that the little pond down beyond his cottage goes dry regularly, every seven years, whether the season is wet or dry, and is therefore poisonous to cows. I think it is an excuse to save himself trouble when the cows are in that field and he doesn't want to bring them up to the higher pond, but you know the country better than I do. Have you ever heard about it?"

Lord Bond knew Mr. Middleton well enough to be quite sure that picking his brains was only his way of saying that he meant to talk about his own views on folk-lore for at least fifteen minutes, but he was none the less flattered, having a touching belief in professional men, especially in one of his own finding. But Lady Bond put an end to his hopes by asking again in a commanding way what was to be done about it and answering her own question by saying that they had better call a meeting in the Village Hall, or better still have a drawing-room meeting first to decide who was to be asked to the general meeting.

"I don't think your room is large enough, Mrs. Middleton," said Lady Bond, "so it had better be at Staple Park."

If Mrs. Middleton felt annoyed at this cavalier treatment of her house she gave no sign of it.

"You must all come, of course," said Lady Bond graciously. "You of course, Mr. Cameron."

Mr. Cameron said with great presence of mind that his work made any day except Sunday impossible.

"—and Mrs. Stonor and her young people," her ladyship continued, Juggernauting over Mr. Cameron as if he were not there.

Daphne, who had been bursting to speak ever since her stepmother checked her, saw an opening and said Denis loathed that sort of thing but she would come and help with pleasure. She was, she added, pretty good at meetings and could typewrite the notices if Lady Bond liked.

"Oh, do you typewrite?" said Lady Bond. "That is delightful. You must come over to lunch and we will make out a list of useful people to invite."

Daphne at once took possession of Lady Bond and so absorbed did her ladyship become in her plan of campaign that the rest of the company, to their great relief, were able to talk among themselves. Mr. Middleton and his sister sat together on the sofa while Mr. Cameron and Mrs. Middleton talked comfortably about nothing in particular. Denis, rather bored, was wondering if he could slip out and go home to bed, when Lord Bond, almost apologetically, reminded him of his offer to play some ballet music.

"I do so like a good tune," he said, "and I never feel the wireless is the same as a piano. I used to play a little piece by Chopin myself once. It was quite short. I wonder if you know the one I mean. It had three of those things like noughts and crosses at the beginning, and three quarters written on the lines. Of course I only played it by ear. De-*doo*-de-doo-doo-doo, it goes, and then the same thing over again only the notes are a little bit different. De-*doo*-de-doo-doo-doo. And then the same thing again, only with just a little change, De-*doo*-de-doo-doo-doo—you don't know it?"

Denis recognised the little piece with no difficulty as the little Prelude in three-four time which everyone has played badly at one time or another. He obligingly sat down and played it with the soft pedal so that the conversation of his elders should not be disturbed.

"Thank you very much," said Lord Bond when Denis had finished. "I do like a good tune so much. My wife and my son like this highbrow stuff, but I do like something with a tune in it and not too long. You were going to play me one of your own tunes."

Lady Bond from the other end of the room said, "So amusing to hear some Chopin. Do go on, Mr. Stonor. I can't tell you, Miss Stonor, what a handicap I find it with my secretary away, and her mother's illness will be a very long one, I fear."

Mr. Middleton sang a few bars of the Chopin in a rather tuneless falsetto and said Denis should study Bach.

Mrs. Middleton looked across with great gratitude at any-one who could amuse Lord Bond, and Denis, interpreting her look, sent her one of the smiles that so changed his ugly face. If pleasing Lord Bond would please Catherine, it should be done, though he very much doubted if his ballet music would give Lord Bond any real pleasure, when suddenly, with what he afterwards considered to be the direct guiding of Providence, a thought came to him.

"I'm afraid my stuff doesn't go very well on the piano, sir," he said to Lord Bond. "You see it's written for orchestra, and piano isn't quite the same. But I was wondering if you like Gilbert and Sullivan."

Lord Bond's face, which was usually quite devoid of any expression but earnest dullness, suddenly lighted up.

"If you really could play some, not too loud," he said,

looking nervously at his wife, "I would enjoy it so very much. My dear mother took me to *Pinafore* when I was seven, it was the first play I had ever been to and I shall never forget the impression it made on me. My wife doesn't much care for that sort of thing, but if you really could play some of the songs, I should enjoy it immensely. I suppose you don't know the words, do you?"

"Not very well," said Denis, amused, "but perhaps you would help, sir."

Without waiting for an answer he began to play the Judge's song from *Trial by Jury,* very softly, while Lord Bond, transfigured, half sang, half spoke the words in a hoarse whisper. At the end of the last verse he shook Denis warmly by the hand.

"We'll have some more another time," he said in a low voice. "Come up to Staple Park one day when my wife is in town, mustn't disturb her you know, and we'll have what I call a real concert together. We've a grand piano in the drawing-room and I'll make them find the key, they lost it at Christmas when the piano tuner came, and we'll enjoy ourselves. And I've some really good port; you look as if a glass or two would do you good."

He went over to his wife, leaving Denis to reflect upon the probable condition of a piano whose key appeared to be permanently lost and the best way of avoiding port, which upset him at once. But he liked Lord Bond and was very willing to amuse him.

"Come and talk to us, Denis," said Mrs. Middleton. "We'll go outside, it's so hot indoors."

Denis and Mr. Cameron walked out with her onto the stone flags and sat down on a bench. The late summer twilight still lingered in the north, behind the house, while before them the landscape was fading into darkness.

"You and Daphne are going to be the greatest success," said Mrs. Middleton. "If you can amuse Lord Bond and she can hold her own against Lady Bond, Skeynes will be more peaceful than it has been since I came here."

"She is a good woman," said Mr. Cameron, "but stupid, stupid. I don't know anyone that so exhausts the air from any room where she is. Half an hour of Lady Bond makes you look more tired, Catherine, than three nights in a train. And I know what I am talking about. Mr. and Mrs. Middleton and I," he explained to Denis, "all went on the Orient Express one summer because Mr. Middleton wanted to meet someone who knew more about Balkan architecture than anyone else. You looked like the inside of a mushroom, Catherine, when we got to Prasvoda. But Lady Bond can produce exactly the same effect on you in three minutes. I dislike her."

"Was the interview a success?" said Denis, who felt he ought to slur over Mr. Cameron's very unchivalrous comparison of his hostess to the inside of a mushroom, and rather resented it.

"A great success," said Mr. Cameron. "The man—he was an ex-prime-minister whose name I could not pronounce at the time and have never remembered since—could not talk a word of English and only a few words of French. Mr. Middleton's French is, to be candid, entirely inadequate to any situation. It was the height of summer when Prasvoda is quite empty and there was no interpreter to be found. So Mr. Middleton talked to the ex-premier for three days and three nights without stopping, not even pausing to suck an orange, about the influence of Graeco-Roman civilisation in Prasvoda with divagations on the Greek element in Shelley, Keats and Goethe."

"And then?" said Denis, suddenly very tired, but amused by the story.

"We came home," said Mr. Cameron, "and Mr. Middleton wrote a most remarkable article on the architecture of the Orthodox Entente, Prasvoda and all those little states, between 1900 and 1936."

"But did he need to go there to write it?" asked Denis. "I mean if he couldn't understand what they said and they couldn't understand what he said—"

He paused.

"How Mr. Middleton comes to know anything is an eternal mystery," said Mr. Cameron. "He has never been able to communicate with any foreigner unless he can speak English, and as far as I can gather from various interviews at which I have assisted none of the people whose brains he says he picks have ever got a word in edgeways. He has an extraordinary power of absorbing not only atmosphere but facts. And he never forgets anything."

"No, I suppose not," said Mrs. Middleton quietly.

Denis, sensitive to voices, couldn't quite make out if her words were a statement, or a question to herself. But any further reflections on this subject were cut short by his host calling Mrs. Middleton's name. One did not keep Mr. Middleton waiting, so much Denis had already discovered, and all three rose and went in.

"Catherine, I needed you, and you were not there," said Mr. Middleton pathetically.

"I was just outside the window and I heard you at once and here I am," said Mrs. Middleton. "What is it, Jack?"

She laid her hand on her husband's shoulder and he looked up very affectionately.

"I need your advice, Catherine, as always. Lady Bond thinks that perhaps for a preliminary meeting Staple Park would be too large."

He looked round him wildly, like a child who only knows half its lesson.

"What about the White House?" said Mrs. Stonor. "I don't think the drawing-room would hold more than five people at a pinch, what with the way it goes round the corner, but we could pull the piano out into the hall, only then I suppose people could hardly get in."

Lady Bond said with a smile of gracious impatience that she feared it would be hardly what they needed and looked at Mr. Middleton, who appeared to have forgotten his cue.

"We were wondering," said Lady Bond, "if it would in any way upset Mrs. Middleton's arrangements—but you can put it better than I can, Mr. Middleton."

Mr. Middleton groaned.

"We could easily have it here, Lady Bond," said Mrs. Middleton, adding with faint malice, "If we have it in the middle of the week when Jack is in town, it will put no one out."

Lady Bond protested against her host's absence and said it must certainly be on a Saturday when all the weekend residents would be obtainable. "But not that young couple over at Beliers," she said. "They are Communists and the woman wears shorts and the young man has a beard."

As no one had ever heard of the young couple at Beliers Mrs. Middleton was able to promise that they should not be asked.

"Then I think to-day week, no I am busy that day, to-day fortnight will suit us all," said Lady Bond. "Miss Stonor, if you will come up to the Park on Monday we could arrange about invitations and you could begin typing the notices. And perhaps you would look at the accounts for me as Miss Edwards is away and I would give you lunch of course."

"Thanks awfully," said Daphne. "Dr. Browning paid me three guineas a week for doing his secretary stuff, but this won't be a regular job, so shall we say half a crown an hour and then I can come as much or as little as you like. I worked four hours a day for five days for Dr. Browning, so this would work out a little cheaper, but it's the country and nothing important, so I think that's quite fair. Then when your secretary comes back she won't be able to have the Union down on you for using blackleg labour. It'll be great fun."

Several of the party saw in Lady Bond's eye how little she had intended to pay Daphne anything at all and felt that Providence was for once taking an intelligent part in affairs at Skeynes. Daphne's remark about the unimportance of the job also gave great pleasure, for though everyone now hated Sir Ogilvy Hibberd and wished him to be baulked at every point, he was a distant foe, and to see Lady Bond bearded in Mr. Middleton's den was a triumph that could be rolled on the tongue and thoroughly enjoyed on the spot. But her ladyship, who prided herself on doing things in a handsome way, said that the arrangement would suit her very well, and catching up Lord Bond in the whiff and wind of her departure, took her leave.

"I always expect," said Mr. Cameron, "that Lady Bond will pick her husband up under one arm and carry him out of the room."

"Oh, she's all right," said Daphne tolerantly. "You only want to get her where you want her. Most people are like that."

"Want, up to the present, has been my master, and certainly Lord Bond's master," said Mr. Cameron, and then Mrs. Stonor, who had for some time been worried about Denis, said they must go home.

"Yes, my dear Lilian, you must be tired," said Mr. Middleton looking with benevolent solicitude at his sister. "You have done much to-day. Much," he added, so that no one should get a word in while he took breath. "But here you will I hope find complete repose. I like to think that at Laverings and equally at the White House, the influence of many hundreds of years of settled occupation, of peaceful tilling of the soil, of the rearing of cattle, a contribution to the well-being of the country to which I am far from indifferent, having taken an infinite amount of trouble to obtain the best Jersey cows and feed and shelter them on the more modern and scientific lines, all these forces, I say, must work together to create an atmosphere in which the tension of latter day life is relaxed, is dissipated. Laverings—"

"Pucken says Lily is going to calve again in August," said Daphne, her handsome face alight with anticipation.

"Laverings," Mr. Middleton continued, raising his voice several tones against this distasteful interruption, "Laverings was already in existence, though not in its present form, before the Conquest. Wait," he said as no one was doing anything else, though much against most of their wills, "I should like to read you an extract from the Domesday Book in which Gorwulf-Steadings, the site of the present Laverings Farm, and the name yet survives in Guestings, one of Lord Pomfret's places in this neighbourhood, is mentioned in some detail."

"I think I had better take the children home now, Jack," said Mrs. Stonor getting up. "Let's have the Domesday thing to-morrow. I am really rather tired after to-day. I don't know why, for after all the railway journey is quite short, and I had finished practically all the packing the night before and Palfrey and Mrs. Pucken had got everything in perfect order here and I had a most restful sleep this afternoon, but somehow one does get fatigued by any kind of move, so we will say good night."

"Bear with me one moment, Lilian," said Mr. Middleton with a patient yet gay smile. "When my hand is on the plough I do not like to look back. Cameron, you will find the volume of which I was speaking in the third shelf from the top of the shelves to the right of the fire. I know every book as if it were my child."

Mr. Cameron, who had at once got up and gone to look, said it was not there.

"You mistake, unless I am gravely in error," said Mr. Middleton, rising in affronted majesty.

But even as he embarked upon his search for the book his wife said good night to the Stonors with a gentle finality that left them no choice but thankfully to slip away by the open French window.

"I have it, I have it," cried Mr. Middleton, turning from the bookcase. "Lilian! Where is Lilian?"

"She has gone home," said Mr. Cameron, who was standing at the window looking after the departing guests.

"I regret it," said Mr. Middleton gravely. "And the more so as I have just remembered that I have that book upstairs in my room. Shall I go and get it, tired as I am? I will, I will, and I will read you the passage in question."

He made as if to go up by his little staircase, but with such a bowed gait and almost shuffling step, as of a man grown old in the service of his country and now unjustly thrown aside, that his wife went upstairs, found the book and brought it to him before he had finished his noble and vacillating journey from the bookcase to the door.

"There you are, Jack," said Mrs. Middleton. "And now I am going to bed. Good night, Alister."

"Bear with me for one moment, Catherine," said the persecuted veteran. "I must read the account of Laverings to you and Cameron. I had promised myself the pleasure of reading it aloud, and though Lilian and her young have left us, a promise is a promise. I feel I shall not sleep if a promise is not fulfilled."

Mrs. Middleton sat down and smiled at him.

He read aloud for some ten minutes an account, extraordinarily dull to anyone who was not interested, of the manor of Gorwulf-Steadings and its appurtenances, while his wife sat apparently thinking of nothing and his partner smoked a pipe. On coming to the end of the extract he shut the book with some violence, and looked round.

"Bed, bed!" he cried. "It is far too late for us, Cameron. We have to work to-morrow and I shall take you over to Pooker's Piece, where we shall talk to old Margett, who is wise with the wisdom of his ancestors. He knows me well and will talk to me when he would be silent with another man. And you, my Catherine, should have been in bed an hour ago."

So saying he went upstairs.

"Good night, Catherine," said Mr. Cameron. "You look tired."

"You said Jack never forgot anything," said Mrs. Middleton rather vaguely.

"You mean the whereabouts of that book," said Mr. Cameron.

"Yes, I suppose I do," said Mrs. Middleton with what might have been a sigh but was probably, Mr. Cameron thought, a yawn, and she went away, asking her guest to shut the French window before he went to bed. Before he shut it he took a turn on the flagged path outside and saw one light still shining through the trees at the White House. He thought it might be that amusing girl, Daphne Stonor, whose routing of Lady Bond filled him with awed admiration. As a matter of fact it was the light from Denis's room, who was too tired to go to sleep. He was thinking about the evening at Laverings and how he had let himself in for playing Lord Bond's locked piano and having to refuse his excellent port. Mr. Cameron's story of his chief's visit to Prasvoda had been very amusing. Then he remembered how Mr. Cameron had said that Mr. Middleton never forgot anything. Mrs. Middleton's non-committal answer came back to his mind. She had not seemed quite sure if Uncle Jack remembered everything and Denis felt a dawning certainty that the one thing Uncle Jack regularly and unconsciously forgot was his wife. This thought appeared to him so worthy of attention that he turned out his light, the better to consider it. From Laverings Mr. Cameron saw the light go out, shut the window and went up to bed.

❧ 4 ❧

STAPLE PARK

MRS. MIDDLETON AND MR. CAMERON WERE ALONE ON SUNDAY morning, for Mr. Middleton preferred as usual to breakfast in his own room. Sun poured into the dining-room and Mr. Cameron imprisoned two wasps in a glass jam-pot which, as he said, was all very well, but he wished he had taken a second helping before they found their way in.

"I suppose you aren't going to church, Alister," said Mrs. Middleton. "Oh look, one of your wasps is getting out at the spoon hole."

"You ought to have spoons with fatter handles," said Mr. Cameron. He took a small piece of the soft inside of his toast, moulded it in his fingers and stopped up the hole. The wasp, who had twice got his head and shoulders out, fell down again discouraged and lay kicking among the raspberry seeds. "No, Catherine, I am not going to church. I should like to come and sing out of the same hymn book as you, but my employer will probably want to talk with me this morning, or rather to use me as a talking horse, if the expression may be allowed. And apart from the great pleasure of sharing a hymn book with you, I find the so-called music extremely trying. Why are all hymns and psalms so high that one can't get there? And if one sings, as I do, an octave lower, one's voice makes no noise at all."

"Perhaps it is all for the best," said Mrs. Middleton. "I always pretend that the print is too small for me to see the words and don't sing at all and try to look as if I were meditating. I don't suppose it really counts, but one must go or there would be no one in the Laverings pew and the Rector would be unhappy. Alister, would you very kindly go over to the White House and see if any of them would care to come with me? It is so nice if one can make a good show for the Rector and even three in a pew, if one spaces them out, are a help. Church is at eleven."

"Then I'd better go now," said Mr. Cameron, looking at the clock. "It's after ten. Shall I let my wasp out? He might bite Ethel."

"Don't bother," said his hostess. "Ethel likes dealing with insects. She has never forgotten or forgiven an earwig that got away from her last summer by what she considered unfair means. She was just going to stamp on it when Flora ate it, so she is getting her own back on wasps this year."

"That decides me," said Mr. Cameron. "I always was one for cruelty to animals, but unfairness I cannot abide. If Ethel wants to kill earwigs, well and good; but to punish a wasp for the crime of another is beyond the limits."

He took his bread stopper out of the jam-pot. The wasp elbowed its way out indignantly and Ethel, who had come

in a moment too soon, gave Mr. Cameron a glance of cold
disapproval.

"I will go over to the White House now," he said. "What
a delightful sister-in-law you have, Catherine. Why haven't
I seen more of her? I never met anyone whose rather irrele-
vant flow of conversation covered such real heart."

"It was clever of you to see that," said Mrs. Middleton.
"Most people don't get beyond the talk. I think she was
so unhappy when her husband died that she took to talking
as a kind of defence. Not but what talking runs in the
family. How Jack and Lilian ever manage to tell each
other anything, I don't know, as neither of them ever
listens."

"Yes, but you know what my employer is," said Mr.
Cameron. "He talks to you all the time, but six weeks afterwards you find he knows exactly what it was that his flow
of words wouldn't let you say to him."

"Yes, I know," said Mrs. Middleton. "It may be the
same with Lilian, though I don't know her well enough
to be sure. She certainly understands Denis and Daphne,
if anyone can ever be said to understand anyone."

"I like Daphne," said Mr. Cameron. "I wish we could
have a secretary like her in the office. The young lady we
have now is a refined product of the London School of
Economics. I wouldn't mind her trying to run her pink
politics down my throat, for that is a malady most incident
to youth, though I never see why being a Communist
should make one abhor washing and have bad manners, but
she thinks she knows how to run the office so much better
than I do that it leads to unpleasantness."

"Daphne does want a job," said Mrs. Middleton, "but perhaps Jack's office—"

"Yes, you are right," said Mr. Cameron. "My employer has always been against nepotism and though one's sister's stepdaughter is hardly a relation, I don't think it would do. And here am I standing talking with the best of them, while the fate of the Laverings pew hangs in the balance."

He went across to the White House, found the Stonors still at breakfast and was hospitably pressed to join them.

"Well, I wouldn't say no to toast and honey," said Mr. Cameron, "because a wasp got into the jam-pot and I couldn't have a second helping. But what I really came for, Mrs. Stonor, was to say from Catherine that she wants volunteers for church."

There was an immediate and gratifying response to this appeal. Mrs. Stonor said she always went to church in the country, though never in town, because church never seemed quite church in London, if Mr. Cameron saw what she meant, and they had services at such extraordinary times at Westminster Abbey. Daphne said she wanted to see what Lady Bond's Sunday hat was like and if the village idiot was still quite well, while Denis said that he would go anywhere if there was a chance of hearing Jerusalem the Golden, which he liked better than any tune in the world, especially where it went up so high that one had to squeak or stop singing altogether. This led to a very interesting discussion between him and Mr. Cameron on Russian basses which so prolonged itself that Mrs. Stonor and Daphne went over to Laverings to collect Mrs. Middleton, leaving the men to follow them.

As Mr. Cameron and Denis, still deep in argument, were about to separate in front of Laverings, the one to be talked at by his employer, the other to go across the field to the church, Mr. Middleton appeared at the garden door with a furrowed brow. It was, he said, after a perfunctory greeting to his visitors, one of the great griefs of a life now nearing its close that every Sunday brought with it duties that made it impossible for him to go to church. This very morning he had intended to accompany his wife and his sister and refresh himself in that spring of living waters the English Liturgy. But, he continued, after a rapid sketch of the development of the Book of Common Prayer, a cursory survey of the Salisbury Rule and a bird's eye view of the Reformation and its effect on the English language, his wish was not to be fulfilled. There was work waiting for him, Work, he added.

"Will you want me?" said Mr. Cameron, who had a sudden wish, that he didn't trouble to analyse, to go to church himself.

All his life, Mr. Middleton said reverently, he had played a Lone Hand. Others had wives, children, devoted friends, but he had borne the heat and burden of the day alone. Alone.

Denis thought secretly that though Mr. Middleton might not have had wives, he had a wife, but didn't like to say so. Mr. Cameron, who through long practice knew exactly the value to attach to his partner's words, said very well, he would go to church and strode off.

"Didn't he want you?" asked Denis as soon as they were out of earshot.

"Not a bit," said Mr. Cameron. "What he wanted was to smoke a very large cigar and go down and talk to Pucken about the cows and the hay. Which is much better for him than sitting indoors talking to me about Vitruvius. Come on, that's the last bell."

They got into church just ahead of the Rector and went into the Laverings pew, which was right up in front with an excellent view of the Bonds' pew in the chancel. Lady Bond's hat was all that Daphne had hoped. A massive erection of brown velvet crowned with the produce of field, flood and grove, it was perched high on its wearer's head with fine disregard of fashion. Lady Bond, whose mother was Scotch, had been brought up in the best tradition of Edinburgh hats, a tradition which dies hard and still dazzles the rash beholder's eye at afternoon concerts in the Usher Hall, and always got her hats from the same shop in Prince's Street. Mrs. Middleton maintained that she had identified on Lady Bond's Coronation year hat a lobster, two hares' claws, a pineapple, a large bunch of parma violets and a fox's mask and though no one believed her, everyone admitted that she had the root of the matter in her. With Lady Bond were her husband, a female friend, and a young man, unknown to the Stonors. Mr. Cameron had the pleasure of sharing a hymn book with Mrs. Middleton, but as it was one of those hymn books with double columns and *Brilliant* type, and both worshippers were long sighted, neither was able to join in the singing, though in any case they would not have done so. To Denis's great satisfaction Jerusalem the Golden was the second hymn, and he exercised himself very happily in singing in various octaves as

the tune soared or sank. Mr. Cameron greatly admired the
way in which Daphne, who had a pleasant voice and no
diffidence, forged gallantly through everything, when
everyone but the choir (four rebellious little boys and two
farmers' daughters) had failed.

"I say," said Daphne accusingly to Mr. Cameron as they
came out of church. "Why didn't you sing?"

Mr. Cameron answered that no one could sing if they
couldn't see the words.

"Well," said Daphne, "why didn't you put your spectacles on? People *ought* to sing. That's what one goes to
church for."

Mr. Cameron felt unequal to this religious argument and
contented himself with saying that if his spectacles were
double million gas microscopes of extra power he might be
able to read double-columned *Brilliant*. Daphne looked at
him tolerantly, said that was out of Scott or someone wasn't
it, and let the subject drop. Mr. Cameron felt that he was
somehow hopelessly in the wrong: first as a shirker, then
as a highbrow and pretentious quoter, and though reason
told him that Daphne's opinion was of little value, he had
an inexplicable desire to make a better impression on her.

As the Laverings party and the Staple Park party coalesced
in the churchyard, some introducing took place.

"I want you," said Lady Bond to Mrs. Middleton, "to
know my friend, Miss Starter. It is so annoying. Miss
Starter is on a diet and has to have a special bread called
Kornog, which is practically starch-free. She brought part
of a loaf with her—"

"It was what I hadn't finished from the loaf I got on

Thursday," said Miss Starter, a thin middle-aged lady in black, with a faint air of royalty about her and a high black net collar. "I usually get one on Monday and one on Thursday, which last me for a week, as I only have two slices, or at the most three, for my breakfast, very crisply toasted."

"—and," continued Lady Bond, looking with some pride at her exhibit, "Miss Starter unfortunately did not bring an extra loaf, thinking she could get one here, but we find that they do not keep it at Skeynes. My cook has telephoned to Higgins, with whom we usually deal, and to Foxham, the other baker, but they say there is no demand for Kornog."

"Have you tried Mopsall at Winter Overcotes?" said Mrs. Middleton. "When Jack was on a diet two years ago we used to get a special bread from him. It wasn't Kornog, but I'm sure he would get it. I think ours was called Pepso."

"Pepso is only starch-reduced," said Miss Starter earnestly. "Sir Barclay did think of it for me, but he came to the conclusion that Kornog was more what I needed."

"Miss Starter has been attended by Sir Barclay Milvin for some time," said Lady Bond. "He specialises in diets, as you doubtless know. I shall certainly try Winter Overcotes. And I do hope you will come up to tea this afternoon and bring your sister-in-law and her young people. I have my son at home for a few weeks before he goes back to New York. He is doing very well there. C.W.," she called to the young man who had been hanging back during the discussion of starch-free bread, "come and meet Mrs. Stonor, and Miss Stonor and Mr. Stonor."

This formal introduction so paralysed all concerned that they shook hands in silence, and in silence followed Lady

Bond to the lychgate, till Daphne said to Lady Bond's son,

"I say, what's your name? Your mother said C.W., but that's only initials. Haven't you got a real name?"

"Yes," said Lady Bond's son simply, "but I'm rather ashamed of it. My people have always called me C.W., and somehow it stuck. I think they must have been a bit ashamed of it themselves."

"What is it then?" asked Daphne.

"Well," said Lady Bond's son rather nervously, "you know my father is called Alured and there's a sort of superstition that he is a bit Anglo-Saxon or something of the sort, some kind of descendant of King Alfred, only there's a gap of about eight hundred years unaccounted for, so one can't be sure. But anyway Mother thought they ought to keep up the spirit of the thing so they called me Cedric Weyland."

"Good Lord," said Denis sympathetically. "I thought my name was bad enough—it's Denis—but yours must be a perfect curse."

"There's only one thing to be thankful for," said young Mr. Bond, "and that is that schools aren't what they were. In my father's time a boy with a name like that would have been persecuted till he hanged himself or was taken away and sent to an agricultural college, but no one minded it a bit at Hocker's. They thought it was pretty foul of my people and I was always called C.W. And of course at Eton nothing matters."

"Were you at Hocker's?" said Denis, interested. "I was there for two years till I got sent abroad for a bit. Do you remember Miss Hocker's parrot?"

The two young men fell headlong into prep school reminiscences and would gladly have gone on till lunchtime, but Lady Bond after condescending to the Rector's wife had rescued Lord Bond from the senior churchwarden and called to her son to get into the car.

"We're all coming up to tea," said Daphne, "so you and Denis can have a good talk then. Would you like us to call you Cedric or C.W.?"

"Whichever you like," said young Mr. Bond, getting in beside the chauffeur. "No one I liked ever called me Cedric, only governesses and awful things like that."

"All right, we'll take the hoodoo off and say Cedric," said Daphne. "If I'm coming to do secretary stuff for your mother I'll have to call you something."

Young Mr. Bond seemed to be taken aback by this news, but the car rolled away before he could make enquiries.

"C.W. is such a nice boy," said Mrs. Middleton as they walked homewards. "His parents have been a sore trial to him at times, but he bears with them wonderfully. He is in some business firm with a branch in New York. Of course, when Lord Bond dies he will have to live in England and look after the estate and all Lord Bond's interests. Denis, would you care to come over to Laverings before tea and try our piano? Jack and Alister are going for a walk after lunch, so you wouldn't be bothered."

Denis thought that most people would have said You won't be a bother, and gratefully accepted.

SUNDAY lunch at Laverings was always the same; what Mrs.

Middleton called the sacred Sunday joint, followed by a pie
of whatever fruit was in season, which happened to-day to
be cherries. She herself would have liked to order milder
and cooler food for a hot June day, but any attempt to
change the ritual made the iron eat so deeply and loudly
into her husband's soul, that she had quite resigned herself.
What with beef and cherry pie and beer, Mr. Cameron
would gladly have stretched himself on one of the long
chairs outside the house and gone to sleep till it was time to
go to Staple Park, but his senior partner was inexorable,
so Mr. Cameron made up his mind that he would at least
walk him off his legs in revenge.

"Don't forget, Jack," said Mrs. Middleton as the two men
were starting, "that we are all having tea with the Bonds
about five."

Mr. Middleton groaned.

"I had it in my mind," he said, "to take Cameron first to
Pooker's Piece, where we shall talk as man to man with old
Margett, talk racy of the soil, and then to tramp, burning
the long miles beneath our feet; over to Worsted, by the
ruins of Beliers Abbey, to Skeynes Agnes and so home, talking as we go."

"That is about fifteen miles," said Mr. Cameron grimly.

"If you did the walking, Jack could do the talking," Mrs.
Middleton murmured. "If I leave it to you will you get him
to Staple Park by 5 o'clock?"

Mr. Cameron said he would. Mr. Middleton called loudly
for Flora, who was sleeping off her dinner in the sun. She
got up and sauntered towards her master, but suddenly
realising that she was pampering him sat down with her

back to him and thought of other things.

"If you don't want to come, don't," said Mr. Cameron.

Flora at once got up again and approached him, her liquid eyes fixed adoringly on his face.

"Here, Flora," said Mr. Middleton, "carry Master's stick. Many is the mile that she has carried my stick or my newspaper, rejoicing in her dear doggy mind that she can be of help to Master. Here, Flora!"

Flora, who understood and resented this statement, took the proffered stick and trotted into the library, where she laid it on the floor by her master's desk and returned for applause.

"No, no, Flora. Master's stick for walkies," said Mr. Middleton. "Fetch stick for walkies."

But as Flora, who had no intention of encumbering her walk with a large stick, remained deliberately stupid and oafish, Mr. Middleton had to go and fetch his stick and announced himself ready for the walk. Flora, who liked long walks, decided that her master had been sufficiently put in his place, pushed her nose against his hand and led the way to the garden gate.

Mrs. Middleton went into the library and cleared some books and papers from the piano in case Denis wanted to open it. Then she picked up a book and lay down on the large sofa. The summer peace of Laverings reigned undisturbed. Mrs. Middleton opened her book, but her thoughts immediately slid away to the White House. She had a great fondness and a deep admiration for her sister-in-law, although circumstances had never allowed them to become very intimate. Colonel Stonor had not been an easy man to live with and Mrs. Middleton knew that only a woman so entirely selfless as Lilian could have dealt with her difficult situation as she had done. From an embittered and disappointed father and two rebellious children, one of them a perpetual anxiety in his health, she had somehow in the few years that Colonel Stonor had lived made a united if not always an harmonious family. With Daphne and Denis she had never attempted to exercise any authority, but both children had felt that it would be a shame to be unkind to so confiding a creature. Owing to her unceasing kindness and her apprehensive nature, Denis had called her the pleasing anxious being, adding not unkindly that the only forgetfulness she wasn't a prey to was a dumb one, for her vague talk ran on, just as did her brother's more reasoned flow of speech. Everyone felt when Colonel Stonor died that Providence had arranged quite nicely, for Daphne would surely marry and Denis could live with his stepmother and be cared for. Daphne had not yet married and the three of them lived happily together. That she should marry again herself had not entered Mrs. Stonor's head and it is improbable that Denis or Daphne had thought of it either, for though she was so little older than Denis, one's father's wife wasn't a person that one connected with marriage, except of course to one's father, a subject from which one mentally shied, feeling that "that sort of thing" wasn't at all in keeping with a person so obviously destined to look after one as Lilian.

Lilian Stonor was of firmer character than her brother, and this Mrs. Middleton quite realised, having found that behind her vague loquacity there were reserves and reti-

cences that no one could approach. She had no intention of
trying to penetrate these defences herself, in fact liking her
sister-in-law all the better for them. What Lilian thought of
her she could not guess, but she hoped that the summer
would bring a closer relationship, involving no sentiment,
founded on respect and liking; for Mrs. Middleton was
often alone, or lonely, she wasn't sure which word to use.
Her masterful husband leaned so heavily on her for strength
that though she grudged nothing she felt from time to time
a weariness of the spirit. It might be more blessed to give
than to receive, but there had been times when she would
have given a year's life to be the receiver and not the giver.
Her longing to step aside for a moment, to lean on a shoulder, to give gratitude as freely as she gave help was very
great, so she had taught herself that one can't have things
both ways and mocked herself for sentimental weakness.
Good friends she had, but none to whom she spoke much
of herself, except in a gentle sardonic way that made them
find her good if baffling company. Alister Cameron was
probably the nearest to a confidant that she had ever known,
but even so their bond was largely their common wish to
defend her husband, who must be allowed to show his
façade of strength to the world, unhindered by his own
weakness.

So hot it was, and so confusing are one's thoughts of oneself, thoughts that are apt to tend to self-pity unless one
laughs in their face, that Mrs. Middleton went to sleep, or
something so near sleep that Denis, coming in by the garden
door, thought he had better not play the piano and sat down
patiently to wait. Though he was very quiet and didn't even

light a cigarette, the consciousness of a presence in the room troubled her light oblivion and she sat up suddenly, shedding book, spectacles, spectacle case, bag and one shoe.

"Oh thank you so much," she said, as Denis collected her property and restored it to her. "I am so sorry. Why didn't you amuse yourself with the piano?"

"Well, I did think of it," said Denis, "but I thought it would be too affected."

"Affected?" said his hostess. "But you were coming over specially to play."

"I know," said Denis, "but I mean you were asleep and besides being rude to wake you up, it would have been rather too much theatre to awaken sleeping heroine with soft music, don't you think?"

"Perhaps," said Mrs. Middleton absently, suddenly recognising in her guest a spirit almost as self-mocking as her own. "Yes. I expect you were right," she added with more vigour. "But do play now. I can write some letters and not disturb you in the least."

Denis begged her not to as he wouldn't be disturbed whatever she did and then felt this was rather a proud, conceited way of putting it and began to stammer so much that Mrs. Middleton quickly asked him about his ballet music. He looked at her from his dark sunken eyes with a moment's suspicion that he was being offered a toy or a sweet to keep him quiet, but reassured by the entire truthfulness in her face he did tell her about his ballet music, with such growing interest in himself that it was suddenly half-past four, and his stepmother and Daphne were on the terrace.

"Good heavens! Lady Bond!" cried Mrs. Middleton. "I'll

be ready in a moment. Come in, Lilian, and be cool. Denis was telling me about his ballet."

"Did you play that bit to Catherine that I never can remember?" said Mrs. Stonor. "The bit I like?"

Denis, who appeared to recognise this particular bit with no difficulty from her description, said he had only told her about it.

"Denis!" said his sister reproachfully. "Telling's no use at all. Why on earth didn't you play?"

"It was a matter of the finer feelings," said Denis pretentiously. "Come and play the Merry Peasant."

Daphne, all willingness, sat down at the piano with her brother and they performed a version of that beginner's bane arranged by Denis for four hands as vulgarly as possible, which always made them have the giggles, and the giggles they were still having when Mrs. Middleton came down and carried them all off in the car to Staple Park.

Staple Park, the seat of Lord and Lady Bond, had been built by Lord Bond's great-great-grandfather Jedediah Bond, a Yorkshire manufacturer of woollen goods who had come south to spend part of his vast fortune and found a family. He had acquired fame in his own part of the world by paying his operatives less and working them longer than anyone in the South Riding and had with his own hands shot three ringleaders in a gang of machine breakers dead, and dragging two others into his counting-house by their collars had fought them both till they lay bruised and bleeding on the floor. He had then jumped down fifteen feet into the yard, picked up a child of one of the strikers, its arm and leg broken in the tumult after the shooting, galloped with it ten miles to the nearest surgeon and paid for the treatment that led to its subsequent complete cure. A few years after the Repeal of the Orders in Council he was able to retire to the South, and built a mansion upon an approved slope overlooking an ornamental water, a Palladian bridge that led from and to nowhere in particular and a wall the whole way round the estate. It was before him that the regrettable gap of eight hundred years in the Bonds' Anglo-Saxon pedigree appeared, and though he called his eldest son Ivanhoe, no researches were able to supply with even a reasonable degree of probability the thirty generations or so that were missing. Ivanhoe Bond had gone into Parliament for one of Lord Pomfret's rotten boroughs; his son Athelstane Bond had entered the House after an expensive but on the whole honourable election and pushed his way resolutely to the front on philanthropy, and his son Ethelwulf had carefully married money and received a peerage in 1907. Alured the second and present Lord Bond was as good a man of business as his great-great-grandfather Jedediah, and fully as philanthropic as his grandfather Athelstane; but besides being almost more dull than any peer has a right to be, he had an extremely kind heart and looked after his tenants with an amount of real kindness that would have shocked his grandfather, who calculated his love of his fellow men on a basis of two and a half per cent. He had married Lucasta, half-sister of the present Lord Stoke, with whom he had a more or less friendly rivalry in pedigree cows. When he succeeded to the title his wife, who never forgot that she had been an Honourable in her own right, became the great lady of the district to that extent that she had made a good many enemies; but the various charities and deserving causes of the county knew very well that provided she was allowed to be Lady Bountiful her cheque book and her really invaluable services as chairman were always at their disposal.

Their only son, whom we have already met, was a faint, a very faint disappointment to them, for though his career had been steady and he was a dutiful son, he saw amusement in things that his parents did not find at all funny and had shown no wish to marry. A few years earlier he had greatly admired a niece of Mr. Palmer, the most important neighbouring land-owner, but his parents had so fostered and encouraged the attachment that it had died almost as quickly as, under the influence of amateur theatricals, it had arisen. For a family, which with the slight gap before mentioned, ran back to Alfred to have no grandson was a disgrace that Lady Bond did not wish to contemplate, and the disgrace was if possible made more acute by the fact that when her half-brother Lord Stoke died, her son, unless Lord Stoke had absentmindedly married his cook, would also come into Rising Castle, though not into the title, which would become extinct.

The Laverings car, driving up the mile and a half of scented lime avenue, turned round with a swish of gravel in the large sweep and drew up before the majestic flight of stone steps on which so many guests at dinners and balls had got wet until Lord Bond's father had built a little side entrance with a covered way for rainy weather. The immense pillars of the portico were golden in the afternoon light and to pass into the cool black and white marble front

hall was to be dazzled by darkness. Tea was being served in
the long inner hall. This uncomfortable room was the core
on the four sides of which the gigantic. suite of drawing-
room, dining-room, saloons, octagon rooms, garden rooms,
were built, and owing to its position was lighted from a lan-
tern in the roof, except for such light as came through the
great glass doors of the marble hall. On its gloomy walls,
covered with a deep red paper of everlasting quality, the
founder of the family had hung an enormous number of
bad but highly varnished copies of second-rate Old Masters.
The floor was encumbered by tables with gilt lions' claws
and inlaid marble tops, cassoni, copies of Canova and Gib-
son, screens of stamped leather, and two enormous globes,
one terrestrial and one celestial.

The butler steered the Laverings party through the half-
light to where Lady Bond in a useful coat and skirt and
wearing a useful felt hat was installed on a sofa that had
belonged to Pauline Borghese, pouring out tea. Miss Starter
was the only other guest present. The company were ac-
commodated with chairs of various degrees of discomfort
and a couple of Chinese stools which the Prince Regent had
given to young Ivanhoe Bond in very inadequate repay-
ment for certain money lost at cards. Denis and Daphne
politely sat on the stools, which were so low that they felt
like children looking over the edge of the nursery table.

"Spencer. Get some cushions for Miss Stonor and Mr.
Stonor," said Lady Bond.

The butler brought two massive cushions of faded red
velvet trimmed with tarnished gold, insinuated them onto
the stools and departed. Denis and Daphne sat down again

and found themselves so high above the table that the rest
of the company looked like dwarfs. Brother and sister began to laugh.

"Those cushions," said Lady Bond, "were brought from
Brussels by my husband's great-grandfather. They always
used to be on the sofa in the little yellow satin room, but I
had them brought into the hall last year."

This interesting piece of history was of a nature to kill
conversation and everyone sat dumb, Lady Bond apparently
not minding in the least, till Miss Starter said that there was
a shop in Brussels where she had once got some very good
charcoal biscuits.

"I love charcoal biscuits," said Daphne. "When we had
them for a dog of ours I always ate half the tin. I suppose
one gets black all over inside if one eats enough."

"Oh, *no*," said Miss Starter, shocked, but on being pressed
by Daphne for her reasons could not give any.

"I expect your young people would like to see the house,
Mrs. Stonor," said Lady Bond. "When Bond and C.W.
come in I will get C.W. to show them the rooms. He and
Bond have been looking at the heifers. We expect to do
well with our cows at the Skeynes Show. How are yours
doing, Mrs. Middleton?"

"I believe they are all quite well," said Mrs. Middleton.
"Jack talks to Pucken about them every day, not that he
really knows anything about them."

"Lily Langtry will be calving about then; it's an awful
shame," said Daphne. "She'd have loved to go to the Show,
Pucken says. Is Mr. Palmer sending his Phaedra up, Lady
Bond?"

"She is calving too," said her ladyship, with some satisfaction. "But my brother, Stoke, will probably have a walkover. No one has a cowman to touch his. Lord Pomfret would give anything to get him."

So happily did this conversation go on that Miss Starter was able to annex Mrs. Stonor and tell her all about the use of bran as a corrective. Miss Starter, who was really an Honourable, was the daughter of that Victorian statesman, littérateur and bearded impostor Lord Mickleham, whose photograph by Mrs. Cameron, draped in a rug and wearing a kind of beef-eater's hat, is familiar to all students of the Mid-Victorian period. Lord Mickleham was the author of *Cimabue: a Poetical Drama in Prologue, Five Acts and Epilogue,* which was once performed by Irving and never again. As he had married three times his descendants consisted largely of nephews and nieces who were older than their uncles and aunts, thus causing much social perplexity, but the Honourable Juliana Starter, the youngest of his eighteen children, had the whole family at her finger tips and was always ready to explain it to anyone who wanted to know.

"It was when I was In Waiting to Princess Louisa Christina," she said, "that Dr. Williams, a very delightful man and quite in advance of his times, recommended bran to Her Highness."

"We used to have bran pies when we were small at Christmas," said Mrs. Stonor.

"Dr. Williams certainly did not recommend it to Her Highness as a pie," said Miss Starter, doubtfully.

"In a wash tub with red baize round it," said Mrs. Stonor,

her eyes shining wistfully at the thought, "and we always made a frightful mess."

Mrs. Middleton, who had been listening, thought it time to interfere before Miss Starter went mad under her eyes, so she asked if Princess Louisa Christina was not a daughter of old Prince Louis of Cobalt. This at once led the talk onto the Royal Family and its relations, a practically unlimited sphere for people who know their Debrett well to triumph quietly over their friends and even Miss Starter's well-bred, plaintive voice was raised a little.

"Well, I feel quite certain somehow that Princess Louisa of Cobalt was a Hatz-Reinigen," said Mrs. Stonor. "I can't think why I feel it, but I feel as if I had heard it or read it somewhere in the way one does you know."

"I don't quite think so," said Miss Starter. "Princess Louisa's sister married one of them, but the Princess—dear me, I should know her name as well as my own. Here comes Lord Bond, we will ask him. Lord Bond," she said as the owner of Staple Park and his son came to the teatable, "we were discussing the mother of Princess Louisa Christina. Do you remember—?"

"Princess Louisa Christina?" said Lord Bond. "Her mother used to drive a brougham and pair. Married old Cobalt. Her marriage was annulled. Shocking business; shocking. Where's Middleton, Mrs. Middleton?"

Mrs. Middleton said he was out walking with Mr. Cameron and might be back at any moment.

"When you have drunk your tea, Alured," said Lady Bond, "will you take Mrs. Stonor's young people through the principal rooms. I feel sure they would be interested."

Lord Bond obediently gulped his tea and stood up.

"I'll come with you," said young Mr. Bond, who could not abide Miss Starter, and avoiding his mother's eye he joined Denis and Daphne for the tour of the house.

Lord Bond had a real passion for his ancestral seat and if he had not been so well off would have been quite happy to show people round it at sixpence a head every day. Unfortunately for him the house was only shown to visitors when he and Lady Bond were away. He had once made an excuse and hurried back to Staple Park from Aix-les-Bains, hoping to enjoy the pleasure of the sightseers, but his butler had been so unkind and cutting that he had not even dared to ask if he might spend the night in his own house and had to go over to his brother-in-law Lord Stoke, who was not only an archaeologist but very deaf and incredibly boring. So he gladly seized the opportunity that his wife gave him of showing the house to his visitors and led the way through the marble hall to the dining-room.

"That's the marble hall," he said as they walked across it. "Black and white marble. We had a very good central heating system put in a few years ago and that's where one of the mantelpieces was cracked when the men were in the house. Here is the dining-room. We don't use it much unless we are a large party. You can't see it very well with all the shutters closed."

"I'll open them, father," said young Mr. Bond.

"No need, no need," said Lord Bond. "Plastered ceiling and all that, you know. It's very much admired. Portraits of my family and their wives. All want cleaning I think, but my wife likes them as they are. I was talking to a man at the club last time I was in town, forgotten his name. He said he cleaned his with slices of raw potato, but old Carruthers who was there said he did his with soap and water. Now we come into the south octagon room."

The south octagon room, lined with locked bookcases with gilded grills across their front, was admired but Lord Bond left them little time to express their admiration, hurrying them on through a door masked with sham books. Daphne lingered.

"I do like those doors with books on them," she said. "If I had a house I'd have one and choose the names of the books."

"I always thought I'd like to do that," said young Mr. Bond, lingering with her. "My great-something-or-other that built this place hadn't much imagination. He just thought of one book for every shelf and said Vol. 1, Vol. 2, and so on."

"I see," said Daphne, examining a shelf which contained twenty-four volumes of an imaginary work entitled *Historical Survey of Taste*. "If I had a door like this I'd have a lot of names of real books like *History of England* or *Life of Gladstone* and then when people tried to get them out to read they couldn't."

"I don't suppose anyone would want to get out a *Life of Gladstone*," said young Mr. Bond doubtfully. "One would have to have an awfully dull set of friends to want books like that."

"But don't you?" said Daphne. "I mean judging by Miss Tartar I should say you did."

"Miss Starter," young Mr. Bond corrected her.

"Well, I said Miss Tartar," said Daphne. "Oh, Miss Starter. I see. Well, she's dull enough."

"I can't tell you I'll be glad to get back to New York," said young Mr. Bond fervently. "I love this place and my people are jolly decent, but the kind of guests they have. . . . Let's go round the rooms the other way."

Accordingly they went back to the dining-room where young Mr. Bond opened some of the shutters and let in the afternoon sunlight so that Daphne could admire the ceiling, exquisitely plastered in low relief with sheaves of corn, wreaths of vine leaves and tendrils and bunches of grapes, painted in what were called Pompeian colours.

"I don't know why father was in such a hurry," said young Mr. Bond as he closed the shutters again. "Come across the hall and I'll show you the yellow satin room and the musical boxes that my great-grandmother collected."

"And tell me about your cows," said Daphne.

If she and her companion had stayed with Lord Bond they would have discovered the reason for his hurry. His lordship paused inside the room they now entered and said reverently to Denis, "Look!"

Denis looked. In front of him was one of the most nobly proportioned long drawing-rooms he had ever seen, lighted by six long windows almost the height of the room. The ceiling and the walls were decorated with exquisite carvings, painted white and gold, and the fireplace was a master-piece in pale golden marble. A few English landscapes of the early nineteenth century hung on the white walls. The furniture, serene, fitting, unobtrusive, must have been there since the house was built. Denis almost gasped with pleasure at its quiet mellow beauty.

"I thought you'd like it," said Lord Bond. "My old great-great-grandfather and his son spent a lot on the furniture. It's been in Country Life. But there's something I really wanted you to see. Look there!"

Taking Denis by the arm he pivoted him round so that he looked into the corner of the room to which his back had hitherto been turned. In it stood the largest, most hideous, most elephant-legged grand piano that Edwardian money could buy. Over its bloated form a piece of Turkish embroidery, glistening with little bits of looking-glass, was carelessly draped. On it stood two large bronzes of matronly nymphs in the respectful embraces of decent satyrs, a huge green glass vase of coloured pampas grass on an oxidised silver stand representing the Three Graces in Art Nouveau style, three elephants' tusks, at least a dozen signed photographs of royalty in massive chased silver frames and a richly bound volume of the songs of Alicia Adelaide Needham.

"I knew you'd like that," said Lord Bond, as his visitor stood spellbound. "My old pater gave it to my dear old mater the year he got his peerage. The most expensive English piano on the market. And we've always kept it exactly as it was when she used it. The pater bought those bronzes at the Paris Exhibition in 1900. The mater was very fond of flowers. I remember those grasses when I was a boy, and the mater used to sing to me before I was taken to bed."

Denis, gazing awestruck on the late Lady Bond's memorial, wondered how on earth her ladyship had managed to use a piano which could only be opened with the aid of two or three strong men, for each of the bronzes must have weighed half a hundredweight, and came to the conclusion that she preferred to make her effects in a small way.

"She had a way of playing all her own," said Lord Bond, almost echoing Denis's thoughts. "She always put the soft pedal down and played the notes one after the other."

"Arpeggios?" Denis suggested, fascinated by the vision.

"That's it," said Lord Bond. "She said it put more expression into the music. Now, I wonder where the key has got to? The butler used to have it in his pantry, but when the piano tuner came on his yearly visit the Christmas before last Spencer was away for two nights owing to the death of his wife, who lived in Wolverhampton, and the key could not be found. So I put it in the drawer of the writing table and when I went to look the other day it wasn't there. But we'll find it, we'll find it, before you come and play to me."

"I do hope so," said Denis.

"Of course we will," said Lord Bond. "Where have your sister and C.W. gone? Is your sister musical?"

"She's got a nice voice, sir," said Denis.

"We'll have a concert, all to ourselves, some day," said Lord Bond. "My wife isn't musical, she's artistic. Well, now I expect you'd like to see the rest of the rooms. We'll find your sister and my boy somewhere about."

So saying he led Denis through the farther door of the drawing-room.

MEANWHILE in the hall Lady Bond, free from her family and the young Stonors, had outlined to Mrs. Middleton her scheme for the drawing-room meeting at Laverings. As far as Mrs. Middleton could make out it was to be Lady Bond's party, chosen by her, at her own time, but Laverings was to supply the tea.

Mrs. Middleton had often wondered if it was worth while standing up to Lady Bond, but every time she had come to the conclusion that it wasn't. It was in her nature to give way, to be silent, and she followed her nature, not without inner mocking at herself. If her husband wanted Lady Bond to use their drawing-room, it would be less trouble to arrange for a few chairs and some cakes than to argue the point. Sometimes she wondered if there was in her anything strong enough to stand up to facts that she didn't like, but to demand one's own way always seemed an unnecessary and almost ridiculous glorification of self, so she let things slide, contenting herself with keeping her house perfectly appointed, cultivating a few friends and being a loving companion and supporter of her husband's quick moods of overbearing wilfulness or despairing abasement.

Miss Starter said she wished the dear princess were still alive, as she would gladly have taken the chair.

"Of course you must come to the meeting if you are still with us," said Lady Bond. "I think your husband must take the chair, Mrs. Middleton; unless of course my brother—"

She paused. Mrs. Middleton, reflecting that either suggestion would annoy her husband so it didn't much matter, said nothing.

"Then that is settled," said Lady Bond rising. "Your men are very late, Mrs. Middleton. Let us go and see what my husband and the young people are up to."

As they went into the marble hall they met Mr. Middleton and Mr. Cameron.

"We have been waiting for you," said Lady Bond with grim graciousness. "I will have some fresh tea made, or would you prefer a drink?"

Mr. Cameron at once said a drink, so Lady Bond told the butler to bring drinks into the yellow satin room, and swept the whole party onwards. By this time Lord Bond and Denis had been round the whole suite of rooms and rejoined Daphne and young Mr. Bond, who had been amusing themselves by listening to the musical boxes that Athelstane Bond's wife had collected and talking about cows, so her ladyship had no idea of the length of time that her son and Miss Stonor had been alone together.

"It was a marvellous walk, a marvellous walk," said Mr. Middleton, who felt that it was quite long enough since proper attention had been paid to him. "Flora—where is Flora by the way?"

"I told the butler to shut her out," said Mr. Cameron. "She had been twice through the duck pond in the village and the water is low."

"So be it," said Mr. Middleton. "Bond, this was a walk that you would have loved. The whole soul of England was abroad on the hills to-day."

"Crowded, eh?" said Lord Bond. "That's the worst of all these cheap excursions by rail and coach on Sundays. Spoils all the walks. Why didn't you go over by Pooker's Piece? No one goes that way."

"We did," said Mr. Cameron.

"Well, I'm surprised that you found it crowded," said Lord Bond.

"And what a talk we had with old Margett," said Mr. Middleton, ignoring the misunderstanding.

"I expect he did all the talking," said young Mr. Bond. "He's as deaf as a post now, but he does love the sound of his own voice. It was very kind of you, sir. The old fellow doesn't often get an audience."

"I didn't hear Margett say much," said Mr. Cameron to a private audience of Mrs. Middleton and the Stonors. "He did say Good afternoon when we found him and I think he said Good evening when we left him. Middleton was in great form."

Mrs. Middleton looked at him half in amusement, half imploringly, while her nephew and niece burst into delighted laughter.

"It is quite extraordinary how much Jack can talk," said Mrs. Stonor. "It was just the same when we were small. I sometimes think it is because he hasn't quite grown up."

"Darling, I do love you when you are mystic," said Denis. "I am sure you are right, but do tell me what you mean."

"Well," said Mrs. Stonor, frowning in painful chase of a thought, "you know the way children do all their thinking aloud because they are too silly to think to themselves and how dull it is. Jack still does his thinking aloud, though of course it isn't dull, and it must run in the family because I do too, and I know I say a good many silly things, but it seems to me the only way to get at what one really wants to say. I'm doing it now."

She looked round for her audience's opinion.

"I think your criticism is extraordinarily good, but you aren't quite fair to yourself," said Mr. Cameron seriously. "I don't suppose you ever are."

"That's clever too," said Denis. "She isn't."

Lady Bond's voice now dominated the party, asking how far the walkers had been.

"We left Laverings at three o'clock," said Mr. Middleton. "No; no sherry I beg. A whisky and soda if I may. It is now nearly six. Say four good miles an hour, for Cameron and I are stout walkers, that would be ten miles, eleven miles or so. But it did not feel like half so much."

"It often doesn't if you don't notice it," said Lord Bond. "I remember once walking round the park here, nearly five miles that is if you keep to the wall, with Carruthers when he was Under Secretary for India, and when we got back we only had just time to get dressed for dinner. Extraordinary how time flies."

"And I'm afraid we must be going," said Mrs. Middleton.

Good-byes were said and Lady Bond reminded Daphne that she was to enter upon her secretarial duties to-morrow.

"That's right. Half a crown an hour," said Daphne. "Thanks awfully. I'll love it."

Lord Bond courteously came to the door to see his guests off, the Middletons and Mrs. Stonor in the car, Mr. Cameron and the young Stonors walking. When he turned back into the marble hall he found his butler looking at him with an air of disapproving though long-suffering ennui that Lord Bond could hardly bear. Every memory of old wrongs sprang to his mind. The time he had come home from

Aix-les-Bains and had been practically driven out of his home. The key of the piano. His old wounds burned and bled anew.

"Spencer," he said in an off-hand way, "I can't find the key of the drawing-room piano. I left it in the writing table drawer."

"I found it in the eskritaw drawer, my lord, when I was Giving a Look Round," said the butler, fixing his employer with a basilisk eye, "so I took it into My Pantry where it belongs."

"Well, put it back in the escritoire drawer," said Lord Bond, finding himself much to his annoyance using his butler's nomenclature. "I might want it at any time."

"Yes, my lord," said Spencer. "I was merely thinking, my lord, that when the piano tuner came it would be advisable to have the key where I could Put My Hand On It."

"Never mind that," said Lord Bond, too cowardly to remind his butler of the Christmas when the piano tuner had come and the key could not be found.

The butler bowed acquiescence and went away in the opposite direction from his pantry, thus leaving his employer in a state of pleasing uncertainty as to whether he meant to obey orders or not.

The walking party were going back to Laverings by the foot path. It led them by fields of springing wheat, through pasture land, followed the course of disused lanes where the hedges were pink with dogrose and yellow flags grew in the ditches. The heat was intense and no breath of air stirred.

"How far did you really walk, Mr. Cameron?" said Denis. "Was it ten miles?"

"When your uncle said that we left Laverings at three and got to Staple Park before six, he was speaking the truth," said Mr. Cameron. "But he didn't say that we got to Pooker's Piece at half-past three and that he talked to old Margett—notice that I don't say with old Margett—till half-past four, or that we stopped at the Beliers Arms at a quarter to five for a soft drink, where Mr. Middleton harangued the soft drinking public on the iniquity of building on Pooker's Piece. I should say four miles at the very outside."

"Uncle Jack is a bit of a windbag," said Daphne. "I sometimes can't think how Catherine sticks it."

"She is very fond of him you know," said Mr. Cameron.

"Of course she is," said Daphne. "I mean when people are married to each other they have to be, unless they are getting divorced or something. Oh, let's hurry up. I can hear the six-twenty hooting before the viaduct and we'll be in time to see it go over. I love that."

She quickened her pace, followed by her companions, and in a very short time they had reached the top of a hill where some cows were grazing. In front of them lay the valley of the river Woolram, spanned at this point by a handsome viaduct, the work of Brunel. Even as they looked a toy train came puffing out of Mr. Palmer's woods on the left, puffed across the viaduct and ran into the cutting on Lord Bond's property on the right. Daphne drew a deep sigh of pleasure.

"I adore looking at that train," she said. "Come on."

"I'm coming," said Denis, who had been leaning against a tree, surveying the panorama.

Daphne looked at him with a peculiar expression that Mr. Cameron did not understand. They continued their walk at a slower pace and Mr. Cameron thought that Daphne was not in her usual spirits. In fact she almost snapped at him once or twice and so much did this prey on his spirits that he dressed for dinner in a very low frame of mind and did not trouble to set Mr. Middleton right when he boasted again of the long tramp they had taken that afternoon. Later in the evening Mrs. Middleton said she must take a scarf that her sister-in-law had left in the car over to the White House, so Mr. Cameron said he would come with her. They found Mrs. Stonor and Daphne playing six pack bezique.

"How nice of you, Catherine," said Mrs. Stonor as soon as she saw the scarf. "I knew my scarf must be somewhere, because I had it when I started and when I got back it wasn't there. Poor Denis was so tired that I sent him to bed and made him have his dinner there. Luckily it is Palfrey's Sunday out, so I was able to take his dinner up without offending her. Do come up and see him, Catherine. He can never sleep when he is overtired and company is a good distraction. Mr. Cameron, do you play bezique? If you do you could finish the game with Daphne. I never like to leave a game unfinished. Not because of superstition, because I really don't think there is any special superstition about it, but it seems so untidy and one always hopes one might have won."

Mr. Cameron sat down at the card table, when Daphne

startled him by picking up all her cards and banging them down on the table in a heap, saying defiantly that she was a beast. On being questioned she said that anyone who wasn't a beast and also a born fool would have seen that to make Denis hurry up the hill in the heat was an idiotic thing to do and she wished she were dead. Mr. Cameron, trying to comfort her, said it was just as much his fault, but Daphne, scorning such an easy sop to conscience, said rubbish.

"You didn't know," she went on, banging violently at each eye with her handkerchief rolled into a tight ball, and then glaring at Mr. Cameron. "It wasn't your fault a bit. Denis always gets knocked out with the heat and I was an idiot to make him hurry. Now he'll be on Lilian's hands for a couple of days, while I do Lady Bond's silly invitations. I wish I was dead and everyone was dead."

"Not everyone," said Mr. Cameron, as he sorted the cards and put them neatly into their box.

"Well, pretty well everyone," said Daphne with less heat.

"I'll tell you what," said Mr. Cameron. "If Mrs. Stonor sees you have been crying it will be very upsetting for her on the top of Denis being unwell."

Daphne said she knew that, and anyway she hadn't been crying.

"So," said Mr. Cameron, ignoring this untruthful remark, "we had better fake the score for the game we didn't finish and put a good appearance on things. Who would have won, do you think?"

Daphne looked at him with admiration.

"You do have good ideas," she said, "and I was a beast

not to think of it. Lilian was seven hundred and fifty ahead of me, so let's say she won."

"Wouldn't she feel more comfortable if you won?" asked Mr. Cameron.

"Yes, she would be more comfortable, but she'd be a bit suspicious, because I never do win. Give me the markers and I'll fix it."

In this agreeable task of forgery Daphne forgot that she was a beast and confided in Mr. Cameron that she liked doing secretary work, but would much rather live in the country and have a cottage and keep pigs, but she couldn't possibly do that because if she and Denis and Lilian all lived together it was fairly easy, but none of them could really afford to live alone. She then enquired where Mr. Cameron lived and on hearing that it was the Temple said it must be awful to live there, which depressed Mr. Cameron a good deal.

"Of course," said he, after a short silence during which he had been following his own train of thought, "your uncle manages to have his home in the country and do his work in London. It might be possible."

"But Uncle Jack's *quite* different," said Daphne. "I mean he earns pots of money and Catherine is rather rich herself. We'll have to stick to London."

"I wasn't thinking so much of you," said Mr. Cameron thoughtfully.

"Who of then?" said Daphne. "We weren't talking about anyone else."

Mr. Cameron suddenly realised that he couldn't easily explain that he was thinking how to organise his own life so that anyone who happened to be married to him could live in the country while he went up to town every day, but luckily Mrs. Middleton and Mrs. Stonor came downstairs. Mrs. Stonor was much happier about Denis and said he was all the better for Catherine's visit.

"He really is getting stronger," she said as she accompanied her guests to the gate. "Dr. Hammond always said he would outgrow his delicacy and I believe he will. If only he could get away on his own. I do wish he could get a job and Daphne would marry someone very very nice, and then I should feel comfortable."

"And what about you?" said Mrs. Middleton very affectionately. "Wouldn't you be lonely?"

"Oh, I'd be all right," said Mrs. Stonor vaguely. "I might have a very small flat somewhere and take up my painting again. I don't seem to have had time to do any for years. Thank you so much for bringing the scarf, Catherine. I simply knew it must be somewhere, because of having started with it and then not having it when I got back. Good night, Mr. Cameron. Do come again whenever you are down here. Denis likes you so much. I must see if Palfrey remembered to take the back door key, otherwise I'll have to sit up for her, but I don't suppose she'll be late."

Mrs. Middleton and Mr. Cameron walked for a few moments in the garden before they went in.

"That was a tremendous compliment that Lilian paid you," said Mrs. Middleton. "She makes Denis a kind of touchstone for her friends; not a bad one."

"He is a very nice boy," said Mr. Cameron, "but I thought

he was too much wrapped up in himself and his music to notice people."

"I think he sees an enormous amount without looking," said Mrs. Middleton. "Some kind of sixth sense. At any rate you have a passport to Lilian's heart now. Let's go in and talk to Jack. By the way did you and he really go ten miles on this boiling day?"

"Not more than four at the outside," said Mr. Cameron. "But I didn't think it worth mentioning at the Bonds'."

By now they had reached the library door and the light shone on Mrs. Middleton's face as she threw him a look of grateful understanding, and they went in.

⤌ 5 ⤍

DAPHNE GOES TO WORK

❧

ON MONDAY MORNING MR. CAMERON WENT BACK TO TOWN without seeing any of the Stonors. Denis had quite recovered from the effects of the heat and began work again on the score of his ballet, while Daphne pumped up her bicycle tyres and rode over to Staple Park. Leaving her bicycle at the foot of the stone steps she rang the bell.

"I say," she said when a footman appeared, "do you think I could leave my bicycle there, or will someone pinch it?"

The footman thought he had better ask Mr. Spencer and shortly returned with that official, who looked at her bicycle as if it were a new and loathsome species of beetle and told the footman to wheel it into the bottle room. The footman went down the steps and Daphne followed the butler across the marble hall.

"What's the bottle room?" she asked.

"The room where the empties is kept, miss," said Spencer. "Being on the ground level, Charles can wheel your bike in there with no exertion and will bring it round for you when required. Miss Stonor, my lady," he said, opening a door in the dark centre hall.

Lady Bond's sitting-room was a pleasant room at a corner of the house, furnished with bright uninteresting chintzes. Her ladyship in another useful coat and skirt was walking up and down smoking.

"Good morning, Miss Stonor," she said. "Would you like a glass of milk before starting work, or some biscuits?"

Daphne thanked her and said she never ate anything in the morning.

"Quite right," said Lady Bond approvingly. "But Miss Starter has such a habit of glasses of milk at odd hours that one gets into the way of expecting it. You will be glad to hear that the man at Winter Overcotes whom Mrs. Middleton recommended can supply Kornog. I think it is all rubbish myself, but Miss Starter has a very delicate digestion and having no other occupation since Princess Louisa Christina died she thinks a great deal about it. Now, if you will sit at that table I will dictate a list of the names for the drawing-room meeting and a circular letter to accompany each invitation."

This she did in a certain and masterful way that Daphne could not but admire. When she had finished she said she had to go and see the head gardener and would be back in an hour. Miss Stonor would find paper, carbons and everything necessary in the table where the typewriter was. Daphne took the cover off the machine and made a face at it as she recognised a very old out-of-date model, but she had to make the best of it, so she sat down and began her work. After some time the door opened. Daphne who was wrestling rather angrily with the typewriter didn't look up.

"Mother," said a voice, adding "Oh, it's you."

Daphne looked up and saw young Mr. Bond.

"Hullo," he said, "are you secretarying?"

"As far as this machine will let me," said Daphne. "I'm going to tell your mother she ought to have a new one."

"I'd like to see my stenographer's face in the New York office if anyone gave her a machine like that," said young Mr. Bond examining the gigantic and cumbersome superstructure with awe. "Are you staying to lunch?"

Daphne said she was.

"All right," said young Mr. Bond, "I was going to cut lunch to avoid the Starter, but now I shan't."

"O.K.," said Daphne. "Oh, damn this machine."

"When you see me at lunch, please give a start of surprise," said young Mr. Bond and left the room.

When Lady Bond got back Daphne handed her a pile of envelopes correctly addressed, each containing a letter explaining the object of the drawing-room meeting and an invitation card. Lady Bond approved and Daphne asked where she would find the stamps.

"Oh, Spencer stamps all the letters," said Lady Bond. "And now I want to discuss with you a letter to the local newspaper and one to our M.P."

Daphne opened her shorthand book and laid it on the table.

"Before I start taking down the letters, I'd better tell you that this machine is hopeless," she said kindly. "I don't suppose you use it yourself so you couldn't know. It must be a pre-war model and it can't have been cleaned since it left the works."

"Is it really as bad as that?" asked Lady Bond, examining the typewriter, about which she obviously knew nothing. "I can't think why Miss Knowles, my secretary, never mentioned it."

"I expect she hadn't the nerve," said Daphne. "But I'm sure she'd be awfully grateful and work twice as fast if you got her a new one."

"Well, I'll ask my son about it," said Lady Bond. "He knows all about offices. You were right to mention it."

The rest of the morning passed quickly and Daphne found she enjoyed working with Lady Bond, who wasted no time and knew exactly what she wanted to say. When they went in to lunch Miss Starter, who was measuring her medicine at the sideboard, told Daphne how delighted she was to find that Kornog bread was procurable.

"Of course," she said, as she took her place at the table, "I could have written to London for it, but it all takes time and I certainly could not have got a loaf before Wednesday, whereas now, thanks to your prompt action, Lucasta, I shall have it this afternoon. Will you thank your aunt very much, Miss Stonor, for her kind help."

"Well, she's really not an aunt at all," said Daphne. "She only married my stepmother's brother. But I'm awfully fond of her."

Although Daphne did not really much care whether young Mr. Bond came in to lunch or not, she felt he needn't have made such a parade of secrecy over something that he was going to forget at once. The dining-room door opened and she looked up, but it was Spencer, who bending over Miss Starter's chair said confidentially,

"I thought you would be glad to know, miss, that your dietetic loaf is come. I have given instructions for your usual slice, lightly toasted, to be brought to you immediately."

He had hardly finished speaking when a footman came in with a small silver toast rack containing a slice of Kornog, lightly toasted and cut into four small triangles. This he placed beside Miss Starter.

"Thank you so much," said Miss Starter. "Oh, but Spencer, they have cut off the crusts again. I did ask for the crusts to be left on, as my doctor says half the good lies in the crusts."

Spencer said deferentially that he would Let Them Know about it, but with a wealth of implication that froze Daphne's blood. He then signed to the footman to remove the toast rack, but just as that underling was carrying it away young Mr. Bond came in by the service door and nearly cannoned into him.

"What have you, Charles?" he said. "Toast? I adore toast. You didn't think to see me, Miss Starter," he continued, dangling the toast rack from one finger. "I found I wasn't out to lunch after all, so I came back through the kitchen, and Mrs. Alcock said there was cold salmon so here I am. How do you do, Miss Stonor. Have some toast."

"Don't eat that, C.W.," said Miss Starter imploringly.

"Why not?" asked young Mr. Bond, putting about four

ounces of butter on one of the small triangles and munching it. "No, Spencer, no maccaroni, it's too hot. Just the salmon and rather a lot of it, especially if there's one of those bits that have what one might call a little salmon fat between the flesh and the skin. Is it poisoned, Miss Starter?"

"The crusts have been cut off," said Miss Starter.

"I'm all in favour of that," said young Mr. Bond, carrying another butter-laden triangle to his mouth. "I always give my crusts to the dogs since I got too old to hide them under the rim of the nursery tea-tray."

"But practically the whole dietetic value lies in the crusts," the guest persisted. "Besides, toast and salmon entirely neutralise each other. That is why I am not having any. Just the salad."

"It seems awful waste to have salmon if one doesn't eat it," said Daphne, in whose life Scotch salmon did not occur very frequently.

"Well, I can neutralise anything," said young Mr. Bond with fine want of logic. "Cider please, Charles."

"That is really enough, C.W.," said his mother. "And I want your advice. Miss Stonor says the typewriter is not in very good condition."

"I've always wondered how poor old Knowles stood it," said young Mr. Bond, taking an enormous helping of Charlotte Russe and emptying the cream jug over it. "All right, mother, this isn't greedy: it's only taking what you ladies have left. That typewriter must have been left over from the year grandfather got his peerage. I believe he bought one to answer the congratulations."

"Then I had better order a new one," said her ladyship,

"and I shall scold Miss Knowles for not having mentioned it before."

"I don't suppose she dared," said young Mr. Bond. "I'll choose you one and have it sent down. Which machine do you use, Miss Stonor?"

Daphne said she liked a Revotina, but Lady Bond ought to choose. Miss Starter said that the princess's secretary always used a Gladinon, so young Mr. Bond said he would have a Revotina sent down as soon as possible if his mother approved.

When they had had their coffee Daphne asked Lady Bond if the same time to-morrow would do, and said good-bye. Young Mr. Bond opened the dining-room door for her and managed to shut himself outside.

"Shall I run you home?" he asked.

Daphne said her bicycle was in the bottle room.

"The devil it is," said young Mr. Bond. "Do you mean to say you ride one of those things?"

Daphne said she was poor but honest, and why not, so they went across the marble hall, through a door, along a stone passage with several corners, down a flight of stone stairs, past what looked to Daphne like several hundred bells all hanging curled up and ready to spring with their names written above them on a board, and so past the boot room to the bottle room.

"By Jove, we do have a lot of empties," said young Mr. Bond. "I wonder who gets the twopences on them."

"Your butler I should think," said Daphne. "And I bet he does pretty well over the stamps too. Your mother says he stamps all the letters."

"I always wondered how my letters got stamped," said young Mr. Bond reflectively. "I must ask my lordly father to let me see Spencer's book. I have an idea that there is some dirty business on foot. One gets suspicious in New York. I say, may I try to ride your bike? I haven't been on one since I was ten."

Daphne gave permission, and to the uncontrollable joy of three under-gardeners and a couple of under-housemaids who had no business on that side of the house at all, the heir to the estate was seen wavering down the drive till he fell off into the rhododendrons. So enchanted was he with this new toy that he insisted on accompanying Daphne home, sometimes riding the bicycle till he fell off, sometimes running behind her while she rode, and sometimes wheeling it while they both walked. By the end of the journey he had so much improved his style that he said he would get a bicycle for himself and they would go for picnics.

"You'd better hire one," said Daphne. "It's no good your buying one if you won't be staying here. When did you say you went back to New York?"

"Not till September. I'm doing a job of work for them over here," said young Mr. Bond, "but I don't always need to be in town all the week. Could I have a drink of water or something? It's a thirsty sport."

"You'd better stay to tea," said Daphne. So young Mr. Bond did stay to tea, and found Mrs. Stonor so easy to talk to that he told her a great many quite uninteresting things about himself and enjoyed himself vastly.

"I'm sorry I forgot the start of surprise at lunch," said

Daphne when he at last tore himself away. "And I forgot to call you Cedric too. I somehow wasn't sure if your mother would approve."

"Probably not, but she will," said young Mr. Bond. "Call me anything you like so long as it isn't Seedric as matron at my prep school used to say. Was Miss Plimsoll there in your time, Denis?"

"Yes, indeed. It was in my second term that her lower teeth fell out of the bathroom window," said Denis, "and a boy called Pringle thought they were a gift from heaven and kept them in his best knickers pocket for two days, till Miss Plimsoll found them herself when she was getting out clothes ready for chapel on Sunday."

"All right, I'll say Cedric," said Daphne. "And it's awfully nice having you here. What with you and Catherine and all the cows, it's going to be a lovely summer. And Mr. Cameron at weekends. I like him almost better than anyone I've ever met, don't you?"

Upon the artless declaration young Mr. Bond walked all the way home in deep gloom and nearly didn't send for the typewriter after all. But reflecting that if he didn't Daphne might give up coming to Staple Park altogether, he wrote to the Army and Navy Stores that very night.

THE next two weeks passed uneventfully. Lady Bond found Daphne extremely helpful with the accounts and on several occasions kept her on till tea-time. Daphne enjoyed seeing into the works of a big house and garden and made one or two suggestions to Lady Bond which her ladyship passed to her husband, who said Miss Stonor had a head on her shoulders. Young Mr. Bond had to be in town daily, but managed to see a good deal of the Stonor family in his spare time. He and Denis laughed together over their reminiscences of Hocker's, and Mrs. Stonor listened kindly to all he had to say about himself.

When Mr. Middleton was in town in the middle of the week, sometimes spending a night or two at his club, Mrs. Middleton took to dropping in very frequently at the White House to gossip with her sister-in-law, whom she got to like more and more. On the first occasion of her husband's absence she sent word to Denis that the piano would be at liberty and he came over at tea-time.

"I didn't come sooner," he said, "because I thought you might be resting."

Mrs. Middleton, who had indeed been resting but would not at all have minded the piano, was touched by this consideration and told Denis that he must use the piano whenever he liked so long as Uncle Jack wasn't at home. So he gradually lost his shyness and came over every afternoon while his difficult step-relative was away. Mrs. Middleton went in and out, sometimes gardening within earshot of the music, sometimes writing letters in her sitting-room next door, sometimes sitting with a book, or only musing while Denis played and frowned and put down hieroglyphics on scored paper and complained that her good piano was ruining him as a composer. By the end of the second week he had so far conquered his diffidence as to play Mrs. Middleton most of the music that he was composing for a ballet. When he had finished playing Mrs. Middleton said nothing. At last she said, "It sounds very grown-up to me."

"I am grown-up, you see," said Denis. "I rather think it's my misfortune."

"Very few of one's friends are," said Mrs. Middleton. "I'm not; and I think that's my misfortune. So how discontented we all are," she added laughing.

Denis looked at her with one of his quick searching looks.

"I knew that the first time I saw you," he said. "Not when I was here before, when I was ill, but as soon as I saw you the first day we were here."

Ethel now brought tea in and while they partook of it Mrs. Middleton asked Denis when the ballet was likely to be produced.

"That's the trouble," he said, with a quick darkening of his eyes. "The artist is there for the décor—no one you've heard of but very clever; the choreographer is there and understands every note I write; I have nearly done my music and it is right for dancing; that's what makes it sound grown-up probably. But as usual the people who would like to put it on haven't any money to back it. Meanwhile it's fun, and if I go on feeling as well as I do here I'll be able to get a cinema organ job. I wouldn't mind going up and down on a golden lift five or six times a day with bears' grease on my hair and bowing in a pale and interesting way to the audiences. Uncle Jack can build me a super cinema, and Lilian shall be receptionist because she loves fussing over people, and Daphne shall be secretary. A family affair."

"Do I come into the family?" asked Mrs. Middleton.

"Of course. You'll be here, ready to comfort Uncle Jack when he says he is certain he forgot to allow for the weight of the audience on the dress circle. And Daphne and Lilian and I will come down to you all rich and jaded on Saturday night late, in a car full of champagne bottles, and go back after Sunday lunch for the five o'clock session."

"That sounds very nice," said Mrs. Middleton. "And talking of nothing in particular, do you all realise that this Saturday is the drawing-room meeting here about Pooker's Piece?"

"We do, indeed we do," said Denis. "It has cast a blight over our lives for days. Daphne seems to have done nicely with the invitations, and half the county is coming. I hope Uncle Jack will come up to the scratch. Can I bring over some chairs from the White House? There is one in my bedroom that squeaks and one in Daphne's room that has one leg shorter than the others."

Mrs. Middleton said she would love to give the one with the squeaky leg to Lord Stoke, who was deaf, and then Ethel came in to announce that Mrs. Pucken wished to speak with Mrs. Middleton and was waiting in the kitchen to that end. She was told to bring her in and shortly conducted Mrs. Pucken into the drawing-room.

"Good afternoon, Mrs. Pucken," said Mrs. Middleton. "Do sit down."

Mrs. Pucken, feeling the immense moral superiority to be gained from standing, said she would prefer to stay where she was and would like to speak to Mrs. Middleton.

"Is it about Lou?" said Mrs. Middleton.

Mrs. Pucken said Lou was a handful of trouble and then looked so ominous that Denis offered to go.

"Don't you disturb yourself, sir," said Mrs. Pucken. "Lou's a troublesome girl, but it's not what you call trouble this time. Not like my eldest niece. That girl's got herself into trouble again, madam, that is to say she doesn't know if it's trouble yet, so we hope for the best and expect the worst. But Lou is a good girl, at least as far as that goes."

She paused for effect and Denis nervously began to put his music together.

"I'm sure I don't want to disturb you and the young gentleman, madam," said Mrs. Pucken looking severely at Denis, who stopped arranging his music and sat down again. "It's this meeting, madam, about Pooker's Piece. Seems Pucken's old grandfather used to live up there in Margett's cottage as is now, and Pucken always talked a lot about the Piece. He has a kind of fancy his people used to live there in the old days and it used to be called Pucken's Piece. A lot of ideas he gets into his head," said Mrs. Pucken, to whom the word ideas meant rubbish, "but he gets talking about it of an evening sometimes. I don't pay no attention to Pucken, but Lou she's a regular dad's girl and listening to Pucken keeps her out of harm's way, for they do say it's at the pictures that most of the harm gets done."

She looked at Denis, who felt that she suspected him of practising debauchery in the sixpenny seats at the Winter Overcotes Odeon and wished he could get under the piano.

"Well, Mrs. Pucken," said Mrs. Middleton.

"It's this way, madam," said Mrs. Pucken. "Miss Daphne's been talking about this meeting Lady Bond's having about Pooker's Piece and nothing will content my young lady but can she come and hear the speeches. Rubbish, my girl, was what I said when she began about it, don't you get getting ideas into your head, but she goes on about it enough to drive you wild, so at last I said, 'Look here my girl, I've had enough of this. I'll speak to Mrs. Middleton about it and see what she says. But don't think you can scamp your work.'"

"Well," said Mrs. Middleton, "I really don't see why Lou shouldn't come. I'm afraid she'll find it rather dull."

"She's quite a one for an outing," said Mrs. Pucken. "And I'll see she cleans herself proper before she comes. It's very good of you I'm sure, madam. Perhaps I'd better come along of Lou myself to keep an eye on her and I could give Ethel and the others a hand with the washing up afterwards."

"Yes of course, do come with Lou," said Mrs. Middleton, feeling that things were gradually getting out of control.

"Thank you very much, madam, I'm sure. And Miss Palfrey is taking quite an interest in the meeting too."

"Miss Palfrey?"

"Lord, I didn't know Palfrey was a fan of Lady Bond's," said Denis.

"Mrs. Stonor's maid, madam," Mrs. Pucken explained. "Her father was a naval captain in an oil tanker."

"You'd better ask Mrs. Stonor then," said Mrs. Middleton firmly. "If she can spare her maid of course you can bring her. Good afternoon, Mrs. Pucken."

Mrs. Pucken, who always knew when the gentry had had enough of her, withdrew and Mrs. Middleton and her guest fell into helpless laughter. Why the staff of the White House should want to attend a drawing-room meeting on preserving the amenities of rural England was beyond their comprehension. Denis said they could now give Mrs. Pucken the squeaking chair with a clear conscience and let Lou, who was skinny, have the chair with one short leg.

Then he gathered up his music and said good-bye.

"Come again next week for music, Denis," said Mrs. Middleton.

"It's a funny thing, but I still don't say Catherine to you," said Denis irrelevantly. " 'You' is the nearest I can get."

"It's not very near," said Mrs. Middleton, truthfully.

"Well, I wish your eyes didn't look tired," said Denis, and went back to the White House. His stepmother and Daphne were in the garden by the little stream and he told them how Mrs. Pucken and Palfrey wanted to come to the meeting. They were amused, but quite as much at a loss as he was. After dinner they all sat outside again. From the kitchen came a ceaseless babbling of voices, mixed with the clash of silver and china in the sink. Denis said there seemed to be a good deal of company to-night.

"Only Mrs. Pucken and Lou," said Mrs. Stonor. "Mrs. Pucken is always in the kitchen lately. I only pay her for the mornings, but she comes up nearly every night with Lou. She and Palfrey are great friends and it means I never have to think of what to do with remains of pudding or cold potatoes. What they talk about all the time I can't think."

The subjects of the foregoing remarks were finishing the after-dinner wash-up. Lou had just been scolded by her mother for leaving the knives in the sink while she dried the china.

"How many times have I told you that's not the way to do the knives," said Mrs. Pucken to her daughter. "Take all them knives out of the sink and put them in that white jug. Now you can put some hot suds in the jug but don't let it come up to the handles. Rot the handles right off the blades, my girl, that's what you'll do, leaving them in the sink like that. Why the cook I was second kitchenmaid under when I first went out, she'd have thrown the rolling pin at me likely as not if she'd seen me done a thing like that. And no giving sauce back neither," said Mrs. Pucken accusingly to Lou, who had not yet opened her mouth.

"My father used to take the slipper to we girls if we didn't have everything the way he liked it," boasted Palfrey. "I'm glad of it now though. Same as Lou will be glad you spoke to her about those knives. Don't forget what your mother says, Lou. And you do the fish knives and forks the same way, and the little tea knives if they have nice handles, and the carvers. Now you can pour away those suds out of the jug and fill it up with hot water and then take the knives out and dry them."

Lou emptied the suds out of the jug, letting one knife escape with a clatter into the sink, thus causing Palfrey to draw in her breath with a hissing sound. She then put the jug under the tap and refilled it with hot water. As she withdrew it she hit the jug against the tap. A crash was heard and a three cornered piece of china fell into the sink.

"All right, my girl, you don't go to the meeting tomorrow," said Mrs. Pucken in gloomy triumph. "Here, give me the cloth. Miss Palfrey and me'll finish the drying. You're just like your dad, all thumbs. Put the cloth on for supper and don't forget the cruet."

While Lou, sniffing loudly, laid the table, the two elder ladies rapidly finished the wash-up and the dry-up. Mrs. Pucken said she would just wash the cloths through and hang them up, as Miss Palfrey wouldn't be boiling till Monday, if Miss Palfrey would put out the things. By the time she had done this Palfrey had set the cold lamb, the cold potatoes, a bottle of Piccalilli, the remains of a trifle and a large piece of cheese on the table and they sat down.

"That's enough, Lou," said Mrs. Pucken sharply to her daughter, who was still sniffing, "and there's others besides you wants the cruet. Pass it to Miss Palfrey. I shan't be coming up to-morrow night, Miss Palfrey. I'll stop on at Laverings and give the girls there a hand. There'll be a big wash-up after the meeting and tea, and four for dinner with Mr. Cameron coming."

Here Lou stopped sniffing and gave a yelp.

"Whatever *is* the matter," said her exasperated mother.

Lou was heard to mumble that she wanted to go to the meeting.

"All right, go to the meeting, only stop that noise. Nobody said you wasn't going," said Mrs. Pucken, who like a true mother had forgotten her threat as soon as she had uttered it. "You'll be able to have a good look at Lady Bond, Miss Palfrey, and young Mr. Bond too, I expect."

"We've seen plenty of young Mr. Bond round our place," said Palfrey. "Always coming to tea he is. I must say though," she added, wishing to give credit where credit was due, "that it's a treat to see him eat. I don't suppose he's Spoken yet."

"Get on with your supper, Lou, listening like that to what Miss Palfrey says," said Mrs. Pucken to her daughter, whose eyes, ears and mouth were wide open.

"Do you mean Mr. Bond will Ask Miss Daphne?" Lou breathed in a hoarse romantic whisper.

"If you was to get on with your supper, Lou, the way your mother tells you, you wouldn't need to be asking all them questions," said Palfrey, with fine kitchen logic. "It's my belief, Mrs. Pucken, it's as good as Settled. But she's quite right not to be too easy with him. Does them good to wait. I've been walking out nine years now with my friend."

"Quite right too," said Mrs. Pucken. "The worst day's work I ever did was giving up a good place at Staple Park to marry Pucken when we'd only been going together three years and I hadn't even met his mother. A fine old lady she was. She had seven sons and she made them all give her their wages every Friday night. Of course when I took Pucken I took care of his money, so the old lady went off it was a fair treat they say and that's how I never met her after all. Well, we must be going, Miss Palfrey. I'll be in to-morrow early, so don't bother about the rest of the wash-up to-night. Has Miss Daphne got Mr. Bond's photo in her room?"

"I couldn't say, I'm sure," said Palfrey, suddenly becoming a faithful retainer. "Not on the mantelpiece where the other photos are."

"But she's got a snap of Mr. Cameron," said Lou, her virgin heart impelled by Aphrodite to express her passion. "I sor it on the table the day I was doing the room out with you, Mum."

Upon this shameless statement both ladies fell on Lou with accusations of prying and Nosey-Parkering and prognostications of a bad end, so that she went home bellowing loudly, but not on the whole unhappy, for had she not borne witness for her chosen hero, just like Glamora Tudor in *The*

Flames of Desire when she told wicked Lord Mauleverer that it was really the Duke she loved.

As for Daphne, she had taken the snapshot of Mr. Cameron in the garden at Laverings the previous weekend and liked to see her own handiwork. She still thought him one of the nicest people she had ever met, but was also much attached to young Mr. Bond, and really thought very little about either.

6

PRELUDE TO A MEETING

ON SATURDAY MORNING A KIND OF FERMENT WAS GOING ON IN all the houses which we already know and in various others with which the reader of this work may already be familiar. At Worsted for example Mr. and Mrs. Palmer at the Manor House were having one of those differences of opinion which sometimes made breakfast a little alarming to visitors. Mr. Palmer, although professionally a rival of Lord Bond and Mr. Middleton where cows were concerned, felt that public spirit about the amenities of Pooker's Piece should rise above any private feelings. His wife, who was of sterner stuff, regarded any meeting held by the instigation of Lady Bond as anathema, for she had never forgotten the day on which the Bonds' cowman had allowed a bull to get mildly out of control and been indirectly the cause of a slight accident to her youngest niece.

"Yes, yes, Louise," said her husband, "that's all very well, but it wasn't Lady Bond's fault that the bull got loose. And the meeting isn't at Staple Park, it's at Laverings. Nice woman, Mrs. Middleton. We ought to go, my dear. Can't let this fellow build on Pooker's Piece."

Mrs. Palmer said Lucasta Bond was capable of anything, and how Mrs. Middleton could submit to having Lucasta's meeting in the Laverings drawing-room she didn't know. Her husband wisely retreated behind the Stock Breeders' Gazette and when Mrs. Palmer had said a little more of what she felt towards Lady Bond she suddenly remembered that she had heard that Mrs. Middleton's sister-in-law's step-daughter, who was doing secretarial work for Lady Bond while Miss Knowles was away, was a nice girl and good-looking, and might be available as fresh theatrical talent; for Mrs. Palmer's production of Greek plays and Shakespeare in a converted barn was one of the celebrated features of Worsted, and *Twelfth Night* was already in rehearsal. So she said presently that she supposed they would have to **go** and she would order the car for three o'clock and had promised to take the Tebbens. Mr. Palmer replied that Lord Stoke had bought a bull from Mr. Leslie at Rushwater and so the discussion closed.

At about the same moment Mr. Leslie who hated the telephone and Lord Stoke who was very deaf, were deliberately misunderstanding each other on the telephone about the delivery of the bull. After some very unhelpful conversation Mr. Leslie tried to convey to Lord Stoke that he meant to go to the meeting at Laverings that afternoon and would dis-cuss the matter with him there if he were going. As Lord Stoke was reminded by the word Laverings that he had quite forgotten that he had been asked to take the chair or pro-pose a chairman, he wasn't sure which, and took full advantage of his deafness not to hear any of Mr. Leslie's attempts to speak, Mr. Leslie banged down the receiver, though not before he had expressed his views on other people's want of sense, leaving his lordship placidly repeating himself to a dead wire, all to the infinite pleasure of the telephone exchange. And it was owing to the deep interest taken by the young lady operator that Mrs. Tebben at Lamb's Piece was unable to get onto the Worsted shop and order some tinned apricots for a cold supper when she got back from the meeting.

"It is too provoking, my dear," she cried gaily to her husband who had heard her trying to telephone and hoped it wasn't anything he need pay attention to. "The exchange won't answer at all. I wanted to get some of those Empire apricots, cheaper than Californian and quite as good, for our little meal to-night. Well, cheese is always our great stand-by and the piece we have left needs finishing. You are coming to the meeting about Pooker's Piece, dear, aren't you? Louise Palmer said they would drive us."

Mr. Tebben, who wanted with all his soul to stay at home and write an article for the Journal of Icelandic Studies on Bishop Ogmund, said he didn't think he need go. His wife replied, yet more gaily, that needs must when the devil drives and Louise was coming for them soon after three or else a little before and she must go and cut a cabbage.

"Think!" she added dramatically. "Our own cabbage! I shall tell Mrs. Phipps to shred it very fine with just a taste of onion and we shall have an excellent salad from our own garden, except for the onion which I must confess is the last of that string of them I bought from the man who was all looped with them and went bad so soon."

Her husband, vaguely wondering who the devil in this particular case was, and why a man looped with onions had gone bad, turned eagerly to his work again and was re-absorbed into sixteenth-century Iceland.

At Pomfret Towers old Lord Pomfret was in the estate room looking at the Ordnance map with his agent, Roddy Wicklow.

"Can't think why the Government allows people like Hibberd," said his lordship angrily. "Had him once on a committee. Feller was wearing a Guards' tie. Extraordinary the way these new men don't know anything. Pooker's Piece. Nice little bit of meadow-land and Palmer planted a nice screen of larches on the north side," said his lordship, who knew every inch of the country. "Like the feller's infernal impudence to want to build on it. I suppose I'll have to go over to the meeting. Laverings: that's down the narrow lane half a mile outside Skeynes, isn't it? I remember that lane. Nearly killed there when I was a young man. Driving a dog cart and we met a waggon full of hay. I was a silly young fool then and tried to pass it. We went right into the ditch and broke one wheel and the mare couldn't be used again for a month. Well, I'll go, but I know the car will stick in that lane."

"I couldn't go for you, could I?" said Roddy Wicklow, who was not only devoted to his employer, but a kind of connection, as his sister had married Lord Pomfret's cousin and heir.

"No, no, you've got to see Sir Edmund Pridham and the Council Clerk about those County Council Cottages," said

Lord Pomfret. "No good my going, I'd only lose my temper. Confounded counterjumper that clerk is. I'll go to Laverings. Daresay I'll lose my temper there too, but that won't matter. Heard from your sister to-day?"

"Yes sir. They seem to be having a splendid time at Cap Martin and little Giles is getting brown all over."

"That's right," said his lordship approvingly. "I'll be glad to see them back though. House seems a bit empty without the little chap."

And Lord Pomfret fell into a muse as he thought of the six-months-old baby who was later to bear the title of his only son, killed so long ago.

AT Staple Park Lady Bond was being driven almost to frenzy by Miss Starter's anxiety about the tea at Laverings.

"If," said Miss Starter plaintively as they sat down to lunch, "I could be sure that Mrs. Middleton had *real* China tea, I should feel more at ease, but so many of one's friends have what they call China tea and certainly isn't, for half an hour after drinking it I always have a peculiar feeling. Now real China tea, like yours, Lucasta, leaves me feeling absolutely free from any feeling at all. I suppose I shall just have to do without my tea altogether."

Lady Bond always invited Miss Starter to Staple Park for a long visit in the summer because she was an old friend of the Bond family and bore genteel poverty in London lodgings very courageously. But every three or four days her guest so exacerbated even her not very sensitive nature that she heartily wished she had not been so kind. Since the Kornog bread had been got from Winter Overcotes Miss

Starter had been unusually placid, but for the last twenty-four hours she had talked of China tea till her hostess could have bitten her with pleasure.

"Well, Juliana," she said, "we will take some of my tea with us and I'll ask Mrs. Middleton if she will have a pot made specially for you."

"Oh dear me, no," said Miss Starter. "I should feel so nervous and uncomfortable that I am sure all my feelings would come on, worse than ever. You know worry is really at the basis of everything; it can poison the most healthy person. I say to myself every night, 'Do not worry. Do not worry. Do not worry.'"

"That's all wrong, Miss Starter," said young Mr. Bond, who had been hoping for some time that his mother's guest would choke on a fishbone and die. "What you ought to say is 'I am not worrying.' Keeps the old Ego in much better order."

"Oh, is that what you do?" said Miss Starter.

"Well, not exactly. The fact is I simply don't worry at all. It saves me a lot of trouble. More of those nice little new potatoes, Spencer. They look a bit young to have been killed, but they taste uncommonly good."

Miss Starter said earnestly that they were poison, which caused young Mr. Bond to put six into his mouth at once, give a single chew and swallow them. Lord Bond, who came in just then from seeing about a drain down in the seven acre field, said talking of poison they had found a vixen dead down near the stream undoubtedly poisoned, and the question was who had done it.

"Miss Starter says it is potatoes," said young Mr. Bond.

"Potatoes?" said Lord Bond. "Never knew a fox eat potatoes."

"Perhaps vixens do," said young Mr. Bond. "Ladies in an interesting condition have queer fancies—at least that's what one reads," he added hastily, meeting his mother's eye. And then without giving either of the ladies time to interfere he plunged into a discussion of the possible vixen poisoner with his father, leaving Miss Starter so discomposed that she quite forgot about her tea.

"We are leaving at a quarter past three," said Lady Bond as she rose from the lunch table. "Juliana, you will rest of course. Alured, who is to take the chair? My brother or Mr. Middleton?"

"Well, my dear—" his lordship began.

"So it had better be Mr. Middleton, as it is his house," said Lady Bond. "Will you catch Stoke as soon as he comes and make him understand that he is to propose Mr. Middleton?"

"Stoke is getting very deaf," said Lord Bond plaintively.

"I said Make him understand," said Lady Bond. "You can drive us, C.W., as I have ordered the small car. Ferguson is having the weekend off as I shall be taking him to town next week."

Her ladyship swept Miss Starter out of the room in front of her, leaving her husband and son together.

"I didn't know your mother was going away next week," said Lord Bond. "I wonder who will drive me if she takes Ferguson. Young Phipps is the only man I'd trust and he won't be back from his holiday. I suppose you wouldn't, C.W.?"

"I'm awfully sorry, father, I really would if I could," said young Mr. Bond quite seriously, "but I have to be at the office all next week. Can't you hire someone?"

"I suppose I'll have to," said Lord Bond with a sigh. "But I'll tell you what," he added, cheering up. "I'll get that nice young Denis Stonor to come and play Gilbert and Sullivan to me. His sister sings and we'll have a nice little concert together. I do hope Spencer will let me have the piano key by then. I don't like to ask him every time and I can't quite burgle his pantry while he's out. Well, well."

He looked longingly at his son, half hoping that he would offer to knock Spencer out in fair fight and bear away the piano key as the spoils of victory. But young Mr. Bond had not heard the end of his father's remarks for it had suddenly come over him how pleasant it would be to hear a little music, and how easily he could run down for an evening in his car now that the evenings were so long.

At Laverings Mr. Middleton had retired to his dressing-room for the morning to do some work, while the library was made ready for the meeting. As this plan had been arranged the day before it did not come as a surprise to anyone except Mr. Middleton himself, who came downstairs at intervals to tell his wife, Alister Cameron, the three Stonors, and any of the servants who were helping, what it meant to him to be an exile from his own room.

"A precious morning and a precious afternoon wasted, lost!" he exclaimed, suddenly appearing at the door of his private staircase. "The whole world is basking in sunshine and I alone am condemned to toil."

"Why not go down to the field and have a talk with

Pucken," said his wife. "It certainly does seem a pity to be indoors on such a lovely day."

"How can I talk to Pucken when I have work to do? And without the kindly shelter of my own room, I feel outcast, unwanted. Better perhaps had I stayed in London for the weekend."

"If you really did work in here there would be some sense in what you say," said Mrs. Stonor, who was putting paper and pencils on a table at the far end of the room. "But after all, Jack, you keep all your plans and things upstairs, which is a delightful room, and I haven't seen you working here, I mean only writing letters or doing nothing, though sometimes when one is doing nothing one is really thinking very hard. When Denis is composing he often looks as if he were quite mad or thinking about nothing at all."

"I do," said Denis. "I sometimes see myself in a glass and say 'Good God.' But I don't see what that has to do with Uncle Jack working upstairs, darling."

"Good morning, Uncle Jack," said Daphne coming in with a jug of water and two glasses on a tray. "How lucky you are, doing nothing on such a divine day. We are all sweltering to death. I say, could I have those two chairs you aren't using in your work-room? I didn't like to take them without asking you, but I saw them when I looked in, when I went up to Catherine's room to see if she had some blue sewing silk she promised she'd lend me. Your room looked so lovely and cool, and I read a bit of an awfully good book you left on the table where your plans are."

"I am always needing nice books for my library list," said Mrs. Stonor. "What was it called, Daphne?"

"Something about Blood," said Daphne. "And there is an awfully good bit about where the detective gets on the track of an Argentine white slaver and the wardrobe suddenly turns round on a hinge and there he sees a girl's body hanging up by the heels and she had nothing on and has been dead for *days*. Oh, 'All Blood Calling,' that's the name."

Mrs. Stonor said it sounded a very nice book and she would put it on her list. Denis said if he were a white slaver he would make a better job than that and he would never have the same respect for Argentines again.

"And could I take those two chairs, Uncle Jack?" said Daphne.

"Certainly not," said Mr. Middleton. "I want them. I need them. I require them, to put things on. And what is that jug of water for?"

"For the chairman," said Daphne. "At least one glass is for him and the other for anyone else, and the jug is so that they can give themselves some water."

"And who is the chairman?" asked Mr. Middleton, rather glad of a diversion from the subject of his leisure reading.

"Didn't Lady Bond tell you?" said his wife.

"No one in this house tells the master of it what is happening," said Mr. Middleton with tragic dignity. "I know nothing. I cannot work. I cannot go out and enjoy the beneficent sunshine."

"But Jack," said his sister, "why not? If you must work you can't go out, and if you go out you can't work, but you can't have it both ways."

To have it both ways was exactly what Mr. Middleton

wanted and usually got. Crushing a desire to strangle his sister he said coldly that he had better put on a hat, for this was hardly a day to walk in the direct rays of the sun, and see Pucken about that manure.

"Then can I have those two chairs if you don't want them, Uncle Jack," said Daphne.

"NO!" said Mr. Middleton. "Catherine, I appeal to you. Is this my house or is it not?"

"Yes, darling, it is," said Mrs. Middleton. "At least as long as we pay the rent. And if you could possibly spare time to speak to Pucken about that manure I shall be so glad, because we really need it for the marrows. I know how busy you are, but it won't take long. I saw Pucken go down the field just now."

Mr. Middleton stood for a moment irresolute. That he wanted to walk about in the sunshine and gossip with Pucken he well knew, and knew that his wife knew it, but to admit that he didn't feel like work, especially after Daphne's very trying and tactless description of the thriller he had been reading, was a mortification to his spirit. A way out must be found which would not impair his dignity.

"I yield, I yield," he said, making his way among the chairs to the French window. "I sigh as a worker, but I obey as a husband."

Pleased with this neat parody, he repeated it, adding with sudden anxiety,

"And no one is to have those chairs, Catherine. That is quite understood."

"Quite, darling," said his wife.

She stood for a moment at the window, watching him go

down towards the field, and then returned to the work of preparing the library for the meeting. There was really very little to be done now except to wait for half-past three. The chairman's table was neatly laid out with water jug, glasses, paper, pens, ink, blotting paper and pencils. Chairs were arranged without too much formality. In her sitting-room tea-things were laid out for the twenty or thirty guests that might come.

"That is always what happens," she said. "One gets everything ready much too early and then feels flat. It's only a quarter past twelve. I'll tell Ethel to bring some drinks into the garden. Would you ring, Alister."

Mr. Cameron rang, the order was given and the whole party wandered across the lawn to where a willow drooped in a most becoming manner above a stone-rimmed pond in which goldfish swam among green weeds. Here in the shade chairs and a garden seat were set and Ethel came wheeling a double-decked trolley towards them, laden with drinks.

"Beer, and lemonade, and cider, and ice," said Denis gloating. "No sherry, thank goodness, Catherine. How clever of you not to have sherry on a hot day. It makes one come all-overish. May I pour out?"

He helped everyone and sat down with a glass of cider on the edge of the pond, near his hostess. Mr. Cameron joined Mrs. Stonor on the wooden seat, for he always enjoyed her company. Whether it was the country air, or the pleasure of the Middletons' company, or a lessened anxiety about her stepson, or all three, she looked much younger than when she arrived at Skeynes. Mr. Cameron felt it to be quite ridiculous that she should be Mr. Middleton's sister. True she was a very much younger sister, and Catherine had told him that she was about her own age, but Mrs. Stonor, to his mind, looked younger than Catherine. Partly perhaps because she was very fair, partly because her greenish eyes danced so agreeably while she spoke, partly because she had, as she herself had said, a child's way of doing her thinking aloud. With Catherine one never knew what her thought was till it suddenly dashed out at one, and if one didn't understand it she never troubled to explain. Take it or leave it. And she couldn't let life slip easily over her as Lilian, in spite of all her difficulties, had done.

"What are you thinking about?" said Mrs. Stonor.

"I was thinking, Lilian," said Mr. Cameron, and then stopped, confused.

"Yes, Alister?" said Mrs. Stonor.

"I don't know what I was thinking of," said Mr. Cameron. "I do apologise. I always think of you as Lilian."

"Well, it seems to me quite reasonable," said Mrs. Stonor. "You are almost one of the family, in fact in a way you are more in the family than I am because you see a lot of Jack and Catherine and I see so little. I've got to know Jack better as a brother in the last few weeks than ever in my life before. And as for Catherine she is a great deal too good for him, or for anyone else for that matter, but luckily neither of them know it. So I really don't see why you shouldn't call me Lilian. The children always speak of you as Alister behind your back, but of course that means nothing in their generation. Ours is still a little more backward about Christian names."

"That is very nice of you," said Mr. Cameron gratefully.

As usual Mrs. Stonor's talk had ramified into a confusing number of by-paths, each of which he would have liked to explore with her but hardly knew where to begin or how to find time enough. What she said about her brother and his wife appeared to him to be so bristling with home thrusts that he could have reflected upon it for a very long time. And what she said about the children, about Denis and Daphne, was double edged, though he hardly thought she meant it to be so. It was quite true that Daphne and he were of different generations, but really not a whole generation apart, only each fresh crop of young trod so quickly on the footsteps of the last that one felt like a great-grandfather at forty-eight. And probably Daphne felt a grandmother compared with all the young creatures between seventeen and the early twenties. Age, it seemed to him, mattered far less than it used to. Meanwhile it was very pleasant to see Lilian looking better and younger day by day.

"And now, what was it you were thinking?" said Mrs. Stonor again.

"I was really thinking how much better you looked since you came here," said Mr. Cameron.

"It's because I feel better," said Mrs. Stonor, accepting with great calm a compliment that most women would apply entirely to their faces. "The children are so happy here. Daphne is always well, thank goodness, and Denis is so very much better, and when he is better I feel so relieved that I feel much better too, and feeling better usually makes one look better. Did Daphne show you the snapshot she took of you last week? It came out very well. She has it in her room—"

Mr. Cameron's heart rose in his bosom.

"—with all her other snapshots. She takes a lot."

Mr. Cameron's heart swooped down to the very depths of his inside and then came to equilibrium again. After all it was something to be even one among many snapshots. Mrs. Stonor went on talking of her step-children with a fondness and admiration that Mr. Cameron found not only suitable, with special regard to Daphne, but wholly delightful in a stepmother. Denis looked up from trying to tease goldfish and gave his stepmother one of his quick looks.

"Are you talking about me, darling?" he enquired. "If so I will tell you that I am very well as this leaves me at present, and I do like you so much, and if only someone would leave me a thousand pounds, or even five hundred, to get my ballet put on I would be quite well and happy for the rest of my life. Catherine, I am tickling for goldfish. Wouldn't it be dreadful if I caught one? It might die on me before I could put it back in the water. Would you mind?"

"Not so long as I didn't actually see it die," said Mrs. Middleton.

"I love your truthfulness," said Denis laughing. "I won't pursue my tickling. Daphne, I'll have sixpence with you on the Great Goldfish Derby. I am backing that far one with a silver fin."

Daphne objected, on the grounds that all goldfish were exactly like each other and anyway they never raced, only swam about. Denis said they would each put a crumb on the water then, and whichever goldfish got it first would win sixpence for the owner, and there was absolutely no difficulty in telling them apart if you took pains. But as there were no crumbs about the idea had to be abandoned. Denis, who said he felt an overmastering passion to bet on something, offered to go up to the house and find a crumb, when Mr. Middleton and Pucken approached.

"You look hot, darling," said Mrs. Middleton. "Come and sit down and have a drink."

Mr. Middleton accepted the glass of beer which Denis got up and fetched for him, but remained standing.

"What about Pucken?" Denis said softly, bending over Mrs. Middleton as he passed behind her chair.

"Beer? No, please not. He has as much as is good for him when the Fleece opens."

"Right," said Denis, sitting down on the edge of the pond again, feeling a little confused, perhaps from bending so low to whisper to someone in a deckchair.

"What about the manure, Pucken?" said Mrs. Middleton.

"Well, mum, it's this way," said Pucken.

"Denis darling, are you sure the stone isn't cold?" said Mrs. Stonor. "You have been there a long time."

"It may have been cold in the beginning, though I didn't notice it, but it certainly isn't now," said Denis. "The sun was shining violently upon it while I got Uncle Jack's beer."

"Well, do be careful," said his stepmother.

"Bless your innocent heart," said Denis, blowing her a kiss.

"Can't you get it?" said Mrs. Middleton as Pucken remained tongue-tied.

"Well, mum, it isn't exactly that," said Pucken.

After a great deal of questioning it appeared that the Fleece was responsible for the whole affair. Pucken had the promise of a load of manure, not none, he said, of your mucky pig manure, but a good clean load from Lord Bond's farm stables, as sweet manure as a man could wish to see. But words having passed between him and Lord Bond's second gardener, who was down at the Fleece, that gardener had said he was danged if Pucken should have so much as a wheelbarrow of manure off the place, and so the matter had remained. He could, he said, get a load off Farmer Brown, but where was the use? There was nothing in the county to touch his lordship's manure and set his heart on it he had for the marrows.

After hearing this Mrs. Middleton said she supposed she had better speak to Lord Bond about it.

"Or will you, Jack?" she asked her husband. "You will be seeing him at the meeting to-day, you know."

But Mr. Middleton showed such signs of becoming a complete nervous and physical wreck if he had to take the responsibility that his wife said she would do it herself. Pucken was told to be more careful at the Fleece and went happily away talking to himself about the excellent qualities of the Staple Park manure. After this the party broke up for lunch.

THE first arrival was Lord Stoke, who enjoyed any kind of meeting so much that he always came a quarter of an hour too soon, to get his bearings he said, though neither he nor anyone else knew exactly what he meant. As his car drew up at the garden gate Pucken, who was hanging about to watch the arrivals, touched his cap. Lord Stoke, who knew every face connected with cows in the whole county and had twice seen Pucken at the Skeynes Agricultural Show, touched his hat in return.

"You're Mr. Middleton's man, aren't you?" said his lordship. "Pucken, that's the name isn't it?"

Pucken, much gratified, scratched the back of his neck and grinned.

Lord Stoke enquired what cows Mr. Middleton was sending to the Show, expressed great interest, not unmingled with relief, at the news that the Jersey was in calf again and so, gossiping with Pucken, moved slowly down the lane towards the field where the cow sheds were. As Pucken was too shy to answer except in monosyllables, his lordship's deafness did not prevent conversation and time passed very happily.

After Lord Stoke came the Palmers, carrying with them Mr. and Mrs. Tebben. Mr. Tebben torn unwillingly from Bishop Ogmund was heartily wishing that Sir Ogilvy Hibberd, the source of all these woes, were spread-eagled. Mr. Middleton who had come out on hearing the sound of cars to catch Lord Stoke was greeted by Mrs. Palmer.

"I don't think you know my friends Mr. and Mrs. Tebben," she said. "Their daughter married my nephew Laurence Deane. And I've brought Ed Pollett over. Come here, Ed."

A man, stiff with consciousness of his Sunday suit, who was sitting beside the Palmers' chauffeur, dismounted and came awkwardly towards her.

"I thought you wouldn't mind," Mrs. Palmer went on, "his coming with us. He's having his holiday."

"Certainly not," said Mr. Middleton, courteous but perplexed. The name Pollett seemed familiar to him, but the bearer of it he could not place. He had heard that Mrs. Palmer had strange theatrical guests. . . .

"Brother of your chauffeur," said Mrs. Palmer, her quick eye at once detecting her host's dilemma. "You must have heard of Ed. He is the under porter at Worsted Station and has a perfect genius for cars, but a little bit wanting."

In giving this character of Ed, Mrs. Palmer took no pains to moderate her voice, but Ed bore no grudge, appearing indeed to take some pride in this publicity.

"Well, he'd better go and find Pollett, he's somewhere about," said Mr. Middleton. "You didn't pass Stoke's car on the way, did you? I want to speak to him."

Ed gave Mr. Middleton a respectful nudge and pointed towards a car a little further down the lane, saying "That's her."

"Who?" said Mr. Middleton, for no female was visible.

"He means Lord Stoke's car, sir, don't you, Ed," said the Palmers' chauffeur coming to the rescue. "Ed can pick out any car, sir, once he's seen it, can't you, Ed?"

"That's her, O.K.," said Ed.

"Well, I must have missed Stoke somehow. I expect we'll find him in the house," said Mr. Middleton. "Come in."

Mr. Tebben had brightened perceptibly at the name of Lord Stoke, for a labourer while digging a drain on his lordship's estate in a field called Bloody Meadow had lately turned up some bones, which might as well have been those of a Viking as anyone else. It was more or less authentically proved that a battle had been fought in the vicinity of Rising Castle between a local ruler and a Danish force stiffened with a roving contingent of Norsemen, and Mr. Tebben had a secret hope that the bones might prove to be those of a hero called Thorstein Longtooth who was mentioned in a Norse ballad over which Mr. Tebben and the President of the Snorri Society had quarrelled violently through the medium of the Journal of Icelandic Studies. If he could get from Lord Stoke a description of the bones, or better still permission to see them, his afternoon would not have been wasted, so he followed his host with a somewhat lighter heart.

Mrs. Tebben paused to cry aloud in ecstasy over the beauty of some delphiniums, but was hustled along by Mrs. Palmer, who wished to get front row seats as her husband was a little deaf.

"All the same, Louise," said Mrs. Tebben. "I do think my plan of getting a few packets of seed from Woolworth's, quite at random, simply by the delightful coloured pictures on the outside, and sowing them here and there in our little garden in a spirit of adventure has often been most success-ful and seldom more so than this year. You haven't seen that little corner down by the ash-pit lately. I have put nastur-tiums there and it is going to be quite a splash of colour."

Mrs. Palmer took no notice of her friend and bore the whole party into the house where Mrs. Middleton was receiving her guests, most of whom knew each other, though not always on speaking terms, so very little introducing was needed. Mrs. Palmer was moving towards the front row, but Mrs. Tebben lingered to exclaim gustily over the beauty of the view from the library window and so lingering found herself face to face with the Bonds. Mrs. Tebben did not in the least mind Lady Bond's title, wealth, position or domineering ways, but on one subject she would brook no rivalry. She and Lady Bond each had an only son and each knew that her own son was quite perfect, though without prejudice to a good deal of fault-finding in the home. Neither lady appeared to have any idea that her husband was in any way responsible for the qualities of her child, each gathering all credit to herself. The race on the whole had been even. Young Mr. Bond had a very good job and would eventually inherit a title, while Richard Tebben was doing very well in an engineering firm and had excellent prospects. There was however one triumph which Mrs. Tebben could not forget and had no intention of letting Lady Bond forget. A few years earlier, before the two young men went out into the world, Richard Tebben at the annual cricket match between Skeynes and Worsted had caught young Mr. Bond out with a spectacular catch never to be forgotten at the Fleece in Skeynes or the Woolpack in Worsted. The result had been a violent friendship lasting for one day, since when the young men had never met, young Mr. Bond going to New York and Richard Tebben on a three years' job to South America. But neither of the mothers had forgotten the event. At the sight of Mrs. Tebben Lady Bond automatically became more the county magnate than ever, while Mrs. Tebben could not help conveying by her air that she had taken a first at Oxford and had a son who caught other people's sons out.

"How are you?" said Mrs. Tebben to Lady Bond. "And how is C.W.? Still playing cricket?"

Young Mr. Bond, who thought this question was addressed to himself, was about to say that he looked forward to the match against Worsted and was sorry Richard couldn't be there, when his mother, morally elbowing him out of the way, said he was quite out of practice as he only played polo in America. She then wished she hadn't said it.

Mrs. Tebben, horrified by the inverted snobbism that at once overcame her against her will said polo was alas! too expensive a game for Richard, but he had had a perfectly wonderful time during the opera season at Buenos Aires, having heard Strilla and Taglino every time they sang.

Lady Bond, who was usually rather proud than otherwise of being entirely unmusical, felt that this boast was aimed at her and in a voice that she didn't quite recognise as her own said That was very nice. Luckily Lord Bond and Mr. Palmer now began to discuss the Skeynes Agricultural Show in a way that relegated women, even Lady Bond, to their proper place, and no blood was shed.

By this time the room was nearly full and it was twenty-five minutes to four. Lord Stoke had not yet arrived, nor had Lord Pomfret, and Lady Bond was beginning to chafe and told Mrs. Middleton so.

"I know Stoke had started," she said, "because Spencer rang up to enquire just before we left home. I do hope he hasn't had an accident. He is so deaf now."

"But he doesn't drive himself, does he?" asked Mrs. Middleton.

"Stoke? He never tried," said Lady Bond. "He is a perfect fool about machinery. But it is worrying. Mr. Middleton," she called as her host came in. "Stoke hasn't come, has he?"

"He has come all right," said Mr. Middleton, "but I can't find him. His car is in the lane, but I can't see him anywhere about."

"Then he is down in the field talking to your cowman," said Lady Bond, who knew her brother's peculiarities. "C.W., you had better go and look."

"Certainly," said young Mr. Bond. "Which field would he be down, sir?"

Daphne said she would show him and they went off together, to the simultaneous annoyance of Lady Bond and Mr. Cameron, who were both even more annoyed when Lord Stoke came in by the French window.

"Oh, there you are, Stoke," said Mr. Middleton. "It is time we began."

"I've been having a most interesting talk with your cowman," said Lord Stoke. "I remember his father quite well. He fell into a ditch coming back from the Southbridge Cattle Show one year and a waggon of hay overturned just at the same spot. When they got the waggon right next day and reloaded the hay, of course Pucken was dead. Suffocated. Don't suppose he suffered, though. He must have been quite drunk when he fell in. At least they had refused to serve him with any more beer at the Stoke Arms and you know what Glazebury was, old Glazebury I mean; he'd go just as far as the law would let him and if he refused to serve a customer it meant that customer was pretty tight already."

"Well, we ought to move a chairman," said Mr. Middleton. "You are going to do it, I believe."

"Eh?" said Lord Stoke.

"We ought to be getting down to business," said Mr. Middleton, not quite patiently and rather loudly.

"Business, eh? Quite right. Who is that woman sitting in the back row, Middleton? I ought to know her face," said Lord Stoke, who had been surveying the audience with much interest.

"That's Mrs. Pucken," said Mr. Middleton unwillingly.

"Of course, of course," said his lordship. "Sarah Margett she was. Her brother keeps the shop at Worsted. Used to be Lucasta's kitchenmaid. I must have a word with her. Well, Sarah, how are you?"

Mrs. Pucken got up and shook Lord Stoke's proffered hand and said she was nicely.

"And how are the new lowers?" said his lordship.

Mrs. Pucken smiled broadly with a slightly seasick motion of her lower teeth and said there wasn't really nothing she couldn't eat now.

"Lou here wants a set like mine, my lord," she said. "Her teeth are something awful. But I say Just you wait a bit, my girl, we can't have everything we want not all at once, didn't I, Lou?"

But Lou, a step further than her mother from familiar terms with the aristocracy, went bright scarlet and although she opened and shut her mouth several times was bereft of the power of speech.

"That's right," said Lord Stoke approvingly, for he was used to finding his friends inaudible and took it for granted that Lou had spoken. "Always do what your mother tells you. Called after Lady Bond, isn't she?"

Mrs. Pucken replied that in a manner of speaking she was, implying that she fully realised Lady Bond's condescension in lending her name. Lord Stoke would have lingered indefinitely, asking after the various members of Mrs. Pucken's family, but Mr. Middleton, made quite desperate, seized his distinguished guest by the arm and propelled him to the other end of the room. Lord Stoke, seeing an armchair, and being used to taking the chair on every possible occasion, sat down in it and Mr. Middleton, who had rather meant to conduct the meeting himself, was forced to take the inferior seat at his lordship's side. Denis caught Mrs. Middleton's eye and received from her a look expressing amusement combined with despair.

Lord Stoke lost no time in telling his audience that they had been convened to discuss a public meeting to be held about the proposed building of a garage on Pooker's Piece. As everyone had already been informed of this by the leaflet of invitation, and in many cases by word of mouth, the news created very little sensation. He then by easy stages passed to the suitability of Pooker's Piece for grazing land, his own opinion of pure-bred Jerseys as against a mixed strain of milker and a pressing reminder to his hearers of the importance of the Skeynes Agricultural Show. At this point Lady Bond, who had been listening to her brother's words with growing disfavour, wrote on a visiting card the words "Let Mr. Middleton speak" and handed it up to the chairman's table.

"What's that?" said Lord Stoke. "Middleton speak? Of course Lucasta, of course. I am just coming to that. Well, Middleton, what have you to say, eh?"

Seizing this favourable moment Mr. Middleton rose to
his feet and launched into a spirited defence of the amenities
of Pooker's Piece, with special and lengthy reference to the
pleasure it had so often given him to ramble over it with
Flora, who barked at her own name and had to be suppressed
by Mr. Cameron, glad of an excuse to vent an unaccountable
irritation of feeling upon a dumb beast. Mr. Middleton's
rolling periods gave his audience time to think in some cases
about nothing, in others about their own affairs. Flora at
intervals gave an hysterical whimper, till Lou, sitting just
behind Mr. Cameron and at the end of a row, was moved to
an heroic impulse.

"Shall I take her away, sir?" she said hoarsely. "She
knows me."

Flora, on hearing this, made a wild struggle as of a beast
starved and tortured to escape to freedom, for with the profound instinct of her kind she associated Lou with bits of
food surreptitiously bestowed whenever she went into the
Puckens' cottage or the kitchen of the White House.

Mr. Cameron thankfully allowed Lou to pick Flora up
bodily and take her out by the service door and relapsed into
gloomy meditation till he saw Mrs. Stonor looking anxiously
and sympathetically at him. Somehow this sight cheered
him a good deal and he began to wonder what everyone else
had already been wondering for some time, whether Mr.
Middleton would ever stop. This question was suddenly
settled by Lord Stoke, who looked at his watch, and uttered
an exclamation.

"Good heavens, Middleton, it's half-past four," he said.
"Sorry I must be off. Sub-Committee of the County Council

at Southbridge at five. Most interesting meeting. Does a lot of good getting people together."

He then descended among the crowd and began saying good-bye to his hostess. Everyone got up or shuffled their chairs, eager for Mrs. Middleton's good tea. Mr. Tebben, driven to desperation by a wasted afternoon in which nothing whatever had been accomplished except the ruin of his working day, got between Lord Stoke and the door.

"Excuse me one moment, Lord Stoke," he said.

"Yes?" said Lord Stoke stopping courteously.

"It's about that find of bones," said Mr. Tebben.

"Eh?" said Lord Stoke.

"Bones!" said Mr. Tebben at the top of his voice. "Viking's bones! My name is Tebben."

"Tebben?" said his lordship. "Good Lord! Tebben! Snorri Society. I read your paper on the Laxdaela Saga in their transactions. Most interesting. I'd like you to come over and see those bones. At least what there is of them. Most of them were broken and a lot crumbled away, but we've got the rest up at the Castle for the moment."

"And do you think they are definitely of that period?" said Mr. Tebben.

"Couldn't say," replied Lord Stoke. "Bones aren't much in my line. Might be a man's, might be a dog's as far as I'm concerned. But come over to-morrow and have a look. I'll send the car for you. Or come to lunch. That's it, lunch, one-thirty, and we'll have a good look at the excavation. Is this your wife?" he added as Mrs. Tebben who had a passion for Getting to the Bottom of Things came up to see what it was all about. "Will you introduce me?"

Mr. Tebben introduced Lord Stoke to Mrs. Tebben, adding quickly that he was going to lunch at Rising Castle on the next day.

Mrs. Tebben, who held that an invitation to a husband should include a wife, was about to be disappointed when a thought struck her.

"That will be splendid, my dear," she said. "I had meant to have a little bit of neck of lamb for lunch to-morrow and open a tinned tongue for to-night. But if you are going to Lord Stoke we will keep the roast till Monday and I shall have a picnic on some Heinz beans by myself for Sunday lunch. Or, I wonder, would the lamb keep till Monday in this weather? Perhaps it might be wiser to have it to-night. It is such a small piece that there will be time for Mrs. Phipps to put it in the oven for our supper when we get home, and I shall just have time to hurry down the garden and get some peas."

She paused, her hat a little on the back of her head with enthusiasm.

"Well, that's splendid," said Lord Stoke, who had but imperfectly understood Mrs. Tebben, but gathered that her inclinations were friendly. "Now I must really be getting along. My car will fetch you at one o'clock to-morrow, Tebben. Lamb's Piece at Worsted, isn't it? I used to know old Margerison who owned it. Married his housekeeper—high time too."

But just as he was going his eye was caught by Ethel, important and flustered, speaking to her mistress. His lordship, who had a violent curiosity about everyone with whom he came in contact, paused to listen.

"Show him in, of course, Ethel," said Mrs. Middleton. "Jack, Lord Pomfret is here."

"Then we'll get something done," said Lady Bond, whose disapproval of her brother and her host had been increasing rapidly. "Don't let the people have tea yet, Mr. Middleton. One moment," she added to the room in general in her committee voice.

The rush towards tea was stemmed and Lord Pomfret came in.

"I am so glad you could come," said Mrs. Middleton, "but I'm afraid the meeting is almost over. Would you care to say anything?"

"Depends on what's been said," said Lord Pomfret looking suspiciously around.

"Absolutely nothing at all," said Lady Bond. "I understood that this meeting was called to arrange for a public meeting about Sir Ogilvy Hibberd's plan for building on Pooker's Piece, but nothing has been settled at all."

"Not much good my coming then," said Lord Pomfret. "However as I'm here can I have a cup of tea, Mrs. Middleton?"

"Of course," said Mrs. Middleton. "Will you come into the dining-room?"

"Crowd there," said Lord Pomfret. "I'd rather have a cup here with you."

Mrs. Middleton, who liked Lord Pomfret but did not intend to be bullied, said she must look after her guests and would send some tea to him and come back herself before long. She then introduced her sister-in-law to Lord Pomfret and went away.

❧ 7 ❧

EPILOGUE TO A MEETING

❧

IN THE DINING-ROOM THE FUN, AS MRS. TEBBEN SAID, WAS FAST
and furious. Most of the other guests were gorging on Mrs.
Middleton's excellent cakes, telling each other that they were
on a diet but when you were out to tea it didn't count. Denis
and Mr. Cameron were being very obliging with strawberries and ices. Mr. Cameron had always found that hard
work was a good way of taking one's mind off things, and
to fill people's plates seemed better than to wonder where
Daphne and young Bond were; so he industriously did both.

As a matter of fact Daphne and young Mr. Bond, having
conducted the most perfunctory of searches for Lord Stoke,
had gone down to the cowshed and had a delightful conversation with Pucken, who obliged them with his valueless
views on the Milk Marketing Board. They then discussed
the cows, the probable date of Lily Langtry's expected calf
and the chances of the various exhibitors at the Skeynes Agricultural Show, after which young Mr. Bond gave Pucken a
cigarette and followed Daphne to the strawberry beds. Here
they performed a difficult but humane deed by rescuing a

thrush who had entangled himself in the net and deeply resented their kind interference.

"By Jove, he has bitten me to the bone," said young Mr. Bond as the thrush gave one last vindictive dig at his hand and fled shrieking to the wood.

"That always happens if you help people," said Daphne. "I expect you'll see that thrush walking up and down outside your window to-morrow with a placard saying 'Mr. Bond Unfair to Thrushes.' "

"If he does I'll jolly well drive my car up and down outside his wood with a placard to say 'Thrush Ungrateful to Mr. Bond.' "

"Well, that's about all," said Daphne straightening herself. "I don't think there's a single one we haven't eaten. It won't matter because I know Catherine has got all she wants for to-night. I suppose we'd better go back to the meeting."

"Need we?" said Mr. Bond.

"Well, not for pleasure," said Daphne, "but Catherine might want me to help and I'd hate to let her down."

Young Mr. Bond, who really had a sense of duty, at once recognised the justice of Daphne's remarks and admired her for them, so they went back to Laverings, entering the library by the French window just as Mr. Cameron was bringing a tray of strawberries and cream for Lady Bond, Mrs. Palmer and their parties.

"Hullo, Alister," said Daphne. "I'd adore some of those." Mr. Cameron smiled at her and brought his tray.

"I should have thought you'd had enough," said young Mr. Bond. "Guzzling away under the strawberry net."

"Well, they do make me come out all over spots sometimes," said Daphne candidly. "Thanks awfully, Alister, but I'd better not."

Mr. Cameron took his tray away and saw that Lady Bond, Mrs. Palmer and Mrs. Tebben were properly looked after. Lord Pomfret, Lord Bond, Mr. Palmer and Lord Stoke, who had now decided that it was too late for the Sub-Committee, were deep in professional talk about cows, and Mr. Middleton for once in his life found so little attention paid to his remarks that he was glad to give Mr. Tebben his views on the Icelandic sagas. Lady Bond, still annoyed by the very inconclusive character of the meeting and what she inwardly called the maunderings of her brother and Mr. Middleton, was in her most aggressive humour and had already had one or two sharp passages with Mrs. Palmer. Mrs. Middleton, who had come back as she promised, found that Lord Pomfret was immersed in cow talk so she tried to pour oil on the rising billows of their politeness, though without much success.

"What play are you giving this year, Mrs. Palmer?" she asked.

Mrs. Palmer said they were having a complete change from Greek plays and doing *Twelfth Night* in modern dress.

"We are still short of principals," she said. "I suppose Mrs. Stonor, your daughter wouldn't help us by doing Olivia?"

"Well," said Mrs. Stonor, who had been listening with some amusement to the bickerings between the other ladies, "she is really my stepdaughter, but I don't see why she shouldn't be able to act. I'll ask her. Daphne!"

"It is quite in the nature of an experiment," said Mrs.

Palmer. "Everyone is as far as possible to be his or her natural self. My butler, for instance, is doing Malvolio and the doctor's twin girls are doing Viola and Sebastian, and the Rector's parlourmaid will be Maria."

"It seems a pity, Louise, that Ed Pollett couldn't do the fool," said Mrs. Tebben. "Of course he can't ever remember his lines and has no voice, but I daresay someone else could sing his part off."

"Ed isn't a *fool*, Winifred," said Mrs. Palmer sharply. "He's only wanting. Miss Stonor, would you care to do Olivia for us?"

"Not if it's Shakespeare, thank you," said Daphne retreating. "We did a lot of him at school."

"It is in modern dress," Mrs. Palmer urged.

"But that wouldn't feel like Shakespeare," said Daphne, basely changing her tactics. "I mean you can generally get away with it with robes and things, but I'd feel an awful fool in my ordinary clothes."

"Well, think it over," said Mrs. Palmer graciously. "We have a most enthusiastic audience. Our high water mark was the production of *Hippolytus* a few years ago."

"That was the year Richard made his wonderful catch," said Mrs. Tebben, beaming at the thought.

Lady Bond who did not like this allusion to her son's defeat said nothing in a very marked manner, but young Mr. Bond with perfect honesty said what fun it was and what a splendid tea the two elevens had had afterwards.

"That was the year Mrs. Palmer's niece, Betty, did Phaedra so well," Mrs. Tebben continued. "Didn't you think her splendid, Mr. Bond?"

Young Mr. Bond, with less enthusiasm, said she was awfully good.

"We all thought they would be engaged," said Mrs. Tebben aside to Mrs. Stonor and Daphne. "I have never seen anyone so struck as Mr. Bond was. Betty is such a nice girl. She has just taken a first in Greats at Oxford."

Daphne's face expressed her opinion of nice girls that took firsts in Greats so clearly that Mrs. Palmer began to bristle for her niece.

"She tells me she saw quite a lot of you, C.W., while you were in America," said Mrs. Palmer, glad to show Lady Bond that a Palmer niece was properly valued by the heir of Staple Park. "I believe she is going back to Bryn Mawr to do a post-graduate course, so doubtless you will see her when you go back to New York. It will be nice for her to have you there."

Young Mr. Bond, acutely sensible of Daphne's disapproval, said it would.

"I didn't know you were such a friend of Miss Deane's, C.W.," said his mother.

Young Mr. Bond began to flounder so miserably that Mrs. Middleton quickly asked Lady Bond why Miss Starter had not come to the meeting.

"Oh, Juliana had one of her bad days," said Lady Bond. "She has headaches that are quite unlike anyone else's, so she is staying in bed with the blinds down and will just have a little toasted Kornog bread for tea and perhaps come down to dinner. C.W., I think we ought to be going. Tell your father I am ready."

At the same moment Lord Pomfret, saying that the

Bishop was dining at Pomfret Towers and he must get back, broke up the cow conference. A welter of good-byes ensued.

"Good-bye, Mrs. Middleton," said Lord Pomfret. "I never had my cup of tea with you. You must let me come over again one day. I don't get about as much as I did since my wife died. She liked you. You look tired. Don't overdo it."

Mrs. Middleton said it was only the heat and she was afraid that they had rather wasted Lord Pomfret's time.

"Not a bit," said the earl. "I've learnt what I wanted to know. Drawing-room meetings are no good. I'll have to think about that feller Hibberd. My wife liked Pooker's Piece. We used to ride there when we were first married. Can't have a garage on it."

He took his leave, as did Lord Stoke and the Palmers, accompanied by Mr. and Mrs. Tebben, which last named lady expressed the greatest appreciation of her afternoon's treat.

"I do hope you will be able to come to tea with me one day," she said to Mrs. Middleton. "Your tea was delicious, but we have a way of doing cake that I am sure you would like to know. When I have a cake that has got really stale and I don't want to make a trifle with it, I cut it into slices and toast them and spread a little butter on them and pile them up in a dish and leave it in the oven for a few moments. You have no idea how good it is. I had a cake last week that had somehow got into a corner and been overlooked and when I had just cut off the little mildewed bit and toasted and buttered it, we all enjoyed it so much."

Mrs. Middleton thanked Mrs. Tebben warmly. The rest

of the guests were going and after some more handshaking
and thanks for the tea she found herself left with her family
and the Bonds.

"Cows!" exclaimed Mr. Middleton. "The whole subject
of cows is one on which, I say it without pride, I am com-
petent to speak, but I must confess that for the moment I
am tongue-tied. In the face of Lord Pomfret and Stoke and
Palmer I must perforce be silent. How they talked, Catherine; how they talked. Never have I been so borne down,
so overwhelmed by sheer force of words, a veritable Niagara
of talk. Bond, you will bear me out in what I say."

"I'll never do anything against Stoke as long as he has
that cowman," said Lord Bond mournfully. "But he won't
leave. I know for a fact that Pomfret would give him twice
what he's getting now. But I still don't agree with Stoke
about those Frisians. Mark my words. . . ."

While Lord Bond said what he felt about Frisians and
Mr. Middleton explained at great length how impossible
it was for him to speak, Mrs. Middleton, on the sofa which
had been put at right angles to the chairman's table, her
back to the window, wondered what use anything was. The
great drawing-room meeting had taken place, nothing useful
had been said or settled; the one success of the afternoon
had been the tea, and if people wanted tea she would far
rather give it to them in a friendly way, a few at a time,
than have the whole house upset. Denis· sat down beside
her, a glass in each hand.

"One is sherry, one is brandy and a little soda," he
remarked. "Which are you going to have?"

"Thank you so much, but I really don't think I want either," she said kindly.

"I know you don't," said Denis. "Which are you going to have?"

"The brandy please," said Mrs. Middleton meekly. "Not because it brings back the colour to my pale cheeks as in novels, but because I like it better."

Denis gave her a curiously ferocious glance and went away to look after the rest of the party. Lord Bond, on the pretext of mixing his whisky and soda himself, accompanied Denis to the table where the drinks stood.

"About that concert," he said. "My wife's going to town next week and Juliana is going to visit her widowed sister at Tunbridge Wells. Suppose you and your sister come up one evening to dinner and I'll get the piano opened."

"I'd love to, sir," said Denis. "I'll ask Daphne."

He fetched his sister, who was loud in her approval of the scheme.

"But you needn't mention it to my wife," said Lord Bond anxiously.

"Are you concealing something from mother?" said young Mr. Bond, who had naturally gravitated to Daphne.

His father explained the plan.

"Jolly good idea," said young Mr. Bond. "Make it Wednesday and I'll run down for dinner."

"That's right. We'll be four then," said Lord Bond, feeling like Guy Fawkes.

Daphne, without looking at young Mr. Bond, said would Lord Bond think it awfully rude if she asked if Mr. Cameron could come. He was staying at Laverings for some time and was most awfully nice and she knew he liked Gilbert and Sullivan.

Lord Bond, who delighted in hospitality, said of course Cameron must come and wouldn't Mrs. Stonor come too. In view of Lady Bond's well-known gift of spotting at once what was going on the invitations had to be given with great care and secrecy, but both were gladly accepted.

"There, that's splendid," said Lord Bond to the conspirators. "Now we shall be six. Oh, one thing though. My wife is taking the Rolls to town and I haven't got anyone to drive the other car. Young Phipps is the only one I'd trust and he is away on his holiday. Tell you what. I'll get the car from the Fleece to bring you over and take you back. Would that be all right?"

"I could fetch them all on my way down from London, father," said young Mr. Bond, "and take them back."

Daphne said he might have an accident or a puncture on the way down and then where would they all be.

"Quite right, Miss Stonor," said his lordship. "Much better to have the car from the Fleece. Do you remember, C.W., the time you were to fetch Juliana from Tunbridge Wells and forgot all about her? Wouldn't do to forget Miss Stonor. Where were you that day, C.W.?"

Young Mr. Bond, suddenly feeling a profound dislike for his father, said rather sulkily Which day.

"The day you forgot Juliana," said Lord Bond. "I know. You were driving Mrs. Palmer's niece to Oxford. Betty; that's the name. Betty Deane. Handsome girl that. You'd like her, Miss Stonor."

Daphne said she was so glad she had never been at Oxford, because all the girls she had known who went there were perfectly ghastly. Lady Bond then summoned her husband and son and everyone walked to the garden gate with them. By their car Ferguson, the Bonds' chauffeur, and Pollett, the Middletons' chauffeur, were deep in discussion, with Ed Pollett standing by.

"Excuse me, my lady," said Ferguson, who like most of the Staple Park employees looked to his mistress for orders, "but if his lordship was wanting anyone to drive the car while I am away, Mr. Pollett's brother is quite as you might say a wizard with cars. Of course I wouldn't have suggested it, my lady, but Mr. Spencer, who was in the dining-room at the time, happened to pass the remark that his lordship said he didn't know who to have seeing that young Phipps was away."

Lord Bond said almost pettishly that he wished Spencer wouldn't gossip in the servants' hall, but his wife, who never let anything pass without investigation, asked who Mr. Pollett was and, hence, who his brother.

If Ferguson had been among his equals he would have said that Mr. Pollett drove Middleton's car, but in deference to his employer's class prejudice he said that Mr. Pollett was Mr. Middleton's chauffeur.

"Can I speak to your man?" said Lady Bond to Mr. Middleton, thus grossly offending Ferguson's class consciousness. Then without waiting for Mr. Middleton's assent she set up a Board of Inquisition on Pollett, harrying and browbeating him in a way to which his free mechanic's spirit was quite unaccustomed. Pollett's ancestors had lived at Worsted ever since there was a Pollett in England; respect for the gentry had been bred in the family since the days of Gorwulf who lived at Gorwulfsteadings and had a Pollett as serf; and all Pollett's education, his training in motor works, his experience with armoured cars in Mesopotamia during the war, fell from him like dust before the broom under Lady Bond's eye.

"Well, Mr. Middleton," she said after a few moments' talk, "your man's brother appears to be distinctly wanting, but I gather that he has a licence and understands cars, and your man says he is absolutely trustworthy, so I daresay he will do for a few days. Will that suit you, Alured?"

Lord Bond would, on the whole, have preferred not to be driven by what he not unnaturally took to be the village idiot, but if his wife said it was to be he supposed he had better agree. Besides he liked Ed Pollett's face and thought he might get some amusing local gossip out of him. So he agreed.

"Then I'd better have a word with him now," said Lady Bond. "Ed!"

Ed, roughly awakened from the pleasant day-dream about nothing at all which was his normal state, came nervously forward.

"Do you understand, Ed?" said her ladyship in a clear voice. "You are to come up to Staple Park on Monday and your brother will show you the car you are to drive, and you will drive his lordship till the end of the week."

Ed looked at his brother for confirmation.

"Say Yes to her ladyship," his brother prompted.

"That's O.K., miss," said Ed.

"It's a little Denham," said Lady Bond, quite unperturbed by her temporary chauffeur's mode of address. "Do you know them?"

Ed smiled blissfully.

"Of course Ed knows them," said young Mr. Bond, who had been wondering where he and Ed had met. "Do you remember the play at Mrs. Palmer's two or three years ago, Ed, and how Mr. Richard Tebben's car got stuck and you put her right? She was a Denham, wasn't she?"

"That's right, sir," said Ed, smiling more benignantly than before.

"He'll be all right for you, father," said young Mr. Bond, with the happy assurance of the young that their elders are so dull as to be immune from accident. "You'll drive my father nicely, won't you, Ed?"

"That's O.K., sir," said Ed, and then said something to his brother that the audience couldn't catch.

"Excuse me, my lady," said Pollett, "but Ed wants to know if he can have a uniform, because he's only got the one good suit and he wouldn't like to spoil it and he doesn't think Mr. Patten, the station master at Worsted, would like him to wear his railway uniform. I could lend him my old one."

This matter being satisfactorily arranged Lady Bond was just going to get into her car when a thought struck her.

"Oh, Mr. Middleton," she said, "we have arranged nothing about the public meeting after all. I really don't know what my brother was thinking of."

"Of cows," said Mrs. Middleton. "They all do at this time of year. Would it be better to put the meeting off till after the Skeynes Agricultural Show?"

"Perhaps you are right," said Lady Bond. "Daphne, if you will come up to the Park on Monday I will give you a list of people and we will settle a date and then you could get on with the typing while I am away."

Daphne was quite ready to do this at half a crown an hour and at last the Bonds went away. Ed went to get his tea at his brother's cottage before catching the 7.33 from Skeynes to Worsted, a journey which he intended to perform either in the cab of the engine driver, Sid Pollett, his first cousin, or in the van of the guard, Mr. Patten, his aunt's husband.

Laverings and the White House all sat in chairs on the terrace and drank what they fancied.

"I can't think," said Mrs. Stonor, "why people ever have meetings. It really seems to be the one way of not getting anything done. I think it would be so much easier if someone would simply write to Sir Ogilvy Hibberd and explain. He would be much more likely to take notice of a person than a meeting. Jack, why don't you write?"

"I write, Lilian?" exclaimed Mr. Middleton. "No, no."

"But why not?" asked his sister.

"My dear Lilian!" said Mr. Middleton, ever active in avoiding things he didn't want to do. "My dear Lilian," he added, hoping to find something to say. "My dear Lilian, the thing is impossible. My name may carry some little weight. I have tramped the country about Pooker's Piece year in and year out, under blazing June suns, under the bitter blasts of winter, under the slanting showers of April—"

"And do not forget the golden shower of autumn leaves," murmured Denis, catching Mrs. Middleton's eye, who wanted to laugh and frown at once and compromised by a glance of reproving sympathy.

"—till every flower, every hedgerow, every blade of grass is as familiar to me as the palm of my hand—"

Mrs. Stonor said she wondered why the palms of people's hands should be familiar to them. She for one, she said, never looked at hers, because it always seemed to be the back of one's hands that one saw, or one's finger nails if they suddenly happened to be dirty when one thought they were clean, which was always happening in London. It was really, she thought, because London water was so hard, certainly much harder than it used to be when she was a girl and it was an extraordinary thing that the water seemed to be getting harder all over England; and it was all very well to say Collect the rainwater in a butt, but when you lived in London it was quite impossible to have a butt in a flat, because first it wouldn't go in at the front door and then there would be nowhere to put it unless one could have it on the roof and padlock it so that other people couldn't use it and in any case London rain was so dirty, as anyone who left her window open when it was raining and saw the white curtains afterwards would agree, that it would really hardly be worth while unless one had a filter. Her hair-dresser, she added, had a water softener machine which was very nice.

"—but," continued Mr. Middleton, who had been champing while his sister unburdened herself, "though I am, as it were, one with this Saxon countryside, bone of its bone, soil of its soil, there are others who have a yet greater and longer claim on it, affection towards it, and to them I must yield pride of place. Besides I don't know the man."

"But that doesn't matter, does it?" said Daphne. "I mean if you begin Dear Sir it's all right. People get heaps of letters from people they don't know. Lady Bond gets about six or seven every day asking her to be a patroness for a ball, or sell tickets for something."

"Of Lady Bond's post bag I know nothing," cried Mr. Middleton, goaded beyond endurance, "but the cases are entirely dissimilar, entirely. I do not wish to ask for Ogilvy to patronise anything, to take tickets for anything. I do not wish to have anything to do with him at all. I do not know him, I repeat. In fact nobody knows him."

"But they must, Uncle Jack," said Daphne, severely practical. "You can't be a person that nobody knows them, unless it was a kind of mystery film."

Mr. Cameron laughed, so Daphne laughed too, though she didn't quite know why. Then Mrs. Stonor took her family back to dinner, with a promise to return later in the evening.

"How did you and Mrs. Pucken enjoy the meeting?" said Mrs. Stonor to Palfrey while she was carving a chicken and Palfrey was handing breadsauce, gravy, peas and new potatoes.

"It was very nice, thank you madam, I'm sure," said Palfrey with such a wealth of sinister meaning that Denis and Daphne got the giggles.

"Couldn't you hear?" said Mrs. Stonor. "Lord Stoke wasn't very distinct."

· "It wasn't that, madam," said Palfrey in a manner carefully calculated to stimulate curiosity.

"Well, I hope you got a nice tea afterwards," said Mrs. Stonor, dismissing the whole affair in what Palfrey considered an unfair and unsympathetic way.

"Well, I always said no one could make breadsauce like you, Palfrey," said Denis, helping himself to far more than his share. "What was wrong?"

"It was Lou, Mr. Denis," said Palfrey.

"What happened?" asked Denis. "Was she sick after tea?"

"Yes, Mr. Denis. She is very given to be bilious. I was just the same when I was her age, the least thing, like a pork chop, or prawns and cocoa upset me. But it wasn't so much that. Mrs. Pucken was quite shocked, and it's not to be surprised at."

"Well, what was it?" said Denis, "or forever after hold your peace, because I shan't ask you again. I got quite a bit of work done yesterday, Lilian, and I want to try it on Catherine's piano."

"I'm sure I would be the last to say anything," Palfrey began.

"So you are," said Denis, "but do go on."

"Well, madam," said Palfrey, retransferring her patronage to her mistress, "Mrs. Middleton's dog, that Flora, was making quite a nuisance of himself while Mr. Middleton was speaking."

"It's not him, it's her," said Daphne. "She's a bitch, Palfrey."

"Whining and making a nuisance of himself he was,"

said Palfrey, who had a rooted conviction, born of her extreme delicacy, that all dogs were he and all cats, or pussies, she: as indeed they too often are. "Sitting by Mr. Cameron's chair he was, so that everyone where he was sitting passed the remark what a nuisance he was. And then what must my lady do, but take the dog as bold as brass and away she takes him to the stable and shuts him in and then comes back to eat her tea."

"But I think it was very kind of Lou to take Flora away," said Mrs. Stonor. "She was making a horrid noise."

"It wasn't that, madam. It was Putting Herself Forward, just to show off to Mr. Cameron. She won't hear the last of it from her mother. Well, Lou, I said to her, I'm really ashamed of you I am. Of you and for you, I said. If Mr. Cameron was Marleen or Donald Duck you couldn't act more silly, I said."

"Well, that was quite dreadful," said Mrs. Stonor sympathetically. "What is Lou doing now?"

"Mrs. Pucken gave her a dose of salts and sent her home, madam," said Palfrey. "She was crying so much she dropped one of the dessert plates and broke it. That makes only four we've got now, madam."

Feeling that this parting line could not be improved she made her exit to the kitchen, leaving her audience stunned.

"Poor Lou," sighed Mrs. Stonor. "And of course it would be one of the good dessert plates. I had better put the rest away. And yet perhaps I hadn't, because it is silly not to use things just because some of them are broken."

"Wear them and tear them, good body, good body," said Denis sympathetically. "Or why not have them gummed onto plush frames and hang them on the wall? Or have numbers painted round them and stick some hands through the middle and you'll have four tasty clocks."

"Don't go on like a Women's Institute, Denis," said his stepmother severely. "I shall simply take no notice of those plates and go on using them exactly as if nothing had happened."

"That's right, darling," said Denis. "Never let dumb objects get the upper hand. But I think Alister ought to be warned about Lou, or he will find she has stolen his shoes to have the pleasure of cleaning them. Why Lou has to pick on a middle-aged man for the first object of her young passion I can't think. I suppose it is fate. I've never loved anyone so much as I loved Mrs. Miller, the drill sergeant's wife at school and heaven knows she had four married daughters."

"When you call Alister middle-aged, you simply don't know what you are talking about," said Mrs. Stonor, suddenly roused. "And everyone falls in love at one time or another with someone who is much older than they are. I think you are very unkind to laugh at Lou. I might as well laugh—"

She paused, and Daphne who had been thinking along her own lines, paying as usual very little attention to her stepmother, said she liked Alister awfully and people were much more interesting when they were a bit older and she was awfully glad he was going to be at Laverings for some of his holiday and could they have coffee outside because it was so hot.

So they had coffee outside with the last sunlight on

delphiniums and roses, almost too good to be true. Mrs. Stonor was pleased to learn through Daphne that Mr. Cameron would be at Laverings for part of the summer. She liked him very much and didn't mind how much he talked to her about himself and about Daphne. Her only anxiety was on his account, an apprehension that he might be caring for Daphne a little more than would be good for his peace of mind. What Daphne herself felt she could not guess. Her stepdaughter's frank avowal of a preference for older people might be personal, might be general. She had noticed for some time past that Daphne was more than ready to express a flattering desire for Mr. Cameron's company, but all these young Dianas hunted the prey of the moment with wholehearted gusto, leaving no room for sentiment. It had also crossed her mind that Daphne liked young Mr. Bond, but young Mr. Bond's pitch had been queered that afternoon by Mrs. Tebben's indiscreet remarks about Betty Deane. It was possible that Daphne was punishing poor Mr. Bond for an earlier flame by throwing herself with even less than her usual hail-fellow-well-met lack of reticence into Mr. Cameron's arms; tropically so, of course, for Daphne was all against what she called sloppiness. It looked to Mrs. Stonor uncommonly as if young Mr. Bond were going to be hurt by her unrestrained Daphne, and though she had no fear that he would die of it, she hated to see anyone suffer. This thought led her to wonder with her ever anxious stepmother's mind if Daphne were going to let herself be unhappy about young Mr. Bond, and from this it was but a step to wondering how much Mr. Cameron might be hurt if Daphne used him as a whip for young Mr. Bond. Altogether there was too much chance of people being hurt and the sunshine took on a livid hue and the roses became dun. If Mr. Cameron were going to suffer she would not at all enjoy standing by and seeing it. Not at all.

Then her mind wandered to Denis. She was glad she hadn't finished what she had begun in a spirit of resentment to say. It was not fair for Denis, who found so much pleasure in Mrs. Middleton's society, to laugh at poor Lou, whose affections were set on an equally unattainable object. Mrs. Stonor was extremely fond of her sister-in-law, but had no guess as to what was in her mind. So kind was Catherine Middleton to everyone that her kindness to Denis was nothing to notice, but if Denis were going to be a little too grateful for the kindness, it might hit him as hard as a real passion. He would not die of his emotions any more than young Mr. Bond would. Mrs. Stonor had not nursed him through a difficult youth without knowing that his music was on the whole his life and would always be so, but she suddenly felt a little pang of jealousy in case anyone should by a kind look innocently undo some of the good work that she had patiently been building up for years, set her nervous Denis back a step on the road to health that was so necessary if he was to use his music seriously. For the moment everything looked twisted. Everyone she cared for was in danger. Not ferocious danger, but danger of a little pain, a little disillusionment, a little spiritual hardening. It had looked as if it would be a perfect summer, but that was ridiculous to expect. Probably she was worrying and exaggerating quite morbidly. Quite unnecessarily. Better to think of something real, like the dessert plate, a definite annoyance.

"It is all too difficult," she said half aloud.

"What is, darling?" said Denis. "Lou and the dessert plate?"

"Yes," said Mrs. Stonor, looking affectionately at her stepson's mocking affectionate eyes. "Lou and the dessert plate and life. I suppose we had better go over to Laverings now. Are you going to bring your music, Denis?"

"No, darling. Being a genius it is all in my head," said Denis modestly. "I did finish writing it down this afternoon in case I died and then a great work would be lost to the world, but as far as playing it on Catherine's piano goes I need nothing but my musical brain and my long, agile, yet powerful fingers."

They found the Middletons and Mr. Cameron in the library because of mosquitoes, so Denis had to keep his music to himself while Mr. Middleton discussed, if a monologue may be termed a discussion, the events of the afternoon.

"He has never stopped since the beginning of dinner," said Mr. Cameron to Mrs. Stonor, surveying his senior partner with exasperated pride. "It is true that he has managed to include the Conquest of Peru, the Thermae of Diocletian, the philosophy of Confucius, the Repeal of the Corn Laws and the Counter-Reformation in his survey of this afternoon, but the principle is the same."

"It is quite extraordinary how many things Jack manages to talk about," said Mrs. Stonor. "He has always been exactly the same since I first remember him when he was a big schoolboy and I was a very little girl. I can't think how he thinks of so many things to say. I mean I could think of a fair number of things to say about things like sewing, or nursing, or books I'd been reading, or cooking, or places I'd been to, but I wouldn't ever get so far as thinking them worth saying. Of course I daresay they wouldn't be. My mother used to scold me a little because when she took me abroad I wouldn't speak French, which I really knew fairly well, though I never can think why when people say abroad they mean France as a rule, and yet most other places are much abroader than France, but people who have been to Russia and Turkey and Iceland never say they have been abroad, and I used to try to explain to her that it wasn't that I was too shy to talk French, but I never had very much to say in English, so there didn't seem to be any more to say in French. I wonder how Catherine bears it. I suppose it wouldn't do any good if she didn't. No one has ever stopped Jack talking. And then of course she is very, very fond of him and that makes one so happy that one minds nothing," said Mrs. Stonor a little wistfully as she thought of her difficult moody husband and how their great affection had made a working partnership which was becoming easier and more peaceful every year, when he had to die.

"Yes, Catherine is very fond of him, bless her," said Mr. Cameron. "And I think she could bear anything quite happily for someone she loved; certainly not show it if she were hurt in any way. She has unusual self-control."

That word Hurt again, thought Mrs. Stonor a little angrily. Too many feelings about as usual.

"And Jack is extremely fond of her," said Mrs. Stonor almost defiantly.

"Yes, he is," said Mr. Cameron. "He sometimes dissembles his love almost to the point of kicking her downstairs, but he is entirely dependent on her affection."

"Nobody is entirely dependent on affection," said Mrs. Stonor, half to herself. "You only think you are. My husband and I were just as fond of each other as Jack and Catherine, but he is dead and here am I still alive. And if he were suddenly alive again there would be one heavenly moment, and then so embarrassing. Not so bad as the Monkey's Paw of course, but bristling with difficulties."

"You are marvellous," said Mr. Cameron, almost laughing. "I never knew anyone who put things as you do."

"I don't put them at all," said Mrs. Stonor in serious surprise. "I was only telling the truth."

But at that moment her brother, anxious for the whole company to benefit by what he was saying, broke across their conversation.

"You my dear Lilian, you Cameron," he said, "will bear me out when I say that the whole of the unfortunate débâcle of this afternoon is due to one man, and that man—"

He paused dramatically. His wife and Mr. Cameron, who were accustomed to these rhetorical pauses which he merely introduced in order to have the pleasure of filling them up himself, said nothing. His sister, who had seen so much less of him in late years, was rash enough to say Lord Bond.

"No, no, Lilian, *not* Bond," said Mr. Middleton. "Bond, a well-meaning ass, would have done his best. He was, I understand, prepared to explain to Stoke, whose deafness makes him really unfit to transact any sort of business now, that he was to propose me as chairman. But if Stoke, knowing that his presence at the meeting is essential, chooses rather to go and inspect my cows with my cowman than to do his duty as a citizen, what is to be expected? It was useless for Bond to try to tell Stoke what was expected of him. He came in late, would listen to no explanation, took the chair himself and talked about cows. I may say without undue pride that I know as much about cows as most men, but a drawing-room meeting convened for the purpose of defending a piece of our national heritage against an invader is not a fit moment to discuss Jerseys and Frisians. I wash my hands of the whole thing."

"Well, Uncle Jack," said Daphne, anxious for fair play. "You did mostly talk about Flora when you made your speech, you know."

Mr. Middleton was about to quell his niece by marriage with his thunder when a thought struck him.

"Where is Flora?" he asked. "My doggie has not come to see her master to-night. Was she at dinner, Catherine?"

Mrs. Middleton said she thought not and appealed to Mr. Cameron, who said he didn't remember seeing her. Mr. Middleton's agitation became very marked. Mrs. Middleton rang the bell. Denis and Daphne, rather bored, went over to the bagatelle board. Ethel came in.

"Do you know where Flora is, Ethel?" asked Mrs. Middleton.

Ethel said she was sure she couldn't say and Cook had said she hadn't come for her supper. She then waited in a baleful and unhelpful way, hoping for tragedy.

"My doggie," said Mr. Middleton, agitated. "She will not sleep unless she has her good-night talk to master. Perhaps she has gone to my bedroom to look for me."

He looked round helplessly.

"She's not upstairs, sir," said Ethel, rejoicing in the bad news, "because Alice looked for her when she went up to tidy the rooms. Cook said You might as well look for Flora, Alice, while you are up there, so she looked, but there wasn't a sign nowhere. Cook thinks she's gone hunting."

"She would never go alone," said her indignant master, "never. She always waits till master has hat on head and stick in hand before she will cross the threshold."

"She brought in a partridge last Tuesday, sir," said Ethel, "but Cook said not to mention it in case you was upset, so she gave it to Pollett."

"Thank you, Ethel," said Mrs. Middleton, "that will do. I expect she will come back soon."

"A light must be kept burning," said Mr. Middleton.

"Really, Jack," said Mrs. Stonor, "it isn't as if Flora was your erring daughter that had run away, and a candle in the window to guide her home."

"Of course we can leave the electric light on, darling," said Mrs. Middleton, "but the question is which. As all the doors and the ground floor windows are shut, she couldn't get in and I am afraid she would howl."

"Then," said Mr. Middleton nobly, "I should hear her."

"And so would everyone else in the house," said Mrs. Middleton, "except the maids who never hear anything and wouldn't get up if they did. We might go down to the wood and call her."

"No. I will not go down to the wood. She will expect to find master at home," said Mr. Middleton. "But I will sit on the terrace and call her from time to time. She may hear me and come."

Accordingly he went out onto the terrace and established himself in a garden chair. Mrs. Stonor accompanied him.

"I say, Uncle Jack," Daphne suddenly shouted from the bagatelle board. "I say. I have only just thought of it. Flora is in the stable. Lou locked her up when she was interrupting your speech and then Mrs. Pucken gave her a dose of salts and sent her home, so I expect she forgot."

It naturally took some time for the united forces of the company to explain to Mr. Middleton that it was Lou, not Flora, who had had the dose of salts, and why Lou, who was not on the Laverings establishment, happened to be in the drawing-room that afternoon, but when he did understand his indignation knew no bounds.

"Flora was being a devilish nuisance to put it mildly," said Mr. Cameron, "and deserves all she got. I'd leave her there all night."

Before Mr. Middleton could marshal his indignation in suitable words, Daphne said she would go and fetch Flora and invited Mr. Cameron to go with her. Followed by Mr. Middleton's voice beseeching them quite unnecessarily to be kind to Flora, they vanished into the dusk towards the stable where the monster cart horse lived, laughing as they went. Mrs. Stonor felt again the little stir of uneasiness that had assailed her earlier in the evening, but put it away and drifted back into talk about old days with her brother.

"I suppose," said Denis rather diffidently to Mrs. Middleton, "this wouldn't be a possible moment for me to play a few soft notes on your piano, would it?"

Mrs. Middleton, seeing her husband and sister-in-law comfortably gossiping farther along the terrace said she would love him to play.

"I'll keep the soft pedal down all the time," said Denis. "It's just a movement of my new ballet. I've got it all down on paper and I want to have a little debauch and play it on the piano. I'll swear not to tell you when the oboe comes in, or how nice the 'cellos sound just here. May I put one or two books on my chair? I like it a little higher."

Without waiting for permission he took a couple of large volumes that were on a table by the piano.

"Duets," he said, looking at one.

"Yes. I used to amuse myself with them," said Mrs. Middleton.

"I didn't know you played," said Denis.

"I don't," said Mrs. Middleton, "I did before I was married and when I lived in London, but one can't play duets alone somehow. I ought to have a little piano in my sitting-room, but even so it would make rather a noise."

Denis at once realised that Mr. Middleton would find music disturbing and wondered what the point was of having a grand piano in the library if no one could use it. But he did not say this. He said what an amusing collection of duets she had and how he adored all that modern French stuff.

"We might try some of them one day when Uncle Jack is away," he said, sitting down to the piano. "Or would it bore you?"

Mrs. Middleton said it would be great fun, only she must have the bass and the pedals, so that she could cover up all her mistakes.

"That will be perfect," said Denis, beginning to play with the soft pedal down as he had promised, "and I will do the counting. Do you like One and, two and, or Wuh-un, too-oo? Some people are proud about counting, but I think it's half the fun of duets. Now," he went on, half speaking, half following the melody, "this is where all the lovers have had a picnic in a grove, all very Watteau, and they all go off two and two and there is one unfortunate gentleman left who has no one to make love to, all in lovely blues he is to be if only I can keep the designer and the producer off putting him into white tights, and he has a sad little pas seul to himself to express the pangs of having no one to love, all graceful and melancholy. And this is where the critics will say 'Mr. Stonor should guard against the primrose path of a too facile gift for melody.' Facile! Catherine, I would sooner invent six hundred pages of stark atonality than one real tune. I nearly killed myself over this facile little melody."

"Keep the pedal down," murmured Mrs. Middleton.

"I will keep it down if it is with my last drop of blood, not that that would be much use," said Denis, "although a pint of pure water does weigh a pound and a quarter. And what is more I will stop playing at once if it is likely to inconvenience anyone," he added, with a quick glance unlike the leisurely mode of his speech.

"It is no inconvenience," said Mrs. Middleton and resigned herself to the facile melody if Denis liked to call it that. A long tiring day. Denis, looking once more at her, decided that she ought to be allowed to rest, and he amused himself on the piano, always keeping the soft pedal down, till the sound of voices and an odious sound of barking shattered his music.

"That," said Mr. Middleton loudly from the terrace, "is Flora."

No one contradicted him.

"I shall call her," said Mr. Middleton. "Flora!"

" 'Tell me, shepherds, have you seen,' " Denis remarked as he shut the piano and put the duets back on the table.

The whole party now met on the terrace.

"And what did my doggie think, shut up alone, no master to love her?" cried Mr. Middleton. "How her faithful heart was tried!"

"She was having a marvellous time, Uncle Jack," said Daphne. "There are a lot of rats in the stable and she had a splendid fight. When Alister and I got there, there was such a row we couldn't hear ourselves speak."

"I didn't know spaniels had it in them," said Mr. Cameron, "but all the blood of the Macdonalds must be in Flora. The way she got that rat down was a pleasure, a grisly one I admit, to the connoisseur."

"So I gave her some coffee sugar that I'd taken with me," said the practical Daphne, "and she buried the rat and then we took her for a walk and I got my shoes absolutely sopping. There's a lot of dew about. I *have* enjoyed myself. I say, Uncle Jack, could Denis and I play our duet? I feel I ought to celebrate the death of the rat. I know you aren't musical, but it wouldn't take long and it doesn't make much noise, not really much."

Flushed with excitement she dragged Denis back into the library and opened the piano.

"Catherine!" said Mr. Middleton, "I appeal to you. That I loathe and abhor this modern cacophony that goes by the name of music is true enough, but of the classics there is no more ardent worshipper than I. Bach, wise, serene, human in the deepest sense; Beethoven, a troubled mortal like ourselves, foretelling in his later works all the struggle, the turmoil of the world we live in to-day, a true prophet crying in the wilderness—"

Mrs. Stonor said one must always remember that he was deaf.

"—Mozart, that prince among his peers," Mr. Middleton continued, raising his voice, "who filled his brief life with pure bright sound. One cannot but love him. There is a little melody of his from a violin-sonata that I whistle to Flora. She loves it," he said looking round for possible disagreement. "That universal language is music even to her doggie ears. Flora!"

"I think she has run away again," said Mr. Cameron.

"You and Daphne had better go and find her then," said Mrs. Stonor, "or Jack will talk all night. Daphne!"

"Hullo!" shouted Daphne from the library where she and Denis were fighting for the pedals.

"Flora is lost again," said Mrs. Stonor. "Hadn't you and Alister better find her?"

"I expect she's gone to unbury the rat," yelled Daphne.

"Come on now, Denis. Ready?"

The cheerful sound of a duet to celebrate the death of a rat filled the evening air. Mr. Middleton winced in a noticeable way, but owing to the gathering darkness no one saw him. Mr. Cameron began to talk about Daphne to Mrs. Stonor. Mrs. Middleton wandered down the path to look at the white Canterbury bells which were her pride at the moment. In her white dress she was almost indistinguishable among them now. Luckily the duet was short and before Mr. Middleton could arrange suitable periods in which to express his disapproval the performers had finished and come out again.

"There is Flora," said Daphne, as a brown form came lightly trotting over the lawn. "What did I say?"

Flora, a look of conscious pride on her face, came up to her master and deposited at his feet with tender care the mangled and mould-covered corpse of her rat.

"Oh Diamond, Diamond, what hast thou done?" said Mr. Middleton, shrinking from the offering.

"I say, Uncle Jack, you oughtn't to talk to her as if she was Cain," said Daphne indignantly. "She has killed a jolly good rat and I expect Pucken will be as pleased as anything. I'll ask him to bury it properly so that she can't dig it up again."

"Flora! Good dog!" said Mr. Middleton, feeling that this was the attitude required of him.

But Flora, having paid this formal tribute to her master, turned her back to him and attached herself to Denis with loving and unwelcome gambols.

"Well, good night, Uncle Jack," said Denis, feeling that the end of the evening had not been a success.

"Yes, you go to bed, Denis," said Mrs. Stonor, who was a little anxious about the night dew for her stepson since Daphne had so vividly described its effects. "I'll come along with Daphne in a few moments."

Denis walked down the path towards the gate. On the way he stopped by the Canterbury bells.

"Good night and thank you so much," he said to his hostess.

"And thank you for the music," said Mrs. Middleton. "We will try the duets when Jack is in town."

"White flowers, and you all in white," said Denis. "Could you keep Flora? She has taken an embarrassing affection for me."

Mrs. Middleton stooped and held Flora by her collar till she heard the latch of the garden gate click behind Denis. Then she went back to the house, asked Mr. Cameron to take the rat in the library tongs and put it in the dust bin, and applied herself to soothing her husband. Flora, pleased with a well-spent day, was obliging enough to go to sleep at Mr. Middleton's feet, so the evening ended more harmoniously than might have been expected. Mr. Cameron walked back to the White House with Mrs. Stonor and Daphne and it was not till well after midnight that Mrs. Middleton heard him come back. She guessed that he had been talking to Mrs. Stonor about Daphne and about himself, and it is probable that her guess was not far out. As she went to sleep she wondered how soon Mr. Cameron would find himself impelled to talk to her about Daphne. Friends come and go. Alister might be a friend that was soon to go a little from her. Would any newer friend come a little nearer?

❦ 8 ❧

HUNTING THE FOLK-SONG

❧

ALTHOUGH LORD BOND FULLY REALISED THAT HIS WIFE WAS A woman of inflexible determination who could carry out her intentions at whatever cost to others, it was not until he had seen her set off for London in the large car that he breathed freely. But not for long, for a difficult task lay before him.

He had been so well brought up, first by an autocratic mother and then by an autocratic wife, not to speak of a black period during which he had been brought up by both ladies, who sometimes used him as a pawn against each other and at other times joined forces to crush him, that he had a feeling of guilt on those very rare occasions when he set out to enjoy himself in his own way. When he met Denis Stonor and was deluded by his kindness into thinking that he had discovered a fellow-enthusiast for Gilbert and Sullivan, he had invited Denis to dinner and music without thinking of the consequences. When he came to think of them he was uneasy, but kept his uneasiness to himself. Then the slight intoxication of being in league with a fellow

man against the regiment of Lady Bond had encouraged
him to the further excess of inviting Daphne, Mr. Cameron
and Mrs. Stonor. And as his son was coming they would
now be a party of six, but of this he had not breathed a word
to his wife. The only drawback to this secrecy was that he
knew Lady Bond had gone to London leaving word that
his lordship would be alone that evening, and he would have
to face Spencer with the news that there would be a small
party. Desperate ills need desperate remedies, so Lord
Bond went into the library and rang the bell. Spencer
appeared, with the faint and provoking air of relaxation
which Lady Bond's absence always produced in the household and which was bitterly if dumbly resented by the
master of Staple Park.

"Yes, my lord," said Spencer.

"Oh, did her ladyship mention that we should be six
to-night?" said Lord Bond, plunging into the subject.

"No, my lord," said Spencer.

"Yes, six," said Lord Bond, temporising.

"And that, my lord, would be . . . ?" said Spencer with
irritating deference.

Lord Bond wanted to say Five friends of mine and it
doesn't matter to you who they are and give me the key of
the piano at once and take a month's notice and I hate you.

"Mrs. and Miss Stonor and Mr. Stonor and Mr. Cameron,"
he said in an unnatural voice.

"That would be four, my lord; five together with your
lordship," said Spencer. "Shall I tell Mrs. Alcock five?"

"No, I said six; didn't you hear me?" said Lord Bond,
beginning to revolt. "Mr. Bond is coming down."

"Very good, my lord. Anything else, my lord?" said Spencer with weary tolerance.

"Yes. That champagne in the fourth bin," said Lord Bond, "and the 1875 brandy. And the key of the piano."

Spencer bowed and went away. Neither side had won; or more correctly both sides had lost. Spencer had been ordered to produce wine and brandy which he considered suitable for better dinner parties and knew that he could not disobey. Lord Bond had demanded the key of his own piano, but Spencer would not give it up till the last moment and even then Lord Bond feared that he might be reduced to the ignominious position of having to beg for it again in front of his guests. On the whole, Spencer's game. The only person who was pleased was Mrs. Alcock, who was always on the verge of giving notice because her employers did not entertain on a scale suited to her ambitions. Six was hardly a party, but it would at least give her an excuse to harry the scullerymaid and the two kitchenmaids.

At eleven o'clock the small car came to the front door to take Lord Bond over to Southbridge on business. Something unfamiliar struck him, which on investigation turned out to be a strange face in the chauffeur's seat.

"Who is that driving?" he asked Spencer, forgetting for the moment the blood feud between them.

Spencer, who never forgot what was due to himself, said coldly that he understood that Pollett's brother was taking Ferguson's place while Ferguson was in town with her ladyship and he supposed that was the young man. He accompanied these words with a look of such thinly veiled contempt that Lord Bond, feeling for Ed Pollett a sympathy which Ed, blissful in his brother's old uniform, did not in the least require, seated himself in front beside his temporary chauffeur. Spencer, who knew to a nicety how employers should behave, nearly gave notice on the spot, but remembering that the piano key was still in his keeping, decided to rest on his laurels and reserve the question of notice till a more pressing occasion. He stood on the steps till the car disappeared and then returned to the establishment which he felt was, with the trifling exception of that second window in his pantry, almost all that a butler could wish, especially when his employers were not contaminating it with their presence.

At Laverings Mr. Middleton had decided to take a week at home, partly to recover from the meeting on Saturday, partly because things at the office were slack enough at the moment to justify the absence of the two senior partners, and if it came to that he and Mr. Cameron could discuss the preliminaries of the new buildings for the College of Epistemological Ideology which a gentleman, described by the Press as a super-steel magnate, had just forced upon the unwilling University of Oxbridge, just as well in the country as in town. So Mrs. Middleton and Denis had not yet played their duets.

On the day of Lord Bond's dinner party Mr. Cameron, wandering as he so often did into the garden of the White House, found Mrs. Stonor peacefully getting the peas for lunch, and accompanied her on the other side of the peasticks, talking through the prosaic but exquisite trellis of leaves and tendrils.

"Daphne isn't helping you with the peas, is she?" said Mr. Cameron.

Mrs. Stonor, after looking carefully round, said she wasn't. In fact, she added, Daphne had gone into Winter Overcotes in the bus with Denis to see if they could get a copy of the *Gondoliers,* as Denis had felt it in his bones that Lord Bond would want him to play "Dance a Cachuca" and wasn't quite sure if he remembered it, while Daphne had equally felt it in her bones that Lord Bond would require "Poor Wandering One" and wanted to get a copy of the *Pirates.*

Mr. Cameron said how very kind Daphne was, adding that he had never heard her sing and how much he looked forward to the evening.

"She doesn't really sing," said Mrs. Stonor. "She knows all the words and the music of lots of songs, but it isn't a voice. She and Denis just have fun together."

Mr. Cameron was faintly shocked by this criticism. However doubtless Mrs. Stonor wasn't really musical and didn't know. Mrs. Stonor, sorry for his obvious disappointment at not finding Daphne, said they would probably be back on the twelve o'clock bus and wouldn't he stay till half-past twelve on the chance, and if he would excuse her while she took the peas in they could sit in the garden. So she took the peas in to Palfrey, and came back to Mr. Cameron.

The next hour was not an easy one for Mrs. Stonor. Her guest, while trying to conduct polite conversation on ordinary topics, was so obviously pulled back to the subject of Daphne again and again as if he were a tethered golf ball on an elastic cord, that she felt a great deal of pity for him. Even when she led the conversation to the work that he and

Mr. Middleton were engaged upon at the moment, he could only bring a limited amount of his attention to bear, and Mrs. Stonor well knew that if a man is incapable of being a bore on his own subject, it must mean that his feelings are very deeply occupied. Her compassion led her to relate a number of very dull stories of Daphne's school career, of her subsequent training at a Secretarial College and of the various positions she had held, winding up with the Dr. Browning whose death had thrown her temporarily out of employment.

"I suppose one oughtn't to call him selfish," said Mrs. Stonor, "because death seems to be something beyond one's control, but it really was annoying, just as Daphne had settled down to the work. One really would think doctors could do something about it, but I daresay they get so used to the idea of people dying that they don't really notice it in themselves."

Mr. Cameron, paying but scant attention to this interesting theory, said he wondered if Mrs. Stonor would let him ask her something, but perhaps there was hardly time now.

Mrs. Stonor looked at him. What she had half feared must be only too true. She liked Alister Cameron very, very much. He was now going to hurt himself a good deal, and hers would be the unpleasant role of seeing him suffer and not being able to help him; for sympathy is often difficult to offer and difficult to accept and even so does not get to the root of the matter. That foolish child Daphne had called him middle-aged, which just showed how silly the young were, for Alister Cameron was what Mrs. Stonor regarded as a very reasonable kind of age and was moreover, she felt, the sort of person one could depend on, the sort of person it would be a very blessed relief and relaxation to depend on.

"I don't think," said Mr. Cameron, who had expended some ingenuity in preparing this approach to his subject, "that you have ever seen my rooms in the Middle Temple."

"No, I don't think I have," said Mrs. Stonor. "In fact," she added in a burst of candour, "I am sure I haven't, because I have never been in them."

"I have a particularly delightful view," said Mr. Cameron. "Very green and peaceful."

"That must be enchanting," said Mrs. Stonor. "It is extraordinary what lovely views there are in London. Absolutely as quiet and green as the country. At least not at all really, because there is always the noise and the smuts, but one would hardly notice the difference except for the way you can't hear yourself speak and the seats come off on your clothes. When I was little we lived in Cadogan Square and I used to get absolutely filthy in summer, playing in a corner of the Square under some laurels."

"Perhaps," said Mr. Cameron with a visible effort, "you would come to lunch or tea with me one day."

Mrs. Stonor said she would love to.

"And bring anyone you like, of course," said Mr. Cameron.

"Well, I don't think that would matter," said Mrs. Stonor, "because the Temple isn't like Albany."

"Do you have that feeling about Albany?" said Mr. Cameron, more human than he had been that morning. "How splendid."

"I am absolutely convinced," said Mrs. Stonor, "that a

Guardsman is lurking in every set of chambers in Albany to Ruin people's reputation."

"Instead of which it is women now, and young men with beards," said Mr. Cameron morosely. "If you wanted to have your reputation ruined there is really nowhere to go nowadays. I'm afraid we can't even make a pretence of it in the Temple, but I do hope you'll come all the same. And of course," he added, with a return to his former nervous manner, "do bring someone with you if you'd care to."

"I'm sure Daphne would love to come," said Mrs. Stonor, sorrier than ever for Mr. Cameron's difficulties.

"Oh, Daphne. Yes, that would be very nice," said Mr. Cameron, with an airy manner which he flattered himself entirely disguised his feelings. He then fell so uncomfortably silent that his hostess was paralysed and hunted wildly for some remark to break the embarrassment.

"It's funny," she said desperately, "how well we have got to know you this summer, Alister, without really knowing anything about you."

She then wished she had not said it, for it sounded exactly as if she were a real mother asking her daughter's suitor what his intentions and position were. But Mr. Cameron appeared to be rather glad than otherwise of the opportunity.

"There's practically nothing to know," he said. "My parents died when I was at school and left me pretty well off, and when I left Oxford I went into an architect's office and then I came in as partner to Middleton and the firm is doing very well."

"I *am* sorry about your parents," said Mrs. Stonor, with such genuine sympathy that Mr. Cameron was moved to tell her a great deal more about himself. In the course of this narration it was discovered that he was almost exactly two years older than Mrs. Stonor, that his father had been in Colonel Stonor's regiment and that his old nurse came from the same village as Palfrey. By this time it was one o'clock and Mrs. Stonor said the children were probably having lunch at Woolworth's and would come out by the half-past one bus, so Mr. Cameron said good-bye and went back to Laverings. Half-way down the garden he remembered that what he really went to the White House for was to ask Mrs. Stonor whether she thought he would have any chance if he urged his suit upon Daphne, but he had so much enjoyed himself that the moment never seemed to arise. He wished she had not spoken of Daphne and Denis as the children. The word child seemed to open a wider gulf than he liked between him and Daphne. On the other hand it had put him and Mrs. Stonor into a pleasant conspiracy together against the disturbing element of youth. Daphne was horribly disturbing, no doubt of it. So very friendly, so very remote; so sympathetic, so unconcerned. A riddle well worth solving, but it was sometimes dangerous to read a riddle aright.

After lunch Mr. Middleton went up to his room to do some concentrated work, leaving his wife and his partner in the library. Mrs. Middleton described rather amusingly how she had wrestled with a Women's Institute Committee meeting in Skeynes and then asked Mr. Cameron how he had spent his morning. He said he had been over at the White House.

"I thought Daphne might be there," he said, "but she and Denis had gone to Winter Overcotes, and I stayed and talked to Lilian. I hope she and Daphne will come and lunch in my rooms in the autumn. You must come too, Catherine, and make a fourth."

"Too many women," said Mrs. Middleton. "One too many certainly; possibly two too many."

"What do you mean?" asked Mr. Cameron.

"I don't exactly know," said Mrs. Middleton. "Do you know yourself, Alister?"

"I still don't understand," said Mr. Cameron. "You wouldn't be one too many ever, Catherine."

"Not as a general rule," said Mrs. Middleton, "but on occasion, yes. And on such an occasion I am rather wondering who else would be a little superfluous."

"Dear Catherine," said Mr. Cameron, "how straight you look at things. I don't know what I'd do without you. Of course you know what I feel about Daphne."

"Yes," said Mrs. Middleton, "and I am not going to talk about it. I'll give you my blessing, or I'll bind up your wounds, but not now. Not till one or the other is needed. Was Lilian nice?"

Mr. Cameron said she couldn't have been nicer. One of the most sympathetic women he had ever met. They had had, he said, a perfectly delightful conversation.

"About what?" said Mrs. Middleton.

Mr. Cameron said she had asked him a good deal about himself. Then, with a little hesitation, he said did Mrs. Middleton think that was a good sign.

"It depends," said Mrs. Middleton. "It is certainly a sign that Lilian is a very intelligent person, but I have known that for a long time. Very intelligent."

"Oh!" said Mr. Cameron.

"As you ought to know if you have any intelligence yourself, Alister," said Mrs. Middleton in a detached way. "But I rather think you haven't just now. You will never find out what Daphne thinks by talking to her stepmother."

"You couldn't—?" Mr. Cameron began.

"Certainly not," said Mrs. Middleton. "I believe in nonintervention. If Daphne is your fate, Alister, speak to her yourself."

Mr. Cameron pointed out to his hostess that he had already waited all morning in vain to try to see Daphne and then by degrees began to talk about Daphne and himself, gradually widening his treatment of the subject to include himself and Daphne and at length treating it on so ample a scale that Daphne vanished and he only spoke about himself. Mrs. Middleton listened kindly and sometimes let her thoughts wander. By the time tea came Mr. Cameron, who as a rule spoke so little, had talked himself nearly dry, but after a refreshing cup he showed every symptom of running on, when luckily Mr. Middleton summoned him to his workroom to discuss the central heating system for the Epistemological Ideological College. Mrs. Middleton, feeling the need of a change, went for a walk by herself down the fields to the coppice and thought with her accustomed tolerance of several things. Alister was certainly to go a little further from her, taking all he could before he went, all the attentive listening, the cool advice which she never gave unless asked, never spared if it was really wanted. And Denis was coming to play duets with her one day, when Jack was in London and would not be disturbed by the piano.

AT a quarter to eight Lord Bond's little car, with Ed Pollett at the wheel, came to collect the Stonors and Mr. Cameron. Denis, who had heard that Ed knew one of the local folk songs hitherto unedited, went in front to explore his unworked mine. Ed, with the true countryman's caution, heightened in his case by his slightly defective mentality, would not commit himself, on the grounds that "she," by which he meant the song, belonged to old Margett at Pooker's Piece. Denis, enchanted by this survival of the singer's property in a song, asked Ed if he thought old Margett would sing it, but was dashed by hearing that Margett, apparently a Puritan in his mode of thought, considered it unsuitable for the lay ear.

"Now if you was old Mr. Patten up at Skeynes Agnes," said Ed, "old Mr. Margett he'd sing her for you."

On further enquiry Denis learned that old Margett and old Patten each had a song which he guarded jealously but would sing for the other, honour among bards being a marked quality. Ed, being a nephew of Mr. Patten the station master at Worsted, grandson of old Mr. Patten, and well known to be wanting, had from time to time been admitted to these bardic feasts and with an intellect unspoilt by schooling, to which he had been practically immune, had retained the songs in his mind.

"You'd had ought to be there last Christmas," said Ed, "when old Mr. Margett sang her and old Mr. Patten he played the mouth organ. That was a fair treat."

Denis, with the cunning of the collector on the warpath, asked Ed if he liked mouth organs.

Ed expressed the greatest admiration for that instrument and said he had a lovely one but it fell on the line and was flattened by the 6.47 down. His mother, he said regretfully, to whom he gave all his wages, wouldn't allow him two shillings to buy another and them sixpenny ones didn't seem to sing like. Enflamed by this poetic flight Ed, to Denis's great terror, took both hands off the wheel and went through the actions of playing a first class mouth organ.

"That's how she goes," said Ed, carelessly taking the wheel again.

"I'll tell you what, Ed," said Denis. "I've got a mouth organ at home. She cost five shillings and sings like a crooner. If you sing me old Mr. Patten's song, you can have her."

On hearing this Ed would undoubtedly have upset the car into the ditch in his rapture, but for the opportune arrival of the Winter Overcotes motor bus which debouched upon the road they were following. As the driver, who also gave out tickets and knowing all his passengers was agreeable about giving credit to ladies who had left their purses at home or spent all their money at Woolworth's, was a second cousin of Ed's, Ed felt obliged by family pride to play a kind of cup and ball with the bus, finally outdistancing it by the narrowest of margins and turning triumphantly into Staple Park. Denis, who had been almost rigid with fright, realised that Ed's skill in driving was something out of the common and was quite ready to laugh at his own fears by the time they arrived.

"Now this is what I call really pleasant," said Lord Bond as he greeted his guests. "You will all have some sherry, won't you. Dinner nearly ready, Spencer?"

"Mr. Bond is not yet here, my lord," said Spencer reproachfully. "I was given to understand, my lord, that he would be here for dinner."

"Well, if he isn't, we won't wait," said Lord Bond pettishly.

Spencer managed to express without speaking that he could easily reduce Lord Bond to a charred cinder by a glance and only refrained from doing so out of consideration for the guests assembled. He then left the room and shortly reappeared to announce in a voice of Christian resignation that dinner was served.

"I must apologise for that boy of mine," said Lord Bond as they took their seats. "He was to be next to you, Miss Stonor, between you and your brother."

Daphne said it didn't matter a bit and very likely he had forgotten. She then devoted herself to talking to Denis and Mr. Cameron, while Lord Bond and Mrs. Stonor laid the foundations of a sympathetic friendship, each talking on the subject uppermost in his or her mind, but listening with great courtesy to what the other had to say and never interrupting.

"I hope you are liking our part of the world, Mrs. Stonor," said Lord Bond, speaking not so much as royalty, as representing the landowners of the county.

"I simply love it," said Mrs. Stonor. "And do you know,

talking of the country, my maid Palfrey, whom you wouldn't know, though she did come to the meeting and enjoyed your speech so much, comes from the same village as Mr. Cameron's nurse. Isn't it extraordinary?"

"Cameron's nurse, eh?" said Lord Bond, looking at Mr. Cameron rather nervously.

"His nurse when he was a baby," said Mrs. Stonor. "He doesn't have one now, though I believe he has quite a nice housekeeper, but of course it's not the same. Foxling-in-Henfold."

"Eh," said Lord Bond.

"The village," Mrs. Stonor explained.

"Oh, Foxling; of course, of course. Used to go there when I was a boy. The Rector was a friend of my father's. He used to shoot jackdaws in the church tower and used incense. Now I'll tell you a remarkable thing. There was a farmer at Foxling who had a good Jersey, splendid milker. He tried crossing the strain with a West-Midland Shorthorn. What do you think happened? The calf, nice little heifer she was with a crumpled horn, won every prize she could at the Barchester Agricultural next year, but she never did any good after that. I told the farmer so, Hopgood his name was, I told him the heifer hadn't got the stamina. And I told Stoke so. That heifer won't have any stamina, I said. Extraordinary how often I've been right in things like that."

"One often is," said Mrs. Stonor. "And what is even more extraordinary his father was in my husband's regiment."

By the time Lord Bond had elucidated the fact that it was Mr. Cameron's father, not the father of Farmer Hopgood or the Rector of Foxling that was in question, Spencer was pouring champagne with a scorn that no one noticed.

"I hope my chauffeur brought you here comfortably," said kind Lord Bond, turning to Daphne on his left. "He is only temporary, but Mr. Middleton's chauffeur, whose brother he is, highly recommends him."

"He's a jolly good driver," said Daphne. "I thought he'd hit the motor bus but he didn't."

"He is going to sing me one of old Margett's songs," said Denis. "Do you know them, sir?"

"Yes, yes," said Lord Bond. "We'll have a talk about them after dinner."

And with what Denis thought a curious want of interest in one so devoted to his neighbourhood, Lord Bond changed the subject and then young Mr. Bond came in, full of apologies, having been detained he said in town. He slipped into his seat between Daphne and Denis, apologised again to everyone for not having changed, and applied himself to catching up on the two previous courses, which he quickly did, talking to Daphne at the same time. But Daphne, not as a rule a stickler for etiquette, seeing her stepmother and Mr. Cameron in talk, found that duty compelled her to turn to the deserted Lord Bond and discuss cows with great animation, having had a talk with Pucken to that very end during the afternoon. Young Mr. Bond was not altogether happy. He had been looking forward to this evening with almost excitement. To snatch an evening with Daphne without his mother's rather cramping presence had seemed to him a delightful adventure. He found Daphne one of the nicest girls he had ever known, perhaps the very nicest, and had no reason to think she felt otherwise than kindly disposed towards him. Now all was changed. Daphne was distinctly avoiding his conversation. Not so had the nymphs of New York treated the heir to an English title; not so did the nymphs of the London season treat a good dancer with a good car. Was it for this that he cut a very dull dinner and even duller dance and had motored forty miles on a lovely summer evening? He turned to Denis and gave him an account of a new ballet company he had lately seen, which turned out to be the company who might do Denis's ballet. What with the champagne and a very good ice pudding and the subsequent strawberries the two young men were quite happy when Lord Bond called down the table.

"I heard some news to-day that will interest you, C.W.," he said. "Palmer told me. He was on the bench with me at Southbridge. It's about his niece Betty, your great friend. Nice girl. She's just back from America—"

Whether this was the end of the sentence no one ever knew, for Mrs. Stonor suddenly remembered that she could not remember whether or not she had remembered to tell Palfrey to remember to tell Mrs. Pucken to catch the butcher's boy at the end of the lane about the cutlets, and as they had all finished dinner Lord Bond asked Mrs. Stonor if she and Daphne would care to have coffee in the library where the men would shortly join them. Owing to the position of the dining-room door Daphne was able to turn a scornful shoulder on young Mr. Bond as she got up, at the same time issuing a pressing invitation to Mr. Cameron not to be long.

The two ladies were not long alone, but long enough for Mrs. Stonor to wonder uncomfortably whether Daphne was behaving badly by accident, which was not at all like her, or on purpose, which was not like her either. What the ins and outs were, Mrs. Stonor was not quite sure, but that Lord Bond's reference to Mr. Palmer's niece had annoyed Daphne was to her almost maternal eye only too clear. If pique with young Mr. Bond was going to make Daphne, no good hand at dissembling her feelings, show an even more open interest in Alister Cameron, she was afraid of the consequences. It seemed to her that in this unnecessary game of hurting people, not only were Alister and Daphne to be involved, but also C.W., whose only fault was that he had a great many female friends and perhaps a tactless father. If Daphne, so tolerant, so easy-going, had to be rude because Lord Bond said he had news of Mr. Palmer's niece, it was all a pretty kettle of fish. She looked at her stepdaughter, but that young lady, whom she had never tried to control except by kindness, was scowling so truculently at herself in a mirror that Mrs. Stonor dropped any idea she had of trying to make her reasonable.

"Well now," said Lord Bond, as the gentlemen came in from the dining-room where, owing to the blessed absence of the ladies, they had all got on very well, "what about our little concert? Let's go into the next room."

He led the way to the drawing-room at whose grace and beauty in the level sunset light Denis marvelled anew.

"You see I've had the bronzes moved," Lord Bond said proudly as he went up to the piano. "Oh dear! Spencer has forgotten the key. Stonor, would you mind ringing. Or no, I'll ring myself."

With a feeling that he could not assert himself too strongly

Lord Bond went over to the fireplace and pulled one of the bell ropes that were part of the original decoration. While the vibration travelled over several hundred yards of bell wire to ring one of the seventy-two bells in the basement and summon a footman to tell Spencer that it was the drawing-room, Lord Bond fussed uneasily over his guests, pressing various chairs, ottomans and sofas upon their notice.

"Did you ring, my lord?" asked Spencer, standing majestically in the doorway.

"The piano key," snapped his lordship. "I told you this morning I wanted it."

"I am sorry, my lord," said Spencer, which convinced nobody and was not meant to. "I did not understand that it was for this evening that your lordship was requiring it. It is in its usual place of safety in My Pantry. Shall I get it, my lord?"

Lord Bond angrily assented and Spencer presently came back with the key. Walking, as Denis subsequently averred, straight through his employer, he unlocked the piano, raised the lid from the keyboard and made as though to retire.

"You can leave the key," said Lord Bond, staking all on one throw.

"I understood that the key was to be in My Charge, my lord," said Spencer.

The whole room was mute in admiration of the battle now joined.

"Hi!" said Daphne. "You'd better let me have the key, Spencer. I'll want to lock up when we've finished."

It was part of Spencer's code that though employers could hardly be in the right, it was almost impossible for guests to be in the wrong. He therefore handed the key to Daphne, for whom he had acquired an unwilling admiration, and withdrew.

"Good *girl*!" said Lord Bond, patting Daphne on the arm. "Now Stonor, we are all ready. I am really looking forward to this little treat. What shall we have first?"

"Anything you like, sir," said Denis.

"Let's have a good chorus to start with then," said his lordship, pulling a chair close up to the piano the better to enjoy himself. "There's a very nice tune in the *Gondoliers*. Something about a fandango—you'll know what I mean."

Denis, exchanging a satisfied glance with Daphne, began to play. Lord Bond, his eyes closed in ecstasy, conducted with a paper knife, tapped the measure with his feet on the floor, and sang all the words he could remember in a tuneless baritone, assisted by Daphne, who had a pleasant voice and no illusions about it and sang soprano, alto, tenor or bass or all four with equal abandon. The years fell from Lord Bond as he demanded tune after tune and when Daphne sang "Poor Wandering One" tears stood in his eyes. Apart from an occasional brief pause while Lord Bond spoke of the glories of the Savoy in his young days, the concert went on without interruption till nearly eleven, when Lord Bond suddenly remembered that he had been neglecting Mrs. Stonor for more than an hour and a half.

"Bless my soul!" he exclaimed as he looked at his watch. "What will your stepmother think of me? I don't know when I've enjoyed an evening so much. Made me feel quite young again. You must come again, Denis, and you too, Miss Stonor."

"I wish you'd say Daphne," said that young lady. "I never know who people mean when they say Miss Stonor."

"Daphne is a very pretty name and couldn't suit you better," said Lord Bond. "Now I must really go and talk to Mrs. Stonor. Nicest evening I've had for a long time."

"I suppose I'd better lock the piano again," said Daphne. "Suppose I put the key in the drawer of that writing table, Lord Bond. Isn't that where it ought to be?"

"It really ought," said Lord Bond, "but Spencer won't leave it there."

"All right," said Daphne. "I'll lock the drawer. You keep the key of the drawer and then you can get the piano key whenever you like. Tell Spencer I've got it if he gets fresh."

With profound admiration for Daphne's courage and strategy Lord Bond pocketed the key of the bureau and went over to Mrs. Stonor, with many apologies.

"But I liked the music," said Mrs. Stonor. "It always seems so peculiar to have musical children, though of course people don't call Gilbert and Sullivan music nowadays, because I'm not in the least musical myself, but of course being only my step-children does make a difference. And I had a talk with your son, Lord Bond. How nice he is. He told me a lot about himself."

Lord Bond, gratified, said that C.W. was a good boy, and observed with pleasure that his son was approaching Daphne, doubtless to compliment her on her performance. He then fell into chat with Mrs. Stonor.

Young Mr. Bond, accompanied by Mr. Cameron, came up to Denis and Daphne.

"I say, Daphne, I did like your singing," said young Mr.

Bond. "I don't like Gilbert and Sullivan as a rule, but you make it sound quite different."

Daphne said in an unpleasant voice that she adored Gilbert and Sullivan more than anything in the world and if she made it sound different she must have been singing very badly. She then begged Mr. Cameron to tell her all about the pictures in the room, because he was an architect and they always knew.

Mr. Cameron felt far from comfortable at being asked to do cicerone in front of the son of the house and was just beginning to say that pictures weren't exactly his line and here was Mr. Bond who would know all about them, when Daphne, taking his arm in a flattering way, walked him off with determination to the other end of the room where a large painting of the Campagna, entirely in tones of brown varnish and attributed on no particular grounds to Wilson, claimed her attention.

Young Mr. Bond looked so stunned that Denis felt very sorry for him. What exactly was happening he did not yet know, but Daphne had been surprisingly rude to one of her hosts, with no visible grounds, and Denis felt he ought to make up for it. So he offered young Mr. Bond a cigarette.

"It's a bit stuffy in here," said young Mr. Bond. "Suppose we go outside."

Accordingly the two young men slipped out of the drawing-room and went into the garden. In the deepening light of late evening Ed could be seen, his head in the bonnet of the car.

"Hullo, Ed, anything wrong?" asked young Mr. Bond.

Ed said he was only waiting to take Them, by which and

a jerk of his thumb he indicated Lord Bond's guests, back to Laverings, and the engine was running that sweet it was a treat to look at her.

"What about that song of old Margett's, Ed?" said Denis, sitting on a stone balustrade. "Do you know anything of old Margett, Cedric? He seems to have a song that is his peculiar property and I rather wanted to find if it is worth collecting. Ed says he knows it and I want him to sing it."

Young Mr. Bond said that Margett had a wonderful memory for old country songs, mostly quite unprintable, but he thought they had all been collected by a society with a gramophone and put into a collection with slightly chastened words.

"Old Mr. Margett he didn't sing her to no gramophone," said Ed firmly.

"Then it's probably even less printable than the rest and that's saying a good deal," said young Mr. Bond. "I heard some of them at the Fleece and I can assure you that I didn't know which way to look, though it's just possible that old Margett exaggerated a bit that evening because the curate was there exuding fellowship. Let's have it, Ed."

Ed grinned sheepishly.

"Come on, Ed," said Denis. "Remember you get my mouth organ if you sing me that song. What's it called?"

"Old Mr. Margett, he calls her 'The Old Man's Darling,'" said Ed.

"Good God!" said Denis. "We have probably struck the juiciest folk song on the market. Fire away, Ed."

Ed twisted his body about and said his mother didn't like him singing it.

"I expect you are right then," said young Mr. Bond to Denis. "Mrs. Pollett isn't at all particular. That's why Ed is a bit queer. They say it was one of Lord Pomfret's under keepers who had to be discharged for selling pheasants, but no one ever knew. If she objects to the song I'd very much like to hear it. Come on, Ed."

After a little more persuasion Ed with an expressionless face suddenly uplifted a tuneful tenor into the following refrain, in rollicking waltz time.

> "She was a dear little pussycat, pussycat,
>   Soft little velvet paws.
> But now all my money is gone, little kittycat
>   Shows me that kitties have claws."

On hearing this interesting fragment Ed's auditors were struck dumb and then laughed so much that they couldn't stop. Young Mr. Bond was the first to recover himself.

"Good eighteen-ninety vintage, I should say," he remarked to Denis.

"I would even put it a little earlier," said Denis as seriously as he could. "It has to me the definite ring of the Lion Comique, which would place it a little further back."

"Don't you like her?" said Ed, puzzled.

"We like her very, very much," said Denis.

"Thanks, Ed," said young Mr. Bond. "She's a winner."

"When I had my mouth organ," said Ed mournfully, "I did used to play a bit of a worlse like at the end."

"Well, if you are driving us back I'll give you the mouth organ to-night," said Denis, "and you can play waltzes all over the place."

Ed grinned seraphically and returned to his loving inspection of the car. The two young men went back towards the house.

"I don't know what has come over Daphne," said Denis. "But one often feels a bit queer and excited after doing music."

"I expect I was butting in at the wrong moment," said young Mr. Bond. "I ought to be getting back to town. Look here, Denis, will you tell father I had to hurry, and say good night to Mrs. Stonor for me. I'll be down again sometime soon."

So saying he got into his car and drove away.

Denis went back to the drawing-room and gave the messages. Lord Bond and Mrs. Stonor were sorry not to have said good-bye and continued their conversation, which was about Miss Starter's family and very dull. Denis thought that Daphne must be tired by all her singing, for the life had suddenly gone out of her and she returned very stupid answers to Mr. Cameron's remarks. Very soon Mrs. Stonor said they must go. Lord Bond saw them to the car, repeating that he hadn't had such a nice concert for years.

"You must come again, you and your sister, Denis," he said as they went down the steps. "I do like to hear a girl sing without any fuss. When that niece of Palmer's comes down to Worsted we must have her over. You'd like her, Daphne. You'd get on very well."

As they drove away Daphne surprised her family and Mr. Cameron by bursting into loud unrefined sobs and saying she hated Staple Park and never wanted to go there again. Her stepmother who had been anxiously observing her all the evening and had heard her being rude to young Mr. Bond about Gilbert and Sullivan, saw that the trouble she anticipated was coming upon them. What to do about it she couldn't yet say, so she applied herself to comforting Daphne, ably seconded by Denis, who was also beginning to guess the reason of his sister's peculiar behaviour. She had behaved very badly to Cedric, but she was his own Daphne and he was going to take her side whatever she did.

As for Mr. Cameron he was disappointed that the evening, so pleasantly begun, was for no visible reason ending in disaster. Daphne's tears moved him deeply, yet he felt at the same time that her abandon was perhaps excessive and admired her stepmother's calm handling of the situation. At the gate of the White House he took leave of the Stonors.

"I do hope Daphne will be all right to-morrow," he said to Mrs. Stonor. "I expect so much music was too much for her. She is rather sensitive."

"I shall put her to bed at once and she will be quite all right to-morrow," said Mrs. Stonor.

"One couldn't help being all right with you," said Mr. Cameron and went into the Laverings gate. As he undressed he suddenly thought that Mrs. Stonor had looked tired. However he had settled it in his mind that it was Daphne who was sensitive, so he dismissed the thought, which then kept him company until he went to sleep.

Denis found the mouth organ and gave it to Ed with a parting injunction not to play any waltzes till he was safely in the garage. Ed smiled mysteriously, mumbled a few words of heartfelt thinks and drove the car back to Staple Park, hardly using his right hand at all.

MR. CAMERON IS WARNED

NEXT DAY DAPHNE HAD QUITE RECOVERED AND NO ALLUSION was made to her outburst. Mr. Cameron went to Oxbridge about the new college and was to be away for ten days or so. Lady Bond came back at the end of the week and as she was not particularly interested in her husband's doings she did not enquire closely how he had spent his time, and the dinner party remained a secret from her. Not that Lord Bond would have denied it, but in his opinion when Lucasta was quiet it was as well to let sleeping dogs lie. Then Miss Starter came back for the rest of her visit with a new diet which she had collected at Tunbridge Wells and there was the usual excitement about the Skeynes Agricultural Show on Bank Holiday, for which Lord Bond was entering some livestock, and Lady Bond was full of fresh plans about a public meeting to save Pooker's Piece, and the wheels of life went on.

Denis went up to town several times about his ballet. His stepmother thought London in the heat a bad plan, but as he came back none the worse and indeed in very good spirits except for the permanent difficulty of getting any backers for the company, she stopped worrying. Daphne was over at Staple Park every day, so Mrs. Stonor spent a good deal of time with her sister-in-law.

The friendship, the growing intimacy between Mrs. Middleton and Mrs. Stonor was of a very gentlemanly kind. Each had an immense respect for the other, unexpressed; each deliberately refrained from looking closely into the life of the other. Mrs. Middleton's silences, Mrs. Stonor's vague talk, were in their essence the same, a screen for personal feelings, a shrinking from any betrayal of deep emotion. Mr. Middleton, with one of his occasional alarming flashes of insight, said he did not know which was the more significant in moment of stress, Catherine's agony of silence or Lilian's agony of speech.

Mrs. Middleton, who rarely made intimate friends, was finding in Mrs. Stonor what she had always hoped to find, an intimacy untouched by sentiment. She knew that whatever she did she would find Lilian exactly the same, anxious and changing on the surface, absolutely dependable in herself. Apart from their affection from different angles for Mr. Middleton, neither woman with many illusions about her husband or brother, each ready to protect him, they had a further bond in their affection, again of quite different degrees, for Alister Cameron and Denis. But each of them saw something the other couldn't or wouldn't see and each had a hidden anxiety for her friend.

If Mrs. Middleton had been asked by the right person what she felt about Alister Cameron she would probably

have said without any particular emphasis that she was
devoted to him, or that she loved him, which would have
been true enough. His association with her husband, their
constant meetings, a silence of nature that agreed with hers,
a tacit understanding that Mr. Middleton must have life
made smooth for him, had created a very strong bond. She
and Alister were perfectly at their ease with one another,
often met, often corresponded, trusted each other and would
have felt very deeply any crack in their friendship. She had
grown so used to his companionship, together or apart, that
it would be impossible for her not to feel an emptiness when
another door opened and he went forward without her. She
had long ago made up her mind to have no sentimentalising
when that moment came, but now the moment seemed to be
near she found it difficult to be entirely happy. That Alister
should care for Daphne did not pain her at all; that was
natural, perhaps inevitable. But if Alister were going to
break his late flowering affection against Daphne's young
indifference, that would be hard to watch. And she wondered, never even putting her wonder consciously into
words, whether Alister were not overlooking his true happiness in his pursuit. But of this she could not speak to
Lilian, nor indeed to anyone else. To Denis, who was so
genuinely devoted to his stepmother, she might have spoken,
but the oftener Denis came to Laverings the less there was
to say. Denis would play to her and there had been long
peaceful silences; at least she supposed he had found them
peaceful, for if he wasn't playing he would sit quietly in the
sun, looking better every day. She found them peaceful, as
she thought, but there was a disconcerting quality in them

as well. Sometimes she raised her eyes from a book or some work and looked at Denis; sometimes as she read and sewed she was conscious that he had looked at her. But the occasions when their eyes met were rare. A sudden, answering look, gone before she was fully aware of it.

Mrs. Stonor's anxiety about Alister and Daphne had not lessened since the evening at Staple Park. Of young Mr. Bond there had been no sign. Daphne had shown an irritability most unlike her usual self, but was always at her nicest with Alister. Mrs. Stonor had asked him over a good deal, hoping he would cheer Daphne up, but now he was away and she was wondering whether she had done a foolish thing. It was so clear to her that he came to the White House only to talk about Daphne, and she saw no solution to the problems involved. If Alister were really in love with Daphne she would not in any way discourage him, but it all looked out of drawing to her. Daphne's feeling for young Mr. Bond and his for her was an unknown quantity, liable to make an explosion at any moment. She had tried to discuss it with Denis, but he had shrugged his thin shoulders and said one couldn't interfere and been more than usually affectionate to her. Her vague apprehension of some hurt to come to Denis remained. She made no pretence of understanding him and had never invited a confidence, but her sensitive affection for her stepson, who was in a way a creation of her own making, of her own saving, made her too aware of undercurrents in his mind. As far as she knew his heart had never been seriously touched. He had laughed at himself with her over various passing fancies, had always protested that she was the only woman he could bear to live with. But she had observed that Catherine was a person about whom he had not laughed, and she would like to have known whether this meant that he didn't think about her much, or thought about her a little too deeply. Her one secret comfort was that whether Denis was affected by Catherine or not, he never wavered in his devotion and kindness to herself; and she hoped that as she had never failed him in the past when he was a delicate, hideous fledgling, she would never fail him in the future.

Mrs. Middleton and Mrs. Stonor were doing a little quite preposterous gardening at Laverings, where the gardener took a tolerant view of employers and let them cut off dead roses or pick freely among his sweet peas.

"How is Lady Bond getting on with her meeting about Pooker's Piece?" Mrs. Middleton asked.

"Daphne has typed a lot of letters about it," said Mrs. Stonor, "but she can't fill in the date till after the Skeynes Agricultural Show. Why, I do not understand, but the Agricultural appears to wreck the county for so long before and after it takes place that nothing can be decided. I am just going to put these dead roses on the rubbish heap. Shall I take yours?"

"Don't bother," said Mrs. Middleton. "Put them on the border and Pucken can clear them away when he comes. I do hate green fly when it gets squashed on one's hand. Jack asks about the meeting at least once a day. He has worked himself up to feeling that he ought to write a personal letter to Sir Ogilvy Hibberd and I expect he will do it. His letters are apt to be intemperate."

"I should think Sir Ogilvy would be intemperate too," said

Mrs. Stonor. "I daresay they will both boil over into the *Times*. They'll print anything and Pooker's Piece would make a good Silly Season heading. Denis went to play to Lord Bond last night when Lady Bond was at the Women's Institute Meeting at Winter Overcotes and he says there is no talk of Mr. Bond coming down till the Agricultural. He has to make a speech then. Oh, dear!"

"Is Daphne still cross?" said Mrs. Middleton, who knew quite well what her sister-in-law's exclamation meant.

"Suppressed crossness," said Mrs. Stonor. "It's good of her to suppress it, but I sometimes think it would be less trying if she didn't. She and Denis went to lunch at Skeynes Agnes, but they'll be back to tea."

"Alister will be down this afternoon," said Mrs. Middleton. "He got back from Oxbridge yesterday and wants to have a few days with Jack."

"Oh, dear!" said Mrs. Stonor again.

"I know," said Mrs. Middleton. "But I don't see what we can do about it. Come and have some tea. I believe Lady Bond is coming over, but that can't be helped either."

Mr. Middleton joined them for tea, full of the letter he proposed to write to Sir Ogilvy Hibberd.

"There is much to be said," he began, "for the personal approach."

"I am sure there is, Jack," said his sister without malice.

"Much to be said," Mr. Middleton repeated, glaring suspiciously at his sister. "I have weighed every pro and con in my own mind. Whether, I have said to myself, would it be better to hold this public meeting which owing to Stoke's very selfish behaviour here seems to be fated never to come to birth, and in any case I very much doubt whether Hibberd, a hard-headed business man, hard-headed in every sense of the word, would be in any way influenced by an appeal of that kind, or, taking up the cudgels myself and laying aside all personal pride—and I am a proud man, Catherine, you know it; you too know it, Lilian—to put clearly and dispassionately before Hibberd what the wanton vandalism that he proposes to inflict on this precious corner of England would mean to Me. I have thought long and painfully on the subject and come to the conclusion that there is no more to be said. Do you agree?"

"I am sure there is no more to be said, darling," said Mrs. Middleton, "and if there were you would certainly say it. And as Lady Bond is coming to tea you had better discuss it with her, for Lilian tells me that Daphne says notices for the meeting are all typed and only waiting to go out till the Agricultural is over."

As his wife spoke Mr. Middleton's face assumed an expression of horror which she rightly interpreted as a wish that her ladyship were not coming.

"It's no good, Jack," she said. "You told me that you had asked her to tea yourself when you met her in town last week."

"You will make my excuses," said Mr. Middleton piteously, rising as he spoke. "Tie up the knocker, say I'm sick, I'm dead."

"That would be quite impossible," said Mrs. Stonor, turning with some severity upon her brother, "because well you know that there isn't one."

"And well you know, too," said Mrs. Middleton, "that

Lady Bond never comes by the front door in summer. She always comes round by the garden to show that she knew you before I did."

"And here," said Mrs. Stonor antiphonally, "she is."

Mr. Middleton, groaning more audibly than the rules of hospitality admit, sank back into his chair as Lady Bond appeared at the library window.

"Here is Lady Bond, darling," said his wife, looking at him with mocking affection.

Mr. Middleton got up again.

"Don't move, don't move," said Lady Bond. "Here I am you see, Mr. Middleton. And I am so glad to find you, Mrs. Middleton, and Mrs. Stonor too. I have brought—now where are they, oh, here they are, they were merely admiring your border—Miss Starter, who I am glad to say is finishing her summer holiday with us, and Mrs. Palmer's niece, Betty Deane, of whom you have heard me speak."

Miss Starter came in followed by a tall, handsome young woman with dark hair, heavy eyebrows, a well-shaped nose and mouth and a general air of overpowering statuesqueness.

"Betty is staying with her aunt Mrs. Palmer for a few days," said Lady Bond, "and they came over to lunch. Mrs. Palmer had to go on to Southbridge, so I thought you wouldn't mind if I brought Betty to tea. I shall drop her at Worsted on my way home."

Having made this very frank and handsome apologia for her guest she seated herself by Mr. Middleton and began to tell him about the public meeting.

"We cannot fix the date till after the Agricultural, as

everyone is so busy at that time," she said. "But possibly about the tenth. Most of the people who matter will be down here then and we shall avoid the twelfth."

"What twelfth?" asked Mr. Middleton, no sportsman in spite of his feudal status.

"The moors," said Lady Bond, leaving Mr. Middleton to brood, perplexed, upon a procession of swarthy Africans who were somehow to be avoided. "Juliana, have you told Mrs. Middleton about the new bread that Dr. Picton recommended to you at Tunbridge Wells? It is quite a new discovery. Not only is it almost starch free, but you can eat any quantity of it without any effect whatever, good or bad. What did you say its name was, Juliana?"

"That is exactly what I can't remember," said Miss Starter, lamenting. "When Dr. Picton told me about it I said, 'Now do write it down, Dr. Picton, for everything you tell me goes in at one ear and out at the other,' so he wrote it down on a piece of paper. I am sure I put it into my bag, but I cannot find it anywhere."

"That is a Dememorising Fixation," said Betty Deane, who had not hitherto spoken, being, as she said, entirely opposed to people speaking unless they had something of value to say. "You ought to go to Prack at Cincinnati and be analysed. He is *the* man on all Memory Fixations. I went to some of his lectures when I was over there. I couldn't understand much because he is a Mixo-Lydian refugee but his book is very good. You ought to read it."

Miss Starter said that she felt herself that quite enough was done for refugees and there was a woman psychopath in Surbiton who had done wonders for a friend of hers.

Betty Deane favoured her with a baleful stare and was silent, obviously finding Miss Starter of no value at all.

"I think," said Miss Starter, who as an ex-lady-in-waiting on minor royalty was immune to snubs, "that although many people get great help from such healers, it is better—I speak for myself of course—to trust to the Church. The Bishop of Barchester wrote an article in the *Evening Headline* on the subject of faith which would I am sure interest you, Miss Deane."

Betty said that religion was all very well for people who believed in that sort of thing, but she herself had been an agnostic since she was sixteen and could not take any interest in creeds which simply atrophied the intellect.

"Isn't it interesting," said Miss Starter mildly, "to find that young people are still agnostics. I thought that had quite gone out. My grandfather was an agnostic, he was a great friend of Huxley and in many ways one of the most deeply religious men I have ever known. I must lend you a little book of his, Miss Deane, *Essays in Anglican Agnosticism,* you would like it. We were all brought up as agnostics and of course one's early training counts for so much, but I remember my father, a great friend of Bishop Colenso, saying, 'Without the Church of England where would we agnostics stand?' And it has always seemed so true to me. This new bread of Dr. Picton's is called Ita-lot, pronounced Eat-a-lot, and I get it by post twice a week from Bishop's Stortford which is the only place where it is made. You should try some, Mrs. Middleton."

Betty Deane, her guns spiked, publicly convicted of a Mid and Late Victorian creed was darkly silent, meditating on Milton's Satan, a character for whom she had an intellectual affinity, or so she felt, waiting for an opportunity to crush someone.

"I have given much thought to the matter," said Mr. Middleton to Lady Bond, "much thought. I am not a man to take lightly any step in which my own name, my position such as it is, are involved but when I see a duty plainly before me, that duty becomes to me a sacred—what at the risk of tautology I find myself unable to call anything but a sacred—duty."

"You will come to the meeting then," said Lady Bond.

"No, no, dear lady, you misapprehend," said Mr. Middleton. "Without undue pride I may say that my name carries a little weight. I shall write to Sir Ogilvy Myself."

"Well I wouldn't if I were you," said Lady Bond, entirely unimpressed. "No good writing to a man like that. He can always be ruder than you can. I think we'll have the meeting on the ninth rather than the tenth. The tenth might clash with the Barchester Infirmary Fête. Ah, here is Daphne. That is very nice. I want her and Betty to meet. Betty has some very interesting news for us."

As when two bulls of milk-white fleece, ranging the slopes of Illyrian Timavus, espy afar off the heifer, grazing, ah! beneath the ilex whose cold shadow the careful farmer will avoid to seek as roof for the golden swarm lest haply the stored sweetness of the honey turn to maleficent vinegar baneful as the Centaur's blood on the fatal shirt doomed to lead the club-bearer to the gloomy realms of Dis, anon they paw the ground with equal foot, this flashing forth fire from his eyes as the careful husbandman strikes the spark

from tinder that will burn the dried stalks of beans to a
rich ash meet for increasing tenfold the produce of his pater-
nal fields (twenty lines of description of various forms of
artificial fertiliser are here omitted), that, similar in shape
and form to this, shaking wide his flowing locks and with
the ivory spears of his forehead turning the turf till sods fly
fast as the scudding sails upon the Adriatic what time
Boreas plunging from where Taygete the Pleiad westers to
the Median Hydaspes, causes fishes to be caught up from the
waters, where they, ah! now in vain, guard their thousand
young destined now to perish waiting a father's care, whirl-
ing them aloft on his wings till they, bereft of Neptune's
element, lie gasping on the shore where to-morrow maidens,
washing linen in the sea foam, may haply weep for silver
scales stained with blood purple as the Tyrian's dye, gained
by him in no not remote seas from the shelly flocks of
Proteus—

To be short, taking young Mr. Bond as the heifer, so did
Daphne and Betty take a violent dislike to each other at
sight, having determined to do so long before they met.
Daphne had heard quite enough, she felt, of how good-
looking and nice Betty Deane was from Lord Bond, while
Betty did not wish to hear any more thank you about
Daphne Stonor who was such a help to Lady Bond and so
much liked by everyone. Their antipathy sent out such
waves of dislike that everyone except Lady Bond became
acutely conscious of it and talked in an unnatural way.

"Did you have a nice time in America?" asked Mrs.
Stonor.

"It is difficult to say yes or no when America, or rather

the United States, is such a large place," said Betty, "but I enjoyed what I did see very much. I had an extremely interesting time in New York and made lots of friends. I hope to go back again and do a course at Bryn Mawr. Cedric Bond goes back in the autumn and I might go with him. You ought to go," she added looking at Daphne.

Daphne said she was sure she would loathe New York.

"You can't say till you've been there," said Betty. "No one can understand it till they have."

Mrs. Stonor, distracted, said she had once been to New York, the year Denis was so ill at Laverings, and thought the flower shops were so nice. She remembered, she said, what particularly beautiful gladiolus there were in the shops that winter.

"Oh, do you say gladiolus," said Miss Starter. "I always say gladiolus."

A short and ill-informed discussion on the subject was terminated by Betty, who said coldly that as both were incorrect it was of little importance. The i and o of gladiolus were both short she said, and an equal stress should be laid on each syllable, as far as possible approximating to the form gladyolus.

"Well, Betty must know. She got a first at Oxford," said Lady Bond.

"When do you expect your son down again, Lady Bond?" asked Mrs. Middleton, seeing Daphne about to express her opinion of the female members of that University.

"We don't quite know," said Lady Bond. "He is very busy at the office at the moment. For the Agricultural in any case. Betty dined with him last night. She had something very special to say to him which we shall all know before long," said Lady Bond with a stately archness that froze her hearers.

She then collected Miss Starter and Betty and went away. Daphne said in an uncertain voice she wanted to write some letters and would go home. Her departure was watched with sympathetic anxiety by her stepmother and Mrs. Middleton. It had not escaped the notice of either of these ladies that Betty Deane was wearing on the fourth finger of her left hand a very expensive-looking sapphire ring, and they could not imagine that Daphne had not observed it. It was no use going after Daphne in her present condition, so Mrs. Stonor sat unhappily with the Middletons, comforted alternately by her brother's entire want of perception and Mrs. Middleton's unspoken sympathy. Mr. Cameron arrived a little later.

"Ha, Cameron!" said Mr. Middleton, who was longing to finish a thriller that he had left upstairs. "We will have a talk indeed about all you have done. We will tire the sun with talking, though Summer Time makes the feat more of a test for us than for our old Samian friend. But for the moment, for the moment, Cameron, I must leave you with Catherine and Lilian. You will not be in bad hands. Later, washed and refreshed, we will meet again."

Upon which he went quickly out of his private door and upstairs.

The two ladies did their best with Mr. Cameron, but he was not very attentive and looked often towards the garden. Finally he interrupted Mrs. Stonor to ask if Daphne was coming over or if he would find her at home.

"I really don't know," said Mrs. Stonor. "She was here, but then she went away. She isn't very well. At least she is very well indeed but rather upset—I don't mean upset so much as harassed, really about nothing at all and I must say she didn't behave at all well, did she, Catherine?"

"Lady Bond brought Mrs. Palmer's niece Betty Deane to tea," said Mrs. Middleton, "and the two girls didn't get on well. I think Daphne was a little rude and went away to get over it. I must say Betty is very trying."

"I'll go and find her," said Mr. Cameron. "I brought a new kind of film for her camera that she said she wanted to try."

"You have been warned," said Mrs. Middleton, a little sadly, but Mr. Cameron did not hear, or did not notice, and went over to the White House. The ladies said nothing and returned to their gardening, snipping off dead, dying, or even slightly faded heads with savage intensity, Mrs. Stonor even going so far as to walk deliberately on a couple of small snails, a thing she would in calmer moments have shrunk from.

Poor Daphne went back to the White House with a swelling heart. Betty's words, the ring on Betty's finger, had told her only too clearly what had happened. It wasn't that she loved Cedric in the least, in fact she looked upon him with indifference if not with hatred, but hypocrisy and deceit were what she could not bear, and of all the horrid, stuck-up, affected girls she had ever met, Betty Deane was the one. Betty would make a very good wife for such a stupid creature as Cedric and she hoped they would both be very unhappy, or be drowned on the way to America, or gored by bulls; and the more she thought of these delightful consummations the happier and more exulting she felt, till at last her happiness took the form of a prickling behind the nose, a gulping in the throat, a wish to tell everyone, especially the Honourable C. W. Bond and Miss Betty Deane, exactly what she thought of them, and such an uprising of hysterica passio that all she could do was to rush, blinded by tears, past the back door where Lou was sitting on a kitchen chair shelling peas into a colander, and bury herself in the darkest recesses of the garden. So it was that when Mr. Cameron came to the front door and asked Palfrey if Miss Daphne was in, he was told that she had gone over to Mrs. Middleton's, but Mr. Denis was at home. Denis was writing out a score.

"Hullo, Alister," he said, "I say, I simply hate to behave as if it mattered, but if I don't get this bit written down I'll forget where the bassoon comes in. I shan't be a minute."

He plunged furiously into his notes again and Mr. Cameron, not at all offended but slightly dashed, wandered out again, not even daring, such was his layman's respect for the musician's frenzy, to ask if he knew where Daphne was. Without thinking much where he was going he walked past the back door and seeing Lou shelling peas he said Good evening. Lou, whose young movie-struck mind viewed the world as little but a setting for love and who would willingly have laid her heart in a puddle that Mr. Cameron might walk dry-shod, was suddenly visited by one of the most noble and entrancing thoughts ever vouchsafed to mortal. She had seen Miss Daphne go down the garden in tears. Now came Mr. Cameron, looking anxious and moody. The inference was clear. They had had a lovers' quarrel and had Broken Apart, Miss Daphne to cry herself into her grave, Mr. Cameron (probably) to go with set face and reckless courage where the danger was hottest. Lou knew well, too well, that Mr. Cameron could never be her Ideel Lover except in day-dreams, but here was an opportunity to display a nobility which even Greta or Norma could hardly hope to emulate. All in a flash she saw the lovers reunited by her help. Together they would visit the little grave marked by naught but a fresher turf where daisies sprang, together their tears would mingle as they thought of Little Lou who had given her life for their happiness. Tears of melancholy bliss welled to Lou's eyes as she carefully put down the colander of peas, for even romance paled for a moment when she thought of her mother's wrath if they were spilt, and followed her secret heart.

"Please, Mr. Cameron," she said.

"What's the matter, Lou," said Mr. Cameron. "You've got a nasty cold, haven't you?"

At these words Lou nearly died of maudlin bliss, but true to her ideal she sniffed and said,

"It's Miss Daphne. She went down the garden. She was crying. She's in the pea-sticks, Mr. Cameron."

"WHAT?" said Mr. Cameron. And without a word of thanks, he hastened towards the pea-sticks, leaving Lou literally gasping with excitement and romance. There, sure enough, was Daphne, standing between two rows of peas, shelling the youngest pea-pods and eating their crisp contents in a melancholy way, pausing every now and then to blow her nose violently.

"Daphne!" said Mr. Cameron. "Darling, what is it?"

Daphne looked up. There was Alister looking as kind and nice as he always did, and the thought of a kind shoulder to cry on was too much for her. With a gulp she hurled herself against him and abandoned herself to the full luxury of grief, repeating amid her sobs how glad she was he had come. Mr. Cameron, hardly able to believe his luck, patted her shoulders, kissed the top of her head, said everything was all right and gradually managed to restore her to sanity.

"I *am* so glad you have come back," said Daphne. "Everyone was *ghastly* and I thought I'd die. Oh, Alister, I *am* so pleased to see you. How did you know I was here?"

"Lou saw you go down the garden," said Mr. Cameron. "Daphne, are you sure I'm not too old?"

"For what?" said Daphne.

"Well, I am a good deal older than you are," said Mr. Cameron, "but it's better than being a good deal younger. After all Jack Middleton is much older than Catherine and they are very happy."

It then occurred to Daphne for the first time, like a thunderbolt, that she was now engaged to Mr. Cameron. Being of a practical turn of mind she thought she had better get it clear.

"You mean," she said, looking at him steadily, "that if we get married you will be older than I am."

"Just about that," said Mr. Cameron.

At the bottom of her heart Daphne knew that though Alister was quite the nicest person in the world, she didn't

in the least want to marry him. But everyone else was
ghastly and it would be too difficult to explain now that
crying on a person's shoulder wasn't at all the same as
being engaged, still less married, so like a soldier's daughter
she determined to make the best of a forlorn hope.

"Well, I daresay by the time I'm about forty you won't
seem so much older," she said cheerfully. "One gets used
to people. Oh Alister, shall we have to tell everyone?"

"I should like to sow the fact in mustard and cress all
over the garden like the gentleman in the song," said Mr.
Cameron, "but we'll do just as you like. Would you rather
only tell your people and not have it in the *Times* just yet?"

"The *Times*!" said Daphne. "Oh no. It would look as if
we were really going to get married."

"But we are," said Mr. Cameron.

"I know," said Daphne. "But people get broken off too.
Oh, not the *Times*, Alister. I'd feel safer if we didn't."

Mr. Cameron naturally found her folly the most delightful thing that he had ever seen and they walked back to
the house, eating a handful of young peas with which
Daphne had thoughtfully provided herself. At the back
door Lou, who had finished the peas, was peeling far more
potatoes than were wanted, hoping to see the result of her
noble action before her mother called her. Her expression
of open-mouthed rapture was such that the lovers stopped.

"It's all right, Lou," said Mr. Cameron kindly. "I found
Miss Daphne."

"They say finding's keeping," said Lou, moved by her
romantic spirit to literary flights which she had never suspected in herself.

"So it is," said Mr. Cameron. "Only don't tell your mother, or Palfrey, or anyone else, because it's a secret for the present."

"Won't you have no ring, Miss Daphne?" said Lou, who had somehow hoped that a ruby the size of a pigeon's egg would materialise on Daphne's finger.

"Oh, Alister, I needn't have a ring, need I?" said Daphne, to whom the word ring brought back such searing memories of Betty Deane's sapphire that she nearly went back to the pea-sticks.

"Of course not," said Mr. Cameron. "But I would like to give you one. Perhaps a little later, when it is in the *Times*."

But at the word *Times* Daphne's face began to crumple so suspiciously that he quickly said they must go and tell Lilian and Denis, and leaving Lou with their secret they went into the house, where Denis was still furiously scribbling spidery hieroglyphics on a huge sheet of scored paper.

"Hullo, Alister," he said, "back again? Give him a cigarette, Daphne. I must get this thing off my chest," and he applied himself again to his music.

"I'm not staying," said Mr. Cameron, emboldened by love, "I only want to tell you that Daphne and I are engaged."

Denis blinked himself into the daylight from the inner world where he had been furiously living and looked startled.

"Everyone was ghastly," said Daphne, "and I went into the pea-sticks to cry, but we aren't going to tell anyone yet except you and Lilian and Uncle Jack and Catherine. Oh, and we told Lou, but she promised not to tell."

"Well," said Denis, getting up and giving his sister a hug, "that's very nice indeed. I really couldn't think of anyone nicer for Daphne to marry. I can't say that I feel like a brother to you, Alister, because never having had one I don't know the feeling, but I am delighted. I shall give you a breakfast service and a very large Persian cat. Have a drink, Alister."

Mr. Cameron accepted some sherry and Denis toasted the bridal pair and expressed again and again his pleasure in the engagement, but it was rather uphill work. Something seemed wrong to him. Daphne looked happy, Alister looked happy, but he missed the rapture which in his mind should go with an engagement and then blamed himself for being so particular.

"I shall have to go now," said Mr. Cameron. "Will you be all right, darling?"

"Quite all right," said Daphne. "And, Alister, if you see Lilian at Laverings you'd better tell her and Catherine. I don't suppose Uncle Jack would notice if you told him or not."

Mr. Cameron laughed, put his arm round Daphne's shoulders for a moment and went away. Denis arranged his music paper and his rough drafts with meticulous care.

"You don't mind, do you?" said Daphne suddenly.

"Of course I don't mind, you goose," said Denis, his conscience pricking him for the want of enthusiasm he had shown. "Alister is a very good chap indeed, who would do anyone credit as a brother-in-law. And what's more, though I don't suppose it has occurred to you, he is what is known as quite a good match. You will be able to live in luxury, darling, which is more than any of the Stonors have ever done yet."

"Denis," said Daphne, and then stopped.

"Out with it," said Denis. "Do you want me to forbid the banns? I've always dearly longed to see it happen and I can imagine no greater pleasure than to get up in church and say 'I do,' and be invited to the vestry to explain while all the audience die of curiosity."

Denis had rambled on simply to fill in time, because his sister had an inscrutable expression to which even he, who knew her so well and so fondly, had no clue.

"It all sounds very nice," she said dolefully, "but oh! Denis, I'd much rather stay with you and Lilian."

Upon which she went upstairs and could shortly be heard having a bath.

Denis tried to tell himself that girls often had a moment's revulsion or fright at having committed themselves, but he was uneasy. If it were in his destiny, which he felt it never would be, to love and be loved, he could imagine a way of love quite different from what he had just seen. Probably Alister and Daphne's matter of fact behaviour was the best and safest for life as it was now, but he had thought of half-lights, undertones, reticences, a hand that trembled when it brushed against his, silences that hung like perfume about him, quick answering glances.

"Romantic fool," he said aloud to himself. And as there was no chance of getting at the bath till Daphne had finished, he applied himself once more to his ballet and was presently immersed in the music of his mind.

MR. CAMERON found Mrs. Middleton and Mrs. Stonor still hard at work in the rose garden and stood about in so marked a way that they were in no doubt as to what had happened.

"Did you find Daphne?" asked Mrs. Stonor, who had never yet been afraid to face a situation.

"We found each other," said Mr. Cameron in a tense voice.

Again both ladies knew quite well what he meant, but with a touch of vindictiveness towards the male sex in general each determined that he should jolly well explain himself and not leave them to take the trouble of extracting his meaning for him. So they remained silent, snipping off roses.

"Lilian," said Mr. Cameron, "could I say something to you?"

"Certainly," said Mrs. Stonor in a cheerful voice.

"I do hope you won't mind," said Mr. Cameron, "but Daphne and I are engaged. I thought I'd better tell you."

Mrs. Stonor put down the basket of dead roses and came round the flower bed to him.

"I am perfectly delighted, Alister," she said, "and I am sure her father would have been pleased. And I hope you will accept me as a very affectionate stepmother."

As she said this she took both his hands.

"And I am enchanted too," said Mrs. Middleton. "I hope you will be as happy as Jack and I are and have dozens of children."

"It is all rather private for the present," said Mr. Cameron uneasily. "Daphne didn't like the idea of the *Times*."

Mrs. Middleton said she quite understood the feeling and when they had told her husband they would not let anyone else know. Mr. Cameron, feeling vaguely that he ought to shelter Mrs. Stonor, offered to see her home, but she preferred to go alone. When she got back to the White House she found Denis still at his work.

"Well, darling, I see you have heard the news," said Denis. "I do like Alister and I do love Daphne, but—oh, I don't know. Am I a beast not to feel very happy?"

"If you are a beast, I am a beastess," said Mrs. Stonor. "I'd like nothing more in the world than for Daphne to be happy—and Alister to be happy—but—oh, I don't know either."

She and Denis sat and looked at each other with concern, each longing to persuade the other that everything was all right, but quite unable to work up any conviction about it.

"I'm being very silly," said Mrs. Stonor firmly.

"You are not, darling," said Denis. "Well, we will give Daphne a slap-up wedding and live on bread and cheese for a year and settle down together to a bachelor life. No one will ever want to be engaged to me, and just as well, and I shall be the prop of your declining years. In youth you sheltered me and I'll protect you now."

"I wish you could, Denis," said his stepmother.

"So do I," said Denis ruefully. "Never mind, you shall protect me, which will really give you much more satisfaction, being a motherly sort of woman. There is the water running off and I'll rush and have my bath if you don't mind."

Dinner passed off peacefully. Daphne appeared to be

quite herself again and though she went to bed early it was
not to toss on a wakeful couch, but to sleep off in a very
natural way the effect of so much excitement.

DINNER at Laverings fell alive into the hands of Mr. Middleton, who read aloud to himself from rough drafts visible
to his inner eye, the various letters he had thought of sending or not sending to Sir Ogilvy Hibberd, calling occasionally upon his wife or his partner for their comments, to
which she paid no attention at all. Under cover of this his
hearers were able to think their own thoughts, which were
not altogether comfortable ones. Mrs. Middleton had the
doubtful pleasure of seeing some of her gloomier prognostications verified with every probability of the rest coming
true; for anything less like her idea of a blissfully engaged
lover there could not be. Mr. Cameron, after an instant of
pure happiness when Daphne had cried in his arms, had
experienced a peculiar sinking of the stomach which reason
told him was excess of bliss but instinct defined as a mixture
of terror at what he had done and irrevocable regret for
something, not very clear to his mind, that he had not done.

"So," said Mr. Middleton when the dessert was on the
table, "I shall send the letter, but not till after the Agricultural."

"Why put it off?" said his wife.

"My dear," said Mr. Middleton, "when you live at Rome,
do as the Romans do. At this time of year every event in
our Country Calendar is calculated from before or after the
Agricultural. Probably a survival from the old Hiring Fair
at Beliers which used to take place at about this time, but

was unfortunately allowed to fall into disuse, together with the Abbey of Beliers, after the Reformation. As a loyal inhabitant of this part of the world it pleases me to conform."

"Then your letter to Sir Ogilvy and Lady Bond's notices of the public meeting will go out at about the same time," said Mrs. Middleton.

"Precisely," said Mr. Middleton. "The one will add weight to the other."

"You don't think they'll interfere with one another, do you?" said his wife.

Mr. Middleton, who had just had that thought, said with great dignity that there were certain subjects on which women were hardly qualified to judge, and became remote.

"And now that that is settled," said Mrs. Middleton, "I am going to tell you something. Alister and Daphne are engaged."

"Blind that I am!" cried Mr. Middleton, striking his forehead with his clenched fist, though cautiously. "An exquisite story has been playing itself out before my very eyes and I have seen naught. You must forgive me, Cameron. My perceptions are usually far more acute, but I have been an old, a weary man, I have had much on my shoulders."

He paused and became Atlas, the world's weight upon his neck.

"As a matter of fact we were all surprised," said Mrs. Middleton.

"Yet I knew, I knew," said Mr. Middleton, brushing this tactless remark aside, "that something was astir, something burgeoning, the eternal miracle of high summer reflected in the mirror of human hearts. This news has made me very, very happy. The friend with whom I have worked, with whom I have always had such cordial relations, has plighted his troth to my sister's stepdaughter, whom I love as if she were my own, my own daughter I mean not my stepdaughter, and under this very roof."

"It was at the White House," said Mr. Cameron, "and as a matter of fact not under a roof at all, because Daphne was in the pea-sticks."

"No matter, no matter," said Mr. Middleton. "And you love her, Cameron, and she returns your love. Forever will you love and she be fair. Make much, Cameron, of these golden hours."

He mused, a little obtrusively, for a moment, while his wife and his partner exchanged an amused glance of embarrassment.

"Time like an ever rolling stream," said Mr. Middleton, by way of a suitable quotation for a newly engaged couple. "And that reminds me, Cameron, we shall have to reconsider the whole question of the water supply for that College. There has been a question of contamination in the reservoir and I must find out exactly what is happening."

Mr. Cameron said he knew a man on the Town Council at Oxbridge whose father had been a scout at his old College and thought something might be done through him. Then the talk became so happily and enthusiastically technical that Mrs. Middleton left the men and thought she would go over to the White House, feeling vaguely that her sister-in-law might need her. Laverings dined much later and sat much longer over its dinner than the White House, so it was now after ten o'clock. When she got to her own garden gate she found Denis in the lane.

"Lilian and Daphne have gone to bed," he said, "and if I could stop working, I'd go too. I suppose you know about Alister and Daphne."

"Yes," said Mrs. Middleton.

"I wish," said Denis, leaning his elbows on the top of the gate, "that I had a nice contented easy-going disposition. But I haven't. And Daphne was really all I've got except darling Lilian, and now I have lost her. Oh, I don't mean because she's engaged, but I suddenly have no clue to her and I don't like it at all."

"Yes, I suppose she and Lilian are all you have," said Mrs. Middleton quietly and then was silent. The silence became so deep that it menaced like a betrayal. "I wish," she said, forcing herself to speak, "that there were more rapture about it. But I suppose I am romantic."

"Oh, yes," said Denis. "You are romantic."

He took his elbows off the gate and melted away into the dark shadow of the lane. Mrs. Middleton did not move for some time. Then she went back to the house, where she found her husband and Mr. Cameron still deep in technicalities, so she said good night.

"You are tired," said Mr. Middleton accusingly.

"I don't think so," said Mrs. Middleton, suddenly conscious, as if his words had released a spell, of boundless fatigue.

"I know you so well, Catherine," said Mr. Middleton,

"and every shadow on your face. Don't get tired."

Mrs. Middleton lingered, her hand on her husband's shoulder.

"No, Jack, I won't get tired," she said. "Good night, Alister."

ৰ্জ 10 ৈৈ

THE AGRICULTURAL AT SKEYNES

ৰ্গ

BY A MIRACLE OF SELF-RESTRAINT ON THE PART OF EVERYONE
concerned, helped by Mr. Cameron's return to London and
his work, Daphne's engagement remained a secret for the
next fortnight. There was a kind of agreement that it
should be announced in the *Times* after the Skeynes Agricultural Show, that Grand Climacteric of the rural year. Mr.
Cameron came down twice to spend the day at the White
House and on each of these occasions Daphne was urgently
wanted at Staple Park. She explained to her stepmother
that if she made excuses to Lady Bond and her ladyship
happened to discover, as she certainly would, that the excuses
coincided with Mr. Cameron's visits, the county would know
the news within twenty-four hours. So Mr. Cameron talked
to Mrs. Stonor, who listened and listened, doing very fine
sewing which needed a great deal of attention.

Mrs. Middleton and Mrs. Stonor were a great deal together, gardening, working, talking on some subjects, silent
on others. Mrs. Middleton, kneeling among damp rock

plants, a smear of mud across her face from pushing her hair back with a dirty gardening glove, did once go so far as to say that life was very tiring, and Mrs. Stonor, picking up from the flagged path a large basket of very earthy weeds which she had just upset, added as a kind of rider that she hoped transmigration wasn't true, because one life was quite enough. Otherwise, being philosophers in their own way, they left philosophy alone.

As invariably happened the weather got worse and worse as the Agricultural drew nearer, till on the weekend of the Bank Holiday a kind of equinoctial gale arose, accompanied by driving rain and a falling barometer. A chimney pot crashed onto the terrace at Laverings, hurting no one; the smoke poured downwards from the White House kitchen chimney, smothering the kitchen in fine soot and forcing its way out through hitherto unsuspected crevices into Palfrey's bedroom. Over at Skeynes the big marquee was nearly blown over in the night and Pucken said with gloomy relish that if Lily didn't calve on Monday night he was a Dutchman. What with the engagement and the weather and the prospect of a wet Bank Holiday and Lord and Lady Bond's dreadfully dull dinner party which they gave every year after the Show, partly to do their duty by the county, partly to show that Bank Holiday made no difference to their well-organised staff, everyone was cross. Denis, obsessed with musical composition and the improbability of ever getting his ballet produced, was almost snappish with his stepmother, who in her turn rather crossly told Mr. Cameron, at Laverings for the weekend but spending most of his time at the White House, that he and Daphne must really make up their minds about announcing the engagement and thinking of the wedding, while Mr. Cameron sat with Mrs. Stonor and Mrs. Middleton alternately, in a state of gloom very unlike him. Daphne had a cold and when having tea at Laverings on Sunday, blew her nose so often that Mr. Middleton became almost demented with fear of infection and drenched his handkerchief with eucalyptus. Mrs. Middleton was very quiet and did her best to smooth matters, for there seemed to her little else to do.

On Monday morning the weather was worse than ever and the kitchen chimney more disordered. Lou, whose nerves had been much affected by her oath of secrecy, sulked when Palfrey told her to wash the kitchen dresser and mind she got all the soot off, and answered back. Her mother for once took her side and rounded on Palfrey, saying that it was a shame to put upon the girl and what was the use of washing the dresser with the soot coming down like that. Palfrey said there were some that were glad of *any* excuse not to do their work; Mrs. Pucken retorted that Lou was only coming to oblige, being as she wasn't getting any wages; Palfrey sniffed, all three ladies cried and the bacon was burnt.

Daphne's cold was better, but her stepmother made her stay in bed till lunch, as a preparation for Lady Bond's dinner party, and when Mr. Cameron came over after breakfast Mrs. Stonor was so short with him that he went back to Laverings and shut himself up with the plans of the new water system.

After lunch a treacherous gleam of sun appeared and everyone said in a hollow way that it would be quite nice for the Agricultural after all. With umbrellas and mackintoshes and in some cases galoshes the inhabitants of Laverings and the White House made their way up the sloppy lane to Skeynes. Only Mr. Middleton remained at home, alleging an anxiety about Lily and her calf that deceived nobody.

The Agricultural was an event eagerly looked forward to by a large part of the county. All those landowners, great or small, who were interested in cattle, pigs, sheep, dead bunches of the greatest variety of wild flowers collected by school-children, and whatever else is shown at an Agricultural Show which is also a Flower Show and a Fun Fair, found it an invaluable opportunity for seeing the friends and enemies that they had been seeing on and off all the year round. Perhaps the best known and most important figure was Lord Stoke, wearing a kind of truncated grey top hat, copied from the hat his father always wore, tweed jacket and leather leggings, and followed in a feudal way by his cowman Mallow, cousin of Mr. Mallow the station master at High Rising. Mallow, as befits the best cowman in the county, was dressed in his hideous Sunday best, but not even the thought of what Mrs. Mallow would say when he got home with his boots and the bottoms of his trousers smeared with the sticky clay of the field where the Agricultural was always held prevented him from enjoying every moment of the afternoon to the full. The only competitor he had feared was Mr. Middleton's Lily Langtry, and in her absence the Rising Castle entries had had little or no opposition to face. Rosettes of the first class decorated every one of his entries, while Lord Pomfret, Lord Bond, and Mr. Palmer had to be content with second and third class or even Highly Commended.

Lord Pomfret usually attended the Skeynes show in person to encourage local industry, but his agent Mr. Wicklow had telephoned that morning to say that his lordship had to be in Barchester to fight the County Council who were trying to build ten cottages in a lane that had been impassable when the floods were out every year since the oldest inhabitant could remember. But Lord Bond and Mr. Palmer had been there ever since nine o'clock and after lunch were joined by their wives. Mrs. Palmer, who was wont to boast with considerable truth that she didn't care what she looked like, was squelching about in gum boots, despising Lady Bond, who, in very neat woollen stockings and heavy brogues, felt an equal contempt for her friend's footgear.

Lady Bond had determined to use the day, with its chances of meeting most of the neighbouring landowners, to prepare the ground for her campaign against Sir Ogilvy Hibberd. The invitations for the Public Meeting were now all ready to be sent out and Lady Bond had planned to enlist everyone's sympathy at the Show, give them Monday night to think it over, and post the invitations on the Tuesday afternoon, so that they would be found on every breakfast table on Wednesday and clinch the matter. Seeing Mrs. Stonor and Denis at the entrance to the grounds, she bore down on them, demanding Daphne, whom she wished to accompany her on her crusade and make mental notes of likely converts. Mrs. Stonor, looking rather draggled in a shapeless old tweed coat and an old tweed hat which was the most suitable toilette she could think of for a wet after-noon among animals, said she was keeping Daphne in bed with a cold.

"That is very annoying," said Lady Bond. "I wanted her to go round with me. I hope she is coming to our party to-night."

"Yes, that's exactly why," said Mrs. Stonor. "I thought if I kept her in bed till tea-time she would be able to come to your dinner, because it isn't an infectious cold, or I would have rung you up at once to say so, but she sneezed twice and I never think sneezing colds matter, it is the ones that begin with a sore throat that are infectious and she has no throat, absolutely no throat at all. But what with the wet walk here and standing about in all this mud among bulls I felt she would be far better in bed."

"Open air is much the best thing for colds," said Lady Bond eyeing Mrs. Stonor's coat with disfavour, and forget-ting, as she was apt to do, that a well-cut tweed suit, an expensive felt hat and a Burberry are not within everyone's reach.

"But not for Daphne's," said Denis agreeably. "Hers are quite different from anyone else's, or anyone's else, if one can speak of an else. She will be quite well to-night."

"Well, I shall look forward to seeing you all," said Lady Bond with vice-regal graciousness and passed on, thinking as she went that Denis, bareheaded and wearing a mackin-tosh which had obviously spent much of its life on the floor of a car, near an oil can, was even more unsuited to an Agri-cultural Show than his stepmother.

"Why did we come here, darling?" said Denis to Mrs. Stonor.

"I can't think," said she, "except that everyone seemed to think we were. I suppose one would call it mass hysteria. Besides we ought to see Lord Bond's cows as we are dining with them to-night. It would only be polite."

"If it is to please Lord Bond, I will take you to see the cows at once," said Denis, "though at dining with them I draw the line. I do like his lordship. His misfortunes do but mellow his character."

"Misfortunes?" said Mrs. Stonor, startled.

"I mean Lady Bond," said Denis. "If I had a wife like that I'd take it out on everyone younger and poorer than myself. Few deeds in my ill-spent life have given me greater pleasure than playing bits from *Pinafore* to Lord Bond of an evening, bless his heart."

"Well, I hope you will have a *very* nice wife," said Mrs. Stonor, seizing on what struck her as the most important feature of his remark.

"Don't hope too much, darling," said Denis. "One can't have everything and I am very happy as I am."

He led his stepmother away in the direction of the cows. Each wondered a little what the other was thinking, but for all their intimate affection neither of them would trespass on the other's reserves, now or ever.

Lady Bond had a very shrewd guess as to where her next objective, her brother Lord Stoke, was to be found, and wasting no time on any hens, ducks, wild flowers, or vegetables from the allotments, she went straight to the pens

where Barsetshire's squarest, most bristly pigs were en-
shrined. Here, as she expected, she found Lord Stoke gloating over a hideous matron, gently scratching her scaly back
with his stick. His herdsman, Mallow, who thought but
poorly of animals with less than four stomachs, was standing
by registering contempt for employers.

"I want you, Tom," said Lady Bond, laying her hand on
her brother's arm.

"Eh!" said Lord Stoke, asserting his deafness in a defen-
sive way. "Now look at her, Lucasta. There's a sow!
Pomfret's showing her. When I look at her I wonder how
I ever came to go in for cows. Isn't she a beauty?"

The beauty, who was the shape of a giant petrol tin with
a snout at one end and a twirly tail at the other, looked with
hatred at Lord Stoke out of her small, vicious eyes, and
turned herself a little to indicate a spot at which more
scratching would be acceptable.

"She got a man down the other day and nearly did for
him," said Lord Stoke, as proudly as if the sow were his
own. "Nasty thing a pig's bite. I'd sooner be bitten by a
mad dog than by most pigs I know. Remember that old
fellow that used to work about the place when the governor
was alive? Old Ted they called him. He used to go wherever the bees were swarming because he said bee stings were
good for rheumatics. Nasty thing happened to him with a
pig when he was a lad. I don't quite remember the rights
of it, but he wore one of the pig's teeth on his watch chain
on Sundays. I think they got the tooth out of his arm.
Ought to write all these things down, you know. Make a
book about them like that book of Pomfret's that everyone

talked about. Come over now, old lady," said his lordship, prodding affectionately at the sow's portentous flank.

"I've been looking for you, Tom," said Lady Bond in a louder voice. "You are coming over for dinner, aren't you?"

"Dinner, eh?" said Lord Stoke. "Bless my soul, yes, Lucasta. Always dine with you after the Skeynes Agricultural. Anything wrong?"

"No, nothing's wrong," said Lady Bond. "But I want you to beat up everyone for the meeting about Pooker's Piece."

"Pooker's Piece?" said Lord Stoke. "Now, it's a curious thing about that field, Lucasta, but you cannot get good butter from any cow that grazes in it. No one can account for it, but there it is. I let old Margett who was farming it in nineteen-two have one of my best Jerseys there for a week, and the butter wasn't fit to eat. Old Mrs. Margett, Margett's mother, said her grandmother told her a highwayman was buried there, but that wouldn't account for the taste of the butter. No, there's more in it than meets the eye."

"Well, you don't want Sir Ogilvy Hibberd to build on it, do you?" said Lady Bond, who had barely been able to control her impatience during her brother's recital.

"Build on it, eh? Certainly not," said Lord Stoke. "Wonderful thing, Lucasta, not a bit of a pig goes to waste. Hams, pork pies, roast lion, hand of pork, pig's face, Bath chaps, pettitoes, sausages, bacon, black puddings, pigskin, leather; and that's only a beginning. I never heard," said Lord Stoke, giving the sow a final prod behind her ear, "of anyone eating their eyes, but I daresay old Margett did. He once ate three live frogs for a wager. You wouldn't find a man to do that now. It's all the Education Act."

Lady Bond, far from being depressed by this evidence of modern decadence, once more shouted commands at her brother not to forget the meeting, and as an afterthought asked him how his cows had done.

"Four firsts and the silver cup, my lady," said Mallow, breaking silence for the first time. "Good thing Mr. Middleton's Lily wasn't showing this year, my lady, or we might have got a second. If Lily knew what she was missing, my lady, she'd be in a rare way."

Lord Bond, who had just come up, asked if there was any news of Mr. Middleton's cow, and was informed by Lord Stoke's cowman that Mr. Middleton's cowman expected to be up all night, not being one to take any chances. Mr. and Mrs. Palmer now added themselves to the party. Mr. Palmer's cows had only got seconds, but his butter and cheese had secured several firsts, popularly attributed to his dairymaid having stirred the milk with a twig from Hangman's Oak, a large, blasted tree near the common, known historically to have been so called because a certain Lucius Handiman, Gent., had in 1672 planted a number of acorns brought back by him from Virginia, of which this was the only survivor, but naturally connected in the popular mind with gibbets and a mild form of magic.

"Afternoon, Bond," said Mr. Palmer, whose success in butter and cheese had made him well-disposed towards all the world, "I see your bull-calf has done well. But what about that duty on mangolds, eh? I always said that third clause of the Root Vegetables Bill would mean trouble. Said so to Louise, three years ago, wasn't it?" he said, appealing to his wife. "The year Leslie's bull got loose in our lane. I said to Louise, I see Bond has been voting against the third clause of the Root Vegetables Bill and that will mean trouble. Now they're going to take that duty off Brazilian mangolds and where shall we be then? No, no; bad business, bad business."

Lord Bond said that clause was still in Committee.

"We all know what *that* means," said Mr. Palmer. "Lot of old women—no offence, Bond—that don't know a swede from a turnip."

Lord Stoke said that his governor had always stood for a sliding scale duty on mangolds, and began to scratch the back of a small black pig in the next sty.

"Now that we are all here," said Lady Bond, whose determination to stick to her point was one of her most annoying and sterling qualities, "what about the Pooker's Piece meeting? I have all the invitations ready to send out for the ninth, and I think if we all made an effort to-day to interest the farmers and the local people we could work up a very good feeling. Mrs. Middleton," she called, as that lady together with Mr. Cameron came up, "I am sure you will help us to beat up supporters for the Pooker's Piece meeting on the ninth. We count on your husband of course."

"Well, you know what Jack is like," said Mrs. Middleton, acting on her usual instinct to protect her husband. "If he can come he will simply love to come, but he might be away."

"I shall count on you in any case," said Lady Bond, "and on Mr. Cameron, I hope."

"Did you say the ninth, Lucasta?" said Lord Stoke, suddenly taking an interest. "Can't have it on the ninth."

Lady Bond asked why not.

"Now, wait a moment, Lucasta," said Lord Stoke. "Never flog your horses. There's something against the ninth, can't tell you what. If I had my old note-book here I'd tell you. I find it a great help," said Lord Stoke, deserting the black pig and leaning his back against its pen as he addressed his circle of auditors, now swelled by several pig fanciers, "to jot down everything of importance in a note-book. Addresses and dates and things of that sort. I usually carry it in my breast pocket, but I suppose I forgot it to-day. Funny thing," said Lord Stoke, taking handfuls of small portable property out of various pockets, looking at them and putting them back again, "I seem to have everything else here. Must have left my note-book in my other tweed jacket. Always have two tweed jackets going at once, Palmer. Then if one wants mending or a button sewing on, I have the other to slip on. My governor taught me that. 'If you are ordering one suit, Tom my boy,' he used to say, 'always order two.' You wouldn't remember that, Lucasta. You were in the nursery."

As Lord Stoke's autobiography showed no signs of coming to an end, Lady Bond used a sister's privilege and cut across what he was saying to make another appeal for the public meeting on the ninth.

"The ninth," said Mr. Palmer. "Louise, there is Mrs. Tebben. You must tell her, Lady Bond. She will be a most enthusiastic helper."

Mrs. Tebben, who had come by the day excursion from

Worsted to Skeynes and was very hot from walking up the hill in her mackintosh, greeted everyone and said it reminded her of some pastoral scene near Vergil's Mantua.

"Banbury?" said Lord Stoke. "Beastly bit of country. I bought a cow there once. Only time I've been really disappointed, except that time in 'thirty-seven when Pomfret got a mare from me ten pounds too cheap, and of course that time when—"

Lady Bond, who was by now almost pawing the ground with impatience, said she hoped Mrs. Tebben would tell everyone in Worsted about the public meeting on the ninth about Pooker's Piece. Mrs. Tebben, her face shining with damp heat and enthusiasm, said she would tell *everyone*, though she believed it was the Buffaloes' Outing. And did Lady Bond, she said, know the excellent plan for reserving seats which she herself always practised.

"We get so many cards of invitation for societies and private views and meetings," said Mrs. Tebben, "and I keep them all, in a drawer. Then if I need a card for anything I take one of them and use the blank side of it. I have quite a collection, and if they would be of any use to you I would willingly send you some, either by post or by the train to Skeynes. They will always take small parcels and any of your people that were down at the station could pick them up. I usually make a large cross on the printed side in red or blue chalk to show that the invitation has nothing to do with the meeting in question, and then on the blank side you could write the numbers of the seats. I have had a great success with this plan at scout concerts."

Lady Bond thanked Mrs. Tebben very much but said she would not trouble her as she did not intend to reserve seats.

"Nonsense, Lucasta," said Lord Stoke, suddenly hearing very well. "Must reserve seats. How do you suppose people will hear if they come late and have to sit at the back of the hall?"

The number and complication of the issues raised by this question appalled everyone except Mrs. Tebben, who said, Then they could just write Reserved on some of the biggest cards, for instance the cards of which she and her husband had not been able to make use for the Royal Academy Soirée, the Conversazione of the Royal Society and an invitation to a reception at the Liverpool Guildhall, though why they had been invited to that she had never been able to make out.

"And now," she added, "I shall visit the exhibits and then I must get the 4.10 back, as our good Mrs. Phipps is out to-night and I must be the cook. Just an omelette, made in a delightfully economical way with hardly any butter and a little chopped parsley out of the garden, and the cold semolina pudding cut into slices in a glass dish with some of my home-made rhubarb jam. I can't tell you how much my husband enjoyed his visit to your excavations, Lord Stoke. He hasn't been able to talk about anything else since."

"Not able to talk, eh?" said Lord Stoke. "What's wrong? Talked all right the day he lunched with me. Tonsils, I expect. You ought to take him to Slattery. He's the man for tonsils. Has 'em out as soon as look at you."

But Mrs. Tebben was so occupied with good-byes to everyone that she did not hear him.

"I shall take off my mackintosh and carry it," she said

brightly. "Now that the rain has stopped I find it hardly necessary. Good-bye, good-bye. I shall not forget the cards, Lady Bond."

She went briskly off towards the big tent and the Palmers followed her. Mrs. Middleton asked whether Miss Starter was at the Show. Lady Bond explained, rather proudly, that her guest could not go near cows without getting hay fever, so she was spending the afternoon resting in preparation for the dinner party that night.

"C.W. ought to be here," said her ladyship. "He was going to drive over from Rushwater House where he spent the weekend with the Leslies and said he would come to the Show before he went home. He felt, rightly, that he ought to show that he takes an interest. Oh, Mrs. Stonor, there you are again. You haven't seen C.W. anywhere, have you?"

"Yes," said Mrs. Stonor. "Denis and I saw him in the cow enclosure. He said he was going to look for you."

And even as she spoke young Mr. Bond came up. He had already learnt from Denis that Daphne was not at the Show and did not quite know if he was sorry or glad. He had spent so much time trying not to think about her that he had thought of very little else, and while one half of him wished to show proper pride, aversion and scorn, the other half wanted nothing better than to cast itself at her feet and offer her its heart and hand. And if anyone disbelieves the strength of young Mr. Bond's attachment, we can only say that even the thought of what his mother might say did not weigh with him in the slightest degree. He congratulated his father and his uncle on their various successes and enquired from Mrs. Middleton about the cow Lily's health.

"Pucken says he is going to sit up all night with her," said Mrs. Middleton. "I don't think there is any real need to, but he enjoys it. He takes a lot of old sacks and a can of tea and some bread and fat bacon down to the cowshed and gets away from Mrs. Pucken. If it weren't for your dinner party I expect Daphne would be there too."

"I could easily run her over if she is really keen," said young Mr. Bond eagerly, but Mrs. Middleton made a non-committal reply.

The sky, which had been lowering hideously for the last half-hour, now made up its mind to spoil the rest of the Agri-cultural Show as thoroughly as possible. Heavy drops came spattering across the ground on a chill gust. Mrs. Tebben put on her mackintosh again, saying gaily that she must foot it swiftly to the station. The Palmers said Rubbish, they would take her home in the car, which they very kindly did, while Mrs. Tebben discussed with herself at great length whether the railway company would refund anything on the return half of a day excursion ticket, price one and seven-pence halfpenny. It was not till Mr. Palmer had pointed out that the day return cost exactly as much as an ordinary single that she was at all appeased, but the subject rankled and she was able to continue it, as what she called a purely academic discussion, with her husband over the economical omelette and the cold semolina pudding.

Young Mr. Bond offered to drive Mrs. Stonor home, hoping to see Daphne, but Mrs. Stonor said she was so wet she would rather walk. The Bonds were just moving to their car when Lord Stoke, who despised all forms of weather and intended to finish doing the Show thoroughly, called them back.

"What is it, Tom?" said Lady Bond. "Be quick, because Ferguson doesn't like to be kept waiting when it's raining."

"Remember I said something about the ninth?" said Lord Stoke, turning his coat collar up. "It came to me just now what it was. I knew there was something wrong with that day."

"Well, you must come, Tom, whatever it is," said his sister.

"You remember old Uncle Fred?" said Lord Stoke. "No, you wouldn't; before your time. He died when I was a youngster. The governor was very fond of him and Uncle Fred left him those Chinese Chippendale cabinets. The money all went to his children—illegitimate of course, but blood's thicker than water. I saw the boy not long ago. When I say boy, he's about my age and doing very well on the Stock Exchange. Don't know what happened to the girl, married a feller in India, I think. Well, as I was saying," he continued, suddenly becoming aware of his sister's expression, who looked as if she would like to run him through with her shooting stick, "Uncle Henry never liked the number nine. His unlucky number. No accounting for these things. I knew I'd remember what it was."

His lordship then went off to look at a ploughing contest.

The walk back to Laverings was far from pleasant. The lane was shoe-deep in slippery clay, the wind lashed hair and hat furiously and penetrated with icy breath Mrs. Stonor's shabby old tweed coat. Mr. Cameron, who was walking beside her, had one of his shoes sucked off in a particularly sticky rut and swore violently under his breath as he tried to get it on again. As they turned the last corner a blast met them that nearly took Mrs. Stonor off her feet and she was thankful to clutch Mr. Cameron's coat sleeve to steady herself, so he quite naturally went into the White House with her.

"Oh my goodness!" said Mrs. Stonor, taking off her hat and coat and kicking her shoes into a corner. "You'd better stay to tea, Alister, and I'll have your shoes dried. I'll just go and see if Daphne is coming down. Denis must have gone back with Catherine."

She ran upstairs and came back with a pair of Denis's shoes for Mr. Cameron and the news that Daphne would be down in about half an hour. Palfrey brought in the tea and took away the wet shoes.

"Alister," said Mrs. Stonor, so suddenly that he nearly jumped. But having let loose this word, she appeared unable to go on.

"Yes?" said Mr. Cameron, eating a cake that he didn't want.

"Alister," said Mrs. Stonor again. "It is dreadful to talk like a parent, but after all there is no one else to do it and though Denis is really the head of the family he is even less her parent than I am."

"It is certainly very difficult to think of you as a parent," said Mr. Cameron. "You don't look fit to be responsible for Denis and Daphne."

"I really do my best," said Mrs. Stonor apologetically.

"Good God, I don't mean that," said Mr. Cameron. "I

mean—I really don't know what I mean. I'd better go back to Laverings."

"But I must say it before you go," said Mrs. Stonor. "Your engagement with Daphne. It was to be put in the *Times* after the Agricultural."

"What does Daphne say?" asked the fervent lover.

"She won't talk about it at all," said Mrs. Stonor mournfully. "She always says wait a few days. I did mention it to her just now and she said to ask you. And will you *please* tell me what to do."

Mr. Cameron looked at her with despair. Mrs. Stonor suddenly felt her heart wrung with anguish for all the muddle, and because in spite of all her vagueness she had a very clear mind about people she loved, she saw that her concern was far more for Alister Cameron's happiness than for the happiness of her much loved Daphne. Then she was so ashamed of this revelation that she sat quite silent, in a violent storm of confusion. Mr. Cameron, looking at her, allowed himself to know what he had known ever since the day among the pea-sticks, and wondered exactly how deeply Lilian Stonor would despise him if she knew. As soon as Daphne would make up her mind he would put the engagement in the *Times* and pray that Lilian would never know the disloyalty of his heart. That Daphne might ever suspect it did not occur to him at all.

"I suppose," said Mrs. Stonor at last, in a conversational voice, "people occasionally make mistakes."

"Yes," said Mr. Cameron. "And then they have to back up their mistakes like gentlemen, or as near gentlemen as possible. Would you mind if I went now, Lilian?"

"No," said Mrs. Stonor, not looking at him.

So he went into the hall and suddenly finding that he had Denis's shoes on, went to the kitchen to ask for his own. Lou was alone, keeping guard for Palfrey, who had gone off to the Show as soon as she had brought tea in.

"Are my shoes here, Lou?" said Mr. Cameron. "And why aren't you at the Show?"

"I'm going to-night, Mr. Cameron," said Lou, reverently fetching his shoes from the kitchen fender. "It's lovely at night with the lights and the boys throwing crackers. Excuse me asking, Mr. Cameron, but aren't you going to say nothing? I mean about you and Miss Daphne? I never said a word, the way you told me."

"Quite soon, Lou, I expect," said Mr. Cameron, tying his damp shoes. "You've been a good girl."

"Miss Palfrey and Mother and me always thought it was to be young Mr. Bond," said Lou, emboldened by her hero's praise and the delightful intimacy of a tête-à-tête in the kitchen. "Miss Daphne seemed quite taken by him. She had his photo under her pillow, because I found it one day when I was helping Mother make the beds, but I hid it away ever so quick, so Mother shouldn't see, in Miss Daphne's handkerchief drawer. I hope I did right," she added anxiously, seeing a peculiar expression on Mr. Cameron's face.

"Quite right, Lou," said Mr. Cameron.

"You hadn't ought to sit in those wet shoes, Mr. Cameron," said Lou as her guest rose to depart.

"I shan't," said he. "I shall go for a long walk."

When Lou went into the drawing-room a few minutes

later in answer to the bell, Mrs. Stonor asked her to bring
fresh tea for Miss Daphne, who was coming down. Lou,
who cried loudly and freely herself on the slightest provoca-
tion, knew at once that Mrs. Stonor had been crying. As Lou
could see no reason for the gentry to cry except Lovers'
Quarrels, she was much exercised. For Miss Daphne to cry
would have been reasonable, but why Mrs. Stonor?

"Has Mr. Cameron gone?" said Mrs. Stonor.

"Yes, Mrs. Stonor, he came into the kitchen to get his
shoes and said he was going for a nice long walk. He *is* a
nice gentleman, Mrs. Stonor, and said it didn't matter a bit
when I told him about Miss Daphne's photo."

"What photograph?" said Mrs. Stonor, not much interested in the girl's chatter.

"Mr. Bond's photo that Miss Daphne put under her
pillow," said Lou, half frightened, half full of a delightful
sense of power and the unchaining of unknown forces.
"Mother didn't see it, Mrs. Stonor. I slipped it into Miss
Daphne's handkerchief drawer as quick as anything."

"All right, Lou, that will do," said Mrs. Stonor, much to
her informant's disappointment. "And bring the fresh tea
the moment Miss Daphne comes down."

When Daphne did come down she looked so wretched
that her stepmother had not the heart to say anything about
the engagement, and very soon went upstairs herself to lie
down before dinner, for her head and her heart were both
aching so much that she didn't know which she disliked
more.

WHILE Mrs. Stonor and Mr. Cameron turned into the little

gate of the White House, it was but natural that Denis, who had been walking with Mrs. Middleton, should accompany her into Laverings. Ethel, who was just bringing in tea, said that Mr. Middleton had taken Flora and gone for a tramp over Worsted way.

"He will do it on wet days," sighed Mrs. Middleton, "and Flora is one mass of mud. However it doesn't seem to do him any harm. You had better have tea with me, Denis, and we will look at those duets. Jack won't be back till six at least if he has gone to Worsted."

As they drank their tea before the fire that Ethel had thoughtfully lighted, rain and wind beating on the windows outside, Mrs. Middleton asked Denis how his ballet was. He was not much inclined to speak of it at first. The excitement of the mood had passed and he was in the Slough of Despond that so often follows some prolonged mental exertion. He saw all its faults and more clearly still he saw the extreme improbability of its ever being performed. But the temptation to unburden himself was too great, and gradually he found himself talking about his hopes and plans just as he so often did.

"And now I have tired you," he added, in a fine glow of self-accusation. "You shouldn't let me."

"How can I help it?" said Mrs. Middleton.

"Do I know what you mean by that?" asked Denis after a silence.

Mrs. Middleton said she wished he would tell her again exactly how much money would be needed to get the ballet company going. Denis mentioned the sum that would put the company on its feet. Ethel came in and cleared tea away.

While she was in the room Mrs. Middleton and Denis talked about the Agricultural. When she had gone there seemed to be no need to talk and a silence fell that was full of disquietude. Mrs. Middleton tried to speak, but as no sound came from her she gave it up and reflected, with the nightmare clarity that is given by an anaesthetic, that not to speak was the very best way of laying up irremediable trouble for two people, and possibly for a third for whom her long affection and devotion were very deep. It did not help her at all when Denis said in a carefully ordinary voice, "If you look so tired I don't know how to bear it." But seeing that she must help him even if she couldn't help herself, she wrenched her mind back savagely from its far wanderings, got up, and said she would look out those duets. The music was piled on the piano. She began to turn it over. Denis threw his cigarette into the fire and came to her side.

"I think," said Mrs. Middleton, "not duets, Denis. Duets are a perpetual battle for the loud pedal. Music for two pianos is much more fun. If we had two pianos in the library—"

Then because Denis's hand touched hers she was speechless and powerless.

"I think you are quite right about duets," said Denis, speaking to the top of her head. "You always are right. Also kind. Also too tired. I am going home to see how Daphne is. I am only talking because it is extremely important that someone should talk at this moment. When I first saw you again at Laverings I wanted more than anything in the world to make you look less tired. I still want that, but I have made no kind of success of it. Indeed a

failure. I shall see you at Lady Bond's horrible dinner
to-night."

Then Mrs. Middleton was left alone. So she put away
the music and wrote some dull letters and before long Mr.
Middleton came back.

"A giant refreshed, Catherine," he called to her as he
came in. "I have walked in good English rain and mud
since three o'clock. So has Flora. She delights in everything that her master loves. Now to prepare for Bond's
dinner party. I feel that I shall be in vein to-night. Did you
enjoy the Agricultural, my dear?"

Mrs. Middleton said it had been very nice and they went
upstairs to dress. While they were waiting for the car Mr.
Middleton looked anxiously at his wife.

"There is a cloud," he said. "Can you tell me?"

"It is just a small, secret grief," said Mrs. Middleton,
faintly amused that she was capable of so accurately ana-
lysing her own feelings.

"Keep it then, my dear," said her husband with all his
kindness. "I wouldn't interfere with your secret griefs. But
let me know when I am needed."

❦ 11 ❧

MR. CAMERON ESCAPES

❦

THE DINNER TABLE AT STAPLE PARK WAS ROUND ON ORDINARY occasions, and by the addition of various leaves it could seat as many as twenty-four. To-night there were to be eighteen, so it was not developed to its greatest extent, but even so it looked highly impressive and Spencer felt that it was on the whole worthy of him. Lord Pomfret was always invited to the Agricultural dinner and always declined. The other local landowners present were Lord Stoke, Mr. and Mrs. Palmer with their niece Betty Deane, the Middletons and Mr. and Mrs. John Leslie, a very nice, rather dull couple who came as representatives of Mr. Leslie and Lady Emily Leslie at Rushwater. These, with Miss Starter, Mr. Cameron, the Stonors and the Dean of Barchester and Mrs. Crawley made up the party.

Poor Daphne found herself between Mr. Cameron and young Mr. Bond, and as Mr. Bond was getting on extremely well with Betty Deane on his other side, she wished more than ever that her cold had been bad enough to keep her in bed. On the same side of the table Mrs. Stonor in the intervals of talking to Mr. Leslie and renewing an old acquaintance with the Dean, was able to look across at Denis, between Mrs. Leslie and Mrs. Palmer, and wonder what exactly had happened that afternoon, for that something had happened she was perfectly sure.

"I hope, Mr. Dean," said Lady Bond to her left-hand neighbour, "that you and Mrs. Crawley will be able to come to a meeting in the village on the evening of the ninth about preserving Pooker's Piece. You will have an invitation by Wednesday morning."

The Dean said that if there was an Evangelical humbug in England it was the Bishop of Barchester, who had arranged a meeting at the Palace for that evening. What the meeting was about he could not at the moment precisely remember, but if it was intended to further any of the Bishop's plans, he ought to be there and lead the opposition.

"You know it is Sir Ogilvy Hibberd who has bought Pooker's Piece," said Lady Bond. "He wants to build a road house."

"Hibberd?" said the Dean. "A pestilent fellow. One of those clerically-minded laymen that are such a thorn in our flesh. I had the pleasure of blackballing him for the Polyanthus. I'll come if I can, Lady Bond, and if not I'll send my secretary. He is young and vigorous to a degree that quite exhausts me and will lead any movement with the greatest of pleasure. In fact if you would switch him onto the Preservation of Pooker's Piece it would be a real godsend to me and perhaps he would allow me to answer some of my own letters."

As the talk between Lady Bond and the Dean was long
and animated, lasting well into the saddle of lamb and red
currant jelly, Mrs. Stonor on the Dean's other side had to
go on talking to Mr. Leslie, which was easy enough if one
asked him about his two young children; and the next
couple, Betty Deane and young Mr. Bond, were similarly
thrown into each other's arms. As they had many American
friends in common, and young Mr. Bond took no notice
of Betty's peculiar manner, they got on very well and indeed
made a good deal of noise, which was far from inspiriting
to poor Daphne. And, as a stone thrown into water spreads
a ripple over the pond, so did the ripple from the Dean and
Lady Bond reach Daphne, forcing her to talk to her affianced
on her other side. In justice to this unhappy pair it must be
said that they did their best. Daphne told herself again and
again that Alister was one of the nicest people she had ever
met and asked him a great many questions about the College
of Epistemological Ideology, but she couldn't help hearing
the gay and heartless chatter between young Mr. Bond and
Betty Deane, nor could she help turning her head from time
to time to lacerate her eyes with the sight of the huge
sapphire on Betty's left hand. Mr. Cameron told himself
what a darling girl Daphne was, and how well she looked
even with the remains of a cold and how nice it would be to
have a wife who took an interest in damp courses and rein-
forced concrete, but he thought a good deal about Lilian
Stonor and people making mistakes and honourably living
up to them, and often answered Daphne's questions rather
at random, which made no difference, as she was not listening to the answers.

On Mr. Cameron's other side Mrs. Crawley was talking comfortably to Lord Bond about the shocking state of the Deanery coal cellar, while beyond them Mrs. Middleton fed Mr. Palmer with questions about his dairy and how his nephew Laurence was getting on. She could not see Denis, two couples away, and wished she could and was glad she couldn't. As for Miss Starter and Lord Stoke they became almost inseparable at once, for Lord Stoke's mother had once been proposed to by Miss Starter's father, and after crying for twenty-four hours, for Lord Mickleham was poor and a poet and quite ineligible in spite of his title, had married old Lord Stoke, while Lord Mickleham had immediately married the first of the three wives who had brought him his eighteen children. Miss Starter, having lived with semi-royalty, was extremely good at Debrett, a book of which Lord Stoke made an almost religious study, and cousins and connections by marriage flew between them like so many shuttlecocks, till Miss Starter quite forgot her diet and took melted butter and a piece of ordinary toast, both of which were well known to be death to her. Beyond them Mrs. Leslie talked gently to Denis about her two young children, her sister-in-law Agnes Graham and her six children, her brother-in-law David who always had such an amusing time, her nephew Martin Leslie who was down from Oxford now and working in his grandfather's estate office, and how much she liked Littlehampton. Her mild babble gave Denis every chance of wishing he could see Mrs. Middleton, two couples away, and being glad that he couldn't. And Mrs. Palmer and Mr. Middleton were doing their best to talk each other down on the subject of the Post Impressionists, both

having very decided views combined with a distinct difficulty in remembering whether Manet and Gauguin were
Monet and Van Gogh or someone else.

Altogether Lady Bond was able to tell herself, as she
always did, that her party was being a complete success and
even Spencer relaxed a little as the roar of contented diners-
out rose louder and louder. But the happiest of parties must
be broken up when the fatal moment comes for the hostess to
take a gracious leave of her first partner and set to her second.
Much as Lady Bond would have liked to go on talking to the
Dean, who was speaking evil of his Bishop in a way that
was balm to her staunch High Church spirit, she saw that the
turning point had arrived, said the Dean must tell her more
about the Palace later on, and seizing a lull in the discussion
on Post Impressionism asked Mr. Middleton for news of
Lily, thus releasing Mrs. Palmer to talk to Denis.

"What's the matter with your stepmother?" said Mrs.
Palmer. "She doesn't look well."

Denis said she had been nursing Daphne, who had a cold.

"I suppose she wears herself out over you young people,"
said Mrs. Palmer, and then softening to Denis, for she had
no children and was very fond of her nephews and nieces
and the young in general, she put him through a rigorous
cross-examination about his own past life, health, work and
prospects. Denis liked her blunt kindness and answered all
her questions as well as he could.

"Of course a wife is what you need," said Mrs. Palmer.
"Someone like Betty who would look after you. Pity you
didn't meet her sooner. How well she looks to-night, and
no wonder."

Denis looked across at Betty, who certainly looked handsome and animated beyond her wont talking to young Mr. Bond, and shuddered at the thought of managing her.

"You young men will not wear enough clothes," said Mrs. Palmer, noticing the shudder. "This weather is very treacherous. I'll tell you what you ought to do."

So she told him, and next to him Mrs. Leslie told Lord Stoke about her children, and her husband's relations, and Lord Stoke thought she was a nice sensible little woman and told her about the new kitchen range at Rising Castle.

Miss Starter, abandoning with regret her genealogical talk with Lord Stoke, turned to Mr. Palmer, and asked him, for she had acquired a royal memory for faces and names, whether she had not seen him and his wife at Homburg before the war. Mr. Palmer, who had never forgiven the Germans for making it impossible to take his usual cure for several years, said they were a bad lot and now he had quite stopped trying to see any good in them he felt much more comfortable. Miss Starter was able to tell several harrowing stories of insults accorded to her at minor German courts where she had been in attendance on H.H. Princess Louisa Christina, courts where, in spite of their intolerable stickling for rank and precedence, she, an English Honourable, had been treated as a commoner. Mr. Palmer put forward the comprehensive view that all foreign titles were rubbish and there was nothing abroad to touch an English Duke, to which Miss Starter agreed so heartily that she ate some ice pudding, a delicacy absolutely forbidden by her physician.

"You look a little tired," said Lord Bond to Mrs. Middleton. "It was very good of you to come to the Agricultural, but it's too much for you on a day like this. Sorry Middleton couldn't come."

"He was rather busy with work," said Mrs. Middleton, feeling that any kindness was more than she could bear.

"Nice of Mrs. Stonor to turn up too," said Lord Bond, in great content with his party. "She looks a bit run down. Nice girl that stepdaughter of hers. Plenty of character Miss Daphne has. Only person I ever knew that got the upper hand of my butler. I've had the piano key ever since she told him to give it back to me. And Denis is a nice boy too, a very nice boy. I'd as soon listen to him playing Gilbert and Sullivan as anything. What's he going to do with his music, eh? Not much money in music, I suppose."

Mrs. Middleton said he had written the music for a ballet but it cost a lot to get that sort of thing produced, naming the sum that Denis had mentioned.

"Ballet, eh?" said Lord Bond, looking down from the head of the table at his young guest with increased respect. "Pretty girls in tights and crinolines, eh? Is it pretty music? I did mean to ask him to play me some, but we always got back to Gilbert and Sullivan. He likes it as much as I do."

Mrs. Middleton said it was very pretty music.

"I must have a talk with that young man," said Lord Bond. "Now you know what you need is a good holiday, Mrs. Middleton. Go off on a cruise or something."

So he gave her a great deal of very kind and quite useless advice, and she wondered why to say a person's name was so difficult and was thankful that she had been able to speak of Denis as "he" when Lord Bond was asking about him.

Mrs. Crawley and Mr. Cameron both knew Mr. Barton,

the architect who was doing some repairs to Hiram's Hospital in Barchester, an old building in which the Crawleys were much interested, so they got on very well, and now Daphne found herself left with young Mr. Bond.

"I've been longing to talk to you ever since dinner began," said young Mr. Bond.

Daphne wanted to say "So have I," but a stranger that had got inside her and was hurting her dreadfully said in a rather horrid voice that he had seemed very happy with Miss Deane.

"She's a splendid girl," said young Mr. Bond enthusiastically. "I wish you could know her better, but she's going to America so soon. You know we are going on the same boat. I wish you were coming too."

The stranger said she knew she would simply loathe America.

"I say, Daphne," said young Mr. Bond anxiously, "I haven't done anything stupid, have I? I thought I might have annoyed you about something last time I was down here and you know I'd die sooner than be a nuisance. Can't you tell me what it is and I'll apologise like anything, even if I haven't done it."

"It's nothing," said Daphne, pushing the stranger aside. "It's only—"

But before she could finish, Betty Deane, deserting her other partner, Mr. Leslie, leant over to young Mr. Bond and said, "I say C.W., did you know your father means to announce it when he gives his Agricultural Toasts? It's a bit shame-making, but I don't like to spoil his fun."

"Good girl, Betty," said young Mr. Bond, patting her on

the arm. "Please excuse me," he continued to Daphne, "I couldn't help it."

"It doesn't matter a bit," said the stranger with icy politeness. "I never noticed you doing anything particular. I really wasn't thinking about it. I just thought you might like to know that I am engaged to Alister Cameron. It's a secret, at least it was, but we're going to have it in the *Times* at once, so I thought I'd tell you."

Young Mr. Bond went perfectly white and said he congratulated her with all his heart and Cameron too.

"Thanks awfully," said the stranger. "I expect we'll be married almost at once, even before you are."

"What on earth do you mean, Daphne?" said young Mr. Bond. "You are mad, or I am. Why should I get married? You know perfectly well—"

But here he was interrupted by a genteel banging of spoons or handles of dessert knives on the table. It was Lord Bond's very embarrassing annual custom to give a few healths at the dinner after the Skeynes Agricultural Show and make a little speech. Much as his wife detested this outburst she was for once powerless to check him. Luckily most of the guests were old friends who were used to their host's mild form of eccentricity, and Lady Bond had to conceal her disapproval as best she could, drawing but faint comfort from the knowledge that Spencer was the only person who fully shared her feelings. In fact every year Spencer determined to give notice after the dinner, but realising what he owed to himself, he always thought better of it next day.

Holding a small piece of paper on which he had made

some illegible notes, Lord Bond ran through practically the whole list of prize winners and gave an historical survey of the Agricultural Show from its inception in 1890 to the present day, reminded his hearers after a little calculation that the fiftieth anniversary would shortly be upon them, regretted the absence of Lord Pomfret, applauded the presence of Lord Stoke, Mr. Palmer and Mr. Middleton, thought of making a joke about the Dean being a kind of shepherd himself but suddenly felt it might be in bad taste or at any rate more applicable to a Bishop than to a Dean, and so floundered happily through nearly twenty minutes of intolerably dull and sometimes, when he had to look very closely at his notes, almost inaudible oratory. Young Mr. Bond tried hard to get Daphne's attention, but with averted head she took an apparently absorbing interest in what his father was saying.

When he suddenly found himself at an end of what he had to say Lord Bond raised his glass.

"I will now give you our usual toast, the Skeynes Agricultural Show," he said, "but before we drink it I want to tell you all a delightful piece of news. Miss Betty Deane, our old friend Palmer's charming niece, has allowed me to congratulate her publicly on her engagement."

He ceremoniously bowed to Betty and sat down.

"You didn't say who to, Lord Bond," said Betty in her usual commanding tones.

"Bless my heart, no more I did," said Lord Bond. "What is his name, my dear? I know he's a friend of C.W.'s but for the life of me I can't remember it."

"Woolcott Jefferson van Dryven, father," said young Mr.

Bond. "One of the nicest fellows in New York."

Betty's health was politely drunk by the company, who were only too thankful for a change from the Agricultural, and a buzz of congratulations surrounded her. With a smile of gracious exasperation Lady Bond rose and led her ladies from the room. As young Mr. Bond held back Daphne's chair for her to go out she looked at him with such a piteous plea for forgiveness in her eyes that he nearly kissed her on the spot, and if he refrained it was not so much from fear of what anyone, even his mother, would say, as the knowledge that a girl who has just told you she is engaged to another man is not the person you honourably ought to kiss.

Daphne toyed for a moment with the idea of suicide as the ladies made their progress to the long drawing-room, but it all seemed too difficult, so she did the next best thing, planted herself firmly by Betty Deane and said how awfully glad she was about the engagement.

"Thank you so much," said Betty. "It will be in the *Times* to-morrow, but Lord Bond wanted to tell people to-night and it is always a mistake to thwart people's impulses, even at his age. You never know what kind of complex you may be creating."

Miss Starter, settling herself in an uncomfortable chair with her back extremely straight, added her congratulations to Daphne's and said she had known Mr. van Dryven's father when he was American Minister at the Grand Ducal court of Schauer-Antlitz.

"He's dead," said Betty. "He got a lot of inhibitions in the diplomatic service and when he tried to get rid of them in America it was too much for him. Woolcott is quite different. He has had every inhibition psychoed and is perfectly free. You'd like him."

"And what does he do?" enquired Miss Starter, with the gracious temporary interest of fallen royalty.

"He looks after his money, and does a spot of archaeology. He took a Classical Excavation Diploma at Pittsburgh. Of course it doesn't carry the same weight as a First in Greats," said Betty, who never underestimated her own achievements, "but it's pretty good to get that Diploma in three months."

"His father was a really scholarly man," said Miss Starter severely. "And where will you be married?"

"Oh somewhere," said Betty. "Marriage is doomed as an institution of course, but one might as well please one's parents. St. Margaret's, I suppose."

"It makes me feel quite young to hear you say that," said Miss Starter. "My dear father did not believe in marriage at all, which was quite advanced in those days. It is quite amusing to hear you young people still holding those views. He was married three times, first at St. George's, Hanover Square, then at St. Peter's, Eaton Square, and finally, to please my dear Mother, at St. Jude's in Collingham Road. I am sure you will be very happy. You must bring Mr. van Dryven to see me in Ebury Street, number two hundred and three, the top floor."

This invitation was so clearly in the nature of a royal congé that Betty, who had meant to pulverise Miss Starter, found herself to her great surprise getting up and going away.

"Cutsam Porck van Dryven would certainly not have liked her as a daughter-in-law," said Miss Starter, surveying

Betty's departing form dispassionately. "Now tell me about yourself. I have always been so grateful to your delightful aunt Mrs. Middleton for finding out about Kornog bread for me. Are you staying here long?"

"I don't know," said Daphne, and then said desperately, "You see I'm engaged too, to Alister Cameron, and we might get married quite soon. I don't want to leave the White House, but I suppose if one is going to be married one might as well get it over, don't you think?"

"Or break it off," said Miss Starter, looking at nothing in particular.

"Oh, but one couldn't," said Daphne, too surprised and too wretched to resent this advice. "I mean if one is engaged to someone awfully nice and one is very fond of, even if one finds someone else one thought was engaged to someone else really isn't, one can't exactly back out."

"I think I understand you," said Miss Starter. "I have eyes in my head and I have seen a good deal of life. You wouldn't do badly at Staple Park."

Upon this paralysing remark she got up and joined the elder ladies, leaving Daphne a prey to conflicting emotions. She knew now so fatally what she wanted and what she didn't want that it was quite unbearable. Suicide being out of the question she felt that even at the cost of being rude she must get away and if possible get home. Her stepmother was now deeply engaged in talk with Mrs. Crawley and Daphne thought if she went round the other way, by the room with all the musical boxes in it, she could find Spencer and ask him to tell Pollett that she wanted to go home at once and send a message to her stepmother that her cold was coming on again and apologise next day to Lady Bond. It was a very muddled, ill-conceived scheme, but all she could think of for the moment. It was dusk outside and only a few lights were turned on, so Daphne was able to slip away unnoticed and make her way to the yellow satin room, from which she knew she could get hold of one of the footmen by the little stone passage that led to the servants' quarters. In the room was young Mr. Bond.

"Hullo," said he. "Father wants to show the Dean the Marie Antoinette box and I'm not sure which it is; the one with the bird that flaps and twitters when you press the spring. Do you know which case it's in?"

"I must go home," said Daphne. "I can't tell you why, but I must."

"I'll drive you, if it's important," said young Mr. Bond. "Only please tell me first that I didn't hear you properly. You aren't really engaged to Cameron, are you?"

"Yes I am," said Daphne, "and it's too awful, because I do think he is the nicest person almost I ever met, but I thought you were engaged to Betty Deane and I hated her, and I thought if I got engaged to Alister it would stop me minding, but it made it much worse, and I do think he is so very nice, but then you weren't engaged to Betty and it was all too ghastly, and I wish I was dead. I think the Marie Antoinette box is in the table with the glass top and the red plush lining."

"Oh damn the box and the table," said young Mr. Bond. "You aren't going to marry Cameron and you are going to marry me. Is that clear? Besides you haven't even got an engagement ring. It's all nonsense."

"I didn't want a ring," said Daphne. "I thought it wouldn't seem like being really engaged so long as I didn't have a ring and didn't have it in the *Times*."

"Then it isn't an engagement at all," said young Mr. Bond.

And at that moment the door opened and Mr. Cameron, who had a passion for musical boxes and thought he might play with some quietly while the others discussed cows, came in and looked piercingly at the guilty couple.

"It isn't Cedric's fault, Alister, it truly isn't," cried Daphne, with visions of a duel.

"What isn't?" said Mr. Cameron.

"I do really think you are the nicest person I have ever known, Alister," said Daphne, "and I am terribly fond of you, but it was so awful and I always thought Cedric was engaged to Betty."

Mr. Cameron was not surprised. He understood Daphne's incoherent words quite well. Lou's indiscretion had only been the last eye-opener and he knew he had known from the beginning that the whole thing was a mistake. Not unnaturally he experienced for a moment a pang of intense mortification, but even as that subsided a hope rose to fill its place.

"If you would like our engagement to come to an end, Daphne," he said, "it can do so this very minute."

"Alister, *darling*," cried Daphne, flinging her arms round his neck and embracing him heartily.

"Are you sure you don't mind?" said young Mr. Bond.

"To be perfectly truthful, though I am very, very fond of Daphne, I was never so relieved in my life," said Mr. Cameron.

Then he and young Mr. Bond shook hands and began to laugh so much that Daphne had to join them, though she didn't quite know what it was about, and as they were laughing Lord Bond came in.

"Well, amusing yourself, young people?" he said benignantly. "Can't you find the Marie Antoinette box, C.W.? I do want Crawley to see it."

"It's in the glass table, Lord Bond," said Daphne, lifting the lid and taking out the little chased golden box with its royal monogram.

"Good girl. You know the place better than I do," said Lord Bond.

"Oh, father," said young Mr. Bond, "Daphne and I are engaged if that's all right."

"Bless my soul! And on the Agricultural night too," said Lord Bond. "Well, I couldn't have been more pleased if I'd got every first prize at the Show. She's a treasure, C.W. A girl that can get the better of Spencer will do anything. But what about your mother, my boy?"

"I think, Father," said young Mr. Bond, "that if I didn't tell her till to-morrow I'd feel stronger then. Could we have it for a secret to-night?"

Lord Bond kissed Daphne warmly and said they would say nothing till next day and he must get back to the dining-room or the Dean would be wondering where he was.

"And I'll get back too," said Mr. Cameron. "I suppose no one else is to know till to-morrow? What about Lilian?"

"Oh I'll tell her, of course, and Denis when we get home," said Daphne. "And it will be lovely to tell Uncle Jack and

Catherine to-morrow, and Palfrey and Mrs. Pucken. Oh—!" she added with a kind of shriek.

"What?" said young Mr. Bond.

"I've just remembered Pucken said Lily would probably have her calf to-night," said Daphne. "Oh Cedric, do you think anyone would notice very much if we drove back to see? I do *adore* new calves."

"I should think they'd notice like anything," said young Mr. Bond, "but we may as well be hanged for a calf as a lamb. Come on. Cameron, you can make some excuses, can't you."

He swept Daphne away, leaving Mr. Cameron with his shattered romance and much happier than he had been since the dreadful day among the pea-sticks. He went back to the dining-room and took a pleasant part in the conversation, though occasionally embarrassed by the looks of complicity that Lord Bond cast in his direction. When the men joined the ladies Mr. Cameron mentioned to Miss Starter, who would, he thought, spread the news as well as anyone else, that Daphne and young Mr. Bond had gone over to Laverings to enquire about a calf.

"A good thing too," said Miss Starter, eyeing Mr. Cameron in a way that made him jump, so clearly did it tell him that she knew exactly what was going on.

But apparently no one else did, and on such an Agricultural evening it seemed perfectly natural that two of the party should drive five miles each way on a rainy night to make enquiries after a cow.

The Leslies, who were the first to leave, offered to drop Mrs. Stonor and Denis at the White House, an offer they gladly accepted, as the Middletons showed no sign of moving. Lord Bond, who had immensely enjoyed being host at so pleasant a gathering, came to see them off.

"One minute," he said, detaining Denis. "Can you come up and see me to-morrow morning? Come when your sister comes. We'll have a little talk about music. Don't forget."

Denis, pleased to give pleasure, and feeling that anything would be better than being at home, where Lilian's keen sense would detect that he was troubled, said he would certainly come up, and so went off with his stepmother and the Leslies.

When the Laverings party got back Mr. Cameron, who had controlled himself heroically all the evening, said he would just see if Daphne had come home, and went across to the White House. Mrs. Stonor and Denis were in the drawing-room and almost at the same moment Daphne burst in, followed by young Mr. Bond.

"Lilian darling," she shrieked, hugging her stepmother violently, "it's a divine calf and I'm engaged to Cedric. Oh Denis," she continued, hurling herself at her brother, "isn't it heavenly. Pucken says it's the nicest little heifer calf he ever saw and he's going to call it Daphne if Uncle Jack doesn't mind."

There was a perfect welter of joyful congratulations, much better ones, Mr. Cameron sardonically reflected, than his ill-starred news had produced.

"Well, I must get back," said young Mr. Bond. "I suppose you'll be coming up to-morrow, Daphne, as usual. I'll come and fetch you. You have kissed everyone except me to-night, Daphne. It's unreasonable."

Daphne checked a gigantic yawn, kissed everyone with great impartiality, including her betrothed, and fled upstairs to bed.

"Do I have to ask any one's permission?" said young Mr. Bond.

"Technically, no," said Denis, "as Daphne is twenty-one and no one has ever attempted to control her. But Lilian and I, unofficially, are enchanted, and if she shows any signs of backing out, rely on us to bring her up to the scratch."

Young Mr. Bond thanked them cordially and went away.

"Is it all right, Alister?" said Denis, looking over the stairs on his way up to bed.

"I've not felt so happy since I can't think when," said Mr. Cameron.

"Good," said Denis, disappearing.

"Good-night," said Mr. Cameron to Mrs. Stonor.

"Is it really all right?" she asked.

"Really. And more than ever right if you will forgive me for anything and everything," said Mr. Cameron.

"If you are really content, that is perfect," said Mrs. Stonor, giving him her hand.

He went back to Laverings, and Mrs. Stonor remained quite still till she had heard both the garden gates click.

After midnight the wind fell, the clouds shredded and melted, the stars were seen again. In the hush after the storm, in the grey hours before the summer dawn, Mrs. Middleton was able to tell herself how glad she was that she had had no further opportunity of speech with Denis that evening. Denis waking again and again in panic from nightmare dreams was able to point out to himself, with all the coolness and detachment suitable to the hour, how it was really for the best that he had been unable to exchange so much as a look with Mrs. Middleton during the dinner party. Nothing could have been more calming and satisfactory for both of them.

❧ 12 ❧

BEFORE LUNCH

❧

ON THE FOLLOWING MORNING LORD AND LADY BOND AND MISS
Starter were seated at breakfast. Sunshine flooded the room.
Outside the gardeners were busily removing every twig and
leaf brought down by the storm and raking over the gravel
sweep. Young Mr. Bond was not there and his mother con-
cluded that he was still asleep.

"I must tell you a very interesting thing, Lucasta," said
Miss Starter. "Last night I actually took some melted butter
and a piece of toast; not my own toast, but ordinary toast. I
was so much interested in your brother's conversation that I
quite forgot about myself for once. And the extraordinary
thing is that I have felt no bad effects at all."

"I always told you you imagined a lot of your complaints,
Juliana," said Lady Bond, who was rapidly going through
her correspondence.

"You have such a wonderful constitution that you don't
understand suffering as I do," said Miss Starter, which was
most provoking of her, for however well people may be

themselves they like to think that they are more sensitive than their neighbours. "And another really most extraordinary thing that has just, only just occurred to me is that I ate some ice pudding, which every doctor I have been to says is Poison for me."

"Sounds like faith healing, or Christian Science or something of the sort," said Lord Bond. "Glad to hear it, Juliana. I hope we'll see you eating a leg of mutton before you leave."

"I fear not," said Miss Starter reprovingly. "One can do much when mentally distracted—I do not mean deranged, merely entertained or amused—that one cannot do under ordinary conditions. The whole flow of the bile is affected."

"We must get Stoke over again then while you're here," said Lord Bond. "You ought to try a pinch of bicarbonate, Juliana. Never known it fail."

"When I leave you on Thursday," said Miss Starter, speaking very pointedly to her hostess, "I shall go to my doctor at once and tell him what happened here. He will be immensely interested."

"Spencer," said Lady Bond, "remind me that I shall have a number of letters for the afternoon post. It's important."

"Very well, my lady," said Spencer.

Presently Miss Starter went to her room to write letters, a Victorian accomplishment which she had never lost, driving the housemaids mad wherever she went, as they had to have her bedroom tidied and cleared far earlier than they thought suitable. Lord and Lady Bond discussed some plans and congratulated each other on the party. Lady Bond then expressed some dissatisfaction at her son's late hours.

"I think C.W. had breakfast more than an hour ago, my dear," said Lord Bond. "I saw him going off in his car while I was shaving."

"He might have said good-bye," said his unsuspicious mother.

"I don't think he has gone to London," said Lord Bond. "Only to Skeynes."

"What would he want to go to Skeynes for?" said Lady Bond in an annihilating way, and gathering up her letters she went to her sitting-room, where, to her surprise and annoyance, her husband followed her and began fidgeting with the books on a table till she could hardly bear it.

"Do you want anything, Alured?" she asked.

"No," said Lord Bond. "No," he added thoughtfully, looking out of the window, "no. Not exactly. There's C.W."

"Then I suppose we shall know why he went to Skeynes," said Lady Bond, seating herself at her desk and opening her engagement book. "Could we dine with the Leslies at Rushwater on Friday week, Alured? Lady Emily sent a message over by John last night. Well, C.W., you were up very early. Good morning, Daphne. Did you bicycle?"

"Good morning, Mother," said young Mr. Bond, kissing the side of his mother's forehead. "I brought Daphne over, because we are engaged and I thought you'd like to know."

Lady Bond behaved very well, merely asking her son to say again what he had just said.

"We got engaged last night," said young Mr. Bond. "You must have seen it coming, Mother. So I thought I'd better bring Daphne over this morning and I brought Denis too, Father, because he said you wanted to see him about something. He is in the drawing-room because you said something about music."

"Quite right, my boy," said Lord Bond. "I'll go to him in a minute. Well, Daphne my dear, I'm just as pleased about it this morning as I was last night. And so will my wife be."

"Do you mean to say you knew last night, Alured?" said Lady Bond.

"I couldn't help telling father," said young Mr. Bond, now joyfully reckless of all consequences, "because he saw us when he came to look for the Marie Antoinette musical box."

"I don't understand this at all," said Lady Bond.

"Well, I'm awfully sorry, but Cedric and I got engaged last night," said Daphne.

In Lady Bond's rather slow-moving mind a struggle was going on between her natural tendency to disapprove of everything which she had not originated herself and a real wish to show pleasure in her son's choice, even if it were not quite her own. She also would much have liked to relieve her feelings by bullying her husband for his complicity. The result was that she remained completely silent and everyone felt uncomfortable, none more so than Lord Bond, when a distraction was mercifully offered by the sound, too rare alas, of horses' hoofs on the gravel.

"Good God," said Lord Bond, who was still at the window. "It's Pomfret and young Wicklow. Wonderful the way Pomfret goes on riding. Over eighty and I've hardly ever seen him in a car in his own part of the country. I wonder what he wants. If it's the Barsetshire Benevolent

Association I suppose I'll have to be steward again, though fifty guineas is pretty stiff."

Daphne and young Mr. Bond did not know whether to stay or to slink from the room, but before they could decide Lord Pomfret was announced and came in followed by his agent Roddy Wicklow, whose sister Sally had married Lord Pomfret's heir.

"It is very nice to see you so early, Lord Pomfret," said Lady Bond getting up.

Lord Pomfret shook hands with Lord and Lady Bond and nodded to young Mr. Bond.

"You know Wicklow," he said. "Just got engaged to Barton's daughter Alice. Nice girl she is. Come on a lot lately."

"Good luck, Wicklow," said young Mr. Bond, seeing a good opportunity to consolidate his position. "I've just got engaged too," he added, taking Daphne's hand.

"That's right," said Lord Pomfret. "Young man like you, coming into a nice little place, can't get engaged too soon. Keep you steady. Congratulations, young lady. What's your name, eh?"

"Daphne Stonor," said Daphne, a little overawed by Lord Pomfret's impressive size, his bald head, his bushy eyebrows and his fierce little eyes.

"Any relation of Stonor of the twenty-third?" said Lord Pomfret.

"He was my father," said Daphne.

"My boy was in the twenty-third," said Lord Pomfret, alluding to his only son Lord Mellings who had been killed as a young man in a frontier skirmish. "Good regiment. Glad to have met you, young lady. Now, Bond, I daresay you want to know why I've come. I was riding round with Wicklow to look at that drain where the vixen got drowned last February, and I thought I'd look in to say I've settled Hibberd for good."

"Do you mean he won't build on Pooker's Piece?" said Lord Bond.

"Wait a minute. Let me tell it my own way," said Lord Pomfret, glaring at everyone. "No, I won't sit down. Sit quite enough as it is. I met Hibberd yesterday afternoon in Barchester at the County Club. Can't think how the feller got in, but they have anyone nowadays. So I told him what I thought. Didn't mince matters. Said it would be damned uncomfortable for him in the county if he went on like that only I put it a bit more strongly."

"Then what will he do with Pooker's Piece?" said Lady Bond.

"Won't do anything," said Lord Pomfret with a bellicose chuckle. "I bought it. He said he'd take a hundred more for it than he gave. No, no, I said, that won't do. No profiteering. I'll give what you gave, or you can take the consequences. I frightened him, I think," said his lordship meditatively.

"Well, that's very public-spirited of you, Pomfret," said Lord Bond. "We are all extremely grateful. Have you decided what to do with it? It's rather far from your property."

"Now don't think you or Palmer are going to get it," said Lord Pomfret. "Too old a bird to be caught by that sort of chaff. No, I'm going to make it over to the National Trust or one of these damned meddling affairs, to be kept as it is, in memory of my wife. Children can play there and that sort of thing. Edith would have liked it."

There was a moment's silence, for everyone knew that Lord Pomfret missed his countess more than he would allow. Then Lord and Lady Bond congratulated and thanked him again warmly.

"I'm going on to tell Middleton," said Lord Pomfret. "Bit of a gas-bag, that feller, but I like his wife. Well, good-bye. Good-bye, young lady. This place needs a few children about. Brighten things up."

"Thanks awfully, Lord Pomfret," said Daphne. "I mean to have about six."

"Do you really think so many, Daphne?" said young Mr. Bond, slightly alarmed by this access of maternity.

"Young lady's quite right," barked Lord Pomfret, "and don't you meddle with her, young man. She knows her own business."

Upon which he went away, followed by his silent and devoted agent and accompanied by Lord Bond.

During the interruption Lady Bond had managed to get her feelings under control and was quite ready to accept and embrace Daphne, but the thought of victory was still uppermost in her mind and she had to express it before yielding to the softer emotions.

"Lord Pomfret has done the county a great service," she said impressively. "It will be a great weight off everyone's mind."

"Then now we needn't send the invitations to the Public

Meeting," said Daphne. "I'll tear them up. Where are they, Lady Bond? I thought I left them on your desk, to go this afternoon."

"Are you sure you didn't put them in a drawer?" said Lady Bond.

"Quite. They couldn't have got posted, could they?"

"I gave Spencer special orders that they were to go by the afternoon post," said Lady Bond.

"Then I bet he's sent them by the morning post," said Daphne. "Shall I ring?"

Without waiting for an answer she rang with a violence that set every bell in the basement jarring and made the third footman rush to Spencer's pantry without putting his coat on to say that her ladyship's sitting-room was ringing like mad. Spencer crushed his underling and proceeded at his own pace to Lady Bond's room.

"I say, Spencer," said Daphne, "did you post those letters?"

"What letters, miss?" said Spencer.

"I particularly said I wanted my letters to go by the afternoon post," said Lady Bond, "and I can't find them anywhere."

"I understood your ladyship to say that the letters was to go particularly by the afternoon post," said Spencer, "and as one of the men was going down to Skeynes on his bike I thought I would take advantage of the event to give him the letters. They will catch the twelve o'clock post, my lady, and be delivered earlier than by the afternoon post."

"It is most vexatious," said Lady Bond.

"Yes, my lady," said Spencer. "Was that all, my lady?"

"No, it wasn't," said Daphne, roused to indignation on her future mother-in-law's behalf. "It was frightfully interfering of you, Spencer, when Lady Bond said the afternoon post, and it's going to make a frightful muddle and be a great nuisance to everyone and all your fault. What is the good of people telling you things if you don't listen? Don't do it again."

Of course under any other circumstance Spencer would have given notice on the spot, but Something, as he reverently said when describing the scene to Mrs. Alcock the housekeeper later on, told him that something was up between Miss Stonor and Mr. Bond and under these peculiar circumstances he felt he had better leave things be.

To everyone's intense surprise he said,

"I'm very sorry, my lady, very sorry indeed, miss. It shall not occur again," and left the room.

Lady Bond gazed at Daphne with an admiration past words.

"I'll tell you what," said Daphne. "There's still time to get the letters back. It's only eleven, and we'll all look awful fools if they are posted now that Lord Pomfret has settled it all."

"But, my dear, we can't," said Lady Bond piteously. "They are in the post now."

"Miss Phipps will get them out if I ask her," said Daphne negligently. "Look here, Cedric, you run me down at once and we'll rescue them before the twelve o'clock collection. Would you like to come?" she added kindly to Lady Bond. "I'm afraid you'll have to hurry."

Luckily Lady Bond kept a felt hat and some gloves in the

hall against sudden incursions into the garden and in two minutes young Mr. Bond was driving much too fast down the drive, with Daphne and Lady Bond in the back seat.

"Don't go right up to the Post Office," said Daphne, poking her affianced in the back. "Miss Phipps mightn't like it if it was you. I'll go in."

So young Mr. Bond drew up in front of the Fleece and Daphne went over to the Post Office. Opening the door of the little cottage, she walked into the office and said good morning.

"Good morning, miss," said Miss Phipps. "I'm sorry I haven't got those peppermint bull's eyes in yet, but I'm expecting them at every minute."

"That's all right," said Daphne. "I'll come in again. Oh, and that idiot from Staple Park posted a whole lot of letters I'd written for Lady Bond by mistake. Be an angel and let me have them out or I'll get into frightful trouble. They're all typewritten, with the crown thing on the flap, so they'll be quite easy to find."

"Well, miss, I really oughtn't," said Miss Phipps.

"Of course you oughtn't," said Daphne. "But you'll save me a frightful blowing up from Lady Bond if you do. Let's have a look." •

Very obligingly Miss Phipps emptied the contents of the mail bag onto the counter. Daphne sorted out the invitations with no difficulty.

"Thanks awfully, Miss Phipps," she said. "You're an angel. And if you hear something about me in a day or two, don't be surprised. I'll come in for the peppermints later."

She ran back to the car with her treasure. Miss Phipps, also guided by a Something, followed her to the door and looked out. What she saw evidently satisfied her, for she remarked aloud to herself, "And a very nice young lady-ship too," and went back to her Post Office, where she served her next customers with such scorn, born of a secret knowledge which she had no intention of using except to mystify and tantalise her clients, that several of them said she was on her high horse again.

"Here you are, Lady Bond," said Daphne, putting the pile of letters on the back seat and getting in beside young Mr. Bond.

"I can't thank you enough, my dear," said Lady Bond. "Kiss me."

Daphne turned round in the seat and leaning into the back of the car gave Lady Bond a very hearty hug.

"I'm afraid," she said, "I had to make you out a bit of a Tartar to Miss Phipps. I hope you don't mind."

"I daresay I deserved it," said Lady Bond magnani-mously. "And now, my dear, I think we will go on to the White House. I would like to tell your stepmother how delighted Lord Bond and I am, and we can discuss the date for the wedding. I suppose you and C.W. will want to get married before he goes back to New York."

As the millennium appeared to have arrived Daphne and young Mr. Bond accepted the miracle gratefully and the car's head was turned towards the Laverings Lane.

MR. AND MRS. MIDDLETON and Mr. Cameron had also breakfasted very comfortably in the sunny dining-room.

Mr. Cameron had decided to tell his host and hostess about his lucky release when breakfast was over, but he could not conceal a happiness which came as a relief to Mrs. Middleton after all the gloom of the last fortnight, though she could not quite account for it. When breakfast was over they went out onto the terrace, where the form of Pucken, who had been hanging about to catch them, presently became manifest.

"Well, Pucken, did you get that manure?" said Mr. Middleton.

Pucken said he thought he'd got her all right and a lovely load she was, and then stood twirling his hat in his hands. Mrs. Middleton, understanding that he had something else to say, asked after Lily. With a broad grin Pucken said she had a fine little heifer calf.

"And I never knew!" cried Mr. Middleton. "This event upon which all my thoughts, my hopes have been centred, has come and gone, and this is the first I hear of it."

"Well, darling, if it only happened last night you could hardly have heard sooner," said his wife. "Besides you do remember, don't you, that Daphne and Mr. Bond left the party early last night to see how Lily was, so you must have known that something was happening, and really you are practically the first person to know."

"Practically!" said Mr. Middleton bitterly. "However, we must now find a name for this newcomer. Have you any suggestion, Cameron?"

"Beyond Epistemological Ideology, none," said Mr. Cameron, rather bored with cows and wanting to get on to his own news.

"Miss Daphne she wants to call her Miss Daphne," said Pucken, "but I said to my old woman this morning, Miss Daphne is a pretty name for a heifer, but Mrs. Bond would be better. My old woman she told me to hold my tongue, but I've eyes in my head as well as another I said to her, and you mark my word, I said—"

"That will do, Pucken," said Mrs. Middleton. "Daphne will be a very nice name for the calf and now you might stake those dahlias."

Pucken went off, chuckling at his own wit, and Mrs. Middleton looked at Mr. Cameron.

"It happened last night," he said guiltily, "but when I got back from the White House you had gone to bed. I was going to tell you now, when Pucken came pushing in. I think Daphne and Bond will be very happy and to be perfectly frank I'm very happy myself. Daphne couldn't have been nicer about it nor could Bond and we are all safely out of a foolish mistake, which was really a great deal my fault."

Mrs. Middleton expressed her pleasure with a warmth that Mr. Cameron again mentally compared with her lukewarm congratulations over his engagement. Mr. Cameron, who had seen young Mr. Bond driving off with Daphne and Denis a little earlier, said he thought he would go for a walk, and sauntered elaborately down the garden and into the field.

"I am very glad that engagement is over," said Mr. Middleton. "Daphne was much too young. Someone like Lilian would be much more suitable for Cameron."

"I think so too," said Mrs. Middleton.

The morning passed on. Mr. Cameron did not come back from his walk and Mr. Middleton read the Journal of the R.I.B.A. in the sun. Mrs. Middleton drove down to the village to get some more stuff to spray the green fly and then cut roses for the house, talking to him as she came in and out of the library window. A little after half-past eleven the sound of hoofs made them both look up and in the lane they saw Lord Pomfret and his agent.

"This is very nice to see you," said Mrs. Middleton over the gate. "Will you come in?"

"No thanks," said Lord Pomfret. "Got to get back. Morning Middleton. I just stopped to tell you that you needn't worry about Pooker's Piece. I'm buying it from Hibberd. Thought you'd like to know. That's the end of him. No more meetings. Well, I must be moving."

Touching his hat he rode off, followed by the silent and devoted Roddy Wicklow.

"What a relief," said Mrs. Middleton. "It was all such a muddle, and I'm sure Sir Ogilvy would have won. Now you can walk over Pooker's Piece quite happily for the rest of your life."

"I know one person who will rejoice even as I do," said Mr. Middleton.

"Lots, I should think," said his wife, "but who specially?"

Mr. Middleton pointed to Flora, who was lying half asleep on the hot flags. A fly passed too near her and she twitched angrily.

"My doggie knows, even in her sleep," said Mr. Middleton, making a statement for which there was not the slightest foundation. "She knows that Pooker's Piece is free for her to run in with Master, that Sir Ogilvy has retreated, leaving us our unsullied English countryside, that—"

His voice suddenly died away. The look of panic that Mrs. Middleton knew so well suddenly invaded his face and dissolved its apparently firm lines as if a sponge had been passed over it.

"What is it, Jack?" she said.

"Fool that I am," said Mr. Middleton, hitting himself not too hard, "fool, fool."

"Yes, darling, but how?" said Mrs. Middleton.

"I wrote to Hibberd last night," he groaned. "With all the force that is in me, all the passionate love of England which is the one thing that my worst enemy cannot deny, I wrote to him. I made it clear that I would be grievously offended by what he proposed to do, that it would be a blow aimed against ME. I humbled myself, Catherine; proud though I am I abased myself to that man, and now Pomfret has in his usual high-handed way taken the very ground from under my feet. I shall be a laughing-stock."

"When was it posted?" Mrs. Middleton asked.

"What do I know of posts?" Mr. Middleton groaned. "I wrote it last night when you, Catherine, were I hope asleep. I left it on the hall table with the other letters, including one, as I remember, to the Army and Navy Stores about Pollett's uniform."

"Then the postman would have fetched them when he brought the morning post," said Mrs. Middleton, "and they would go by the twelve o'clock delivery. I think we can save it. It's lucky I didn't put the car away."

Before her husband could ask her more than twice where

she was going, she had driven off towards Skeynes, leaving him with a bitter sense of desolation which he expressed in vehement language to the uninterested Flora. As Mrs. Middleton stopped outside the Post Office the church clock struck eleven which meant twelve, owing to Summer Time. An attempt had been made a good many years previously to alter the clock, but its works so deeply resented being put on an hour in spring and even more being put on eleven hours in autumn (for to put it back an hour was found to be a mechanical impossibility) that it had been found better to leave it to itself. Mrs. Middleton clicked the latch of the Post Office door and went in.

"Good morning, Miss Phipps," she said. "Mr. Middleton has posted a letter he didn't mean to post, as usual. Do you think I could get it back?"

"There now, if you aren't in luck, Mrs. Middleton," said Miss Phipps. "I ought by rights to have had the bag ready, but I was doing a bit of ironing, so I told the postman to call back in ten minutes. It was an organdie blouse for my niece to wear to go to the cinema at Winter Overcotes with her young man and she wanted to get the ten-past-twelve bus, and I'd just got the iron nice and hot, so I said 'You'll burn it if you do it, Gladys,' for she never thinks what she's doing. 'Let auntie do it,' I said, so I've just finished it as you come in. Here's the bag."

For the second time that day Miss Phipps generously poured out the letters on the counter. Mrs. Middleton saw her husband's letter to Sir Ogilvy Hibberd, took it and thanked Miss Phipps.

"I hear we may expect some joyful news about Miss

Daphne before long," said Miss Phipps, suddenly becoming extremely genteel.

"Well, I don't know anything official," said Mrs. Middleton and escaped before Miss Phipps could begin asking questions. She did wonder a little how Miss Phipps came to suspect what was, as far as she knew, only known to the immediate family and Pucken, but the subject did not hold her mind long. No subject could hold her mind very long from its anxious avoidance of one thought. She remembered a message for the President of the Women's Institute, an excellent creature who lived three miles out of Skeynes, and with a faint and affectionate vindictiveness towards her husband for giving so much trouble she decided to go round that way before lunch.

MR. CAMERON, having walked down to the field in a way that certainly did not deceive Mrs. Middleton, took the footpath that led back to the garden of the White House, passed the pea-sticks without a tremor, and came to the little stream, where Mrs. Stonor was grubbing about with rock plants. She looked up anxiously when she saw him, half afraid that he might have been exaggerating his relief the night before and be now contemplating suicide. But he asked after Daphne in such a cheerful voice that she felt her fears to be groundless.

"Daphne is very well," she said. "All the excitement seems to have cured her cold and Cedric took her and Denis to Staple Park about half an hour ago. I must tell you, Alister, because it is rather funny and I hope you won't think it brutal, how she celebrated her engagement to Cedric, which was by throwing all her photographs of her men friends, which is a dreadful expression but what else can one say, into the waste paper basket. I thought it rather heartless, but after all what *can* one do with photographs and snapshots that do clutter up the house so? I found her waste paper basket in the kitchen, so I just looked to see what it all was and that snapshot she had of you wasn't there, so I expect it is the only one she kept, which is in a way rather touching."

Mr. Cameron thought he had never heard anyone talk such delicious nonsense and said he had come to say he was going back to town that afternoon and wasn't likely to be down again for the present, as they were going to be very busy at the office and he would probably be spending his weekends at Oxbridge. On hearing this Mrs. Stonor poked a small plant very viciously into a hole and forced the earth down round its roots till it nearly screamed. Mr. Cameron, rather frightened by her determination and her silence, went on talking about the office and the new college and various plans in a very blithering kind of way, not quite knowing what he was saying.

"Do you *ever* talk about anything but yourself?" said Mrs. Stonor in a pause, pulling up one or two small weeds as she spoke. "You and Jack are just the same. I wonder how Catherine and I can stand it."

"I am sorry," said Mr. Cameron, abashed.

"Of course Catherine is very fond of Jack," said Mrs. Stonor, "which makes a difference."

"Well, I am very fond of you, if that makes any difference," said Mr. Cameron. "I know I've no right to say so after the way I've behaved, but as I'm going away to-day it doesn't much matter, and I am going to say it. I am very fond of you. In fact I love you quite dreadfully. I won't say it again, but I must say it this once, I absolutely adore you and if I thought there were the faintest hope of your considering marrying me I'd ask you at once, but as there isn't, will you forgive me and let me go on being a friend. Only I shan't be able to help loving you. Damn it all, Lilian, everything I say sounds quite idiotic and like people in books, but I do mean it and you can't help my wanting to give you everything I have to give even if you don't want to take it. Good-bye."

He put out his hand. Mrs. Stonor looked up from where she was kneeling on the edge of the little stream.

"I was thinking of Denis," she said, ignoring Mr. Cameron's farewell gesture.

Mr. Cameron felt so strongly that stepsons were not suitable subjects for the thoughts of people to whom one was offering one's whole heart, that he could have killed Mrs. Stonor on the spot, loving her as he did.

"You see," said Mrs. Stonor, looking up very seriously at her admirer, "I have really brought Denis up by hand, as you might say, and I do feel responsible for him. He gets on very well with me and it would be quite dreadful for him if suddenly he had no home. He is so much better this summer that it is really very encouraging, but I couldn't bear him to feel that he was being turned out, and you know what lodgings are. Of course he might be lucky and some landladies are very kind, but one never knows. If we could perhaps wait for a little. I don't mean to be grasping, and of course one can't have one's cake and eat it, but do you think that would be possible?"

"You mean," said Mr. Cameron, thinking very hard over his beloved's rather jumbled speech, "that if it weren't for Denis you wouldn't mind marrying me?"

Mrs. Stonor looked up with swimming eyes.

"*Don't*," said Mr. Cameron.

"Very well," said Mrs. Stonor and did her best not to.

"Denis could quite well live with us," said Mr. Cameron, "and I'd like it. I like Denis very much indeed."

"It wouldn't do," said Mrs. Stonor decidedly. "It is silly enough for me to be his stepmother considering how old he is, but you would be a step-stepfather, if there is such a thing, and I don't think it would work. Besides, he is apt to play the piano a good deal."

"Look here. Will you marry me?" said Mr. Cameron.

"Of course," said Mrs. Stonor patiently. "That's what I've been saying for ages, but you don't seem to understand. Only I must think of Denis."

"There is Denis," said Mr. Cameron, looking up the little garden as he heard the gate click. "Now we'll settle this thing at once. I won't be thrown into the waste paper basket twice in one day. Denis!" he called.

WHEN Lord Bond had seen Lord Pomfret off, he went to the drawing-room, where Denis was waiting his pleasure. But instead of asking him, as he had expected, to play him something from the *Mikado*, Lord Bond had enlarged upon the pleasure he felt in having Daphne for a daughter-in-law, till Denis glowed with pleasure at hearing his dear

Daphne so well appreciated.

"And now there's one more thing," said Lord Bond, walking up and down. "You've given me a lot of pleasure, Denis. You've played me all the old tunes I like, and I know you young people like something more up to date. Now, about this ballet of yours. From what I hear what is wanted is a backer."

"Yes, sir," said Denis.

"Well, I believe in you, and I am willing to put up something," said Lord Bond, naming a sum that Denis had come to look upon as impossible. "Mind you, it's business. I shan't expect to see any of it back, but there have got to be accounts. If I lose money I like to know exactly how. And if your ballet pays, then I shall get some interest. Now don't thank me, because I like to do it."

"I hardly know how to thank you, sir," said Denis. "How did you guess what we wanted?"

To Denis's incredulous joy Lord Bond said that a little bird had told him how much money was needed. He longed for Lilian to be there and share his pleasure in actually hearing those words said.

"You'd better go to town as soon as possible," said Lord Bond, "and see my lawyer. I'll write to him about it to-day."

"There's only one thing," said Denis, "my stepmother. You see the ballet people are in Manchester now and it would mean living up there for a time. Lilian will be losing Daphne and I don't quite like to think of her alone. I have always looked after her since my father died—at least we have looked after each other."

Lord Bond very kindly said that Denis was quite right

to think of his stepmother, but she was a sensible kind of woman and would see that a young man couldn't always live at home. Denis finally said that he would consult her and at any rate go up to town and see Lord Bond's lawyer at once. He tried again to express his thanks, but was silenced by his kindly host, who ordered the little car to take him home. The drive to Laverings was not long enough to give Denis much time for consideration. The anxious avoidance of one thought was always uppermost in his mind. To go to London, then to Manchester would perhaps be flight, but it would be quite worth while being a coward oneself if it would make life easier for anyone else. Then he thought he was perhaps being a little conceited to imagine that his presence or absence might affect anyone. But his heart told him quite fatally that there was no conceit about it; merely a statement of fact and a fact that needed facing.

He thanked Lord Bond's chauffeur and went in at the garden gate. Mr. Cameron's call reached him and he went down to the little stream. If he had been feeling less peculiar himself he would have noticed that his stepmother and Mr. Cameron were looking a little peculiar themselves, but between excitement and the foreboding of grief his usual sensitiveness to atmospheres was rather dulled.

Mrs. Stonor in whom no amount of emotion could dull her perception of what was happening to one of her nurslings asked Denis if anything had happened. He said it had, but he hardly knew where to begin.

"I really don't know where to begin either," said Mrs. Stonor.

Mr. Cameron began to behave like a man, but was at once squashed by Mrs. Stonor, who begged with the utmost firmness to be allowed to explain things in her own way. On hearing this Mr. Cameron sat down on a dry stone and lit a cigarette, ready to bear with the utmost possible patience his beloved's serpentine methods.

"Of course Daphne getting married will mean that you and I will only be two instead of three," said Mrs. Stonor to Denis. "Of course if you ever *wanted* to be a bachelor, I mean technically a bachelor, at least you know what I mean, and live in lodgings where I am *sure* the landlady would neglect you, you mustn't worry about me, because I can always manage very well. Only you must consider that our two incomes separately aren't as much as they are together, not on my account, I mean, but you would be surprised how expensive housekeeping is when you are on your own, so please do consider very carefully, because I'd love to have you to live with me always but not if you felt you couldn't bear someone else in the house."

Mr. Cameron knew that he would burst soon, but managed to control himself.

"Darling," said Denis, pulling up a few long grasses and plaiting them together, "heaven knows I don't want to leave you, because nothing can be nicer and more spoiling than being with you, but after all I have to do something some day. You know I'm much better what with all this hot weather and the fresh milk and that damned cock that wakes me at three every morning, and I really ought to be up and doing. Only I'd much rather do nothing for the rest of my life than desert you: it sounds rather gigolo but you know what I mean. If you happened to get a bit sick of me I could manage quite well on my own; but as long as you like to have a man about the house, count on me."

"I really think, Denis, you ought to know—" Mr. Cameron began.

"No, Alister," said Mrs. Stonor. "Denis is my stepson, not yours. Well, darling," she went on, "nothing on earth could induce me to get sick of you and I do like a man about the house, so let's just leave things as they are for the present, shall we?"

"But Lilian—" Mr. Cameron protested.

"Very well," said Denis, trying hard not to feel a dull disappointment, "if you really like having me and I am any kind of help, we'll leave things as they are, just as you say."

"Then we'd better go in. It will be lunch-time soon," said Mrs. Stonor, annoyed with herself for feeling so unhappy. "Will you stop to lunch, Alister?"

Mr. Cameron wanted to say No and walk off into the infinite, but he couldn't. So he said Yes and followed Lilian and Denis to the house. And no sooner had they reached it than Lady Bond and young Mr. Bond and Daphne came in, all of them radiant, Lady Bond's majestic felt hat for once a little crooked after Daphne's daughterly hug.

"I can only hope, Mrs. Stonor," said Lady Bond, advancing upon her hostess, "that you are as pleased as I am. C.W. couldn't have chosen better and I hope you will let them be married before he goes back to New York."

"And we are going on the *Normandie*, first class!" said Daphne. "And I could get a lot of clothes in New York. Oh, Lilian darling, do say yes."

"It wouldn't do any good if I said no," said Mrs. Stonor to Lady Bond, "so certainly I say yes. And thank you so much for being pleased. And Lord Bond has always been so very kind to Denis. It couldn't be nicer."

"So Denis has told you, has he?" said Lady Bond. "My husband mentioned it to me last night and I quite agreed with him that it would be an excellent thing. Denis has given my husband a great deal of pleasure this summer, when I'm sure he would really much rather have been playing jazz. Bond told me what a delightful evening you had when I was away."

After this kind speech Denis did not like to protest against Lady Bond's conception of his character as a jazz fiend.

"Told me what?" said Mrs. Stonor.

"I hadn't mentioned it, darling, because of not wishing to seem ungrateful if you needed me," said Denis, "but Lord Bond did most nobly offer this morning to put up the money for the ballet, and that would mean living in Manchester for a bit. But if you'd rather not I can quite well, without being a bit noble about it, go on as I am."

"But I'd like you to go more than anything in the world," said Mrs. Stonor, in a voice that carried no reservations at all. "It's the best news I could possibly have. We'll have a talk about it. How very, very kind of your husband, Lady Bond."

Lady Bond said graciously that they looked upon Denis as one of the family now and she must be getting back to lunch.

"Thanks most awfully, Mrs. Stonor," said young Mr.

Bond. "It's ripping of you. And could Daphne come back to lunch?"

"Of course," said Mrs. Stonor, mildly surprised that any-one should ask her permission. "I suppose I ought to kiss you, Cedric, but it seems so unusual."

"That's all right," said young Mr. Bond and taking her hand he kissed it quite naturally, a gesture that left Daphne speechless with admiration.

"Well, mother-in-law," said young Mr. Bond very imper-tinently to his mother, "come along."

But as they went into the hall such a dreadful noise of unrestrained crying from the kitchen smote upon their ears that Mrs. Stonor, with an apology, went to the kitchen door, followed by Lady Bond, who had a lively curiosity about domestic affairs. An informal court of justice was being held by Mrs. Pucken and Palfrey, with Lou, her face swollen with tears, in the dock.

"What *is* the matter?" said Mrs. Stonor.

Palfrey said she shouldn't wish to say.

"Well, Sarah, what is it?" said Lady Bond to her ex-kitchenmaid.

Mrs. Pucken, at once recognising and reacting to the voice of authority, said it was quite shocking the way girls carried on nowadays. As good as stealing , she called it, and her own daughter, called after her ladyship and all.

"Ah yes, that is Lou, isn't it," said Lady Bond. "What has she been doing?"

"I didn't steal it," blubbered Lou. "Miss Daphne threw it in the waste paper basket and I didn't think there was no harm in taking it."

"Taking what?" said Lady Bond.

"Mr. Cameron's photo that Miss Daphne threw in the waste paper basket, my lady," said Mrs. Pucken. "When a young lady gets engaged she does quite the right thing to throw away the photos of the other gentlemen. And what does my lady do," she continued, pointing at her unhappy daughter, "but pick Mr. Cameron's photo out and had it down the front of her dress of all places. Nice goings on. And it fell out of her when she was washing the scullery floor and that's what all the noise is about, because I threw it on the kitchen fire. I'm reely very sorry, Mrs. Stonor, all this disturbance with Miss Daphne just engaged and the joint in the oven. Lou can't come up here no more, not if she can't behave."

"And how did you know about Miss Daphne?" said Mrs. Stonor.

"Pucken he was up with Lily last night," said Mrs. Pucken, "and Mr. Bond and Miss Daphne they came to see the calf and Pucken said anyone with half an eye in his head could see what was up. I gave Pucken a piece of my mind, talking like that, but I'm sure I wish them joy."

"A big girl like Lou ought to be in proper service," said Lady Bond. "I shall need a vegetable maid next month. Tell Lou to wash her face and go up and see Mrs. Alcock this afternoon, Sarah. And tell Pucken not to talk so much."

Lady Bond retreated feudally from the kitchen, leaving Lou to receive all the good advice and terrifying prognostications that her mother and Palfrey could give. She did not stop crying, it is true, but her tears and yells gradually passed from sheer despair to an expression of pleasurable

anticipation about Staple Park, where she would no longer
be under her mother's domination. Young Mr. Bond drove
his mother and Daphne off to Staple Park, so that they
wouldn't be late for lunch.

"I didn't know you were Clark Gable," said Denis, who
together with the rest of the party had been a fascinated
spectator of the scene in the kitchen, to Mr. Cameron.

"Poor Lou!" said Mrs. Stonor.

Something in her voice made her stepson look at her
piercingly.

"I'm so pleased about the ballet," said Mrs. Stonor. "And
I'm sure it will be the greatest success and I'll come to your
first night. And if you are really going to Manchester it
will be in a way most convenient, because it sounds rather
stupid that Alister was engaged to Daphne and of course I
was really delighted about it if I thought either of them
would have been happy, which they obviously wouldn't, so
probably things are much better as they are and you will
always, always come to us when you are in London, won't
you, darling?"

"I suppose—" said Denis hesitatingly.

"Yes," said Mr. Cameron. "Lilian, I *will* speak. Your
stepmother, Denis, has forgiven me for being the most blithering ass that ever was. I can't explain to you how the muddle happened, but thank God it was cleared up. We shall
be married, though not in such a violent hurry as Daphne,
and if you don't object to a kind of step-father-in-law, I'll
be very, very glad."

"And if you felt like giving me away, it would be quite

perfect," said Mrs. Stonor, "unless of course Jack wanted to. He might take offence."

Denis, feeling that nothing was left remarkable beneath the visiting moon, kissed his stepmother most affectionately and said he would do anything she liked and it couldn't be nicer.

"I daresay I'll look on you as Mr. Murdstone at first," he said to Mr. Cameron, "but it will pass."

"And now Alister can stay to lunch," said Mrs. Stonor.

Mr. Cameron said he had better go and tell Mrs. Middleton that he wouldn't be back.

"I'll tell her," said Denis. "If you are going up this afternoon, Alister, will you take me with you? I've got to go and see Lord Bond's lawyer."

"Certainly," said Mr. Cameron. "Only I've got to start directly after lunch. Two o'clock too early?"

"Perfect," said Denis. "I might have lunch at Laverings to make up for your having lunch here. I'll just put some things in my suitcase and go over and tell Catherine."

He went upstairs and packed his clothes for a few nights in town. Laverings lunched later than the White House, so there would be time to go over. What with Daphne and Cedric and Lilian and Alister, not to speak of Lou's contribution, he felt a little dizzy. His own safe world had suddenly cracked under his feet. A new world was before him, thanks largely to Lord Bond, a world unknown, unsafe, difficult, but the world where he ought to be if there was anything in his music. In his musician's self he had the terrifying confidence of the artist; as for his private self he thought it would often be very homesick and lonely. And all that remained to be done now was to make his loneliness more desolate, lest a natural longing to comfort and be comforted should bring bitterness in the end to a heart that he hardly knew. He went out into the hot sunshine. In the lane he saw Mrs. Middleton, who had just put the car into the garage. She had a letter in her hand.

"I've been rescuing a letter from the Post Office," she said, falling into step with Denis and walking slowly down the lane. "One of the letters Jack repents when he has written them. I don't know what we would do without Miss Phipps."

"Alister asked me to say he wouldn't be back for lunch, if you will excuse him," said Denis. "He is going to marry Lilian. It is all rather complicated, but she will explain it to you. It seems very satisfactory to me."

"I'm so glad," said Mrs. Middleton. "I've thought so for a long time."

"I'm going up with him directly after lunch," said Denis. "Lord Bond has been extraordinarily generous. He is putting up money for my ballet. How he knew how much we need I don't quite know. Did you tell him?"

"Not exactly. I mentioned it," said Mrs. Middleton.

"You would," said Denis. "Thank you. I am going to see his lawyer and then go to Manchester, where the ballet company is working just now."

"And then back here?" said Mrs. Middleton.

"I think not at present," said Denis. "It seems better not to."

Mrs. Middleton stopped, determined, whatever darkness

and roaring of a thousand waters overwhelmed her, however the ground seemed to rock under her feet, that she would not take Denis's arm or ask him for help.

"Is that—" she began, and couldn't go on.

"Is that—" she said again, with extreme care but no more words would come from her.

Denis wondered to what point self-control could be borne, and what defence there was against the terrifying weight of silence.

"Is that," she said for the third time, speaking as if each word had to be brought with pain from some infinitely remote darkness, "for you or for me?"

"For us both, I think," said Denis, and began to walk back towards Laverings. Mrs. Middleton walked beside him, but her steps so lagged that he was afraid.

"I am pretending to Lilian," he said when they reached the gate, "that I am having lunch with you. As a matter of fact I shall go for a walk and come back when Alister is starting. I don't know what I'll do without you."

"You will do quite well; oh, very well," she said, opening the garden gate.

"And you, which is all I care about?" said Denis.

"Oh, I shall do well; quite, quite well," she said searching for each word in that darkness where she was helplessly bound.

"Good-bye," said Denis and took her hand.

She held his hand closely to her in both of hers for a moment, then turned and walked away down the flagged path without a backward glance. Denis watched her till she went in by the library window. Then he shut the gate and went down the lane into the fields. In three quarters of an hour he could start with Alister.

In the library Mrs. Middleton found her husband, his face still ravaged, what hair he had in wild disorder.

"Here is your letter, Jack," she said, handing it to him.

"Thank God, thank God," said Mr. Middleton, tearing it open and reading it. "I regret in a way that Hibberd could not have seen it. It is well expressed, Catherine, well expressed. When something has to be said, Catherine, I can always say it. Facts marshal themselves, my pen becomes a trumpet. You may remember the letter I wrote to Tolford-Spender about the restoration, rather the wanton desecration of the church at Monk's Porton; that was a letter. He was forced to admit himself in the wrong all along the line and that little gem of pure East Anglian Transitional was saved. And now Pooker's Piece is saved," said Mr. Middleton triumphantly, as though his intercepted letter to Sir Ogilvy Hibberd had been the means of its salvation.

Mrs. Middleton was still standing, for she felt that if she sat down she would never get up again. She made no answer.

"You are tired, my dear," said her husband with real concern. "You went to the Post Office in the fierce noontide heat and by your own methods, whether legal or illegal I shall not enquire, rescued my letter and saved me from eternal shame and opprobrium. You must lie down this afternoon."

He put his arm kindly round her. Mrs. Middleton rested

her head on his shoulder, thankful for support and affection.

"I don't know what I would do without you, Catherine," said he earnestly.

"Nor do I, darling," said Mrs. Middleton.

Ethel then announced lunch, with deep disapproval of the intimate attitude of her employers, so they went into the dining-room.

"We are alone?" said Mr. Middleton. "I thought Cameron was with us till the afternoon."

"I quite forgot to tell you," said Mrs. Middleton, "that in the middle of everything else he and Lilian have decided to be married, so he is having lunch at the White House."

"An excellent thing, an excellent thing," said Mr. Middleton. "Will I have to give her away?" he added with sudden terror.

"Not if you don't like, Jack," said his wife. "Denis could always do it. Lord Bond has been most generous and put up some money for Denis's ballet scheme, so he is going to Manchester."

One might as well say his name. People said if you had been thrown from a horse it was best to ride again at once, to show your nerve had not gone. She had said his name twice.

"Good God!" said Mr. Middleton. "A day of wonders. Daphne and young Bond, Hibberd, Pomfret, the calf, the manure, Denis, Lilian and Cameron, your brilliant *coup* with the letter. I stand amazed. That so many things should have happened at once. And all before lunch."

And Alister has gone, Mrs. Middleton thought, and Lilian will go. Then shutting her mind resolutely against the deeper pain, which she knew would pass with time, though it was at the moment almost unbearable, she said,

"Yes. It is extraordinary how many things can happen before lunch."

FINE WORKS OF FICTION AND NON-FICTION AVAILABLE FROM CARROLL & GRAF

☐ O'Hara, John/A RAGE TO LIVE	$4.95
☐ O'Hara, John/TEN NORTH FREDERICK	$4.50
☐ Proffitt, Nicholas/GARDENS OF STONE	$4.50
☐ Purdy, James/CABOT WRIGHT BEGINS	$4.50
☐ Rechy, John/BODIES AND SOULS	$4.50
☐ Reilly, Sidney/BRITAIN'S MASTER SPY	$3.95
☐ Scott, Paul/THE LOVE PAVILION	$4.50
☐ Taylor, Peter/IN THE MIRO DISTRICT	$3.95
☐ Thirkell, Angela/AUGUST FOLLY	$4.95
☐ Thirkell, Angela/CHEERFULNESS BREAKS IN	$4.95
☐ Thirkell, Angela/HIGH RISING	$4.95
☐ Thirkell, Angela/MARLING HALL	$4.95
☐ Thirkell, Angela/NORTHBRIDGE RECTORY	$5.95
☐ Thirkell, Angela/POMFRET TOWERS	$4.95
☐ Thirkell, Angela/WILD STRAWBERRIES	$4.95
☐ Thompson, Earl/A GARDEN OF SAND	$5.95
☐ Thompson, Earl/TATTOO	$6.95
☐ West, Rebecca/THE RETURN OF THE SOLDIER	$8.95
☐ Wharton, Williams/SCUMBLER	$3.95
☐ Wilder, Thornton/THE EIGHTH DAY	$4.95

Available from fine bookstores everywhere or use this coupon for ordering.

FINE MYSTERY AND SUSPENSE
TITLES FROM CARROLL & GRAF

- [ ] Allingham, Margery/NO LOVE LOST $3.95
- [ ] Allingham, Margery/MR. CAMPION'S QUARRY $3.95
- [ ] Allingham, Margery/MR. CAMPION'S FARTHING $3.95
- [ ] Allingham, Margery/THE WHITE COTTAGE
  MYSTERY $3.50
- [ ] Ambler, Eric/BACKGROUND TO DANGER $3.95
- [ ] Ambler, Eric/CAUSE FOR ALARM $3.95
- [ ] Ambler, Eric/A COFFIN FOR DIMITRIOS $3.95
- [ ] Ambler, Eric/EPITAPH FOR A SPY $3.95
- [ ] Ambler, Eric/STATE OF SIEGE $3.95
- [ ] Ambler, Eric/JOURNEY INTO FEAR $3.95
- [ ] Ball, John/THE KIWI TARGET $3.95
- [ ] Bentley, E.C./TRENT'S OWN CASE $3.95
- [ ] Blake, Nicholas/A TANGLED WEB $3.50
- [ ] Brand, Christianna/DEATH IN HIGH HEELS $3.95
- [ ] Brand, Christianna/FOG OF DOUBT $3.50
- [ ] Brand, Christianna/GREEN FOR DANGER $3.95
- [ ] Brand, Christianna/TOUR DE FORCE $3.95
- [ ] Brown, Fredric/THE LENIENT BEAST $3.50
- [ ] Brown, Fredric/MURDER CAN BE FUN $3.95
- [ ] Brown, Fredric/THE SCREAMING MIMI $3.50
- [ ] Buchan, John/JOHN MACNAB $3.95
- [ ] Buchan, John/WITCH WOOD $3.95
- [ ] Burnett, W.R./LITTLE CAESAR $3.50
- [ ] Butler, Gerald/KISS THE BLOOD OFF MY HANDS $3.95
- [ ] Carr, John Dickson/CAPTAIN CUT-THROAT $3.95
- [ ] Carr, John Dickson/DARK OF THE MOON $3.50
- [ ] Carr, John Dickson/DEMONIACS $3.95
- [ ] Carr, John Dickson/THE GHOSTS' HIGH NOON $3.95
- [ ] Carr, John Dickson/NINE WRONG ANSWERS $3.50
- [ ] Carr, John Dickson/PAPA LA-BAS $3.95
- [ ] Carr, John Dickson/THE WITCH OF THE
  LOW TIDE $3.95
- [ ] Chesterton, G. K./THE MAN WHO KNEW
  TOO MUCH $3.95
- [ ] Chesterton, G. K./THE MAN WHO WAS THURSDAY $3.50
- [ ] Crofts, Freeman Wills/THE CASK $3.95
- [ ] Coles, Manning/NO ENTRY $3.50
- [ ] Collins, Michael/WALK A BLACK WIND $3.95
- [ ] Dickson, Carter/THE CURSE OF THE BRONZE LAMP $3.50
- [ ] Disch, Thomas M & Sladek, John/BLACK ALICE $3.95
- [ ] Eberhart, Mignon/MESSAGE FROM HONG KONG $3.50

☐ Fennelly, Tony/THE CLOSET HANGING	$3.50
☐ Freeling, Nicolas/LOVE IN AMSTERDAM	$3.95
☐ Gilbert, Michael/ANYTHING FOR A QUIET LIFE	$3.95
☐ Gilbert, Michael/THE DOORS OPEN	$3.95
☐ Gilbert, Michael/THE 92nd TIGER	$3.95
☐ Gilbert, Michael/OVERDRIVE	$3.95
☐ Graham, Winston/MARNIE	$3.95
☐ Griffiths, John/THE GOOD SPY	$4.50
☐ Hughes, Dorothy B./THE FALLEN SPARROW	$3.50
☐ Hughes, Dorothy B./IN A LONELY PLACE	$3.50
☐ Hughes, Dorothy B./RIDE THE PINK HORSE	$3.95
☐ Hornung, E. W./THE AMATEUR CRACKSMAN	$3.95
☐ Kitchin, C. H. B./DEATH OF HIS UNCLE	$3.95
☐ Kitchin, C. H. B./DEATH OF MY AUNT	$3.50
☐ MacDonald, John D./TWO	$2.50
☐ Mason, A.E.W./AT THE VILLA ROSE	$3.50
☐ Mason, A.E.W./THE HOUSE OF THE ARROW	$3.50
☐ McShane, Mark/SEANCE ON A WET AFTERNOON	$3.95
☐ Pentecost, Hugh/THE CANNIBAL WHO OVERATE	$3.95
☐ Priestley, J.B./SALT IS LEAVING	$3.95
☐ Queen, Ellery/THE FINISHING STROKE	$3.95
☐ Rogers, Joel T./THE RED RIGHT HAND	$3.50
☐ 'Sapper'/BULLDOG DRUMMOND	$3.50
☐ Stevens, Shane/BY REASON OF INSANITY	$5.95
☐ Symons, Julian/BOGUE'S FORTUNE	$3.95
☐ Symons, Julian/THE BROKEN PENNY	$3.95
☐ Wainwright, John/ALL ON A SUMMER'S DAY	$3.50
☐ Wallace, Edgar/THE FOUR JUST MEN	$2.95
☐ Waugh, Hillary/A DEATH IN A TOWN	$3.95
☐ Waugh, Hillary/LAST SEEN WEARING	$3.95
☐ Waugh, Hillary/SLEEP LONG, MY LOVE	$3.95
☐ Westlake, Donald E./THE MERCENARIES	$3.95
☐ Willeford, Charles/THE WOMAN CHASER	$3.95